Crowbone

Robert Low has been a journalist and writer since the age of seventeen. He covered the wars in Vietnam, Sarajevo, Romania and Kosovo until common sense and the concerns of his wife and daughter prevailed.

To satisfy his craving for action, having moved to an area rich in Viking tradition, he took up re-enactment, joining The Vikings. He now spends his summers fighting furiously in helmet and mail in shieldwalls all over Britain and winters training hard.

www.robert-low.com

ROBERT LOW

Crowbone

HARPER

Harper
An imprint of HarperCollins*Publishers*
77–85 Fulham Palace Road,
Hammersmith, London W6 8JB

www.harpercollins.co.uk

This paperback edition 2013
1

First published in Great Britain by
HarperCollins*Publishers* 2012

A catalogue record for this book is
available from the British Library

ISBN: 978-0-00-729856-3

This novel is entirely a work of fiction.
The names, characters and incidents portrayed in it,
while in some cases based on historical figures, are the work of the author's imagination.

Set in Sabon LT Std by Palimpsest Book Production Limited,
Falkirk, Stirlingshire

Printed and bound in Great Britain by
Clays Ltd, St Ives plc

MIX
Paper from
responsible sources
FSC www.fsc.org **FSC® C007454**

To my wife, Kate,
who keeps my eyes on the real prize

10th Century Europe

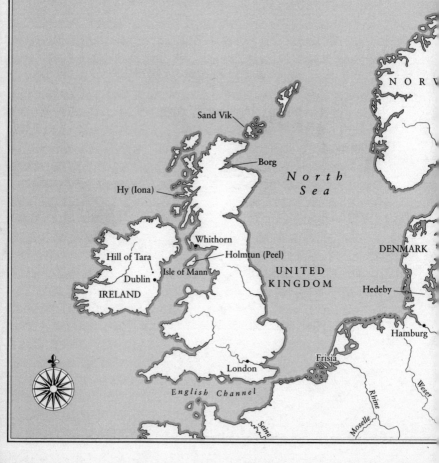

In the hilt is fame.
In the haft is courage,
In the edge is fear.

Lay of Helgi Hjörvarðsson

Finnmark, A.D. 981

THEIR skin was already slack and waxen yet unsettling, with meltwater frozen from their final cooling beaded like new sweat. Black and orpiment bruising, red wounds gaping like lipless mouths, black blood thick as porridge crusting in the cold.

One face seemed to be looking at everyone who looked at it, a bewildered question frozen in the glassed eyes. His knuckles were clenched so tight on his belly that the rough pelt he wore oozed between fingers clamped on either side of the great gash, as if trying to force it shut on the blue snakes coiling from it. His hair was wild and uncombed and his nose needed wiping.

Too late for all of that, Crowbone was thinking.

They were tough, these dark little Sami from the snow hills, feared even by the Norse from Gjesvaer, who hunted whale and walrus and ice bears over the northern floes. They knew that the Sami could stalk a man and he would never know it until the bone tip of an arrow came out of his heart.

Even in a stand-up fight they are killing us, Crowbone thought, carving us like chips off a great tree. Men lay not

1

far off, arms folded on their breasts and faces covered by cloaks. Men of skill and wit, gone from boasts and laughter to sacks of clothing, laid out like fresh-cut logs and just as stiff in the cold.

As for the Sami, they had now fought these mountain hunters too many times, but this was the first time they had seen so many of them dead in the one place. The crew moved among them silently, save for a muttered growl here and there, peered and prodded, knelt now and then to search in the blood and splintered bone. They were trying hard to ignore the strangeness of these beast-masked warriors and all the old fear-tales of Sami wizards.

It was Murrough, cleaning the great hook-bearded Dal Cais axe with one of their skin masks, who gave voice to all their fears, as he squinted at one lolling body and nudged it with his foot.

'Sure,' he said, 'and I killed this one yesterday, so I did.'

ONE

Island of Mann, A.D. 979

THREE sheltered in the fish-reeked dim of the *keeill*, cramped up and feeling the cold seep into their bones – but only one of them did not care, for he was dying. Though truth was, Drostan thought, glancing sideways at the red-glowed beak-face of the Brother who lived here, perhaps this priest cares even less than the dying.

'I am done, brother,' said Sueno and the husked whisper of him jerked Drostan back to where his friend and brother in Christ lay, sweat sheening his face in the faint glow from the fish-oil light.

'Nonsense,' Drostan lied. 'When the storm clears tomorrow we will go down to the church at Holmtun and get help there.'

'He will never get there,' said the priest, voice harsh as the crow dark itself and bringing Drostan angrily round.

'Whisht, you – have you so little Christian charity in you?'

There was a gurgle, which might have been a laugh or a curse, and suddenly the hawk-face was thrust close, so close that Drostan bent backwards away from it. It was not a comfort, that face. It had greasy iron tangles of hair round it, was leached of moisture so that it loomed like a cracked

3

desert in the dark, all planes and shadows; the jaws clapped in around the few teeth in the mouth, which made black runestones when he spoke.

'I lost it,' he mushed, then his glittering priest eyes seemed to glass over and he rose a little and moved away to tend the poor fire, bent-backed, a rolling gait with a bad limp.

'I lost it,' he repeated, shaking his head. 'Out on the great white. It lies there, prey to wolves and foxes and the skin-wearing heathen trolls – but no, God will keep it safe. I will find it again. God will keep it safe.'

Shaken, Drostan gathered himself like a raggled cloak. He knew of this priest only by hearsay and what he had heard had not been good. Touched, they said. A pole-sitter who fell off, one or two claimed with vicious humour. Foreign. This last Drostan now knew for himself, for the man's harsh voice was veined with oddness.

'God grant you find it soon and peace with it, brother,' Drostan intoned piously, through his gritted teeth.

The hawk-face turned.

'I am no brother of yours, Culdee,' he said, his voice a sneer. 'I am from Hammaburg. I am a true follower of the true church. I am monk and priest both.'

'I am merely a humble anchorite of the Cele Dei, as is the poor soul here. Yet here we all are,' answered Drostan, irritated. 'Brother.'

The rain hissed on the stone walls, driving damp air in to swirl the scent of wrack round in the fish-oil reek. The priest from Hammaburg looked left, right and then up, as if seeking God in the low roof; then he smiled his black-rotted smile.

'It is not a large hall,' he admitted, 'but it serves me for the while.'

'If you are not one of us,' Drostan persisted angrily while trying to make Sueno more comfortable against the chill, 'why are you here in this place?'

He sat back and waved a hand that took in the entire

4

keeill with it, almost grazing the cold stone of the rough walls. A square the width of two and half tall men, with a roof barely high enough to stand up in. It was what passed for a chapel in the high lands of Mann, and Drostan and Sueno each had their own. They brought the word of God from the Cele Dei – the Culdee – church of the islands to any who flocked to listen. They were cenobites, members of a monastic community who had gone out in the world and become lonely anchorites.

But this monk was a real priest from Hammaburg, a *clerk regular* who could preach, administer sacrament and educate others, yet was also religious in the strictest sense of the word, professing solemn vows and the solitary contemplation of God. It stung Drostan that this strange cleric claimed to be the united perfection of the religious condition – and did not share the same beliefs as the Cele Dei, nor seem to possess any Christian charity.

Drostan swallowed the bitter bile of it, flavoured with the harsh knowledge that the priest was right and Sueno was dying. He offered a silent apology to God for the sin of pride.

'I wait for a sign,' the Hammaburg priest said, after a long silence. 'I offended God and yet I know He is not done with me. I wait for a sign.'

He shifted a little to ease himself and Drostan's eyes fell to the priest's foot, which had no shoe or sandal on it because, he saw, none would have fitted it. Half of it was gone; no toes at all and puckered flesh to the instep. It would be a painful thing to walk on that without aid of stick or crutch and Drostan realised then that this was part of the strange priest's penance while he waited for a sign.

'How did you offend God?' he asked, only half interested, his mind on Sueno's suffering in the cold.

There was silence for a moment, then the priest stirred as if from some dream.

'I lost it,' he said simply. 'I had it in my care and lost it.'

'Christian charity?' Drostan asked without looking up, so that he missed the sharp glitter of anger sparking in the priest's eyes, followed by that same dulling, as if the bright sea had been washed by a cloud.

'That I lost long since. The Danes tore that from me. I had it and I lost it.'

Drostan forgot Sueno, stared at the hawk-faced cleric for a long moment.

'The Danes?' he repeated, then crossed himself. 'Bless this weather, brother, that keeps the Dyfflin Danes from us.'

The Hammaburg priest was suddenly brisk and attentive to the fire, so that it flared briefly, before the damp wood fought back and reduced it once more to a mean affair of woodsmoke reek and flicker.

'I had it, out on the steppes of Gardariki in the east,' he went on, speaking to the dark. 'I lost it. It lies there, waiting – and I wait for a sign from God, who will tell me that He considers me penance-paid for my failure and now worthy to retrieve it. That and where it is.'

Drostan was millstoned by this. He had heard of Gardariki, the lands of the Rus Slavs, but only as a vague name for somewhere unimaginably far away, far enough to be almost a legend – yet here was someone who had been there. Or claimed it; the hermit-monk of this place, Drostan had been told, was head-sick.

He decided to keep to himself the wind-swirl of thoughts about his journey here, half carrying Sueno, whom he had visited and found sick, so resolving to take him down to the church where he could be made comfortable; he would say nothing of how God had brought them here, about the storm that had broken on them. It was then God sent the guiding light that had led them here, to a place so thick with holy mystery they had trouble breathing.

The cynical side to Drostan, all the same, whispered that it was the fish oil and woodsmoke reek that made breathing hard. He smiled in the dark; the cynical thought was Sueno's doing, for until they had found themselves only a few miles of whin and gorse apart, each had been alone and Drostan had never questioned his faith.

He had discovered doubt and questioning as soon as he and Sueno had started in to speaking, for that seemed to be the older monk's way. For all that he wondered why Sueno had taken to the Culdee life up there on the lonely, wind-moaning hills, Drostan had never resented the meeting.

There was silence for a long time, while the rain whispered and the wind moaned and whistled through the badly-daubed walls. He knew the Hammaburg priest was right and Sueno, recalcitrant old monk that he was, was about to step before the Lord and be judged. He prayed silently for God's mercy on his friend.

The priest from Hammaburg sat and brooded, aware that he had said too much and not enough, for it had been a time since he had spoken with folk and even now he was not sure that the two Culdees were quite real.

There had been an eyeblink of strangeness when the two had stumbled in on him out of the rain and wind and it had nothing to do with their actual arrival – he had grown used to speaking with phantoms. Some of them were, he knew, long dead – Starkad, who had chased him all down the rivers of Gardariki and into the Holy Land itself until his own kind had slaughtered him; Einar the Black, leader of the Oathsworn and a man the Hammaburg priest hated enough to want to resurrect for the joy of watching him die again; Orm, the new leader and equally foul in the eyes of God.

No. The strangeness had come when the one called Drostan had announced himself, expecting a name in return. It took the priest from Hammaburg by surprise when he could not at once remember his own. Fear, too. Such a thing should not have been lost, like so many other things. Christian charity. Long lost to the Danes of the Oathsworn out on the Great White where the Holy Lance still lay among fox turds and steppe grasses. At least he hoped it was, that God was keeping it safe for the time it could be retrieved.

By me, he thought. Martin. He muttered it to himself through the stumps of his festering teeth. My name is Martin. My name is pain.

Towards dawn, Sueno woke up and his coughing snapped the other two out of sleep. Drostan felt a claw hand on his forearm and Sueno drew himself up.

'I am done,' he said, and this time Drostan said nothing, so that Sueno nodded, satisfied.

'Good,' he said, between wheezing. 'Now you will listen more closely, for these are the words of a dying man.'

'Brother, I am a mere monk. I cannot hear your Confession. There is a proper priest here . . .'

'Whisht. We have, you and I, ignored that fine line up in the hills when poor souls came to us for absolution. Did it matter to them that they might as well have confessed their sins to a tree, or a stone? No, it did not. Neither does it matter to me. Listen, for my time is close. Will I go to God's hall, or Hel's hall, I wonder?'

His voice, no more than husk on the draught, stirred Drostan to life and he patted, soothingly.

'Hell has no fires for you, brother,' he declared firmly and the old monk laughed, brought on a fit of coughing and wheezed to the end of it.

'No matter which gods take me,' he said, 'this is a straw death, all the same.'

Drostan blinked at that, as clear a declaration of pagan heathenism as he had heard. Sueno managed a weak flap of one hand.

'My name, Sueno, is as close as these folk get to Svein,' he

8

said. 'I am from Venheim in Eidfjord, though there are none left there alive enough to remember me. I came with Eirik to Jorvik. I carried Odin's daughter for him.'

Sueno stopped and raised himself, his grip on Drostan's arm fierce and hard.

'Promise me this, Drostan, as a brother in Christ and in the name of God,' he hissed. 'Promise me you will seek out the Yngling heir and tell him what I tell you.'

He fell back and mumbled. Drostan wiped the spittle from his face with a shaking hand, unnerved by what he had heard. Odin's daughter? There was rank heathenism, plain as sunlight on water.

'Swear, in the name of Christ, brother. Swear, as you love me . . .'

'I swear, I swear,' Drostan yelped, as much to shut the old man up as anything. He felt a hot wash of shame at the thought and covered it by praying.

'Enough of that,' growled Sueno. 'I have heard all the chrism-loosening cant I need in the thirty years since they dragged me off from Stainmore. Fucking treacherous bitch-fucks. Fucking gods of Asgard abandoned us then . . .'

He stopped. There was silence and wind hissed rain-scent through the wall cracks, making the woodsmoke and oil reek swirl chokingly. Sueno breathed like a broken forge bellows, gathered enough air and spoke.

'Do not take this to the Mother of Kings. Not Gunnhild, his wife, Eirik's witch-woman. Not her. She is not of the line and none of Eirik's sons left to the bitch deserve to marry Odin's daughter . . . Asgard showed that when the gods turned their faces from us at Stainmore.'

Drostan crossed himself. He had only the vaguest notions what Sueno was babbling, but he knew the pagan was thick in it.

'Take what I tell you to the young boy, if he lives,' Sueno husked out wearily. 'Harald Fairhair's kin and the true line of Norway's kings. Tryggve's son. I know he lives. I hear, even in this wild place. Take it to him. Swear to me . . .'

'I swear,' Drostan declared quietly, now worried about the blood seeping from between Sueno's cracking lips.

'Good,' Sueno said. 'Now listen. I know where Odin's daughter lies . . .'

Forgotten in the dark, Martin from Hammaburg listened. Even the pain in his foot, that driving constant from toes that no longer existed – clearly part of the penance sent from God – was gone as he felt the power of the Lord whisper in the urgent, hissing, blood-rheumed voice of the old monk.

A sign, as sure as fire in the heavens. After all this time, in a crude stone hut daubed with poor clay and Christ hope, with a roof so low the rats were hunchbacked – a sign. Martin hugged himself with the ecstasy of it, felt the drool from his broken mouth spill and did not try to wipe it away. In a while, the pain of his foot came back, slowly, as it had when it thawed, gradually, after his rescue from the freeze of a steppe winter.

Agonising and eternal, that pain, and Martin embraced it, as he had for years, for every fiery shriek of it reminded him of his enemies, of Orm Bear-Slayer who led the Oathsworn, and Finn who feared nothing – and Crowbone, kin of Harold Fairhair of the Yngling line and true prince of Norway. Tryggve's son.

There was a way, he thought, for God's judgement to be delivered, for the return of what had been lost, for the punishment of all those who had thwarted His purpose. Now even the three gold coins, given to him by the lord of Kiev years since and never spent, revealed their purpose, and he glanced once towards the stone they were hidden beneath. A good hefty stone, that, and it fitted easily into the palm.

By the time the old monk coughed his blood-misted last at dawn, Martin had worked out the how of it.

Hammaburg, some months later . . .

Folk said it was a city to make you gasp, hazed with smoke and sprawling with hundreds of hovs lining the muddy banks and spilling backwards into the land. There were ships by the long hundred lying at wharfs, moored by pilings, or drawn up on the banks and crawling with men, like ants on dead fish.

There were warehouses, carts, packhorses and folk who all seemed to shout to be heard above the din of metalsmith hammers, shrieking axles and fishwives who sounded as like the quarrelling gulls as to be sisters.

Above all loomed the great timber bell tower of the Christ church, Hammaburg's pride. In it sat a chief Christ priest called a bishop, who was almost as important as the Christ priest's headman, the Pope, Crowbone had heard.

Cloaked in the arrogance of a far-traveller with barely seventeen summers on him, Crowbone was as indifferent to Hammaburg as the few men with him were impressed; he had seen the Great City called Constantinople, which the folk here named Miklagard and spoke of in the hushed way you did with places that were legend. But Crowbone had walked there, strolled the flower-decked terraces in the dreaming, windless heat of afternoon, where the cool of fountains was a gift from Aegir, lord of the deep waters.

He had swaggered in the surrounds of the Hagia Sophia, that great skald-verse of stone which made Hammaburg's *cathedral* no more than a timber boathouse. There had been round, grey stones paving the streets all round the Hagia, Crowbone recalled, with coloured pebbles between them and doves who were too lazy to fly, waddling out from under your feet.

Here in Hammaburg were brown-robed priests banging bells and chanting, for they were hot for the cold White Christ here – so much so that the Danes had grown sick of Bishop

11

Ansgar, Apostle of the North, burning the place out from underneath him before they sailed up the river. That was at least five score years ago, so that scarce a trace of the violence remained – and Crowbone had heard that Hammaburg priests still went out to folk in the north, relentless as downhill boulders.

Crowbone was unmoved by the fervour of these shaven monks for he knew that, if you wanted to feel the power of the White Christ, then Miklagard, the Navel of The World, was the place for it. The spade-bearded priests of the Great City perched on walls and corners, even on the tops of columns, shouting about faith and arguing with each other; everyone, it seemed to Crowbone, was a priest in Miklagard. There, temples could be domed with gold, yet were sometimes no more than white walls and a rough roof with a cross.

In Miklagard it was impossible to buy bread without getting a babble about the nature of their god from the baker. Even whores would discuss how many Christ-Valkeyrii might exist in the same space while pulling their shifts up. Crowbone had discovered whores in the Great City.

Hammaburg's whores thought only of money. Here the air was thick with haar, like wet silk, and the Christ-followers sweated and knelt and groaned in fearful appeasement, for the earth had shifted and, according to some Englisc monks, a fire-dragon had moved over their land, a sure sign that the world would end as some old seer had foretold, a thousand years after the birth of their Tortured God. Time, it seemed, was running out.

Crowbone's men laughed at that, being good Slav Rus most of them and eaters of horse, which made them heathen in the eyes of Good Christ-followers. If it was Rokkr, the Twilight, they all knew none of the Christ bells and chants would make it stop, for gods had no control over the Doom of all Powers and were wyrded to die with everyone else.

Harek, who was by-named Gjallandi, added that no amount

12

of begging words would stop Loki squirming the earth into folds and yelling for his wife to hurry up and bring back the basin that stopped the World Serpent venom dripping on his face. He said this loudly and often, as befits a skald by-named Boomer, so that folk sighed when he opened his mouth.

Even though the men from the north knew the true cause of events, such Loki earth-folding still raised the hairs on their arms. Perhaps the Doom of all Powers was falling on them all.

Crowbone, for his part, thought the arrogance of these Christ-followers was jaw-dropping. They actually believed that their god-son's birth heralded the last thousand years of the world and that everyone's time was almost up. Twenty years left, according to their tallying; good Christ children born now would be young men when their own parents rose out of their dead-mounds and everyone waited to be judged.

Crowbone was hunched moodily under such thoughts, for he knew the whims of gods only too well; his whole life was a knife-edge balance, where the stirred air from a whirring bird's wing could topple him to doom or raise him to the throne he considered his right. Since Prince Vladimir of Kiev had turned his face from him, the prospect seemed more doom than throne.

'You should not have axed his brother,' Finn Horsehead growled when Crowbone spat out this gloomy observation shortly after Finn had shown up with Jarl Orm.

Crowbone looked at the man, all iron-grey and seamed like a bull walrus, and willed his scowl to sear a brand on Finn's face. Instead, Finn looked back, eyes grey as a winter sea and slightly amused; Crowbone gave up, for this was Finn Horsehead, who feared nothing.

'Yaropolk's death was necessary,' Crowbone muttered. 'How can two princes rule one land? Odin's bones – had we not just finished fighting the man to decide who ruled in Kiev and all the lands round it? Vladimir's arse would never have stayed long on the throne if brother Yaropolk had remained alive.'

He knew, also, that Vladimir recognised the reality of it, too, for all his threats and haughtiness and posturing about the honour of princes and truces – Odin's arse, this from a man who had just gained a wife by storming her father's fortress and taking her by force. Yaropolk, the rival brother, had to die, otherwise he would always have been a threat, real or imagined and, one day, would have been tempted to try again.

None of which buttered up matters any with Vladmir, who had turned his back on his friend as a result.

'There had been fighting, right enough,' answered Orm quietly, moving from the shadows of the room. 'But a truce and an agreement between brothers marked the end of it – at which point you axed Yaropolk between the eyes.'

But it was all posturing, Crowbone thought. Vladimir was pleased his brother was dead and would have contrived a way of doing it himself if Crowbone had not axed the problem away.

The real reason for the Prince of Kiev's ire was that Crowbone's name was hailed just as frequently as Vladimir's now – and that equality could not be allowed to continue. It was just a move in the game of kings.

Crowbone fastened his scowl on the Bear-Slayer. A legend, this jarl of the Oathsworn – Crowbone was one of them and so Orm was *his* jarl, which fact he tried hard not to let scrape him. He owed Orm a great deal, not least his freedom from thralldom.

Eight years had passed since then. Now the boy Orm had rescued was a tall, lithe youth coming into the main of his years, with powerful shoulders, long tow-coloured braids heavy with silver rings and coins, and the beginning of a decent beard. Yet the odd eyes – one blue as old ice, the other nut-brown – were blazing and the lip still petulant as a bairn's.

14

'Vladimir could no more rule with his brother alive than I can fart silver,' Crowbone answered, the pout vanishing as suddenly as it had appeared. 'When he has had time to think of this, he will thank me.'

'Oh, he thanks you, right enough,' Finn offered, wincing as he planted one buttock on a bench. 'It is forgiveness he finds hard.'

Crowbone ignored the cheerful Finn, who was clearly enjoying this quarrel among princes. Instead, he studied Orm, seeing the harsh lines at the mouth which the neat-trimmed beard did not hide, just as the brow-braids did not disguise the fret of lines at the corners of the eyes, nor the scar that ran straight across the forehead above the cool, sometimes green, sometimes blue eyes. The nose was skewed sideways, his cheeks were dappled with little poxmark holes, his left hand was short three fingers, and he limped a little more than he had the year before.

A hard life, Crowbone knew and, when you could read the rune-marks of those injuries, you knew the saga-tale of the man and the Oathsworn he led.

Unlike Finn there was no grey in Orm Bear-Slayer yet, but they were both already old, so that a trip from Kiev, sluiced by Baltic water that still wanted to be ice, was an ache for the pair of them. Worse still, they had snugged the ship up in Hedeby and ridden across the Danevirke to Hammaburg, which fact Finn mentioned at length every time he shifted his aching cheeks on a bench.

'Did the new Prince of Kiev send you, then?' Crowbone asked and looked at the casket on the table. Silver full it was, including some whole coins and full-weight minted ones at that. Brought with ceremony by Orm and placed pointedly in front of him.

'Is this his way of saying how sorry he is for threatening to stake me? An offering of gratitude for fighting him on to the throne of Kiev and ridding him of his rival?'

'Not likely,' Orm declared simply, unmoved by Crowbone's attempt at bluster.

'You were ever over-handy with an axe and a forehead, boy,' Finn added and there was no grin in his voice now. 'I warned you it would get you into trouble one day – this is the second time you have annoyed young Vladimir with it.'

The first time, Crowbone had been nine and fresh-released from slavery; he had spotted his hated captor across the crowded market of Kiev and axed him in the forehead before anyone could blink. That had put everyone at risk and neither Orm nor Finn would ever forget or forgive him for it.

Crowbone knew it, for all his bluster.

'So whose silver is this, then?' Crowbone demanded, knowing the answer before he spoke.

Orm merely looked at him, then shrugged.

'I have a few moonlit burials left,' he declared lightly. 'So I bring you this.'

Crowbone did not answer. Moonlit buried silver was a waste. Silver was for ships and men and there would never be enough of it in the whole world, Crowbone thought, to feed what he desired.

Yet he knew Orm Bear-Slayer did not think like this. Orm had gained Odin's favour and the greatest hoard of silver ever seen, which was as twisted a joke as any the gods had dreamed up – for what had the Oathsworn done with it after dragging it from Atil's howe back into the light of day? Buried it in the secret dark again and agonised over having it.

Because Crowbone owed the man his life, he did not ever say to Orm what was in his heart – that Orm was not of the line of Yngling kings and that he, Olaf, son of Tryggve, by-named Crowbone, had the blood in him. So they were different; Orm Bear-Slayer would always be a little jarl, while Olaf Tryggvasson would one day be king in Norway, perhaps even greater than that.

All the same, Crowbone thought moodily, Asgard is a little

fretted and annoyed over the killing of Yaropolk, which, perhaps, had been badly timed. It came to him then that Orm was more than a little fretted and annoyed. He had travelled a long way and with few companions at some risk. Old Harald Bluetooth, lord of the Danes, had reasons to dislike the Oathsworn and Hammaburg was a city of Otto's Saxlanders, who were no friends to Jarl Orm.

'Not much danger,' Orm answered with an easy smile when Crowbone voiced this. 'Otto is off south to Langabardaland to quarrel with Pandulf Ironhead. Bluetooth is too busy building ring-forts at vast expense and with no clear reason I can see.'

To stamp his authority, Crowbone thought scathingly, as well as prepare for another war with Otto. A king knows this. A real jarl can understand this, as easy as knowing the ruffle on water is made by unseen wind – but he bit his lip on voicing that. Instead, he asked the obvious question.

'Do you wish me to find someone to take my place?'

A little more harshly said than he had intended; Crowbone did not want Orm thinking he was afraid, for finding a replacement willing to take the Oath was the only way to safely leave the Oathsworn. There were two others – one was to die, the other to suffer the wrath of Odin, which was the same.

'No,' Orm declared and then smiled thinly. 'Nor is this a gift. I am your jarl. I have decided a second longship is needed and that you will lead the crew of it. The silver is for finding a suitable ship. You have the men you brought with you from Novgorod, so that is a start on finding a crew.'

Crowbone said nothing, while the wind hissed wetly off the sea and rattled the loose shutters. Finn watched the pair of them – it was cunning, right enough; there was not room on one *drakkar* for the likes of Orm and a Crowbone growing into his power and wyrd, yet there were benefits still for the pair of them if Crowbone remained one of the Oathsworn.

Perhaps the width of an ocean or two would be enough to keep them from each other's throats.

Crowbone knew it and nodded, so that Finn saw the taut lines of the pair of them ease, the hackles drift downwards. He shifted, grinned and then grunted his pleasure like a scratching walrus.

'Where are you bound from here?' Crowbone asked.

'Back to Kiev,' Orm declared. 'Then the Great City. I have matters there. You?'

Crowbone had not thought of it until now and it came to him that he had been so tied up with Vladimir and winning that prince his birthright that he had not considered anything else. Four years he had been with Vladimir, like a brother . . . he swallowed the flaring anger at the Prince of Kiev's ingratitude, but the fire of it choked him.

'Well,' said Orm into the silence. 'I have another gift, of sorts. A trader who knows me, called Hoskuld, came asking after you. Claims to have come from Mann with a message from a Christ monk there. Drostan.'

Crowbone cocked his head, interested. Orm shrugged.

'I did not think you knew this monk. Hoskuld says he is one of those who lives on his own in the wilderness and has loose bits in the inside of his thought-cage. It means nothing to me, but Hoskuld says the priest's message was a name – Svein Kolbeinsson – and a secret that would be of worth to Tryggve's son, the kin of Harald Fairhair.'

Crowbone looked from Orm to Finn, who spread his hands and shrugged.

'I am no wiser. Neither monk nor name means anything to me and I am a far-travelled man, as you know. Still – I am thinking it is curious, this message.'

Enough to go all the way to Mann, Crowbone wondered and had not realised he had voiced it aloud until Orm answered.

'Hoskuld will take you, you do not need to wait until you

have found a decent ship and crew,' he said. 'You have six men of your own and Hoskuld can take nine and still manage a little cargo – with what you pay him from that silver, it is a fine profit for him. Ask Murrough to go with you, since he is from that part of the world and will be of use. You can have Onund Hnufa, too, if you want, for you might need a shipwright of his skill.'

Crowbone blinked a little at that; these were the two companions who had come with Orm and Finn and both were prizes for any ship crew. Murrough macMael was a giant Irisher with an axe and always cheerful. Onund Hnufa, was the opposite, a morose oldster who could make a longship from two bent sticks, but he was an Icelander and none of them cared for princes, particularly if they came from Norway. Besides that, he had all the friendliness of a winter-woken bear.

'One is your best axe man. The other is your shipwright,' he pointed out and Orm nodded.

'No matter who pays us, we are out on the Grass Sea,' he answered, 'fighting steppe horse-trolls, without sight of water or a ship. Murrough would like a sight of Ireland before he gets much older and you are headed that way. Onund does not like looking at a land-horizon that gets no closer, so he may leap at this chance to return to the sea.'

He stared at Crowbone, long and sharp as a spear.

'He may not, all the same. He does not care for you much, Prince of Norway.'

Crowbone thought on it, then nodded. Wrists were clasped. There was an awkward silence, which went on until it started to shave the hairs of Crowbone's neck. Then Orm cleared his throat a little.

'Go and make yourself a king in Norway,' he said lightly. 'If you need the Oathsworn, send word.'

As he and Finn hunched out into the night and the squalling rain, he flung back over his shoulder, 'Take care to keep the fame of Prince Olaf bright.'

Crowbone stared unseeing at the wind-rattling door long after they had gone, the words echoing in him. *Keep the fame of Prince Olaf bright* – and, with it, the fame of the Oathsworn, for one was the other.

For now, Crowbone added to himself.

He stirred the silver with a finger, studying the coins and the roughly-hacked bits and pieces of once-precious objects. Silver *dirham* from Serkland, some whole coins from the old Eternal City, oddly-chopped arcs of ring, sharp slivers of coin wedges, cut and chopped bar ingots. There was even a peculiarly shaped piece that could have been part of a cup.

Cursed silver, Crowbone thought with a shiver, if it came from Orm's hoard, which came from Atil's howe. Before that the Volsungs had it, brought to them by Sigurd, who killed the dragon Fafnir to possess it; the history of these riches was long and tainted.

It had done little good to Orm, Crowbone thought. He had been surprised when Orm had announced that he was returning to Kiev, for the jarl had been brooding and thrashing around the Baltic, looking for signs of his wife, Thorgunna, for some time.

She had, Crowbone had heard, turned her back on her man, her life, the gods of Asgard and her friends to follow a Christ priest and become one of their holy women, a nun.

That had been part of the curse of Atil's silver on Orm. The rest was the loss of his bairn, born deformed and so exposed – the act which had so warped Thorgunna out of her old life – and the death of the foster-wean Orm had been entrusted with, who happened to be the son of Jarl Brand, who had gifted the steading at Hestreng to Orm.

In one year, the year after Orm had gained the riches of Atil's tomb, the curse on that hoard had taken his wife, his newborn son, his foster-son, his steading, his friendship with the mighty and a good hack out of his fair fame.

Crowbone studied the dull, winking gleam of that pile and wondered how much of it had come from the Volsung hoard and how bad the curse was.

Sand Vik, Orkney, at the same time . . .

THE WITCH-QUEEN'S CREW

The wind blew from the north, hard and cold as a whore's heart so that clouds fled like smoke before it and the sun died over the heights of Hoy. The sea ran grey-green and froth flew off the waves, rushing like mad horses to shatter and thunder on the headlands, the undertow smacking like savouring lips until the suck was crushed by another wild-horse rush.

The man shivered; even the thick walls of this steading did not seem solid enough and he felt the bones of the place shudder up through his feet. There was comfort here, all the same, he saw, but it was harsh and too northern, even for him – the room was murky with reek because the doors were shut against the weather and the wind swooped in through the hearthfire smokehole and simply danced it round the dim hall, flaring the coals and flattening flame. It made the eyes of the storm-fretted black cat glow like baleful marshlights.

A light appeared, seeming to float on its own and flickering in the wild air, so that the man shifted uneasily, for all he was a fighting man of some note, and hurriedly brought up a hand to cross himself.

There was a chuckle, a dry rustle of sound like a rat in old bracken and the night crawled back from the flame, revealing gnarled driftwood beams, a hand on the lamp ring, blackness beyond.

Closer still and he saw an arm but only knew it from the dark by the silver ring round it, for the cloth on it was midnight

e. Another step and there was a face, but the lamp blurred it; all the man could see clearly was the hand, the skin sere and brown-pocked, the fingers knobbed.

That and the eyes of her, which were bone needles threading the dark to pierce his own.

'Erling Flatnef,' said the dry-rustle voice, rheumed and thick so that the sound of his own name raised the hackles on his arm. 'You are late.'

Erling's cheeks felt stiff, as if he had been staring into a white blizzard, yet he summoned words from the depth of himself and managed to spit them out.

'I waited to speak with my lord Arnfinn,' he said and the sound of his voice seemed sucked away somehow.

'Just so – and what did the son of Thorfinn Jarl have to say?'

The moth-wing hiss of her voice was slathered with sarcasm, for which Erling had no good reply. The truth was that the four sons of Thorfinn who now ruled Orkney were as much in thrall to this crumbling ruin, Gunnhild, Mother of Kings, as their father had been. Arnfinn, especially, was hag-cursed by it and had merely brooded his eyes into the pitfire and then waved Erling on his way without a word, trying not to look at his wife, Ragnhild, who was Gunnhild's daughter.

Erling's silence gave Gunnhild all the answer she needed. As her face loomed out from behind the blurring light of the lamp he was unable even to cross himself, was paralysed at the sight of it. Whatever The Lady wanted, she would get; not for the first time, Erling pitied the Jarls of Orkney and the mother-in-law they wore round their necks.

Not that it was an ugly face, aged and raddled. The opposite. It was a face with skin that seemed soft as fine leather with only a tracery of lines round the mouth, where the lips were a little withered. A harsh line or two here and there on it, which only accentuated the heart-leaping beauty that had been there in youth. Gunnhild wanted to smile at the sight of him, but knew that would crack the artifice like throwing a stone on thin ice. She used her face as a weapon and clubbed him with it.

'I had a son called Erling,' she said and Erling stiffened. He knew that – Haakon Jarl had killed him. For a wild moment of panic Erling wondered if she sought to raise the dead son and needed to steal the name . . .

'I have a task for you, Flatnose,' she said in her ruin of a voice. 'You and my last, useless son Gudrod and that Tyr-worshipping boy of yours – what is his name?'

'Od,' Erling managed and mercifully Gunnhild slid away from him, back into the shadows.

'Listen,' she said and laid the meat of it out, a long rasp of wonder in that fetid dark. The revelations left him shaking, wondering how she had discovered all this, awed at the rich *seidr* magic she still commanded – the gods knew how old she was, yet still beautiful and still a power.

Later, as he stumbled from the hall, the rain and battering wind were as much of a relief as goose-grease on a burn.

TWO

The coast of Frisia, a week later . . .

CROWBONE'S CREW

IT was no properly straked, oak-keeled *drakkar*, but the *Or-skreiðr* was a good ship, a sturdy, fat-waisted *knarr* with scarred planks and the comfort of ship-luck. It had carried the trader safely from Dyfflin to Hammaburg and elsewhere – even back to the trader's home in Iceland. Hoskuld boasted of its prowess as it hauled Crowbone and his Chosen Men out of Hammaburg to the sea, then west along the coast. The *Or-skreiðr*, Swift-Gliding, was Hoskuld's pride.

'Even when Aegir of the waters is splashing about in the worst way,' he declared, 'I have never had a moment's unease.'

Crowbone's eight Oathsworn, jostling for sea-chest space with the crew and the cargo of hoes and mattocks and kegged fish, found little humour in this, though some gave dutiful laughs. But not Onund.

'You should not dangle this stout ship in front of the Norns, like a worm on a hook,' Onund growled morosely to Hoskuld. 'Those Sisters love to hear the boasts of men – it makes them laugh.'

Crowbone said nothing, for he knew Onund had sourness seeped into him, for all he had agreed to this voyage. The other men were less frowning about matters. Murrough macMael was going back to Mann and possibly Ireland and that pleased him; the others – Gjallandi the skald, Rovald Hrafnbruder, Vigfuss Drosbo, Kaetilmund, Vandrad Sygni and Halfdan Knutsson – were happy to be going anywhere with the Prince Who Would Be King. They were all seasoned Swedes and half-Slavs who had been down the cataracts from Kiev with the silk traders at least once and had sailed up and down the Baltic with Crowbone, raiding in the name of Vladimir, Prince of Novgorod and now Kiev.

Ring-coated most of them, exotic in fat breeks and big boots and fur-trimmed hats with silver wire designs, they swaggered and bantered idly in the fat-waisted little *knarr* and made Hoskuld and his working men scowl.

'How do we know their worth?' one seaman grumbled in Crowbone's hearing. 'Who decided on these instead of a decent cargo?'

'They think we are just barrels of salt cod,' Gjallandi announced, appearing suddenly at Crowbone's ear, 'while your new Chosen Men believe it is a day's sail, with a bit of sword-waving at the end of it and yourself crowned king of Norway, no doubt. All will find the truth of matters, soon enough.'

He was shaking his head, which made all those who did not know him laugh, for he was not the figure of a raiding man. He was a middling man in most respects save two – his head and his voice.

His head was large, with a chin like a ship's prow and two full, beautiful lips in the centre of it, surrounded by a neat-trimmed fringe of moustache and beard. The hair on his head was marvellously copper-coloured, but galloping back over his forehead on either side of his ears; when the wind blew it stuck straight out behind him like spines. Murrough said it was not his hair that was receding but his head growing from all the lore he stuffed in it.

That lore and his voice had made his fortune, all the same, first as skald to a jarl called Skarpheddin and then to Jarl Brand. He had left Brand after arguing that it was not right to come down so hard on Jarl Orm for the loss of Jarl Brand's son – which, according to Murrough and others, showed how Gjallandi's voice sometimes worked before his thought-cage did.

Now he had come with Crowbone because, he said, Crowbone had more saga in him and the tale of the exiled Prince of Norway reclaiming his birthright was too good to miss. Crowbone had joined in the good-natured laughter, but secretly liked the idea of having someone spread his fame; the thought was as warming a comfort as a hearthfire and a horn of ale.

'The crowning will come in time,' Crowbone answered, loud enough for everyone to hear. 'Until then, there are ships and men waiting to join us.'

'No doubt,' said the steersman whose name was Halk and his Norse was strange and lilting. 'Do they know you are coming?'

His voice had a laugh in it which removed any sting and Crowbone smiled back at him.

'If you know where you are going,' he replied, 'then – there they will all be.'

It was clear that Hoskuld had told his men nothing much, which was not sensible in a tight crew of six who depended on each other and the trade they made. Crowbone did not much trust Hoskuld, for all he had come from Mann to deliver his mysterious message – without pay, no doubt, for Christ monks were notoriously empty-pursed.

'For the love of God,' Hoskuld had replied when Crowbone had asked the why of this and his face, battered by wind and wave into something like a headland with eyes, gave away nothing. His men said even less, keeping their eyes and hands on work, but Crowbone felt Hoskuld's lie like a chill haar on his skin. Yet Hoskuld was a friend of Orm and that counted for much.

Crowbone sat and watched the land slip sideways past him while the sea rose and fell, dark, glassy planes heaving in a slow, breathing rhythm.

He watched the gulls. Hoskuld never got far enough from the land to lose them and Crowbone listened to them scream to each other of finding something that moved and promised fish. One perched on the mast spar, heedless of the sail's great belly and Crowbone watched this one more carefully than the others. He felt the familiar tightening of the skin on his arms and neck; something was happening.

The crew of the *Or-skreiðr* coiled lines, bailed, reefed sail, took the steering oar and stared at Crowbone and his eight men. He could almost feel their dislike and their distrust and, above all, their fear. Here were the plunderers, pillagers and pagans that peaceful Christ-anointed traders, farmers of the sea-lanes, could do without as they ploughed up and down from port to port.

Here were red murderers, sitting on their sea-chests, talking in their mush-mouthed East Norse way – made worse by all the time spent with Slavs – and eyeing up the crew with almost complete indifference when not with sardonic smiles at watching men work while they stayed idle.

Crowbone knew his eight Chosen well, knew who was more Svear than Slav, who had washed that weekday, who doubted their own prowess.

Young men – well, all but Onund – hard men, who had all, without showing fear, taken that hard oath of the Oathsworn: *we swear to be brothers to each other, bone, blood and steel, on Gungnir, Odin's spear we swear, may he curse us to the Nine Realms and beyond if we break this faith, one to another.*

Crowbone had taken it when he was too young for chin

hair, driven to it as those desperate and lost in the dark will run to a fire, even if it risks a scorching. He had kin somewhere, sisters he had never seen – but mother, father, guardian uncle were all dead and Orm Bear-Slayer of the Oathsworn was the nearest thing he had to any of the three.

He watched his Chosen Men. Only Onund knew what the Oath meant, for he had taken it long enough ago to have marked the warp of it on his life. Most of the others would come to know just what they had sworn, but for now they were all grins and wild beards in every colour save grey, laughing and boasting easily, one to the other.

Hoskuld, beaming at the way they were skipping along, announced that he had many skills, one of them navigation.

'We go out on to a big expanse of water dead ahead,' he added. 'Land on the berthing side, so you cannot really miss it. After a bit, we turn north. That is to the right. The steerboard side. The hand you use to pull yourself off.'

Crowbone forced a smile as Hoskuld moved off into the grins of his crew, while Murrough turned and looked at his fellow Oathsworn lazing there.

'Never be minding, lads,' he bellowed. 'We have bread and fish and water if this short-arsed little trading man loses us. Also, there are Crowbone's birds to steer by, when all else fails.'

Crowbone raised one hand in acknowledgement, while Hoskuld and his crew stared for a moment, stilled. Then they busied themselves and Crowbone smiled, for he knew no Norseman, especially Christ-sworn, liked the idea of a *seidr*-man and none of these liked to be reminded of the strange tales that surrounded Crowbone.

'We will need no magic birds to get us where we are going,' Hoskuld said eventually, with the scowl of an outraged Christmann. 'Nor will I lose my way, Irisher. This is a ship blessed with God-luck.'

Right there, the lone gull on the mast spar took off from

its perch and screamed, a mad laughing as it turned and wheeled away back towards the grey-blue line that was land. Crowbone watched it go, the hairs stiff on him; it does no good to tempt the Norns, he was thinking.

'There was once a Chosen Man in the service of a jarl, don't ask me where, don't ask me when,' he said and the heads came up. Crowbone had not meant to speak; he never did when the tales came on him, but those who had heard him before leaned forward a little. The steersman laughed but Murrough wheeshed him and the silence allowed the wind to thrum the rigging lines.

'As part of his due he used to get bread and a bowl of honey each day,' Crowbone went on, soft and gentle as the breathing sea. 'The warrior ate the bread and put the honey into a stoppered jug, which he took to carrying around with him, lest it be stolen. He wanted to keep the jug until it was full, for he knew the high price his honey would fetch in the market.'

'A sensible trading man, then, this warrior,' Hoskuld offered sarcastically, but glares silenced him.

'I will sell my honey for a piece of gold and buy ten sheep, all of which will bring forth young, so that in the course of one year I shall have twenty sheep,' Crowbone said, the words tumbled from him, like slow, sticky sweetness from the tale's jug.

'Their number will steadily increase, and in four years I shall be the owner of four hundred sheep. I shall then buy a cow and an ox and acquire a piece of land. My cow will bring forth calves, the ox will be useful to me in ploughing my land, while the cows will provide me with milk. In five years' time the number of my cattle will have increased considerably and I shall be wealthy. I shall then build a magnificent steading, acquire thralls and marry a beautiful woman of noble descent. She will become pregnant and bear me a son, a strong boy fit to carry my name. A lucky star will shine at

29

the moment of his birth and he will be happy and blessed, and bring honour to my name after my death. Should he, however, refuse to obey me, I will whack him round the ear, thus—'

Crowbone smacked one fist into his palm, so that the listeners started a little.

'So saying,' Crowbone added softly, 'he lashed out at the imaginary child. The jug flew from under his arm and smashed. The honey ran into the mud and was lost.'

'Heya,' sighed Murrough and stared pointedly at Hoskuld, who laughed nervously. The steersman crossed himself; no-one had missed the point of the tale.

The gull – the same one, Crowbone was sure – screamed with faint laughter in the distance.

Not long after, the steering oar broke.

One blink they were sailing along, scudding under a sail bagged full of wind, with the blue-grey slide of the land distant on one side. The next, Halk was yelling and hanging grimly on to the whole weight of the steering oar, which had parted company from the ship entire and looked set to go over the side. The Swift-Gliding leaped like a joyous stallion spitting out the bit, then yawed off in a direction all its own.

Men sprang to help Halk, wrestling the steering board safely on to the ship. Hoskuld, bawling orders, found the Oathsworn suddenly alive, moving with practised ease to flake the sail down on to the yard and bring the free-running *knarr* to a sulky halt, where it rocked and pitched, the slow-heaving waves slapping the hull.

'Leather collar has snapped,' Onund declared after a brief look. 'Fetch out some more and we will fix it.'

Hoskuld glared at Halk, whose eyes were wide with inno-cent protesting, but then Gorm stepped into Hoskuld's scowl and matched it with one of his own. He had been with Hoskuld ever since they had first set keel on water, so he had leeway. He had hands and face beaten by weather, but his eyes were clear and there was at least a horn-spoon of intellect behind them, even if his nose was crooked from fights and his body a barrel which had been scoured by wind and wave.

'Not Halk's fault,' he growled at Hoskuld. 'Should have stayed in Dyfflin for long enough to fetch such supplies as spare leather, but you would sail. Should have stayed in Sand Vik longer than to pick up this poor dog of a steersman, but you sailed even faster from there.'

'Enough!' roared Hoskuld, his face turning white, then red. 'This is not fixing matters.'

He broke off, glanced at the thin line of land and wiped his mouth with the back of one hand.

'This is the Frisian coast,' he muttered darkly. 'No place to be wallowing, dangled like a fat cod for sharks.'

'Leather,' Onund grunted.

'None,' Gorm replied, almost triumphant. 'Some bast line, which will have to do.'

'Aye, for you never stayed long enough in Dyfflin or Sand Vik,' Crowbone noted and everyone heard how his voice had become steeled.

'Save for picking up a steersman,' he added, nodding towards Halk, who stared from Hoskuld to Crowbone and back, his mouth gawped like a coal-eater.

Folk left off what they were doing then, for a chill had sluiced in like mist, centred on Crowbone and the lip-licking Hoskuld.

Crowbone knew now where the steersman had his lilting Norse from. From Orkney, where Hoskuld had gone from Dyfflin and before that from Mann. Mann to Dyfflin to Orkney.

'You know who this Svein Kolbeinsson is,' Crowbone said, weaving the tale as he spoke and knowing the warp and weft were true by the look in Hoskuld's eyes.

'How many others have you told?' Crowbone went on. Hoskuld spread his arms and tried to speak.

'I . . .' began Hoskuld.

Crowbone drew the short-handled axe out of the belt-ring at his waist and Hoskuld's crew shifted uneasily; one made a whimpering sound. Hoskuld seemed to tip sideways and sag a little, like an emptying waterskin. The crew and the Oathsworn watched, slipping subtly apart.

'You know from Orm what I can do with this,' Crowbone said, raising the axe, and Hoskuld blinked and nodded and then rubbed the middle of his forehead, as if it itched.

'Only because you have friendship with Jarl Orm is it still on the outside of your skull,' Crowbone went on, in a quiet and reasonable voice, so that those who heard it shivered.

'Svein Kolbeinsson,' Hoskuld gasped. 'Konungslykill, they called him. I was younger than yourself by a few years when I met him, on my first trip to Jorvik with my father.'

Crowbone stopped and frowned. Konungslykill – The King's Key – was the name given to only one man, the one who carried King Eirik's *blot* axe. Such sacrifice axes were all called Odin's Daughter, but only one truly merited the name – Eirik's axe, the black-shafted mark of the Yngling right to rule.

Carried by a Chosen Man called the King's Key, the pair of them represented Eirik's power to open all chests and doors in his realm, by force if necessary. It gave Eirik his feared name, too – Bloodaxe. Crowbone blinked, the thoughts racing in him like waves breaking on rocks.

'This ship it was,' Hoskuld said wistfully. 'The year before Eirik was thrown out of Jorvik and died in an ambush set by Osulf, who went on to rule all Northumbria.'

What was that – twenty-five years ago and more? Crowbone looked at Hoskuld and while the gulls in his head screeched and whirled their messages and ideas, his face stayed grim and secret as a hidden skerry.

'Svein Kolbeinsson was taken at the place where Eirik of Jorvik died, but after some time he escaped thralldom and fled to Mann. It seems he turned his back on Asgard since the gods turned their backs on him, so he became a monk of the Christ in the hills of Mann around Holmtun, in the north of the island. He died recently, but before he did, he told this monk Drostan a secret, to be shared only with the kin of the Yngling line.'

The words spilled from Hoskuld like a stream over rocks, yet the last of it clamped his lips shut as he realised what he had said. Crowbone nodded slowly as the sense of it crept like honey into his head.

'Instead, you went to Dyfflin,' Crowbone said softly.

Hoskuld licked his cracking lips and nodded.

'At Drostan's request,' he murmured hesitantly.

'You are no fool, Hoskuld Trader, you got the secret from this monk Drostan, you know what he has to tell me.'

'Only what it is,' he managed, in a husked whisper. 'Odin's Daughter. Not where it lies, though.'

'Eirik's axe, Odin's Daughter itself, still in the world and a monk has the where of it in his head,' Crowbone said.

Now it was the turn of the Oathsworn to shift, seeing the bright prize of Eirik's Bloodaxe, the mark of a true scion of the Yngling line – a banner to gather men under. That and the magic in it made it worth more than if it were made of gold.

'Olaf Irish-Shoes, Jarl-King in Dyfflin?' Crowbone mused, bouncing the axe in his fingers. 'Well, he is old, but he is still a northman and no man hated Eirik Bloodaxe more than he – did they not chase each other off the Jorvik High Seat?'

Hoskuld bobbed his head briefly in agreement and those who knew the tale nodded confirmation at each other; Eirik had been ousted from Jorvik once and Olaf Irish-Shoes at least twice. Gorm muttered and shot arrowed scowls at his captain.

'Well,' said Crowbone. 'You took the news to Irish-Shoes, then Orkney.' Crowbone's voice was all dark and murder now. 'Not to Thorfinn, I am thinking.'

'Thorfinn died,' Gorm blurted. 'His sons rule together there now – Arnfinn, Havard, Ljot and Hlodir.'

'There is only one ruler on Orkney,' Crowbone spat. 'Still alive is she, the Witch?'

Hoskuld answered only with a choking sound in his throat; Gunnhild, Eirik's queen, the Witch Mother of Kings. The tales of her were suddenly fresh as new blood in Hoskuld's head: she it was who had sent her sons to kill Crowbone's father then scour the world for the son and his mother. Now the hunted son stood in front of him with an axe in his hand and a single brow fretted above his cold, odd eyes. Hoskuld cursed himself for having forgotten that.

'Arnfinn is married to her daughter,' he muttered.

Crowbone hefted the little axe, as if balancing it for a blow.

'So,' he said. 'You took the news to Olaf Irish-Shoes, who was always Eirik's rival – did you get paid before you fled? Then you took it to Gunnhild, the Witch, who was Eirik's wife. You had to flee from there, too – and for the same reason. Did you ken it out at that point, Hoskuld Trader? That what you knew was more deadly than valuable?'

He stared at Hoskuld and the axe twitched slightly.

'You are doomed,' Crowbone declared, grim as lichened rock. 'You are as doomed as this Drostan, whom you doubtless betrayed for profit. Olaf will want your mouth sealed and so will the Orkney Witch. Where is Drostan? Have you killed him?'

Hoskuld's brows clapped together like double gates.

'Indeed no, I did not. Him it was who asked to go to all these places, then finally to Borg in the Alban north, where we left him to come to find Jarl Orm, as he asked.'

He tried to keep the glare but the strange, odd-eyed stare of the youth made him blink. He waved his hands, as if trying to swat the feel of those eyes off his face.

'The monk lives – why would I kill him, then bother to come and find Orm – and you?'

'Betrayal,' Crowbone muttered. He leaned a little towards

Hoskuld's pale face. 'Is that what this is? An enemy who wants me dead, or worse? Why sail to Mann if the monk is at Borg?'

'He left something with the monks on Mann,' Hoskuld admitted. 'A writing.'

Crowbone asked and Hoskuld told him.

'A message. I was to pick it up on the return and take it to Orm.'

To Orm? Crowbone closed one thoughtful eye. 'And you delivered it?'

Hoskuld nodded.

'You know what this message spoke?' he asked and watched Hoskuld closely.

The trader shook his head, more sullen than afraid now.

'I was to tell you of it,' he replied bitterly, 'when you asked why we were headed for Mann at all.'

Crowbone did not show his annoyance in his face. It was a hard truth he did not care to dwell on, that he had simply thought Mann was where Hoskuld wanted to go with his strange cargo. Either he was paid more after that, or Crowbone found a ship of his own was what the young Prince of Norway had assumed.

Now he knew – a message had been left by this Drostan, in Latin which Hoskuld did not read – he knew runes and tallied on a notched stick well enough, so he could carry it to Orm and not know the content.

And the thought slid into him like a grue of ice – there was a trap to lure him to Mann.

He said so and saw Hoskuld's scorn.

'Why would Orm set you at a trap?' he scathed. 'He knows the way of monks. They would not have written this message to Orm only once.'

That was a truth Crowbone had to admit – monks, he knew, would copy it into their own annals and if he went to Mann he would find it simply by saying Orm's name and asking with a silver offering attached. For all that, he wanted to bury the blade in the gape-mouthed face of the trader, but the surge of it, which raised his arm, was damped by a thought of what Orm might have to say. He had fretted Orm enough this year, he decided – yet the effort not to strike burst sweat on him. In the end, the lowering of his arm came more from the nagging to know what this writing held than any desire to appease Orm.

'Get me to Mann, trader,' he managed to harsh out. 'I may yet feed you to the fish if it takes too long a sailing – or if I find this message or you plays me false.'

'We are sailing nowhere,' Onund interrupted with an annoyed grunt, bent over the steering oar so that his hunched shoulder reared up like an island. 'We are drifting until this is lashed. Fetch what line you have – I can get us to land safely and then we will need to find decent leather.'

'I would hurry, hunchback,' said Halk the Orkneyman, staring out towards the distant land. 'It would seem the sharks have found their cod.'

He pointed, leading everyone's eyes to the faint line, marked with little white splashes where oars dug, which grew steadily larger.

'It is all of us who are doomed,' Gorm hissed, his eyes wide, then jumped as Kaetilmund clapped him on the back.

'Ach, you fret too much,' he said.

Gorm saw the Oathsworn moving more swiftly than he had seen them shift since they had come aboard. Sea-chests were opened, ringmail unrolled from sheepskins, domed helmets brought out, oiled against the sea-rot and plumed with splendid horsehair.

'Our turn to do the work,' Murrough macMael grunted and hefted his long axe, grinning. 'You can join in if you like, or just watch.'

Gorm licked his lips and looked at the rest of the Swift-Gliding crew, who all had the same stare on them.

Not fear. Relief, that they were not Frisians.

*   *   *

Hrodfolc was smiling, though his teeth hurt. He did not have many left, yet the few he had hurt all the time these days – but even the nagging pain of them could not keep the smile from his face, laid there when the watchers brought word to the *terp* that a fat cargo ship was wallowing like a sick cow just off the coast.

It had been a time since such a prize had come their way. Ships sped past this stretch of coast like arrows, Hrodfolc thought, half-muttering to himself, for they know the red-murder fame of the folk living along it.

He turned to where his twenty men pulled and sweated, grunting with the effort, slicing the long snake-boat through the slow, rolling black swell. No mast and no sail on his boat, which is how cargo ships with a good wind at their back could always outrun us, Hrodfolc thought, leaving us rowing in their wake.

Not this time. This time, there would be blood and booty.

'Fast, fast,' he bellowed, the boom of his voice in his head bursting tooth-pain in him. The riches called to him and he could see them, taste them – wool and grain and skins. Casks filled with salt fish, or beer, or cheeses; boxes stuffed with bone, buckles, boots, pepper. Perhaps even gold and silver. Honey, or some other lick of sweetness after a long winter. His mouth watered.

'Fast,' he called and his men grunted and pulled, wild-haired, mad-bearded, their weapons handy to grab up when they left off the oars and flung them inboard.

Hrodfolc eyed the fat ship, focusing the pain on them, the ones on the ship. He would rend them. He would tear them . . .

They streaked up to the side of the slow-rocking cargo ship and saw pale faces, four, maybe six and that widened Hrodfolc's brown smile. The oars backed water furiously, then clattered inboard a breath or two before the long, sleek boat kissed the side of the *knarr*, a gentle dunt. Men hurled up lines to lash themselves to the side; others grabbed up weapons and scrambled to climb up the thwarts of their higher-sided victim, Hrodfolc snarling ahead of the pack with an axe in either fist.

It was a surprise to them all, then, when a line of shields suddenly rose up and slapped together like a closing door. It was shock when a great, bearded axe on a long shaft arced out from under them, making Hrodfolc shy away sideways, though he was not the target of it. The axe chunked over the thwarts, the powerful arms wielding it snugging the snake-boat to the *knarr* like a lover cinching the willing waist of his girl into an embrace.

Crowbone saw the gaping, snaggle-toothed mouth of the man who led these Frisian raiders, his face a great rune of terror at the sight of the shields and ring-mailed, spear-armed men who stood behind them, scowling from under the rims of horse-plumed helmets.

Crowbone hurled his own spear and it took the man in the middle of his twisted tooth, which flew out of his mouth as he fell backwards, spraying blood and head-gleet all over his own men. He hurled his second spear with his left hand and it went through the thigh of another Frisian, pinning the man to the deck of the snake-boat – his screeches were as high as a gull's.

Yet more spears flicked and the men on the snake-boat screamed and flapped like fox-stalked chickens. A few grabbed up oars and tried to push their boat away, but Murrough's long axe and a grip like a steel band held them. There were splashes as men hurled themselves into the sea rather than wait to die, for the Oathsworn were pillars of iron with big round shields, spears which they hurled and blades which they followed up with, crashing to the rocking deck of the snake-boat. The Frisian raiders had cheap wool the colour of mud and charcoal, spears with rusted heads and little wood axes.

Some did not even have that and Drosbo took a half-pace backwards as a raider with a knife, fear-maddened to fighting like a desperate rat in a barrel, hurled himself forward, screaming, slashing. The knife scored down the ringmail with little hisses of sound and Drosbo let him do it for the time it took him to grin and the Frisian to realise it was doing no good.

Just at the point the Frisian thought of aiming for the face, Drosbo brought his sword down in a cutting stroke that took the man in the join between neck and shoulder, a great, wet-sounding chop that popped the blade out of the man's armpit and the whole arm, knife and all, into the sea.

Then Drosbo booted him in the chest, hard enough to pitch the shrieking raider into the slow-shifting, crow-black water in a whirl of blood.

There was a moment of crouching caution, then Murrough gave a coughing grunt, like a new-woken bear, and offered a final spit on the whole affair as he worked his bearded axe loose from the snake-ship's planks and straightened, rolling the overworked muscles of neck and shoulder. Hoskuld's crew stared at the astounded, gape-mouthed dead, at the blood washing greasily in the bowels of the snake-boat, at those still alive and swimming hopelessly for the far-away shore, black, gasping heads rising and sinking on the glass swell.

'That is that, then,' Onund growled out and clapped the stunned Orkneyman on the shoulder. 'See if you can find some decent rope.'

Holmtun, Isle of Mann, at the same time

THE WITCH-QUEEN'S CREW

The wind rushed the trees and then bowled on over the scrub and broom, ruffling it like a mother does a son's hair. Birds hunched in shelter, or were ragged away from where they wanted to go, steepling sideways and too busy even to make a voice of protest.

The sun was there, all the same, for the heat of it made riding in ringmail and wool a weary matter and the glare of sky, white as a dead eye, made Ogmund squint.

He was tired. They were all tired from plootering over hill and heather, a trail of curse and spit, the hooves of weary horses clacking on loose stones.

Somewhere ahead, Ogmund thought, scanning the distance and squinting until his forehead ached, were the raiders. On foot. How could folk on foot have kept ahead so well? And who were they, who dared to raid this corner of Mann, which had not been raided in years?

'A warrior,' said a voice as if in answer and Ogmund turned to where Ulf, forcing himself taller in his saddle to see better, was pointing ahead to the wooded hill. He had good eyes did Ulf and Ogmund saw the figure, dark against the glare.

'So, we have caught them, then,' he said and felt the relief of the men behind him, for it meant they could get off the horses and ease their arses. Even as he swung a leg over and slid to the ground, feeling his legs buckle a little, Ogmund kept staring at the figure on the hill. Unconcerned, was the word that sprang to his mind, as if the man was picking his teeth after a meal of bread and cheese. Ogmund felt a stir of unease and looked round at his own men for the comfort of seeing them sorting out weapons and tying chinstraps.

'What are you thinking on this, Ogmund?' asked Ulf.

That it smells, Ogmund wanted to say. That the monks whose mean little church was raided spoke of three men only and I have twenty, so should be feeling less like a maiden with a knowing hand on her knee.

Ogmund spread his hands and summed up the situation for his own benefit.

'A monk had his face stirred up a little,' Ogmund said, aware even as he spoke that it sounded like a whine. 'Nothing

40

of value was taken and some of their precious vellum was creased. Seems a strange crime to me, three raiders in ringmail and with good weapons and nothing of value stolen at all. Vellum and parchment taken and read and returned. When did you know ragged-arsed bandits who could read monk scratchings?'

'Try telling that to Jarl Godred,' Ulf replied shortly. It was clear he thought they should all be moving up the slope with shields set and weapons out; Ogmund had no doubt he would say as much to Godred as soon as he could flap his mouth close to the jarl's ear and the jarl would have much to say to Ogmund as a result, none of it pleasant. Not for nothing was the ruler of this little part of Mann called Hardmouth – though never to his face.

For this reason, and because the weather was foul, Ogmund had not complained when not long since Godred chose Ulf to go and ferret out the truth of a report that two dead monks were to be found in a remote hut in the hills. Ulf had found them, two rat-eaten bodies. He was still bragging about it, though he had faced no threat, as Ogmund pointed out. Here was the opposite case, no serious crime had occurred yet the danger was very real. Ulf clearly wanted to show Ogmund, not to mention Jarl Godred, how ready he was to face any threat.

Ogmund sighed and waved the men forward, signalling for three to act as horse-holders. Ulf stayed mounted, which annoyed Ogmund since it made Ulf look like the leader. Ogmund would have liked to command him to get off, but knew that would look petty. He wanted to get back on his own mount but was not sure he had the strength of leg to spring up on it in his ringmail and felt the crushing despair of knowing there had been a time when he would have done it without thinking.

Too old, he thought grimly. Everyone knows it and Ulf grows impatient to be in my place.

The figure on the hill was suddenly close, so that Ogmund was startled at how he had daydreamed a mournful way to this point without realising it. He shook himself like a dog to sharpen his wits and stared at the man on the hill.

He was big and wore a helmet with ringmail covering the front of it so that none of his face could be seen at all; the eyes were no more than points of light in the cave of his shadowed face. It had gilded eyebrows and a raised crest and was altogether a fine helm, which had been greased and oiled carefully. The wearer had a long coat of ringmail, too, was thick-waisted, but not fat, had a shield slung on his back and one hand resting lightly on the hilt of a sword in a tooled leather sheath – though the hilt of the weapon was plain iron and sharkskin grip, without decoration.

All of it only increased the rise of Ogmund's hackles. A little raiding man might well have a fine helmet, but he would not have bothered so much in the care of it, having almost certainly stolen it in the first place. Nor did this one stand like a little raiding man. He stood as if he owned the ground his feet were on.

'Who are you?' Ogmund demanded.

'Gudrod Eiriksson from Orkney.' The voice was metal-muffled, inhuman and that rocked a few back on their heels as much as the name. Bloodaxe's son? Here in Mann?

'Orkney does not rule here now,' Ulf sneered.

'Not now,' replied Gudrod easily, 'but soon enough again, maybe.'

Another man appeared from the trees, ring-mailed and armed, moving quietly to the left and slightly behind Gudrod. He had a sharp face and a weasel smile, hardly softened at all by the trim line of his beard. His nose was broad and spread out, as if he had been hit with a shovel and it fascinated Ogmund.

A third slid out, wearing a red tunic and green breeks, both so faded they held only a distant laugh of colour. He

42

had a sword thrust through a ring in his belt but wore no armour at all, not even a helmet, and his face was round and boy-smooth, unmarked by war or weather so that the black hair which framed it made the youth look like an angel Ogmund had seen painted on the rough wall of the big church in Holmtun. Yet this angel moved strangely; like a padding wolf.

'You robbed a church,' Ulf went on and Ogmund finally had had enough. The casual trio, the whole raid, had him ruffled as a wet cat and Ulf taking on the mantle of leader here was more than enough.

'When I need you to speak, Ulf Bjornsson,' he said, low and harsh as grinding quernstones, 'I will find a dog and have it bark.'

Someone snickered at the back and Ulf jerked his reins so hard the horse threw up its head in protest and scattered bit-foam.

'You lead here?' demanded Gudrod and Ogmund nodded. The man with the squashed nose laughed, a high, thin sound. Ogmund saw his top lip stick to his teeth; that sign of nerves gave him a little comfort. He realised, suddenly, that the man had no bone in his nose, which gave it the look.

'There was no harm done in the church,' Gudrod went on easily in that hollow-helmet voice. 'It was a misunderstanding. We sought enlightenment only, not riches. A priest decided that we were not Christian enough for him. And here is me, baptised and everything, as fine a Christian as yourself, whoever you are.'

'Ogmund Liefsson, of Jarl Godred's Chosen,' Ogmund replied automatically, cursing himself for his lack of manners.

'Godred? Is that Godred, son of Harald? The one who is called Hardmouth much of the time?' demanded Gudrod, his light, amused tone still apparent even filtered through the ringmail over his mouth. 'Does he still bellow like a bull with a wasp up its arse?'

43

A few men chuckled and Ogmund turned a little to silence them.

'What enlightenment?' demanded Ogmund, deciding to ignore Gudrod's question. 'What brings the last of Eirik Bloodaxe's sons all the way to a wee chapel in the wilds of Mann? Is your mam looking for a priest to confess her sins to?'

The implication that there was no-one closer who would absolve Gunnhild did not wing its way past those behind Ogmund and there were more chuckles, which Ogmund was pleased to hear.

Gudrod may have scowled under his helmet, but only he knew. The hands shifted, spreading wide in a graceful gesture, like a smile.

'We sought a priest, certainly,' Gudrod replied. 'Though it appears he is not to hand. So we will leave as peacefully as we came.'

'Ha!' roared Ulf. 'You and your handful will get what you deserve – the end of a rope.'

The head turned to him and even Ogmund felt the wither of those unseen eyes.

'Whisht, boy,' said the metal voice. 'Men are speaking here.'

Ulf howled then and Ogmund heard the snake-hiss rasp as he dragged his blade out.

'Stay!' he roared out, but Ulf had blood in his eye and was kicking the horse, which had started to doze and was now sprung awake. Shocked, it leaped forward and, without stirrups, Ulf swayed off-balance, so that his sword waved wildly.

'Od,' said the flat-nosed man. 'Kill him.'

The beautiful boy-man moved like silk through a finger-ring. Ogmund had never seen anything move so fast – yet he saw it clearly enough, like a form in a storm-night, etched for an eyeblink against the dark by a flash of lightning. The figure flicked the sword up and out of the belt-ring with the fingers of his left hand, swept it from the air with his

44

right, took one, two, three steps and leaped, turning in the air as he did so, bringing weight to the stroke.

There was a dull clunk and a wet hiss, then the man called Od landed lightly on his feet and turned to stride, unconcerned, back to where he had started. Something round and black bounced once or twice and rolled almost to Ogmund's feet.

The horse cantered on, then tasted the iron stink of blood, squealed and tried to run from it, so that the body on its back, blood pluming from the raggled neck, tipped, slumped and finally fell off into the broom.

There was silence. Ogmund looked at the thing at his feet and met Ulf's astounded left eye; the right had shattered in the fall and watery blood crept sluggishly from the severed neck.

'This is Od,' Gudrod said in his inhuman voice, waving one hand at the angel. 'He is by-named Hrafndans.'

Ravendance. It was such a good by-name that men sucked in their breath at it, as if they could see those black birds on branches, joyously bobbing from foot to foot as they waited for the kills this youth would leave them. They looked at this Od, then, as he took to one knee, sword grasped by the hilt and held like a cross, praying. It was when he licked Ulf's blood from his blade that they all realised that it was Tyr Of Battles, the Wolf's Leavings, he was praying to, dedicating Ulf's life to the god. There was a flurry of hands as they crossed themselves.

'You should know that Od is only one of my crew. Nor did I come from Orkney on a little faering,' Gudrod said. 'I am the son of Queen Gunnhild and King Eirik Bloodaxe, after all.'

Ogmund licked his lips. Once he had had to beat a horse until it bled before it would cross a tiny rivulet to the green sward on the other side, and when it did so, the leap took it into the sucking bog that had only looked like a firm bank. Ogmund had spent a long, sweating time hanging on while the horse plunged and struggled itself back to trembling safety, knowing that if he fell in his ringmail he was doomed.

He felt that same fear now, glancing round at the trees where men were hidden, he was sure. How many ships would Bloodaxe's son bring from Orkney? His sister was married on to the jarl, in the name of God – how many ships would he not bring? The trees hid long hundreds of men in Ogmund's mind.

'So we will leave,' Gudrod ended, his voice cold as the metal rings which hid his face. 'You will not stop us.'

Which is what happened. Ogmund considered the sight of them vanishing from him, then stirred Ulf's head with one foot.

'Gather this up,' he said. 'We will take him back and tell everyone that he died for pride and stupidity and that the three miserable bandits who raided were actually a prince of Orkney and many ships of men. Though they outnumbered us, our fierceness chased them off.'

The others agreed, because they had been too feared to fight and knew it, a secret shame they did not want out in the world. It began to rain a little, a cooling mist that refreshed Ogmund as he watched Ulf loaded like a sack on to his uneasy horse. Ogmund smiled to himself, careful not to let it show on his face; it had not been such a bad day.

Two miles away, the three miserable bandits rested on a knee and Gudrod took off the helmet, so that he could raise his face, like a bairn's fresh-skelped arse, to the cool mirr of rain. His short, curled beard pearled with moisture.

'No Drostan,' Gudrod declared. 'But at least we learned something from those monks – old Irish-Shoes is here on Mann, in Holmtun.'

'Aye, well – the church in Holmtun was where Hoskuld said the priest lived. Olaf Cuarans will have him,' Erling said with a certainty he did not entirely feel. 'His hand is closer, after all – he rules here as well as Dyfflin, no matter what Hardmouth Godred MacHarald thinks.'

'You would think that the priests of this place would know this Drostan,' Gudrod said, baffled. 'What news he brought – of a dead companion – is worthy of being written down by them who scratch down everything that goes on. If they did, they kept that writing hidden well – there is no mention of a monk called Drostan coming to them with news of two dead in the hills. You would also think that Godred Hardmouth would know that and tell his Chosen Men.'

Erling shrugged, having no explanation for any of it. Truth was, he had never thought to find any monk or priest and that tales of Eirik's famous axe were just that – tales. As for searching out writings – well, none of them here could read and if the monks had admitted to it, the document they scribbled on would have to have been taken to someone who could unravel the Latin of it. He kept his lip stitched on all this, all the same, for Gudrod was Eirik's son and the Witch-Queen his mother.

'Olaf Cuarans is where we go next,' Gudrod said, settling the helmet in the crook of his arm. 'Old Irish-Shoes wants my da's axe, that is certain and he is sleekit as a wet seal – it would not surprise me if he told no-one his plans, not even his hard-mouthed jarl here.'

Erling swallowed thickly at the idea of sailing into Holmtun proper and facing the might of the Dyfflin Norse.

'Is that wise, lord? Orkney and Ireland have never been friends.'

'My mother wishes it,' Gudrod said and his tolling bell voice was as hard metal as if he still wore the helmet, 'so we must find a way.'

'She will have me be a king yet,' he added bitterly and ran one hand through the iron raggles of his thinning hair. 'Since I am the youngest.'

Erling got stiffly to his feet, saying nothing, though he knew that Gunnhild's youngest had in fact been called Sigurd, by-named the Slaver. Klypp the Herse had killed him some time ago, after Sigurd forced himself on his wife while a guest in his hall. Gudrod was not so much Gunnhild's youngest as the only one of her sons left alive.

This did not, he thought to himself sullenly, give him the right to put them all in danger.

'Next time,' he said bitterly, 'we will take all the crew with us, I am sure.'

Gudrod only grunted, something between laughter and scorn, then jerked his fleshy chin towards Od, who was picking the congealed blood from the blade as he cleaned it, sucking his fingers now and then. He looked up and smiled blandly at Gudrod and Erling from under the dagged black curtain of his hair.

'We have your heathen dog,' Gurdrod said and then unlooped a small bag from his belt and grinned. Erling sighed.

'Lord,' he said, 'we should be moving on. There is no time for *hnefatafl*.'

'There is always time for 'tafl,' Gudrod replied, unfolding the cloth and placing the counters. 'Anyway, it should not take long – you are a poor player.'

Erling sighed, then turned to look at Od.

'Do not do that,' he said. 'You will be sick.'

Od smiled like a summer's day, his lips bright with blood.

'I am never sick,' he answered.

THREE

The Frisian coast, a little later . . .

CROWBONE'S CREW

CROWBONE lay on the lip of the seawall, peering through the grass and meadow flowers. Bees hummed and, next to him, Kaetilmund lay, chewing a stem and squinting across the neat fields to the raised mound and the houses on it.

A *terp* it was called, a mound heaped up above the flood-plain in case the earth dyke that Crowbone lay on was not enough to keep out the sea. The fields might be awash, but the Frisian folk of this place would keep their homes dry on an island of their own making.

'What is that one doing?' Kaetilmund demanded and Crowbone had to admit, for once, that he did not have any idea. The thrall had an axe and looked to be trying to cut a section from a branch that had a slight curve at one end to use on the pole lathe next to him. An old man was watching him, unconcerned, perhaps to make sure he did not use the axe for anything but woodcutting, though the thrall was not having a deal of success with that.

He cut once, twice – then the head flew off the axe and he

went and fetched it, stuck it back on the haft and bent over the thick branch again. One, two, three – and the head flew off the axe. He went to fetch it. The old man shook his head in sorrow and spat.

The idiot thrall, small and dark and ragged, was not what occupied Crowbone. He and Kaetilmund had come to see if this was the place the snake-boat raiders had launched from and, if so, how many men they had left.

By the time the Swift-Gliding had been worked to shore with a makeshift steerboard fastening of poor bast rope there was the raid-thrill on all of Hoskuld's crew, which made the Oathsworn laugh. Thick as linen on those who had never had much chance for raiding, it set them to staring at the land with their hands flexing, as if grasping hilt and shaft. They no longer saw wave or water, only riches and fame and Gjallandi, as grinning and glaured with it as any of them, clapped their shoulders and spoke of gold, boasting of old exploits and new ones to come.

Crowbone and Kaetilmund had gone ahead and now it was clear there were few, if any, fighting men left in the Frisian place. There was the idiot thrall who made Kaetilmund chuckle and that was interesting enough. There was the white-haired Frisian who watched him and the man in the cage nearby.

There was the strangeness that Crowbone studied, his head cocked to one side. The man had been imprisoned for a time, it seemed, and was hard to see into the shadows of the cage. Yet he was a man in a cage and, every now and then, the idiot thrall would stop and peer in, as if anxious, then go back to doing what clearly was fretting to Kaetilmund.

'Odin's arse, man – fix the fucking axehead,' he muttered, as if the thrall could hear him. The thrall thought up a new way and tried many little, fast strokes, since large ones simply loosened the axehead faster. That caused the branch to shift sideways and, after chasing it for a few steps, the thrall put a foot on it and kept cutting, so that Kaetilmund sucked in his breath and at once by-named the idiot No-Toes, since he predicted that as the most likely outcome.

Then the thrall changed the branch round and this time, when he put his foot on it, he did it on the curved end, so that it flew up and smacked his shin. The old man shouted something; Kaetilmund stuffed his knuckles in his mouth to keep from laughing aloud and the effort squeezed a fart from him.

Crowbone did not laugh. Memory washed through him of another time he had lain hidden in the grass, a memory dark as Munin's wings. Lying in the grass above Klerkon's summer settlement on Svartey, the Black Island, having run away yet again. Of course, being an island, there was no escape from Klerkon, the raider who had taken Crowbone and his mother and killed his foster-father. For all that, escape was what Crowbone had done more than once and, each time, hunger had driven him back to see what he could steal – and each time he had been captured he had been punished more harshly than before.

They had seen him this time, too, so that he had crouched down and pretended to be dead, not moving, not breathing, hidden in the long grass and so small at eight that he could easily be missed as they swished a way towards him.

Then a fart hissed out of him. He thought that was good, for he knew that the dead farted, sheep and men both and so would add to his subterfuge. Then the hand had gripped him like a vice and one of Klerkon's men, Amundi Brawl, hauled him up, laughing about how the smell had given him away.

Klerkon, his goat-face twisted with anger, had thrown Crowbone back to Inga, Randr Sterki's wife, snarling at her to make sure the boy knew he was a thrall and not to let him loose again. Inga, furious at having been so embarrassed, fetched sheep-shears and a seax, then cropped Crowbone's head to the bone and beyond, flicking off old scabs and

51

scraping new wounds until the blood got in the way and she gave up.

'There,' she said, wiping her hands clean on dry grass brought by her own son, the grinning Eyvind, full of his ten years and malice at his ma's tormentor.

'Now,' Inga said, 'you will be fixed to the privy by a chain and stay there until you learn that you are a nithing thrall.'

'I am a prince,' he had spat back and she had smashed his mouth with a scream of rage. He had wanted his mother, then, but she was already dead, kicked to death by the man who had put his bairn in her. It was him, Kveldulf, who fastened Crowbone to the privy and left him there.

Revenge. The day Orm and the Oathsworn had come to raid Klerkon and freed him, the day Klerkon's own precious bairn went against the side of a wall and had the life broken from it with a snap and a last wail, that day he got his revenge.

Inga, begging and pleading, snarling and fighting, as the Oathsworn held her down and someone – who had it been? Crowbone squeezed his head, but could not remember clearly. Red Njal, maybe? Finn? No matter – the man who had broken his way into Inga had stabbed her first and a frantic Eyvind had died trying to save her. Orm had taken off the back of his head with a sword-stroke.

Crowbone had bent to Inga as the men had left her, choking in her own blood on the flank of a dying ox.

'I am a prince,' he had said, his breath wafting the dying flutter of her eyelashes. 'You should have listened.'

Princely revenge. He shook the memories from him and shoved them back in the black sea-chest he kept in his head. Stuffed full, it was, of all those matters a prince finds expedient and necessary. Lesser men are allowed to brood on them, Crowbone thought, but princes who would be kings cannot afford them. Vladimir had taught him that, having learnt it from his own father, the harsh Sviatoslav.

'Thor's hairy balls,' Kaetilmund hissed with delight. 'We

52

have to have this thrall, Crowbone, just for the joy of watching him.'

Crowbone stirred out of the past and peered down. The thrall had cut his length of wood and fixed it to the lathe, wrapping the rope round it once, then twice. It was clear the lathe-grip was faulty, for when he pumped the footboard, the lump of wood spun obligingly – then flew off like an arrow from a bow, straight into the open doorway of a house. There was a shriek and a clatter, followed by a scream of woman who lunged out and proceeded to shriek at the old man, who in turn took to battering the thrall round the head and shoulders, grunting and red-faced with the effort.

The thrall took it all, half-curled, like a rock in a storm. When it had washed over him and the woman went off, panting, he got wearily to his feet, fetched the lump of wood, wrapped it in the rope and fastened it on the lathe.

'No, no,' Kaetilmund declared with glee. 'Surely not . . .'

But he did. He pumped the footboard, the lump of wood flew off and smacked the side of the house, then bounced, scattering chickens in an irate din.

Crowbone turned and grabbed Kaetilmund's shoulder, signalling that they should slither away, as the woman burst from the house with fresh howls.

There were more shrieks when men from the sea came down on them not long after, grey and snarling as wolves. Shrieking and running, dragging stumbling bairns by the wrist, what was left of the little *terp* went out across their mean fields like scattering sheep.

The Oathsworn did not bother with them much – there was no room in Hoskuld's boat for slaves and enough of the better-looking ones had stayed, cowering, for men to look over and decide what to do with.

Hoskuld's crew did the fighting and chasing, yelling and waving weapons, slick with the raid-lust that comes on men who never usually get a lick of the *rann-sack* – even Hoskuld himself puffed along with a long, single-edged old seax in one fist and kicked a door, beaming from the great headland of his face. His snarling joy was spoiled a little when the door did not give way and the force of his kick landed him on his arse. He got up, looking right and left, while folk pretended not to notice.

There were only two fighters. One was the white-hair, who came storming round the side of the main steading of the place, an axe in either hand and both wrists with enough old memories in them to show that, in his youth, he would have been feared.

Gorm aimed a wild swing at him, which the man easily dodged and, if he had not been slowed by age and stiffness, the return would have spilled a deal of Gorm's belly into the kale patch. It did enough to make Gorm back off and call for help, so that Halk rushed in from one side and the old man, snarling with the desperation of the doomed, hurled himself on the Orkneyman with a shrill cry, like an owl threading the night with screech.

Crowbone watched Gorm and Halk cut the old man down, flurrying blows long after the blood-speckled grey hair was the only thing that moved on the man, wisping stickily in the wind.

'Bravely done,' Murrough growled and spat. Crowbone said nothing; brave or not, it was done and that was what mattered.

The other fighter was the idiot thrall, who took up the wood axe and moved to the caged man, turning this way and that, standing guard. Hoskuld scrambled up from his episode with the door and launched himself at the thrall, thinking the stub of a nithing would turn and run.

Instead, the axe whirled up and cut. It would have been a death-blow, for sure, save that the loose axehead flew off, back over the thrall's shoulder and made Vandrad Sygni hunch his neck into his shoulders as it whizzed past him. But the thrall's blow was with the haft only, which was battleluck for Hoskuld, since it took him in the left ribs and drove the air out of him as if he was a dead cow. Then the thrall followed it up with a head smack that laid Hoskuld flat with a groan.

'Do not kill him!' Kaetilmund yelled, as Vandrad, scowling, nocked an arrow to his bow. 'That thrall is too valuable to waste.'

The Oathsworn agreed with some chuckles – all save Vandrad, who still had the memory of the axe-bit bird-whirring too close to his head – and closed in on the thrall, who half-crouched with his stick. Inside the cage, the shadowed figure stirred and Crowbone saw the gleam of white hair or beard.

'Hold there,' Vigfuss said. 'Drop that little stick and no harm will come to you.'

A choking laugh came from the shadowed figure in the cage. 'Too late for that,' he wheezed.

The thrall did not move at all, but a young dog the colour of yellow corn suddenly bounded out from behind some huts and skidded up to stand before him, legs splayed and growling.

The Oathsworn tensed a little, for no-one liked dogs, which were just fur bundles with a mouthful of filthy blades.

'Call that hound off, thrall,' Vandrad rumbled. 'Or I will kill it and whack your bottom with your little stick.'

'It is a bitch,' the caged man growled. 'A guard for the village.'

'Not such a good one,' Crowbone pointed out and felt the caged man's eyes appraising him. He did not like to be watched where he could not see and so moved a little way round, to try and see more than just the gleam of white hair or beard; the thrall watched him, flexing his hand on the axe-shaft. The yellow dog wagged her tail and licked the back of the thrall's hand.

'It liked everyone too much,' the caged man observed.

'Now you have your reward,' Crowbone said, 'for if it had

been on guard, perhaps your village would not be leaking blood down the street.'

'Not my village,' said the caged man and now Crowbone saw him clearly – a thin face, like a ravaged hawk, with a shock of white hair and a tangle of grey-white beard. He had a tunic and breeks, which had once been fine but were now smeared and stained with blood and the leakings from filthy wrappings round both of his hands. The eyes that met Crowbone's own were fox-sharp, all the same.

Murrough, hearing women shriek and wanting to be off in that direction, finally had had enough. 'Throw down that stick,' he growled jutting his jaw, but the look he got back caught Crowbone's attention and made him study the thrall intently.

There was no wolf at bay in those eyes, nor was there the wild flare of darting looks that sought an escape. Most revealing of all, there was the stare itself. A thrall who knew that his place was no more than that of a sheep would have stared at the ground. Instead, the thrall's eyes, slightly narrowing, were a blue appraisal of Murrough, as if marking where he would strike for best effect. It was then, too, that Crowbone saw the thrall was fastened by a length of chain to the cage and, for a moment, felt the sharp bite of his own thrall's chain on his neck, tasted the acrid stink of the privy.

Murrough saw the thrall's look, too, and was made wary by it – which showed sense, Crowbone thought, but still he snapped a command for Murrough to be still just in case the Irishman launched an attack certain to include pain for one or the other and possibly a deal of blood. The others watched, wary as hounds round a stag.

'Berto,' said the grey-head, almost wearily, 'I am done. Let their leader come up.'

The youth called Berto let the stick drop a notch and half-turned to the man in the cage, his bland, beardless face furrowed with concern. The tension leached away and, lumbering up like a great bear, Onund Hnufa clapped Murrough on one shoulder and glanced at the thrall.

'Not bad, *fetar-garmr*,' he said and folk laughed at the term, which meant 'chain-dog' and could be directed at both the thrall and the yellow bitch equally. Then Onund turned to Murrough and the others.

'Leather,' he said and they remembered why they had come and went off to hunt some out. Kaetilmund stayed and went slowly up to the cage and cracked it open with a sharp blow that made the dog squeeze out a bark. Murrough hauled out the man, gently enough, and the thrall knelt by his head. When Crowbone moved up, the thrall fixed him with summer-sky eyes dulled with misery.

'My thanks,' the grey-hair said to Crowbone. 'This is Berto. He is from the Wend lands. I am called Grima, from Bjarmaland.'

'A long way from home,' Crowbone noted and Grima chuckled, a moth-wing of sound. His wrapped hands soaked some fresh blood on to the old stains of his tunic. There was gold thread in that tunic, Crowbone noted.

'Need help with those fingers, old yin?' Kaetilmund asked. 'We have a skald who knows some healing runes.'

Grima smiled and raised both blood-swaddled hands.

'Hrodfolc's joke,' he said. 'He fed me bowls of good stew with meat in, but cut a finger off and never let me know which stew it was in. Where is he, by the way?'

Crowbone told him and Grima's grin was sharp and yellow.

'Good. Nithing Frisian *fud* – he thought I would not eat for fear of swallowing my own flesh,' Grima said and then laughed. 'He knew better when I asked him to cook it longer – my own meat is a little too aged to be tender.'

Crowbone and Kaetilmund smiled at this, a defiance they appreciated.

'Balle did this to me, the whore's by-blow,' Grima wheezed.

His eyes closed while pain washed through him, keen enough for Crowbone to feel it as well.

'This flatness is no place for a man from the north mountains to die,' he added. 'Who are you, then, who is here to witness it?'

Crowbone told him, adding that the death was still a way off – then Kaetilmund finished unwrapping the first of the hands and Crowbone saw the ugly black and red and pus yellow of it. He realised the bright glitter of Grima's eyes was fever.

'Good,' said Grima. 'Now all truths are almost unveiled. The gods are kind, for I know your fame. With your help I will leave this cursed place and die where I belong. But I have little time, so listen, Olaf, son of Tryggve, now of the Oathsworn. I am Grima. Once I was known as you are known, for I led the *Raudanbrodrum* – do you know of them?'

The Red Brothers. Crowbone had heard of this *varjazi* band and their leader's name, which meant 'a full helm' in the honest tongue of the north and was usually given to a man whose face was hard and set as iron, so that only his eyes gave anything away. He had not heard these names for some years and said so; Grima nodded weakly.

'This is the last you see here. We are rule-bound – though not as fiercely oathed as you – and most of us did not do well faring out in the east, along the Silk Road, so we came down on to the decent waters of the Baltic and raided the Wend lands, where I thought they would be fat and lazy, since it had not seen *rann-sack* for some years. Well, here I am, dying for lack of luck – the raiding was poor and all we had was Berto here, which a certain Balle did not think enough. He is wrong – Berto is worth a deal as you may discover when the matter is ripe. I hear you were luckier – all the silver of the world, eh?'

'Yet we are here, in the same flat shit-hole,' Kaetilmund pointed out, hoping to take Grima's mind off the second

58

unwrapping, for the bindings were matted to the stumps and Grima hissed blood on to his teeth from his bitten lip.

'You still fare better than me, I am thinking,' he answered wryly, when he could speak, 'since most of your fingers are still on the end of your hands and your life is not unravelled yet. Now here is the way of it. Balle was my Chosen Man, but he grew tired of waiting and did not want to challenge in the usual way, the white-livered tick. He killed all the men who were loyal to me – not many, the years had thinned them, but I realised that too late – and threw me over the side of my own ship. I would have been red-murdered then if Berto had not leaped after and towed me to shore. The gods clearly turned their back on me all the same – for this Hrodfolc took us both.'

Kaetilmund gave Berto an admiring grin.

'Well, No-Toes,' he declared. 'You may have no skill with an axe or a lathe, but it seems you are more fish than chain-dog.'

Crowbone simply wondered why the thrall had done it, for there seemed little reason for it. Grima saw the look and knew it for what it was. When he spoke Crowbone jerked, as he always did when he suspected folk were reading the whirl of his thought-cage.

'Perhaps because I did not kill him and he was no better than a thrall when I took him anyway,' Grima said. 'Nothing much changed for him except he breathed sea air. I am in his debt. I have nothing to give to him but what I can make happen in the short time left me, with my last breaths. He has eighteen summers on him and will prove valuable to you. Trust me in this and free him, in return for what I can give.'

Crowbone smiled.

'What makes you think you have anything I need?' he pointed out and Grima grinned; sweat rolled off him. Gjallandi had come up in time to see and make tutting sounds as he inspected the ruin of the old warrior's hands.

'You are a prince with no princely ship crew I can see,' Grima grunted. 'Unless you have more hidden away. Which means you have no princely ship, either. I am jarl of the Red Brothers, who are a crew with a ship and in need of a prince. Free Berto and I will lead you to them. Kill this Balle and those who follow him and make me jarl again – then I will hand crew and ship to you, for I have no use for them where I am going.'

Crowbone considered it and was thinking the old man might not last long enough for all this. He was set to scowling when Grima chuckled.

'I will live long enough to watch Balle's face when I arrive full in it with a prince and a fistful of the famed Oathsworn,' he growled and Crowbone sat still for a time, put out at the idea of the old man reading his thoughts – or, worse, his own face being so blatant that anyone could see what went on inside his head.

Then he nodded and spoke the words aloud, so there would be no going back. The thrall blinked a little from the bland round of his face and Kaetilmund, grinning, cracked the links of the chain, so that the freed thrall could unravel himself.

'There you have it, No-Toes,' he said. 'Fetch that axehead back and fix it on properly, for you can carry it like a man now. You had better thank Prince Olaf here, for now you are a warrior.'

'I am Berto. I am thanking.'

The voice was high and thick with accent, for the Wend knew Norse only as spoken by Frisians and his own sort, which was as like the true sounds of men as dogs barking. Crowbone held the flat gaze of the Wend with his own odd eyes, seeing the deep blue eyes and round olive face of a youth not yet even into beard. He had seen Wends before, travelling up the Odra River with Orm. He had not thought much of them, so he was surprised to find himself being studied carefully and there was something both attractive and disturbing about that; not much of a thrall in his own lands, this one, he thought, that he can keep his head up and his eyes bold. He found he had muttered as much aloud.

'No doubt a prince at home,' Onund grunted, hearing it as he passed. 'As all thralls are who are raided from others.'

He went away laughing, with others who knew how Crowbone had been rescued by Orm – and claimed his princely rank with his first words – joining in. Crowbone, remembering the slaughter that had come after, could not find a smile and turned to the old man instead, cocking his head in a question.

'We have a *stöðvar*,' Grima said. 'An old seasonal place where we lie up. The crew will be there, for Balle has all the clever of a rock and thinks me dead and gone.'

Berto the Wend bent his head over the old man while the yellow dog whined and tried to shove its scarred ears under an oxter. It was, Kaetilmund thought, a powerful, wedge-headed bitch and as ugly an animal as ever disgraced the earth. A strange friend for a thrall, he thought – but the Norns had woven them a deal of luck and you had to take such matters into account.

Berto cradled the old man's head and waved away the greedy flies as Gjallandi marked out fresh runes on clean wrappings and rebound the blackening stumps. The metallic stink of blood was strong and the sweat ran stinging in Crowbone's eyes.

'This is Prince Olaf,' Grima said to Berto, his eyes closed. 'He will one day be a king and, if your life-luck holds as firm as it has done, you may profit each other yet, for all that he is of the Oathsworn and you follow the Christ.'

Crowbone looked at Berto and saw the fierceness in his round, large-eyed, sharp-nosed face, so that he looked, for a moment, like a hunting owl. He nodded. Grima spasmed with pain as Hoskuld's men picked him up and half-carried, half-dragged him back to the ship.

Onund Hnufa lumbered up as the harsh stink of smoke

61

wafted to Crowbone's nose. The same wind brought distant sobbing and the crackle of burning and Crowbone turned moodily away as the *terp* started to flare and burn, spilling smoke to stain the sky.

Onund lumbered alongside, happily clutching their entire treasure – a stiff, thick square of half-cured leather the size of his chest.

Holmtun, Isle of Mann, some time later . . .

OLAF IRISH-SHOES

Jarl Godred perched on a bench in his own hall while Olaf lolled in his High Seat draped in a winter wolf pelt that ran like a river of milk down on to his shoulders. Under the fur coddling them his shoulders were still wide, despite his hair and the winter wolf pelt being the same colour. The matching white beard was twisted in three long braids weighted with rust-spotted iron rings. Above it, out of a knob-cheeked face, the eyes, feral as hunting cats, glittered like blue ice.

Godred saw that what could be a smile was hacked out of the Jarl of the Dyfflin's lumpy face as he deviously questioned Ogmund about the raiders. Not only was the old war-dog spoiling for another bash at the Ui Neill – a war Godred had always thought beyond foolish – now he was showing an unhealthy interest in monks.

Olaf's royal belly strained the tunic, which had been delicate green trimmed with red knotwork once but was now mainly food stains; standing close to him, Ogmund thought it might be possible to trace the whole life of Olaf Irish-Shoes in those stains, meal by meal, like reading runes on a raised stone.

'This son of Gunnhild said he sought the monk Drostan?' the Jarl of Dyfflin asked, the smile still like a cleft in rock.

Ogmund wished the lord of Dyfflin would not smile, for it

was as off-putting as wolf-breath on the back of your neck. So was the look of his own Jarl Godred and he knew Hardmouth was less than happy with the entire business – especially the arrival of Olaf Irish-Shoes, stamping his authority.

'Not in all those words,' he answered, 'but it was clear that was what he did when you tally matters up.'

He glanced at Godred, who sat next to Sitric, Olaf's younger son. The twig does not fall far from the tree, Ogmund thought, for Sitric, still dark-haired, was round-faced and stocky. One day he and his da would be as alike as two gobs of spit – the eldest boy was a third gob of the same spit and limped so that no-one these days called him anything but Jarnkne – Iron Knee.

There was another son, Raghnall, back in Dyfflin and Ogmund had seen him, too. Tall and cream-haired, from a different mother, he was Olaf's favourite. He liked his women, did Olaf – currently he was thundering himself into the thighs of an Irish beauty called Gormflaeth and showing little sign that his belly got in the way of matters.

'We know Ulf found two dead monks in a *keill* up in the hills,' Sitric growled, shaking his head. 'One looked to have had his head beaten in, but the rats had eaten well on the pair of them, it was hard to tell. Two monks, all the same. This Drostan is dead.'

'Then who was with Hoskuld the Trader?' demanded Olaf, leaning back on the High Seat and spreading his feet to the fire – sensibly shod feet, Ogmund noted with surprise but then, the name '*cuarans*', Irish Shoes, was only given by Norwegians and Danes as a sneer against the Dyfflin Norse, who were all thought to be half-Irish of lesser worth because they had forgotten how to be true people and taken to wearing Irisher sandals.

'Hoskuld came to Dyfflin with a monk, but I never saw him,' Olaf went on, fiddling with his beard rings. 'Hoskuld came with a preposterous tale of how this monk knew where Eirik's old axe was and that this monk he had was prepared

63

to reveal the where of it for money. The monk, Hoskuld said, would only come to me in person once assurances had been given – which was not a little insulting, I was thinking.'

'I thought it the worst attempt to gull you out of silver I had heard in many a long day,' Sitric rumbled and his father nodded and grinned ruefully.

'Aye – but Hoskuld is a good trader and valued, so I let him have his night's hospitality, as if I considered the matter. Truth was I had already decided to send him packing back to his shy monk, or else bring the charlatan before me – but before I could do anything, Hoskuld left my hall. In haste. In the night. That was even more insulting, as if he thought I would do him harm.'

'Not so stupid, though,' Sitric growled, 'since that is what he deserved for such a tale.'

His father looked sharply at him.

'Yet here is Gunnhild's last son, come from Orkney looking for a monk,' he said. 'A man with the sense of a stone can see that this tale of Hoskuld's now has legs on it.'

'Find Hoskuld,' answered Godred and Olaf soured the jarl with a hard look.

'Good idea,' he snarled. 'I had not thought of it at all now that it is clear Gunnhild seeks him hard enough to send her last son.'

Godred's cheeks grew pale, then red, but he said nothing, merely picked moodily at a loose thread on the hem of his own tunic and perched on a bench in his own hall while Olaf lolled in his High Seat and his son grinned.

'I want this Hoskuld,' Olaf declared suddenly, 'but unlike Gunnhild I do not have the ships to spare – I need them and you, Godred, for the war that is coming.'

Godred merely nodded and said nothing. Olaf Irish-Shoes had been thrashing around in a fight with Domnall and the southern Ui Neill for years and, only this year, Domnall had finally decided to throw it all away and enter the monastery at Armagh. Good news all round, Godred thought bitterly – but now the old man had decided to wave his sword at the new leader of the Ui Neill in the north, Mael Sechnaill.

'In five days,' Olaf declared, levering himself stiffly out of the chair, 'I want you and your men in Dyfflin. Then we are off to teach this Ui Neill puppy a lesson. Send your best man after this Hoskuld – but no more than a snake-ship's crew.'

Godred nodded and watched the old man stump off, calling for Sitric and complaining of the damp as he hauled his fur tighter round him. Battles, he thought bitterly. The old fool lives only for battle and will risk everything on the outcome of a stupid fight; he has lost as many thrones as he has gained. The thought of losing everything here on Mann if the old war-dog failed made Godred waspish.

'Find Hoskuld,' he snarled at Ogmund. 'Take the *Swan Breath* and same arses you got to lie for you over the Gudrod business and see you make more of a fist of matters when next you meet that Orkney bitch-tick. Get this Hoskuld and the secret he holds. I was going to send Ulf, but you have contrived to get him killed. Now you will have to do.'

Ogmund watched Hardmouth leave the hall, the anger burning in his chest so hard that he found himself rubbing his knuckles on his breastbone. He would not have taken that when he had been young, he thought, then swallowed the sick despair at that truth.

He was no longer young when the likes of Godred could lash him and walk away.

The Frisian coast, a little later . . .

CROWBONE'S CREW

He had many names. The Arabs gave him Abou Saal. The Church called him Biktor the Nubian and the True People, the Ga-Adagbes, knew him as Nunu-Tettey – Nunu, because all the Nubii males were called after the Divine Celestial Waters and Tettey because he was first-born.

Here, they called him Kaup. Sometimes they called him Kaup Svarti. Kaup came from their mistake when he tried to tell them that he was a Christian, but not one they knew. Copt, he had told them, but they were stinking, ignorant northmen and thought he was saying *kaup*, which meant 'bargain' in their tongue and they thought that thigh-slapping funny, since they had hauled him from the ruin of an Arab slaver and so had got him for free.

Svarti, of course, because it meant black. Black was a poor word to describe Kaup, all the same; Mar Skidasson, closest thing to a friend Kaup had among the Red Brothers, had likened Kaup's colour to the wing of a crow in sunlight, that glossy blue-black colour. He knew a good name when he heard one did Mar – his own by-name was Jarnskeggi, Iron Beard, and Kaup had to admit that Mar's hair was exactly that colour.

Kaup grew no hair on his face and the stuff on his head was a tight nap that never got longer, only a little greyer at the temples, for it had been a long time since the slave ship in the Dark Sea. With little hope of returning home, Kaup had been with the Red Brothers of Grima for years and, after they had crept round the unnerving fact that he looked like a man two weeks dead, most of the northmen found Kaup good company. He laughed a lot and they envied the white of his teeth and the way his black skin always shone, as if buttered.

Still, in all the years with Grima, Kaup had never been sure whether he was a slave or a warrior. He knew slaves of the northmen were treated no better than livestock and not allowed to carry weapons, but Kaup had a spear and a shield and one of their long knives, called a seax. He had killed for them and had his share of loot – yet when something had to be fetched or carried, it was always 'the Burned Man' who was sent to do it and expected to carry it out with no mutter.

Standing watch was another of the matters he was expected to do. Wrapped in a wool blanket he had made into a cloak, standing on one leg like a stork and leaning on his spear, Kaup was less happy than he had ever been, for Grima – whom he had liked – was gone and Balle was now in charge. Kaup did not like Balle and neither did Mar, who had had to twist his face into many agreeable positions to avoid the fate of others who had been good friends with the old jarl.

Not long after Balle had thrown Grima and the Wend into the sea they had come down to this old berth, which they had not visited in many years. At this time of year, no-one expected to see another ship, yet before Kaup's eyes a fat trader muscled in to the shingle and men spilled to the shore.

There was a tingle on him when he ran to report this strangeness and the skin of his forearms was stippled and grew tighter when he and Mar and Balle went to look at the newcomers.

'A fat *knarr*,' Balle said, a shine in his eyes, relief showing in his broad, deep-marked face the colour of old wood. It would be relief for Balle, thought Mar, for he would be eager to show he had better luck than Grima, luck that brought a great plump duck right into the teeth of all these foxes.

'Teeth,' said Kaup and Mar jerked at this echo of his thoughts, then looked at the *knarr*, seeing the helmets and the dull gleam – like still, dark water – of ringmail. His own eyes narrowed at that, for there were more than a few of them and the one who was clearly the leader had a helmet in the Gardariki style, with a white horsehair plume braiding out of it, like smoke from a roofhole. All of his men had similar helms, but his was worked with brass and silver. Truly, this *knarr* had teeth.

'A hard fistful,' growled Balle, studying the men, tallying

the possibilities. 'Yet their leader is only a stripling and there's no more than a handful of nithing sailors.'

The Red Brothers numbered fifty-eight and, after all their bad raid-luck, even the ones who did not like Balle much and thought he still had matters to prove would follow him: it would be an easy prize with the numbers on their side. Even if it was empty, the *knarr* alone was worth it.

Mar felt Kaup shift beside him, tasted the big dark man's unease along with the salt from the sighing sea. It smelled of blood and his hackles stirred a little.

Balle watched and waited, feeling his men filter up in knots and pairs to look, not wanting to turn round to see how many, which would have made him look as if he was anxious. He was pleased, all the same, when he caught sight of some, out of the corner of one eye; they were armed and ready.

He would wait until the crew of this fat trader had finished unloading whatever it was in the bundle they thought to appease him with. The stripling who led them would come, arms out and easy to show he meant no harm but wanted only to share warmth and food and maybe trade whatever was in the bundle. He does not realise, Balle thought, with a lurch of blood-savage, that all he has is already mine.

The stripling came and with him was a worryingly big man with a hook-bitted axe leading the helmeted ones carrying the burden. The stripling came with a spear in each fist and the walk of a man who did not want to appease anyone, which Mar and Kaup noticed and frowned at, glancing sideways at Balle. They all noticed the youth's coin-weighted braids, the neat crop of new beard and the strange, odd-coloured eyes.

Balle had seen it, too, and pushed the worry of it from him as if it was a bothersome dog. The shine of that rich *knarr* was on him and the stripling was still a stripling, who had done as Balle had seen in his head, even if he had a giant at his back, spears in his fists, eyes of different colours and a measure of arrogance which had taken in the Burned Man and showed no shock. Balle had been disappointed at that; the sight of Kaup always made northmen lick uneasy lips and should have made this boy at least blink a little.

Then he saw the truth of what he had thought was a trade bundle and everything in him melted away, running like water out of his bowels and belly, so that he could not move and almost fell where he stood.

It was no wrap of trade goods. It was Grima.

Mar and Kaup grunted, the shock of it stirred through the rest of the Red Brothers like ripples from a stone in a quiet pool. Grima, who was thought drowned and dead, was back, sitting in a throne carried by great mailed warriors, guarded by a giant, preceded by . . .

'Prince Olaf, son of Tryggve,' announced the stripling loudly. 'Come to hold up the falling roofbeams of Grima's sky. Come to bring him back to those who tried to foist red murder on him.'

Now this was real luck to men who knew the shape and taste of it, for Grima had gone into the sea with nothing but the cloth on his back and yet, here he was, sprung out of it, with warriors and a prince at his command.

This was god-favour if ever it was seen and if Grima was so smiled on, then the man who had tried to kill him clearly was not – both those who were Christmenn and those who followed Asgard stepped away from Balle. He felt men draw away from him and anger surged in, which was as good as courage.

Then Grima stirred in his chair and Balle felt the better for seeing how weak and near death the old man was, saw the dark stains on the wrappings round his hands. He saw, also, the little figure appear suddenly from behind the mailed throne-carriers, a yellow dog prowling at his heels.

'Berto,' Kaup called out without thinking how much delight was in his voice, for he had liked the little man.

Berto raised one hand to Kaup in salute, then curled his lip at Balle, who almost went for the man then and there. Arrogant little fuck! A nithing thrall, with a look like that on him . . .

'I speak for Grima,' Berto said, his chin in his chest as he made himself gruff. The fact that he spoke at all in such a way so astounded Balle that he opened and closed his mouth once or twice.

'He challenges Balle for the leadership of the Red Brothers,' Berto went on. 'He declares Balle a white-livered son of a sheep, who lets himself be used as a woman every ninth night by those who supported him in throwing Grima into the sea.'

There was muttering at that and a hissing sound of sucked in air, for there was no stepping back from that insult. The stillness that followed made the sea-breathing seem to roar and a gull cried out like a lost bairn; the stripling leader raised his head and searched for it.

'I take the challenge,' Balle said, 'and after I have won I will not deal kindly with you, Wend.'

Then he twisted his mouth in a nasty smile at Grima.

'Will you stand up long enough for me to kill you?' he asked, knowing Grima was not the one he would have to fight.

The bundle on the throne shifted a little.

'No,' said the husked whisper, which a trick of wind carried down the beach to a lot more ears than should have heard it. 'Yet you cannot kill me, Balle. I will live longer than you.'

Folk made signs on themselves and Balle had to resist the temptation to cross himself, or touch his Thor Hammer, which would have been as sure a sign of weakness as dropping to your knees and babbling for mercy.

'I stand in his place,' said the stripling with two spears.

Mar, looking at Balle as the youth spoke, saw the sudden flood of relief wash the man.

He thought it would be the giant, Mar realised, but thinks

he can beat the stripling. That is wrong; if the stripling fights a big man like Balle, whose name is a warning since it means 'dangerously bold', it means he is their best. Better than a giant with a hooked axe. Mar studied the youth more closely now, but saw nothing in him that spoke of greatness, or even of prince. He was a tall youth with tow hair and a spear in either hand, nothing more. It was clear Balle thought this, too.

'If you have a god,' he growled, low and hackle-raising, 'you had better ask him for help now.'

'I have a god,' the stripling declared, 'and I dedicate you to him. I claim the Red Brothers for Grima and you are the price of it. Will you stand aside or fight?'

Kaup caught the unease that flickered on Balle's face, a moment only, like a flare from a firestarter's spark. Enough, all the same. Balle will lose this and the youth already knows it. Yet the little prince's face was as innocent as a Christ-nun's headsquare.

Balle spat on his hands, hefted the long axe and rolled his shoulders, which was answer enough. The youth smiled and the delight in his voice was a rill of pleasure.

'Odin, hear me – take this Balle, as *blot* for this victory. I, Prince Olaf of the Oathsworn of Orm Bear-Slayer, by-named Crowbone, say this.'

There was a rustle, as if a wind had come up and rushed through unseen trees, as men stirred and sighed. Suddenly, the famed Oathsworn were here, launched out of a clear day and a calm sea like Thor's own Hammer; Mar looked at Kaup and licked dry lips, for the grim mailed men with horsehair smoking from their helmets were now even more fearsome than before.

Balle, too, felt the chill lick of it, but was instantly ashamed and the anger that brought to him was a forge-fire. He hefted the long axe and calculated the distance between him and the stripling – then signalled for Mar to pass over his shield.

Mar paused, then handed it over with a look that flared Balle's rage into his face. He would remember that scorn when this was done and then Mar had better look to himself. Overdue for having his head parted from him, Balle thought.

Kaup watched carefully, for he tucked all such matters of these northmen away in the sea-chest of his head and knew that this was no *holmgang*, with ritual and measured fighting area, but an *einvigi*, unregulated and unsanctified, which most vicious combats were. It did not rely on any god – though Ullr was claimed to be the deity who watched over it – but on skill and battle luck only. Once, when his people were young, Kaup knew that they had worshipped false gods, such as Bes and Apedemak, the god of war, who would have presided over such matters as this.

No matter which of the Asgard gods watched here, Kaup had to admit Balle looked the better man with his long axe on one shoulder, and shield held to cover most of himself against the stripling with two short throwing spears. They faced each other on the sand of a nowhere beach, where the tide-birds scurried, beaking up black mud from a strand silvered by the fading light of an old day.

'You are a big man,' Kaup heard Prince Olaf say said softly to Balle, 'and no doubt of some value to Grima, once, before Loki visited treachery on you. At half your size, I will still be twice as useful to him and three times the fighter you are.'

Balle blinked a bit, worked the insult out and came up spitting and dragging the axe off his shoulder with one hand, though it was unwieldy like that. Yet everyone saw the battle-clever in Balle, for he was about to rush the stripling who had two throwing spears and a seax snugged across his lap.

The youth would get one spear off, which the shield would take – then Balle would throw the shield to one side and close in with the two-handed axe, before the youth transferred his second spear to a throwing hand. Everyone saw it. Everyone knew what would happen – except the youth, it seemed.

Balle lumbered forward; the spear arced and smacked the shield hard – harder than Balle had imagined, so that he reeled a little sideways with it and saw the point splinter through on his side. A powerful throw, but harmless, ruining only the shield.

With a great roar of triumph, he hurled the speared shield to one side and threw himself forward. He had him; he had the youth, for sure.

Something whirred like a bird wing and there was a sharp tearing feeling in Balle's belly, then he tripped and fell, rolled, cursing, scrambling upright and appalled at his bad foot luck. Ready with the axe, he spun in a half circle and almost fell again, looked down and saw a blue, shining rope tangled round his ankles. At the same time as he followed it back to the bloody rip in his shirt and into the very belly of him, a shadow fell and he looked up.

It was the stripling, a thoughtful look on his face and Balle snarled and went to strike, but the axe seemed stuck to the ground. Then something flashed and there was a burning sensation in Balle's throat, harsh and fierce enough for him to drop the axe and spin away. He did not want to touch his throat, was afraid to touch it, but thought to get away from the stripling for a moment, get his breath and then work out how to get back in the fight, for it had clearly gone awry.

He could not hear properly and could not catch his breath and there was a terrible gargling, roaring sound; he found himself on the ground, felt a draining from him, like slow water falling, looked down at the huge bib of red that soaked his tunic.

Never get the stains out of that, he thought. My mother will be furious . . .

Crowbone stuck his seax in a patch of coarse sand once or twice, then wiped the rest of the throat-clot off it on Balle's tunic sleeve, the only bit that was not already covered in the big man's blood. He felt his left thigh start to twitch and hoped no-one had noticed either that or the fear-sweat that soaked him, stinging his eyes to blinking.

No-one spoke, then the Burned Man walked up with Crowbone's second spear, the one that he had thrown with his left hand, the one that had sliced open Balle's belly so deftly that the axeman had scarcely even noticed it until he fell over his own insides. He handed it politely to Crowbone and smiled, unnervingly white, out of the great dead-black of his Hel face.

'Am I leader here?' asked Grima in his hoarse whisper. Men nodded and shuffled.

'Am I leader?' Grima roared and then they bellowed back that he was. Grima, the roar almost the last breath left in him, slumped back in the makeshift throne and whispered to Berto, who nodded and straightened.

'I told Balle I would see his death before mine and so it is and I can let Asgard take me,' Berto said and, for all his piping and thick accent, no-one doubted it was Grima's voice. 'Prince Olaf will be jarl. My silver is his. My ship is his. If you have any clever in you, you will follow him – but mark this. The Red Brothers die with me. You swear to him and the Oathsworn now.'

Men looked at the so-called prince, a stripling digging his spear point into the sand to clean it. The giant with the hook-bitted axe, grinning, worked the other spear point from the shield, then handed the shield back to Mar.

'Sure,' he said, 'there is a fair wee peephole in it now. A good thick leather patch is needed – ask Onund if he has some left from fixing our steer oar. He is the man with the mountain on one shoulder. My name is Murrough macMael.'

Mar looked thoughtfully at the finger-length gash and then nodded to Murrough.

'I will leave it as it is,' he answered blankly. 'The breeze through it will be cooling in the next fight.'

The tension hissed away from the beach. The ring-mailed throne-carriers picked up the chair with Grima in it and started back to the *knarr*; the Red Brothers began to go back in little knots to their fires, but the stripling cleared his throat and they stopped.

He did not say anything, merely pointed – once, twice, picking two men. The third time was at the bloody remains of Balle. The men he pointed out hesitated for an eyeblink; Mar stepped in to that, scowling.

'Pick him up,' he said to the men. 'He was a Christmann so we will bury him.'

He looked at Crowbone. 'Do you have a priest in your crew?'

Crowbone eyed the man up and down, taking in the neat-chopped hair that came down round his ears only, the close-trimmed beard, the cool eyes the colour of a north sea on a raining day. The one, he noted, who had handed his shield to Balle with a look as good as a spit in the eye. A good friend to the Burned Man and the pair of them better on your side than against it. He smiled, for he felt good and the thigh-twitching had ended; he was alive, his enemy was dead and the triumph of it coursed through him like the fire of wine.

'I am a priest,' he said, 'though a good Christ-follower would not think so. Better you say words over him, I am thinking. Better still, of course, if you kept him, for Grima will die tonight and he was no Christmann, I am sure. It would be good to lay this dog at his feet as he burns.'

Mar blinked.

'Is that your command?' he asked and Olaf spread his empty hands in a light, easy gesture and said nothing at all.

Mar nodded, satisfied; here was a follower of the old gods, but not one with his face set against the Christ as hard as he had heard the Oathsworn were. They lifted Balle and carried him away to be buried and Kaup stumbled out some Christ words, as many as he could remember.

Afterwards, they dug him up again and brought him back to the driftwood pyre being prepared for Grima; Mar nodded to Olaf, who smiled at this cunning.

Men came to the pyre, no matter which gods they followed, out of respect for Grima, and Crowbone watched them as Hoskuld, scowling at the cost, spilled expensive aromatic oil on to the driftwood. Crowbone saw which of them mourned, stricken, for Grima and which of them did him honour for what he had once been. There were others and he watched them closer still, the ones who hung at the back and shifted from one foot to the other, trying not to look at each other and make it obvious they were plotting.

Grima burned, hissing and crackling, throwing shadows and lurid lights over the strand. Crowbone stepped into the blooded ring it made and held up his hands.

'You are the Red Brothers of Grima,' he said loudly. 'You have travelled as one, fought as one. You have rules for this and I want to know them.'

Men looked one to the other and Crowbone waited.

'None may steal from another,' said a voice and Crowbone knew who it would be, had already marked it and turned to where Mar was.

'Or?'

'Death,' answered Mar. 'Unless mercy is shown, but Grima was not a merciful man.'

There were grunts and a few harsh laughs at the memory of what Grima had been. Mar folded his fingers, rule by rule, to mark them.

'Equal shares for all. If a man loses a finger in battle, he gets an extra share, but if he loses two he gets no more shares, for one is a sad loss, but two is careless.'

Orm would not have grown rich here, Crowbone thought, thinking of the three lost fingers on the Oathsworn jarl's left hand.

'If a man loses a hand, all the same, he gets a share for

every finger and thumb on it, provided it was taken off with a single blow, for a hand removed by more than one blow shows the owner of it was not fighting well or hard enough.'

Crowbone nodded, but said nothing. These were good rules and he would remember all of them, though they consisted mainly of what a man got for losing pieces of himself. Death gained him nothing, though it was expected that the jarl would pay weregild to any family, if they were ever found, out of his own wealth.

'If one man kills another,' Mar went on, 'there is no crime, provided it puts no-one else in danger, or sends the ship off course. Another may claim the right to settle blood-feud on such killing, but if there is none to right such a wrong, then no wrong has been done. If a Brother insults, offends or otherwise does you injustice, you may kill him for it, unless he kills you first.'

There were more, which were all the same matters, Crowbone noted – those with sharp edges and skill were in the right. Those with dull blades and fumbling were in the wrong.

Mar stepped back respectfully, leaving the flame-dyed space to Crowbone and the lifting sparks that whirled Grima to Odin's hall.

'The Red Brothers die here. We are the Oathsworn,' Crowbone said and it was clear he meant all of them assembled, not just the ones who had come with him on the *knarr*. 'We have no such rules and need none, for we have an Oath. We will all take this Oath while Odin is close, watching Grima come to him as a hall-guest. Those who do not take it will leave at once, for if they are nearby and in sight come dawn, anyone may kill them.'

He stopped and the fire hissed and the sea breathed.

'Be sure of your mouth and your heart, where these words come from,' he said and suddenly did not seem a stripling any longer, seemed to have swelled so that his shadow was long and eldritch. There was flickering at the edges of vision and those who believed in such things tried not to look, for it was clear that the *alfar* were close and those creatures made a man uneasy.

'Once taken, this Oath cannot be broken without bringing down the wrath of Odin,' Crowbone went on. 'You can take it as a Christmann and stay one if you can – but be aware that the Christ god will not save you from the anger of breaking this Oath. This has been tried before and those who did so found all the pain of their suffering a great regret.'

'God will not be mocked,' said a voice and Mar turned to see it was Ozur, one of Balle's men. Langbrok – Long-Legs – they called him and Crowbone listened to all of what he had to say, patient as the man's bile flew like froth. At the end of it, Ozur spat into the funeral fire. Men stirred and growled at this insult, even some Christ worshippers who were friends of Grima; if they did not agree with a pagan burning, they at least wanted to do him honour.

Mar sighed. It would be Ozur, of course, who was hotter for the Christ than this funeral fire and now those who had followed Balle were at his back, uneasy that they were now in the few and not the many.

'I will not foul my mouth with such a heathen thing as your oath,' declared Ozur finally, then stared round the rest of the faces. 'Neither should you all. It is a bad thing, even for you idol-worshipping scum.'

Eyes narrowed, for few men had liked Ozur anyway and none of the Thor and Odinsmen here cared for his tone. Yet there was a shifting, from one foot to the other, like a nervous flock on the point of bolting and Mar heaved another sigh; there had been enough blood and upset. The Red Brothers were gone for sure and nothing was left but for each to go his own way – or become Oathsworn. It wasn't as if men like them had much of a choice, after all.

He said as much, marvelling at the faces turning to listen

to him. Ozur scowled. Crowbone cocked his head like a
curious bird and marked Mar with a smile; he liked the man,
saw the pure gold of him and how he could be worn like an
adornment for a prince.

'You also are a pagan,' Ozur spat back at Mar. 'God alone
knows what you and that burned devil you keep so close to
you get up to, but it does not surprise me that you will take
something as foul as this oath into your mouth.'

Rage sluiced over Mar and he was already curling his fingers
into fists and looking for a hilt when there was a wet chopping sound and men were spilling away from where Ozur
had stood. Now there were two figures, one on the ground
and, as Crowbone and the others watched in amazement,
Kaup – stripped naked and no more than a shadow in the
shadows so that his eyes were the palest thing to be seen of
him – heaved up the body of Ozur after plucking his knife
from the man's throat. He took three steps and threw it on
to the pyre. Sparks flew.

'This Ozur child should have paid more heed to the fact
that I was not so close to Mar tonight,' said Kaup in his thick,
low, smile of a voice. Then he jerked his head at the pyre and
Crowbone.

'Now he goes to the feet of Grima. Say your oath, for I
have a mind to take it.'

Crowbone recovered himself, blinked away the shock and
surprise of what had happened and looked at Kaup.

'That was the last such killing you will do among oathed
crewmates,' he said, 'once you have spoken the Oath from
your heart.'

He and Kaup stared at one another for a long moment
and, in the end, the Nubian nodded. Crowbone said the words
of the Oath and Kaup repeated them, then crossed himself,
as if to clean off a stain and went to find his clothes. Slowly,
in ones and twos, men stepped forward into the pyre light
and intoned the Oath.

We swear to be brothers to each other, bone, blood and steel, on Gungnir, Odin's spear we swear, may he curse us to the Nine Realms and beyond if we break this faith, one to another.

Crowbone stood and listened to them, the stink of oil and burning flesh circling him like a lover's arms. There was a sudden sharp moment of *heimthra*, of longing for that which was gone; Orm's Hestreng, where the jarl had tried so hard to bring the Oathsworn to rest, and failed, for they were raiding men, not farmers. There would be new grass in the valley there, unfolding leaves making tender shadows. There would be a sheen on the fjord and the screams of terns, swooping on everyone who came too close to their carelessly-laid eggs. It was a good jarl's hall and Crowbone had envied Orm for it.

Crowbone wanted that. He wanted that and more of the same, with the great *naust*, the boatsheds, that went with it, huge lattice-works of wood as elegant as any Christ cathedral and, in them, the great ships and all around them the iron men to go in them. Ships and men enough to make a kingdom.

Why have the Norns brought me here, to this beach, Crowbone wondered, binding the thread of my life into the frayed remains of Grima? My greatness is lifted up by the last act of the jarl of the Red Brothers, as sure a sign of Odin watching over me as a one-eyed face appearing in the blue sky.

He brooded on that the rest of that long night and into the dawn, while men moved to fires and left the pyre to collapse into ash and sparks, hushed and reverent and awed by everything that had happened, swift as a stooping hawk, on this dark and lonely beach.

In the morning, they howed Grima's ashes up in a decent little mound, marked out with light-coloured stones plundered from the shingle and circled in the shape of a boat to show a man from the *vik* lay here. Then they packed up their sea-chests and started to board the two ships.

Crowbone, last to leave, turned to look at the stone-ringed

mound of Grima's howe, a fresh scab just above the tideline, as far removed from the north mountains as you could get. Crowbone wondered if his *fetch* would be content with that.

He walked away, feeling the unseen eyes on his back from under that boat-grave, thinking on a band of sworn-brothers and the wyrd of their last leader, old, alone and dying on a distant shore.

FOUR

The Frisian coast, a day's sail later . . .

CROWBONE'S CREW

ONLY the Norse do not fear the dark on the open sea. At least, so any who travel on the whale road tell folk. The truth is that only the whales do not fear the night sea – but men from the north sail it anyway, when the likes of Greeks and Englisc and Saxlanders and Franks give in and snag their ship close to the shore with ropes.

Grima's gift-ship was called *Skuggi* and it well-matched the name, Crowbone thought, for it was pitch-tarred all over the hull so that the wood was as black as if it had been burned, though streaked with salt and gull shit here and there. *Skuggi* meant shadow to most people, but northmen took more from the name, to them it spoke of an ominous shade, a spectre.

The sail did not make the ship or name sweeter, for when it was hauled up it was the colour of old blood. Crowbone was well content, all the same, for this was a proper *drakkar* of twenty oars a side – old, Onund said, and stiff with new wood here and there, but sound.

Fast, too – they had to leash the Shadow so that Hoskuld's

panting Swift-Gliding could keep pace. Crowbone had left Rovald and Kaetilmund on board the *knarr*, just to make sure the new steering oar kept Hoskuld on the same course; he needed Hoskuld yet, to point out this Drostan to him when they found him, but the trader was more reluctant and scowling than ever since Berto had whacked him with an axe handle, ruining his attempt to be the figure of a warrior.

They had a long, good sail that day. Crowbone had confirmed men in their old standings, so that the Shadow's shipmaster was still Tjorvir Asmundsson, who was called Stikublig. Stick-Starer was an apt by-name for him, since he spent a lot of time throwing little wood chips over the side and watching intently to judge the speed, the better to work out where they were.

Crowbone was content; with the men working at familiar things it seemed little had changed save for the jarl standing next to the steersman and a few new faces. Mar and Kaup and some others knew that everything had changed but, by the time they ran up on a quiet shore, the crew seemed happier than they had been at the start of the day.

Fires were lit and food cooked; Kaup surprised Crowbone and others by making something tastier than they could have done themselves from little twisted packets of herbs and spices he had hidden round himself in various places. The crew who knew him well chuckled at the delight on the new faces.

After they had finished eating, in the thin light before sunset, Crowbone sat with Onund and Murrough, waving Mar and Kaup, the Burned Man, to join them.

'How is it with them?' he asked Mar and the man knew at once what Crowbone meant.

'They sit a little apart from your Gardariki men,' he said, 'though that will change over time. Most of the men here are new and have not seen what men who were with Grima for a long time have seen. Those ones are easier in their minds – though no-one is yet comfortable with the Oath they swore.'

'You?' asked Crowbone and Mar nodded. His questioning eyes at Kaup got him back a nod and a grin like the flash of a magpie wing. Crowbone was silent for a time.

'I hope Grima's *fetch* will be content where we put him,' he said eventually, 'in a land far removed from the north mountains.'

Mar looked at Crowbone curiously.

'It is as fitting an end for a Red Brother as any,' he answered then, to Crowbone's surprise, smiled sweetness into his face. 'Do you know how that band got their name?'

That band, he had said and Crowbone marked it. They were already gone, the Red Brothers, sliding into the grey haar of yesterday, the Oathsworn stepping into their worn boots. Crowbone shook his head and waited to hear how the Red Brothers were so called; such a blood-dyed name must have a good tale behind it.

'On their first voyage, with Grima as shipmaster of them,' Mar said, 'they had the Shadow, then a new ship and a fine new sail, dyed with *reád-stán*. When it was rinsed, it came in stripes – dark red and yellow-gold – and Grima was pleased.'

Onund nodded. A sail coloured with *reád-stán* – ochre – was a fine sight, though he preferred, he said, to weave the colours in strips and sew them. Mar smiled again.

'Aye, that's an expense, but worth it, as we found,' he went on. 'When such a dyed sail as we had is sea-washed, the colours are fastened in the cloth – except that when it dries in the wind for the first time afterwards, it gives off a dust and that blew all over Grima and all of us. Everything. Then the damp soaked in and everything was dyed. When the ship came to berth next, it was completely red and everything in it – clothes, faces, hands, sea-chests, everything. We had to pitch-paint the hull to change the colour of it, but the sail had turned mostly as you see it – the colour of blood. It has faded a little, but not by much – it took longer to lose the skelpt-arse look of our faces. That was us. The Red Brothers.'

Murrough chuckled and Mar saw that even the prince they called Crowbone managed a smile. This prince, Mar was sure, knew the power in names, no matter how you came by them – none better, since the name of Crowbone was one any sensible man walked carefully around.

'You were with Grima a long time, then?' Crowbone asked and Mar nodded.

'All my far-travelling life,' he said. 'It is strange that he is missing now. It feels as though I have left something valuable and cannot remember where.'

Crowbone knew that feeling well enough and had the fading memories to prove it – Lousebeard, his foster-father, vanishing over the side of Klerkon's ship, pitched out because he was too old; nowadays, Crowbone could only remember him as a face made up mostly of the black O of his open, surprised mouth as he went backwards into the grey water.

Then there was his mother. Sometimes Crowbone had to squeeze his eyes tight to summon up the face of his mother and, once to his horror, had forgotten her name for a moment. Astrid. He said it to himself, as if to nail it to the inside of his head.

They sat, each man wrapped in his own thoughts, watching the little peeping birds that run at the tideline. As each wave hushed in, the birds would all wheel about and bundle busily away across the gold-gleaming shore, piping anxiously to one another. As each wave slid out, they would advance again, all together as a patter of tiny feet. When the silly yellow bitch ran at them, they rose together, and swirled overhead in a wild whirring of sound.

'Like Pechenegs,' Crowbone said and both Onund and Murrough laughed, for they had seen these steppe gallopers, climbing over and under their little ponies, wheeling and darting as one and with no-one seemingly ordering it. Then Crowbone saw Kaup and Mar nodding and smiling and it came to him that they had seen a lot, too.

Onund sighed a little at the sight of Crowbone and Mar together, for Mar had the same way about him as Crowbone did – as if some old man had settled in a much younger body.

They traded tales for a while and Mar discovered that Crowbone, stripling or not, had been up and down Gardariki, even in the worst of winters, had fought the Pechenegs and worse, it seemed, for Mar had heard of the Oathsworn legend of how they came by all the silver of the world in Atil's hidden tomb. Why they still raided, then, seemed a mystery to Kaup, but he kept his fine white teeth clicked shut on that and most other matters.

Mar told of the Red Brothers faring beyond the Khazar Sea, which the Rus call Khvalyn, and how they had joined in battles there, first with one people, then another. Not that it mattered who they battled as long as they won, for plunder and death was the same and the chance for both equal in any red war.

Then Crowbone told him of the Great City – which neither Mar nor Kaup had seen, for all their Gardariki travel – and some of the marvels in it, such as the clever constructs that throw water in the air, for amusement. And Kaup managed to astound Crowbone when he spoke of meeting a strange people out along the Silk Road. They called themselves the Soong, were yellow as old walrus ivory and had flatter faces than even the Sami and eyes which were not only slitted as if they were always trying for a hard shit, but set slantwise in their heads.

Crowbone and the others looked at him closely once or twice to see if he was just clever-boasting, but in the end had to believe him, even when he told how these folk had made toys out of a fire which roared like Thor with his arse ablaze and then bokked coloured stars up in the air. He had, Kaup confessed, shat himself and then run away when he had first witnessed this.

There was laughter – a good sound, Crowbone thought. Then the Burned Man sucked back to the marrow of the meeting.

'I have taken this Oath,' he declared, frowning, 'but it does not bind me. I am not afraid of it.'

Mar shifted uncomfortably, but Kaup's eyes were like lamps on Crowbone's face.

'I am Christian,' he said, then dazzled out a smile and spread his hands. 'Well,' he added, 'I am, but not a Christian the others like. For all that, they have asked me to speak.'

This was new and Crowbone shifted.

'They?'

Kaup put his fingers to his mouth and let out as good an imitation of a hunting owl as any Crowbone had heard; a few moments later, men slid out of the dark, silent and heavy with unease. They looked at Kaup, who grinned back, not realising the truth was not so much that they had asked him to speak on their behalf, but that they had picked him as the most expendable if Crowbone took offence.

A dozen, Crowbone reckoned – and Berto one of them, the yellow dog at his heels. Crowbone laid a stilling hand on the forearm of Onund, who had started to rise, grunting like a threatened bull walrus.

'I am Thorgeir Raudi,' said one man peering out from under a great tangle of curls, made even more red-gold by the fire-light. 'All of us here are Christmenn.'

'I am Bergfinn,' said the one next to him, a man with hair like padding from a burst saddle and a face beaten by wind and weather into soft, brown leather. 'I took your Oath, like all the rest of us here – but it does not sit well with us.'

'You had the choice,' Onund growled and men shifted, digging the sand with their toes like lectured boys.

'We have been raiding men for so long,' Kaup declared and men nodded agreement. 'What else is there for us? We want to stay as brothers – but your Odin oath is not binding to us.'

'So?' demanded Crowbone, curious rather than angry, since it was clear they had thought this through and found a path they all could follow. Now they are trying to put my feet on it, he thought to himself.

Kaup took a breath, but it was Berto who spoke, his voice lilting and clear as birdsong.

'We will swear to you, prince. Swear on God and Jesus to be your men. As binding as any Odin oath.'

Onund blew down his nose like a startled horse and waved one hand with dismissive disgust – then he saw Crowbone's face and stopped, his eyes narrowing.

Crowbone, smiling at the possibilities, nodded. Onund felt the air shift, as if knotting itself with anger, and listened, silent and stricken, as Berto took one knee and put his hands on Crowbone's hands and swore to be his man. One by one, the others followed.

Later, they went back to the fires and he listened to them boast and insult one another. Two fell into a quarrel about who had the stronger blow and decided on a fight to prove it, which was good entertainment until one, seeing he was losing, hauled out a seax and the event turned nasty.

Crowbone was pleased, though, when Murrough felled one with the haft of his axe and Kaup hammered the other to the ground.

'Once,' Crowbone said as the men grunted shakily to their feet and wiped away blood, 'a frog lived in a pond and made friends with two geese who used to come and visit him there. They were happy for many years, but then there was a freeze that lasted for months. The ponds and rivers started to ice over. People and animals were starving.'

There was silence, profound as snow; the bleeding men dripped quietly.

'The two geese decided to save themselves and fly to somewhere warmer,' Crowbone went on. 'They also worked out how to save their friend too, even though a frog cannot fly. The geese would hold a stick in their beaks and then the frog could hold the stick in its jaws. In this way the geese could fly him south while holding the two ends of the stick.

'The geese flew off with the frog between them. They flew over hills, valleys, fields and fjords, and a city. The people of the city saw them and clapped in wonderment, shouting for others to come and see two geese carrying a toad that way. But this irritated the frog, so he opened his mouth to tell them that he was not a toad, but a frog. He was still telling them when he hit the ground and burst.'

There was silence, save for a few grunts.

'Do not get too annoyed by what others are saying,' Crowbone finished, looking at the two men, who were grinning wryly at him through the blood on their faces. 'It could burst you.'

'Besides,' he added pointedly, 'the jarl always has the strongest blow.'

There were grunts and a few cheers. Folk helped the two men up, so that they staggered back to seats side by side and set to swearing to each other how they had never meant any harm.

It would take time to unravel the old rules, Crowbone thought, so best to start at once. He looked for Onund, for he had seen the hunchback's cold face when the Christmenn had sworn to him and wanted to see if a little time had tempered the look – but the shipwright was nowhere to be seen.

Gjallandi fell to telling tales, having made one up about the death of Balle at the hands of Prince Olaf. It was a good tale, ending with a feather of black smoke coming out of the dead man's mouth, taking the shape of a raven and flying away.

'That did not happen,' said a man.

'Did the story of it make you shiver?' demanded Gjallandi haughtily, pouting his beautiful lips and throwing his considerable chin at the man, who admitted it did. Gjallandi smacked one hand on another, as if he had made a good law-point at a Thing.

'What was the raven, then?' demanded Kaup, fascinated and Gjallandi did not miss a beat.

'Odin, it was, shapechanged and possessing the body of Balle. A test, it was, to see if our Prince Olaf was ready.'

'Ready for what?' demanded Stick-Starer and Halfdan snorted derisively.

'To be king in Norway,' he answered, then turned to Gjallandi. 'Is that not the right of it?'

Gjallandi nodded portentously and men looked at Crowbone, sitting among them and yet apart, his face bloody with flame.

'Now you come to mention it,' said Stick-Starer, 'I think there was some smoke.'

'I saw a raven,' another man offered. 'For sure.'

Gjallandi grinned.

Northeast of Holmtun, Isle of Mann, at the same time . . .

THE WITCH-QUEEN'S CREW

Gudrod sat with Erling Flatnef on the night-stippled beach, apart from the rest of their men as was fitting. He was playing 'tafl with Erling, for the game was his obsession and a good contest pleased him because he invariably won. Erling, with his boneless nose wobbling, was no contest as usual and Gudrod was bored, glancing across to where Od sat alone, for the men did not like him and he did not care for fire, or company or even, it seemed to Gudrod, for food, since Erling had to tell him to eat.

'My sister's boy,' Erling declared moodily, following Gudrod's eyes. 'A strange one, from a birth that killed his mother. His father died in a bad winter four years later, so I got him.'

'Who taught him to fight?' Gudrod demanded and Erling, frowning over moving, took some time to reply.

'I showed him the strokes,' he answered, 'but no-one taught him the things he does, or the way he moves.'

He leaned forward a little.

'You should know this,' he said, low and slow as if the words had to be forced out. 'The boy kills. That is what the gods made him for. Chickens, dogs, deer, men, women, children – he has killed them all in his short life and not one of those deaths meant anything more than another or anything at all to him. I am sure Loki made him, but I have leashed him with Tyr, telling him that the death of people is a god-sacrifice and the best sacrifice is a warrior, dedicated to Tyr. I tried God and Jesus, but could not persuade him of the fighting worth of those two.'

Gudrod felt the skin along his arms creep and he glanced at Od, sitting still and quiet and staring up at the grey-black sky.

'Perhaps Tyr has taken him, after all. Best avoid him,' Erling said and so Gudrod, with a sharp sneering glance at the man, got up and deliberately went to the side of Od. For a time it seemed Od had not even noticed him and Gudrod was not used to that, did not like it.

'Are they eyes?' Od asked suddenly and, for a moment, Gudrod was lost. Then he realised the boy was looking at those stars the clouds unveiled.

'Embers,' Gudrod corrected. 'Flung there by Odin and his brothers, to help guide folk on the whale road. Folk like us.'

He paused as Od's head dropped and turned to look at him.

'Do you play *hnefatafl*?' Gudrod asked and had back a blank stare.

'The game of kings?' he prompted and had back a beautiful, slow smile.

'The game of kings,' the boy replied slowly, 'is to ask me to kill their enemies.'

Gudrod was too stunned to speak for a moment, for it was clear the boy had never played the game in his life. What lad did not learn *hnefatafl*? Or even *halatafl* – the fox game?

'You did well with that upstart warrior Ulf Bjornsson,'

Gudrod said finally, to break the oppressive silence. 'One stroke.'

Od said nothing, his face like a fresh-scraped sheepskin. Gudrod, trying to smile, told him of the first time he had killed a man, when he was fifteen. On a russet hillside slick with rain and entrails, he had shoved his sword into the man's face, leaving him lying there with the wet and blood pooling under him. Later, someone had told him that it was the Rig-Jarl Tryggve, so the first man he had killed had been a king.

He looked at Od, expecting something and nothing came for so long that Gudrod began to get angry, sensing he was being insulted. Then at last Od spoke and Gudrod's mouth was filled with ash, choking his angry words.

'I killed a boy who annoyed me when I was five,' Od said, as if he spoke of cutting down a tree, 'but Erling gave me my first man-kill for my name-day. A thrall we had captured. He was a Jutlander, I think.'

'Gave you?'

Od looked at Gudrod, that bland sea-gaze, as if this was something that happened every name-day, that every uncle gave a nephew such a present. Gudrod felt the back of his neck prickle with a sudden rush of sweat.

'Aye. I was learning how to properly cut throats,' he explained and smiled, warmed with the old memory of his fine day. 'There were ten thralls in all, but I was a fast learner and needed only six.'

Gudrod's armhairs were bristled now and the back of his neck prickled with a sudden rush of sweat. He managed to point out that he was sure the remaining four were grateful and Od turned that bland sea-gaze on him.

'I used those ones to learn how to hamstring,' he said, then stretched and rose up, yawning.

'Best name-day I ever had,' Od said. 'I was seven.'

He went off to find his cloak, leaving Gudrod in the darkness, feeling older than stones and colder than the hissing wind, which had long since upset the abandoned game of kings.

Valland to the Manx Sea, two weeks later . . .

CROWBONE'S CREW

'Each one of these should be coated with gold,' Crowbone growled moodily, waving a crab claw. Kaup, cooking them on a coal-grill by the mastfish, grinned back at him.

'We should not have traded, then, but raided these Franks,' said Berto and one or two nearest him chuckled at his Wend fierceness towards northmen. When they said it was a foolish risk for crabs, he only scowled more deeply and spat back that these Franks were too far removed from northmen nowadays. Then he swaggered off, chewing and spitting out shell, so clearly a boy trying to be a man that men laughed, remembering what that had felt like.

'They no longer speak decent Norse in Valland,' Onund admitted. 'Not for years. They are still northmen, though they have forgotten a lot of that and now call this coast Normandie. Now they cannot sail worth a fuck and have taken to fighting on horseback.'

He spat out shell, so that the wind whipped it away over the side, then worried more meat out of the claw.

'They are Norse enough that it would be foolish to annoy them,' he added and glanced sideways at Crowbone. 'They are ruffled by us. It is this ship. You may as well shake a sword and scream at them. We should paint it an easier colour.'

Crowbone scowled, for he liked the black ship and bloody sail.

'Once there was a fox,' he said and, because the sail was up and rowing men were lounging in sheltered spots out of the wind, he was the centre of all their attention at once;

already the crew knew that Crowbone's tales were even better than those of Gjallandi.

'This fox seated himself on a stone by a stream and wept aloud,' Crowbone went on. 'The crabs in the holes around came up to him and asked: "Friend, why are you wailing so loud?" The fox told them: "My kindred have turned me out of the wood and I do not know what to do."

'Of course, the crabs asked him why he had been turned out. "Because," said the fox, sobbing, "they let it be known they would go out tonight hunting crabs by the stream and I said it would be a pity to kill such pretty little creatures."

'Then the crabs held a Thing on it and came to the conclusion that, as the fox had been thrown out by his kindred on their account, they could do nothing better than engage his services to defend them. So they told the fox and he readily consented, then spent the whole day in amusing the crabs with all kinds of tricks.'

'Sounds like Gjallandi,' said Halfdan, sucking his fingers where he had burned them on the grill; the cloak-swathed skald acknowledged him with a good-natured wave.

'Night came,' Crowbone went on. 'The moon rose in full splendour. The fox asked: "Have you ever been out for a walk in the moonlight?" The crabs had not and told how they were such little creatures that they were afraid of going far from their holes by the riverbank. "Oh, never mind that," said the fox. "Follow me. I can defend you against any foe." So the crabs followed him with pleasure.

'On the way the fox told them all sorts of pleasant things and made them laugh and think they were having such a good time. Then the fox came to a halt and gave a short, sharp bark. Instantly, a horde of foxes came out of the wood and joined their kinsman, all of them hunting the poor crabs, who fled for their lives in all directions, but were soon caught and devoured.

'When the banquet was over, the foxes said to their friend:

"How great your skill and wisdom. You are truly a prince of cunning." Which was only the truth, after all.'

A few laughed, others frowned, for they knew there was a meaning in the tale but did not want to admit they had not understood it. Except Kaup, of course, who always wanted explained what he did not understand about men of the north.

'Does this tale reveal that all crabs are stupid, or all foxes clever?' he asked, smiling.

Crowbone, his head on one side like a quizzical bird, did not smile.

'Perhaps it reveals that there is more than one way to catch crabs,' he answered.

'Perhaps,' Berto offered, looking at Crowbone, 'it is more a tale about how a fox can succeed by seeming to be a friendly prince.'

Crowbone smiled, but others frowned and one or two snorted, saying there had been hardly a mention of a prince in it at all and what did a Wend know of Norse tales anyway?

'Now that you have warmed the pot of your skills,' Gjallandi declared to Crowbone, before Berto boiled over into fighting, 'perhaps you would favour us with another. Such as what they are saying.'

He uncoupled one hand from his cloak and waved it at a distant wheel of wind-ragged birds. Crowbone did not reply for a moment and let folk think he was considering matters, though the truth was that he was wondering whether the skald was worth the effort of keeping. He was more jealous than a woman when it came to his skills, seeing Crowbone as a rival and, though it was always good for a prince to have someone spreading your fame, Crowbone thought, Gjallandi was more irritating than grit in bread.

For a moment, he savoured the sight of the man's big head, the fleshy lips opening in an O of surprise as he was pitched into the sea – but the thought brought back the memory of his foster-father, Lousebeard, and he shivered.

'I can tell you what lies ahead,' Crowbone announced and stared pointedly at Gjallandi. 'Provided you have the stomach for the knowing.'

'You can tell me what lies ahead,' Stick-Starer declared, bustling down one side, following another wood chip's bobbing dance, 'provided it has nothing to do with crabs, for I have eaten too many.'

So Crowbone told them how the birds were struggling back to land, as fast as they were able, because a storm was coming. Men looked at the sky and squinted, but it was grey-blue, scudding with clouds and gave nothing away.

Stick-Starer stroked the grizzle of his face, then the yellow bitch barked once or twice and Berto declared that there was a storm coming, for sure. Men laughed and Stick-Starer shrugged.

'I do not know the workings of birds,' he said slowly, 'but a man with his head up his arse could tell you it is late in the year for heading up to Mann. Storms are more than likely. If you want to follow the barking of an ugly bitch and the wheeling of birds, you must tell me and I will fold my arms and sit.'

Crowbone nodded and men groaned, for the wind was mostly from the shore and now they had to climb on to sea-chest benches and pull hard for land.

Later, when the *drakkar* was keel-snugged in the shelter of a natural scoop of shingled harbour, men huddled round a flattening fire on shore under a wool sail that flapped like a bird wing in the rising wind. They did not mind the wind or the ticking of rain on the canopy and joked about whether to thank Crowbone's birds or Berto's yellow bitch for getting them clear of bad weather.

Crowbone sat and stared into the darkness, wondering where Hoskuld's *knarr* had gone.

The mica panels in the unlit lantern were loose and their trembling woke Thorgeir Raudi.

'Awake are we?' growled Bergfinn, appearing from behind him. 'An eyeblink before I kicked you, so that was rib-luck for you.'

The darkness puzzled Thorgeir for a moment, for he could not have slept, he thought, all through the day and into night. Besides, he said to himself, Bergfinn would never have let him.

Then he realised that the light puling on the horizon still marked the day, but clouds had smothered it like smoke. The wind whipped the raggles of his hair and the lantern swung above him, hung from a hook at the stern; Thorgeir knew that tremble well enough, felt the heavy slap of wave that caused it.

Bergfinn met his gaze.

'Aye – a blow is coming and we are making for land.'

'Where is the Shadow?' demanded Thorgeir and Bergfinn shrugged.

'They could row straight for the shore. I last saw them some time back.'

Thorgeir had been pride-swelled since Prince Olaf chose him, after their trading call on the Franks, to replace Kaetilmund on the *knarr* and he had picked Bergfinn to stand for Rovald, both of them to keep an eye on Hoskuld. Thorgeir didn't feel so pleased suddenly.

'We have been tacking since the wind rose,' said a new voice and Gorm came forward, the wind flattening his tunic against him. 'Hoskuld asks a favour of you.'

Above them men were fighting the sail down another knot and when they came up to the cliff-faced captain he was bellowing aloft like a bull seal. Thorgeir could see that only the least patch of sail was out, but still the ship leaped like a goosed maiden.

'Yonder,' said Hoskuld, pointing, and they all three peered out, the wind whipping their hair and beards back from their faces, at the dark bulk of land, the white cream of waves on the shore.

'If we want to reach it,' Hoskuld yelled at them as the wind roared and whined, 'I will have to take the sail down entire and then we will wallow like a sick whale. If I leave it up even a notch we may never reach land at all. We cannot row but I can get it close – then I need two good men to rope us to shore and we can then haul it in.'

Bergfinn turned to Thorgeir, the hair flying over one ear and whipping his face. He knew the *knarr* was not for rowing, knew what was needed and did not like it. He said as much.

'My men know how to handle this ship,' Hoskuld yelled. 'I need them aboard. You are strong and I can get you within a few strokes of the shore.'

As if to seal matters, Gorm came up with two lengths of bast rope and the Orkney steersman cursed and bellowed for help; men sprang to lend their strength to his, keeping the *knarr* wallowing slowly towards land.

Thorgeir hesitated. He did not like what Hoskuld wanted, but he took the rope and looked at Bergfinn, who looked at the shore, which was even closer now, but at the end of a tack. From now, Hoskuld would have to turn back out to sea, or try and hold where he was and wish for land to come and meet him at some point – hopefully without hidden rocks heralding it.

'Fuck,' Bergfinn said and took his shoes off, stuffing them down the front of his tunic. Then he wrapped the rope around his waist as Thorgeir had done and, with a brief glance, one to the other, they went over the side, whooping and roaring defiance.

The shock of it almost sucked the breath out of Thorgeir and the water smacked him like a hand, great swelling breakers that whipped the feet out from under him and sucked him this way and that.

He half-swam, half-fought, struggling and breathless, his throat burning with swallowed salt water that racked him with spewing coughs. Something banged his feet, then hit them again until he realised it was shore. The next surge took him to his knees in shingle and he struggled up out of the white water, dropping, panting to the stones. His chest burned but elation drove him to his feet – he had made it. Still alive, praise Aegir and his queen, Ran.

He took two or three breaths, red-raw ones that coughed more bad wet air from him, then took his hands off his knees and straightened. To his relief, he saw Bergfinn staggering up the shingle, the rope in one hand and his mouth working like a landed fish.

It was only when he got closer that he heard the words.

'. . . cut the rope. Fuckers. They have cut the rope.'

Thorgeir jerked his own line, felt nothing and hauled it in until he brought up the dripping, fresh-cut end.

Out on the bow of the *knarr*, Gorm peered into the mirk, raised one hand, then the other, arms aloft; Hoskuld heaved a sigh of relief that both men were alive, for he had not wanted deaths over this, only escape from that odd-eyed boy. He offered a pungent curse to Orm who had talked him into this and wished a rotting disease on the monk who had begun it all – though the three gold coins the priest had paid glowed warmly in his mind and he touched the hem where he had sewn them for safekeeping.

He shouted for the sail to be racked up, the wind catching the wet weight of it almost at once; the Swift-Gliding reared up and sped away from the land, where Thorgeir howled unheard and whipped the wet stones in a fury with the treacherously cut rope's end.

Hoskuld had gone.

FIVE

The Manx Sea, days later . . .

CROWBONE'S CREW

SHADOWS shifted as men gathered gear and moved softly under the creak and flap of the old-blood sail; even before Crowbone reached the prow he saw Onund waiting, watching, with the tools in his hand that would unfasten the snarling dragon-prow, keeping it from challenging the *fetch* of this land. More importantly, it would announce that the folk following it came in peace.

Crowbone, Kaetilmund and Onund stood with Stick-Starer, all of them staring out beyond the prow at the distant, silvered horizon and the smear on it.

'Smoke, I am thinking,' Stick-Starer declared and Kaetilmund, his hair whipping ahead of him with the strong wind, gave a grunt that might have been agreement and squinted a little, so that he was looking more sideways at the stained horizon.

'Could be a place with a borg on a hill,' he admitted finally and Stick-Starer looked relieved.

'Of course it is a place with a borg on a hill,' he answered scornfully. 'Holmtun on Mann, as I said.'

'You have not been in these waters for some time,' Crowbone pointed out mildly, 'and we have seen no land on our steerboard side, which should be expected if we have sailed up the west coast of Mann.'

'Where are we then?' Kaetilmund demanded challengingly, curling his lip at Stick-Starer. 'Is this not Holmtun?'

Stick-Starer stroked his chin and looked at the milk-sodden sky. Truth was, he did not exactly know and the prince who was now their leader had the right of it – he had been long out of these waters, so that the warp and weft of old wisdom was being dragged from him with some trouble. He muttered, pored over the tally-marks and the wooden wheels for some time. Then he threw a wood chip in the water, watching it bounce away behind them in the curling wake.

Crowbone leaned, one foot up on the thwart, brooding from under his eyelids. The Great City shipmasters had matters marked on scrolls and drawn on vellum, so that all they had to do was haul them out and look them over to find the description of how to get to a place, whether they were far south in the Middle Sea, or north into the Dark Sea. Yet northmen were considered much better seamen than the sailors of Constantinople and Crowbone wondered why that was.

He looked at Stick-Starer mumbling over his wooden instruments like some Pecheneg shaman casting bones and with about as much chance of solving the problem; he wished he had some of the Great City scrolls. Not that they would be of any help to Stick-Starer since he could not read – but that was unfair, Crowbone thought, for neither can I, not Latin nor Greek. I cannot even decently read runes, he added to himself and made a promise to at least learn that.

When, though, was the problem – there was enough for a prince-who-would-be-king to learn, not least of it using either hand in a fight and getting out of ringmail underwater while still swimming like a fish. All that and how to lead men and read the ways of power – a prince was never done working.

101

'I believe,' admitted Stick-Starer, breaking into Crowbone's brooding, 'that we may be a little bit off. I need a landmark before I can be sure.'

Onund gave his familiar grunt.

'*Engi er allheimskr ef þegja má,*' he said, his thick Iceland accent enough to make decent Norse speakers frown over it. Crowbone smiled as Stick-Starer worked it out and glared – no-one can be really stupid who stays silent.

Not much later, the truth of it was unveiled and Stick-Starer had a single eyebrow from scowling, while the beaten walrus-skin of his seamed face was red as a skelpt arse.

'A place with an island fort,' Kaetilmund jeered. 'You had that right, for sure – but you have managed to miss Mann island entire.'

Stick-Starer hunched into it and stared at the water running in a V from the prow, while Onund and others fought the dragon-beast down from the prow before the Shadow got too close. In the end, most folk were agreed on where they were – Hvitrann, which was stuck on the end of a tongue of land which Murrough knew as Galgeddil. It was, he said, part of the kingdom of Cwymbria, which ran all the way up to the river fort at Alt Clut and was run by a skilled and hard man called Mael Coluim, though the kings of Alba said they owned him.

The locals called it Hwiterne, Murrough went on, which means White House and comes from the white stone church the Christians built, which in Latin is called *candida casa*. It was a good Norse place once, though none of them around here were welcoming to men on the *vik*.

All of which was interesting, Crowbone said, but of no real aid to men looking for Holmtun on Mann and one or two, hoping to be helpful, said that if they were to sail south and a little west for a day they could not miss the island. Crowbone looked at Stick-Starer, who licked his lips nervously and said nothing at all, for he thought the odd-eyed youth had a hard look on him, like a man about to throw his shipmaster over the side.

Crowbone knew what Stick-Starer thought and let him sweat a little; the truth of it was clear to him now – the Norns wove this and Stick-Starer's poor way-finding was another thread that had led Crowbone to this place. The storm had lashed them hard and Hoskuld was gone in it; Crowbone did not think he had sunk, but he had poor hopes for Bergfinn and Thorgeir, who would not have allowed Hoskuld and his men to sail off without arguing out the folly of it.

He knew, all the same, that the great, mysterious tapestry of the world was woven of men's lives and his own thread was bright in it, shining with the men and ships and silver and kings the Norns wove it with. Even the threads of gods, he thought to himself grimly, are braided with my wyrd, for the Norns weave even Asgard's lives.

'Well,' growled Mar as the clang of alarms began to sound, 'do we sail off or try to show these folk how friendly we are?'

'Do not land on the east side,' Stick-Starer added, attempting to redeem himself and remembering something about the place they were sailing to. 'There is a bay there which looks inviting, but it is all stinking marsh.'

There was, thought Crowbone with a frown, no reason at all for stopping here, other than the fact that heading south for Mann would put the wind in their teeth and mean a hard row of it. It was not as if they needed food, though the bread was mushy and more than a little green, nor water, which was still drinkable if you strained it through your linen kirtle first. Yet the Norns were in this, he was sure of it, ever since he had seen the three terns screaming sunwise round the mast that morning.

Then the yellow bitch barked and Berto shaded his eyes with one hand and pointed with the other.

'Looking yonder,' he said in his crippled attempt at West Norse. 'Is that not the ship of that Hoskuld, harboured there?'

There was a flurry of peering and pointing, then Kaetilmund gave a nod and a grunt, smacking the little Wend on the shoulder hard enough to rattle the leather helmet over his brow.

'Good eyes, No-Toes,' he said cheerfully. 'It is that lost ship, for sure.'

Crowbone felt the hairs on his arms raise, tasted the tingle of the Norn-weave moment on his tongue. The sail came flaking down, the prow beast was lifted off and the oars clattered out. On the way to his sea-chest oar bench, Mar offered Crowbone a hopeful grin.

'All we need are some quiet words,' he said and Crowbone looked sourly back at him, then at Kaup, the dark shadow following him. Quiet words. From a black ship with a blood-red sail whose crew contained at least one walking dead man. In every saga told, the villain was always a powerful magic-worker with a pack of trolls, rabid wolves, *alfar* – and black men.

'Aye,' he declared as the men picked up the oar rhythm. 'There is no bother in this at all.'

An hour later, of course, matters had turned out as sour as Crowbone had thought and he stood in the prow, shaking his head at the wyrd of it.

It was, he brooded, ridiculous. Between us all we have command of a fair wheen of tongues, yet I am standing in the prow of a boat trying to find one gods-cursed person we can talk to.

Crowbone, fretting and churning deep in himself, wondered if it was worth pitching Stick-Starer over the side and ignoring the sunwise terns and his own surety of Norn-weaving. All unknown to him, Mar watched the hood-eyed prince and marvelled at his stillness and seeming unconcern as the youth stood, hipshot and silvered by the dawn, as if waiting patiently for his rising-meal.

The Shadow rose and fell in slow, rolling swells, the snarling prow of it removed and safely covered, the strakes grating on the harsh sand and shingle but not driven hard enough up on the beach so that it could not be rowed swiftly out again. To the left, jostling with fishing craft, Hoskuld's *knarr* nudged the stone quay, fastened snugly to an iron ring. Beyond the curve of shingle, sand and stiff grass was a sea wall, behind which huts and houses huddled. To the right was a great rock, hunched as Onund's shoulder and with a stone-walled borg barnacled tight on it; somewhere there a bell clanged.

'Call them again – surely they know even your bad Frankish? The land is only across the water from them.'

Onund glanced briefly at Crowbone, then called out that they came in peace, but held his own council as to how close this place was to the land of the Franks.

Crowbone watched and waited, but no-one came, not even from the borg and he studied the round gate-towers, saw the strength of it – but saw no spear points or helmets. There were folk around, all the same, for a handcart and people hurried across the raising-bridge into the maw of the borg; two of them were girls, their skirts flying. The bridge came up not long after, with a rending screech of cogs and wheels needing greased.

'Well,' growled Kaetilmund, 'we have tried Frank and Norse and Slav and a bit of Wend and some Greek – even Murrough's Irish, which you would think they would know, being even closer to them than the Franks, but unless you know Englisc or the Christ-tongue, then we are done with talking here.'

Mar shrugged as Crowbone looked at him.

'I know the prayers in Latin,' he said. 'Well, a bit, here and there.'

'Well, we did not sail in here to stand and stare at Hoskuld's ship,' Crowbone said and jerked his chin at Kaetilmund. 'Take two men and get aboard her. Murrough, you and Rovald come with me – there may yet be someone who speaks the Irisher tongue. Gjallandi, you speak well and know the Latin a bit.

Berto, you can come as well, since it is the only way to get the dog – it is an ugly animal, but a wagging tail is a soothing sight.'

Then he leaped over the prow into the shallows and sloshed his way to the shore, the others following him. Half-way up the shingle, he turned and called out to Onund.

'If you see us coming back at a fair speed, it would be nice to think that folk were bending the oars for the open sea even as we leap aboard.'

'Not too fast, all the same,' Murrough added with a scowl. 'For it would be nicer if we were actually aboard when you bend them.'

The laughter was nervous and those left behind soon fell silent and watched Crowbone and his four men and a dog trudge up the shingle into the grass-stabbed dunes and over the sea wall. The gulls wheeled and screamed at the yellow dog as it ran back and forth, tail beating furiously.

They came into the fringes of the place, cautious as old cats, past the drunken fences and the plots they bounded, up through the houses with the doormouths of them stoppered and the shutters closed. For all their blindness, Crowbone thought to himself, those wind-holes watch us.

They prowled round a little, in wide, wary circles, stepping light-footed as wolves then went on up to the church which Crowbone thought more gull-grey than white. It had thick walls, small slits set high up and a single massive door, set in an archway and studded with iron-headed nails. As good a fortress as the one to their right, which men eyed warily now that they were far from the ship and in danger of being cut off if anyone sallied out from it.

Gjallandi stepped up and banged the door, yelling out in Latin until a slat opened and eyes looked warily out at him. Men cheered mockingly.

'Whisht,' Crowbone ordered, not wanting to tip the balance of the door-slat into shutting again. Gjallandi gabbled and had an answer, then gabbled some more. Then the slat shut with a bang and he stepped away, his great lips pursed.

'They are wary,' he said. 'I have promised that there will be no trouble and that all here are good Christmenn.'

'Well,' Crowbone declared with princely assurance, 'half right is almost no lie.'

The door of the stone church cracked open like a smile and spat out a priest called Domnall, a tall, thin streak of a man with cool grey eyes and the sort of chin that could never be shaved clean even with the sharpest knife. He had hair cut so that it looked like an upturned bird nest on his head and the centre of it was shaved, which was the way of most Christ priests. More to the point, he spoke Norse after a fashion.

He saw through Crowbone almost at once, despite the prince's attempts to turn his Thor Hammer amulet into something resembling a cross, and refused to speak further until the scowling youth agreed to be prime-signed at least into the company of Christian folk.

For his part, Crowbone permitted the holy water cross-marking on his brow well enough and ignored the black looks of the good Odinsmen of the Oathsworn, though he had more trouble with Onund, who spat almost on the prince's boots and offered the opinion that Orm would not have done this and would not be pleased to hear of it.

Crowbone choked his rage in his throat and swallowed, though it burned his belly. He smiled at Onund, as sweet as his insides were sour.

'Orm will understand,' he said soothingly, while thinking that Onund was right – Orm would never have given in by as much as a finger-length to the Christ priest's demands, for he had done it before and had annoyed, he thought, the gods in Asgard.

Which is why Orm, Crowbone thought, will never amount to more than a raiding captain in this part of the world where he had never set his foot before, since Christ folk would never deal with him. Here, it seemed, the Tortured God held sway and it was a prudent prince who took note of it – prudent gods in Asgard, too.

He dared to say as much, then had to duck under Onund's scowl to go after the now talkative priest. He discovered that the church they had come up on was not the *candida casa*, but a smaller chapel for pilgrims of some Christ martyr called Ninian. Nor had they landed where they had thought to land – in Hvitrann town proper – but only at the port, which was at the end of a thin stretch of land that would have been an island but for the saving grace of a last narrow neck. He learned this sitting out of the wind in a wooden lean-to tacked on to the church wall, drinking nutty ale and eating cheese and bread while some hurrying girl went to fetch the commander of the borg, a keg-shaped belcher called Fergus.

And all this, Crowbone marvelled, because he had muttered some praise for the White Christ and had his forehead wetted. That sort of matter was worth remembering.

Crowbone already knew that Hoskuld's *knarr* was empty as a blown egg and learned from this Fergus that Hoskuld had been grabbed by one Ogmund, who claimed to belong to Olaf Irish-Shoes. They had all left in a snake-boat.

'Like your own, only smaller,' Fergus offered, chewing bread and cheese while the priest sat with his hands in the folds of his sleeves and Crowbone perched on a stool opposite the pair of them, so he could reach the seax in his boot if matters spilled over.

'Was his crew also taken?' Crowbone asked lightly and Fergus grinned, showing two blue teeth in the front of his mouth. He was easier now that he had been assured Crowbone was no threat, but still cautious, for no northman could be trusted.

'No. Held until my lord arrives from Surrby,' he answered, 'and judges whether they are the raiding men this Ogmund claims. Two at least are no traders, but fighting men and claim to come from Gardariki, though I think they are great liars. We picked them up on their own, from further down the coast, but they knew the trader's crew at once.'

Bergfinn and Thorgeir, Crowbone thought and kept his face as bland as fresh-scraped sheepskin.

'The cargo?'

'Held in safekeeping. Berthing fees. Tithes. Custom duties.'

Crowbone was silent while he assembled the weft and warp of this. Hoskuld, for all his cleverness, had sailed into the arms of this Ogmund, who clearly had been sent to find him and bring him back to Olaf Irish-Shoes in Dyfflin. The fact that Ogmund had left *knarr*, cargo and crew behind told Crowbone he had all the clever in him of a stone; bring Hoskuld the Trader he had been told and so he did that and no more.

Fergus had then seized crew, cargo and ship and thought himself no end of a fine fellow for having done so. Crowbone wondered, idly, why Bergfinn and Thorgeir had been on their own and not with the crew; he was pleased they were alive, but curious as to why that was, since it spoke of having done nothing much to thwart Hoskuld's attempts to run away.

A more worrying fact was that this arse Fergus, grinning and spraying crumbs as he stuffed food in his maw with thick fingers, had also sent word to his lord at Surrby – Crowbone wondered where Surrby was and how long it would take to get from there with armed men. The name of it soothed him a little for it was Norse, though it meant 'sour land' which did not have a happy ring to it.

'It would be best,' Fergus added, swallowing ale, 'if you were gone when my lord arrives. Lest there is confusion over your own relationship to these raiders.'

The priest cocked one disapproving eyebrow.

'The holy chapel of Saint Ninian has offered succour to these Christians,' he pointed out and Fergus shrugged.

'There is no confusion,' Crowbone answered lightly. 'Your

prisoners are part of my crew and innocent of such charges. It surprises me that some Dyfflin men can land here and snatch away a trader so arrogantly. I am sure your lord will also see this when it is put to him – who is he?'

The lord, he learned from the scowling Fergus, was called Duegald Andersson, a Dane by the sound of it, or one of those half-Norse the locals called *fion ghaill* – fair strangers – and it told Crowbone that this area called Galgeddil was more Norse than anything else. He said as much and Fergus shrugged and showed his blued teeth in a sneering smile.

'I would not depend on anything coming from that,' he offered, then rose abruptly, scraping the bench back with a screech. He was a lot less sure of matters than he had been when he had woken that morning and did not like this odd-eyed youth for having spoiled his day.

'Get gone from here,' he said, which was a flat blade smacked on the table to the likes of Crowbone, but he was enough of a prince to know that Fergus did it because he was confident of his borg being able to hold out against a shipload of Norse until this Duegald arrived. Since there was nothing to be gained from spitting and scowling, Crowbone smiled and nodded politely instead.

Domnall saw the manners of it and considered that the prince was a better man than Fergus, which was not a hard thought for him; he knew Fergus as a farter and swearer, with nothing much in his head other than where his next drink would come from. Still – he had the right of it in this matter and Domnall said as much to the polite prince.

'It would be best if you sailed, I am thinking,' he added finally. 'Fergus sent for Lord Duegald some days ago and he will be here tomorrow, or the day after.'

Crowbone nodded and feigned sighs at having to leave his men to their fate, then went back to the cookfires and sail-tent camp on the beach and near their ship. He found the crew looking morosely at the canted dragon-ship and the great, slick expanse of seaweed, shell and mud that stretched from it; low tide sucked the water away entirely from the place and Crowbone cursed himself for not having thought of it. Baltic waters had no tide worth the name and all these men were Baltic raiders until recently.

'Well, that is that, then,' Mar declared moodily. 'We should leave when the sea comes back, hoping it does before this lord and his men arrive from this Surrby.'

'I have heard of that place,' Stick-Starer answered, aware that he was also being blamed for not knowing about the tide. 'It is a Norse borg, surrounded on three sides by marshes, which accounts for its name.'

'Interesting,' Crowbone snarled at him, 'but of less use than gull shit on a rope end.'

'What of the prisoners in the borg?' demanded Berto, feeding fish scraps to the yellow dog.

'What of them?' Kaup asked, astonished that anyone would care; they were nothing to do with the Shadow's crew and had been treacherous besides. Folk argued it back and forth while the wind hissed out of the dark land and flattened the flames of the fire.

In the end, Onund silenced them with a smack of one hand on his thigh.

'Bergfinn and Thorgeir are there,' he pointed out and Crowbone saw the puzzled looks on more than a few faces, particularly those of the Christians. He sighed, for he knew it would come to this.

'They are Oathsworn,' he reminded them and saw the cat and dog chase of that across faces until they worked out the power of the oath they had sworn. Crowbone saw Mar and Kaup look at each other and knew what they were thinking – we have sworn only to the prince, so what is this oath to decent Christians? He saw that Onund had spotted this too, and decided it was a princely matter to speak up quickly.

111

'We cannot leave them,' he said. 'Besides – they may know exactly where this Ogmund has taken Hoskuld.'

'Which is what to us?' demanded a tall man, a Saxlander called Fridrek. Good with a bow, Crowbone recalled.

'I mean no disrespect,' the man lied, his bold stare into Crowbone's blank face a clear challenge. 'I just wonder why we are pursuing this trader. I wonder why we are in this part of the world at all, trying to get to Mann. For some axe?'

There was silence enough for the wind to seem to roar, then a stillness came down until it seemed even the world held its breath.

'It seems to me,' Fridrek went on, seemingly oblivious to any silence, 'that we are following a youth of little fighting experience for no gain I can see in it.'

Crowbone shifted a little and spread his arms. He was trying to be liked, though the matter of the tides and this Fridrek's tone was a powering sea to the crumbling cliff of it.

'We seek my destiny,' he said finally, 'which is to be king of Norway . . .'

'Norway has a king,' Fridrek interrupted. 'You seem short on men and war skill to be claiming a throne. Now we are stuck in the mud and at the mercy of some Galgeddil men.'

'It is true that I am a little light in the ways of battle,' Crowbone said, smiling – then he lashed out with one foot and it was only then that folk realised he had shifted to balance himself on the other. The nail-studded sole of his boot took Fridrek in the sneer of his face; his nose burst with a great gout of blood and teeth flew when he went over backwards with a muffled shriek.

'I have some skill in surprise, all the same,' Crowbone added, fierce with the release of the moment. 'Nor do I like folk yapping when I am speaking.'

'You are a little mean-spirited tonight,' Onund growled as men helped Fridrek up and began to look to his nose and mouth.

'I am not,' Crowbone countered. 'I am the happiest of men, for I know how to take that borg away from Fergus and release both the men in it, Hoskuld's cargo and all the other cargoes no doubt stored there.'

Men leaned forward, glaured with the vision of all the plunder that might be to hand. Even those tending Fridrek let him bleed a little as they turned to listen.

'Otherwise,' Crowbone added, looking sourly at the Saxlander, 'I would just have killed him.'

Somewhere, a bleared sun smeared through the mist, making silhouettes on the road up to the borg. It was a cold sun, a dirty grey light that fell on the handcart being pushed by four weary peasants and preceded by two girls in decent overcloaks and white headsquares, carrying covered jugs.

Maccus, who only liked this gate guard duty because of the morning girls with their milk, nudged Cuimer and nodded in their direction, licking his lips ostentatiously. Cuimer grinned, set his spear to one side and pulled off his helmet, the better to free his hair, which made Maccus frown. Cuimer had thick, wavy hair only slightly infested with nits, while Maccus dared not do the same, since the helmet, he swore, had worn all the hair from the front half of his head.

Still, the girls looked winsome enough, and he thought they had probably come from Hvitrann proper, since he had not seen them before. New girls; the prospects made him lick his lips. One was short and plump – that one is Cuimer's, Maccus promised himself, tonguing his loose teeth – but the other was tall and had started to sway lasciviously as she came up and across the raising-bridge.

Not far away, Murrough and Mar turned their heads at the sweet sound wafting from the chapel, where most of the people had sensibly gone including two girls shamed and clutching themselves in their underclothes and four peasants worried about their handcart. Two hard men with spears made

113

sure they stayed there, grinning at the girls and the discomfited monks.

'Like honey to the ears,' Murrough said softly.

'The sound of swan-maidens,' agreed Mar.

Inside the chapel, Domnall led his charges in loud Latin, chanting sonorously that the borg was in danger until Gjallandi stormed in with the great scowl that was Kaup alongside him and gave the priest a look that let him understand the Norse skald knew Latin well enough, even when sung. Domnall shrugged – he had done his best and it had been a forlorn hope, since he knew no-one in the borg, especially keg-head Fergus, understood more Latin than the proper responses.

Yet he had done his duty so that he could face his God and Lord Duegald both with the knowledge that he had tried to thwart these raiders, while also keeping the raiders – who were now certainly in charge of matters – from burning God's house or harming the innocents. Warriors would die, of course, but that was the nature of fighting men, Domnall thought to himself. *Pater Noster, qui es in caelis, sanctificétur nomen Tuum . . .*

The mist and the water blended with vague strokes of rushes, grass and trees. The guards were grey on grey stone as the peasants laboured the handcart of bread and the girls hefted the heavy jugs of milk, a rising-meal for the garrison.

Cuimer, plump and pink, his helmet held in the crook of his arm and his hair flowing over his ears, stepped forward, grinning a yellow smile at the tall, slender girl. He said something the tall girl obviously did not understand, but his wink was lewd and he laughed, even though she had odd eyes, neither one colour nor another.

Then, sudden as a flaring spark, he wasn't laughing at all and the tall, slender girl had whipped a seax out from the jug she carried, slammed the earthware into the man's face and followed it up with an expert slash across his throat.

Maccus, who had been scowling at Cuimer as he stepped

forward to talk to the winsomely tall maiden, gawped as the blade flashed, bright as kingfisher wings in the mirk and Cuimer fell backwards, the blood slushing from his throat and his face full of pottery shards. Maccus opened his mouth to shout and something darted at him from one side like the tongue of a snake, so that he reared back with a little scream, half-turning to see the round face of the plump girl, her eyes wide and bright. He thought he saw reluctant sadness there, but there was nothing reluctant about the fistful of steel she had. The strength went from his legs and then the plump girl stabbed him in the liver and lights and he fell, scrabbling away from this horror, pleading in a voice that wheezed because his lung was burst.

'Leave him – get to the draw-weights!'

Crowbone tore the headsquare off and flung it away, while the peasants grabbed the hidden axes from the handcart and turned, in that instant, into four *rann-sack* nightmares, the sort ma tells her bairns to beware of when they get lippy and foot-stamping. Two of them took wooden wedges and hammers and sprinted for the gatehouse. Berto gathered up his skirts and followed the men with hammers into the gatehouse.

They wedged the cogwheels, cut the ropes and pulleys and, even as the garrison started beating metal alarms, the rest of the Shadow's crew spilled out from where they were hidden and ran screaming at the wide-open gate, across the raising-bridge that could not be raised, scouring the cold out of their mist-frozen bodies in blood and fire while the garrison scattered like crazed geese.

'Just as well we attacked when we did,' growled Onund, lumbering up like a sleepy bear. 'I think that guard with the pretty hair was about to take liberties.'

Crowbone, standing with a seax dripping slow, heavy pats on the hem of his skirt, gave a rueful smile, looked at the handle of the pottery jug still clenched in one fist and tossed it away. The cold dawn wind stroked his freshly-shaved face like a blade. Onund had done it, deliberate and slow and unsmiling while men nudged and jeered at how much of a girl it made their jarl look; Crowbone, as the cold steel had caressed his throat, had never taken his eyes from the hunchback's face, but had seen nothing there but implacable concentration.

Berto had needed no shaving, but insisted that he keep his breeks on under the skirt. Men jeered at him, all the same and pretended to kiss him, so that he flushed. That changed to pale when Crowbone handed him the seax and he realised what he had to do – Crowbone had not been sure the little Wend would manage it up until he had stuck the blade in the guard's ribs.

They killed everything that moved or begged, burned what would burn, stacked what could be carried and unlocked all doors until they found the men they sought.

Hoskuld's crew staggered blinking into the daylight to behold, open-mouthed, the body of Fergus, face as black as Kaup's own, turning slowly as it hung beneath the arch of the gate while ash and sparks whirled round them. Thorgeir and Bergfinn stared at the ground, shamefaced and scowling.

'We were tricked,' Thorgeir told Crowbone and it was Halk the Orkneyman who gave a nervous laugh at that and told Crowbone what Hoskuld had done. Crowbone studied Halk, then the others; Gorm was the only one who returned his stare, eye to eye.

'Now you can take care of the ones who fooled you,' Crowbone said to Thorgeir and Bergfinn and handed Thorgeir the bloody seax. Onund, grim as a wet cliff, handed Bergfinn an axe.

'Do not be tricked again,' Crowbone ordered. 'Take them to the ship and watch them – I will have words and questions later.'

They were moving carping geese and blue-glass goblets, bales, barrels and boxes under the dangle of the dead Fergus when Kaup came up, panting fast and so wild his eyes seemed huge and white.

'Horsemen,' he said, 'coming up fast.'

Crowbone felt his belly turn a little, for he had hoped to be away before this Lord arrived with his men.

'How many?' he asked and Kaup cursed at not telling this important matter immediately. He flashed both hands four, perhaps five times.

'Fuck,' Rovald spat. 'Horsemen.'

'Do they fight on horses here, or on foot?' Crowbone demanded of Murrough, who shrugged and grinned, hefting the long axe off his shoulder and handing Crowbone his sword, rescued from the handcart.

'No matter,' he said. Crowbone nodded and sent laden men to the ships, so that Bergfinn and Thorgeir, with four others, found themselves back on the *knarr* working up a sweat stacking the plunder and shoving her off into the wind. Those with ringmail stayed near Crowbone, moving slowly and standing rearguard, though most of them had plunder, too.

Not for long. Trussed fowls and bread, blue-glass and bales all went one way when the horsemen appeared, milling in some confusion. They had come on at speed towards the smell and sight of smoke, not knowing what to expect; they had not thought to find ring-mailed raiders, so they reined in and waited while a man in a white cloak talked to those on either side of him, waving his hands.

'Horsemen, then,' Kaetilmund declared, seeing the men remained mounted.

Not good ones, Crowbone thought to himself, as a man fought his nervous mount and another clattered his long spear off his neighbour's helmet and had back curses for it. They were clearly new to this business of fighting mounted.

'Perhaps they will let us go away, seeing as the damage is already done,' Vandrad Sygni said, nocking an arrow. Murrough laughed.

Berto was the last laden man to reach the Shadow, having ripped off the dress. Now he waded out to the Shadow clutching a new bow and with the yellow dog splashing at his heels; the great blood sail flapped and filled and it stirred, fighting the clutch of mud still under the keel, for the tide was rolling in as the wind was rolling out.

The horsemen shifted at that sight, but the line of men on the sand stood and waited, then Crowbone yelled out an order and they began to step in rowing time, shields up but moving backwards to the shingle and the shallows, where the tendrils of mist trailed like hag hair.

The white-cloaked man saw them sliding back to the water and the dragon-ship, barked an order and the horsemen shifted into a ragged line; bits spumed with slaver, bridles jingled and the horses pawed and snorted, sensing what was coming.

'Well, then,' growled Mar, stuffing his helmet more firmly on his head, so that the great froth of his iron-coloured hair stuck out like wire, 'they will make a fist and shake it at us, it seems.'

He turned to big Murrough who would be on one side of him in this, their first fight together; they slammed helmets together, forehead to forehead, a rough kiss of greeting and farewell.

'May the Dagda smile on the Ui Neill this day,' roared Murrough and Crowbone felt the fierce fire of the moment; he had a single crew now.

They were matched fairly in numbers, though the Shadow's crew were better armed and better men, which Crowbone bellowed out in as deep a voice as he could manage as they slid into a shieldwall. Murrough stepped forward of the front ranks and began swinging the hook-bitted axe in that killing snake-knot that makes it impossible for a man to get near without suffering and the horsemen checked a little at the sight of him, then moved forward again at a walk. Everyone could see how ragged they were, how they waved their long spears like beetle feelers.

Their voices were brave enough, all the same, for they traded shouted insults on the size of balls and bellies – but it was Kaup who undid them, stepping out from the ranks a little and shaking a spear. Then Kaetilmund yelled 'Oathsworn' so that the others took up the chant.

The sight of a *draugr*, a dead man walking, was bad enough, never mind one armed with a spear and followed by fighting men of the Oathsworn, who were known even here. Crowbone, slapping on his horsetailed helmet and tucking his woman's skirt up into his belt to free his legs, marvelled at how far that fame had reached.

There was a ripple then, a stone of argument in the sure pool of the horsemen. Crowbone could almost hear them thinking – here was something more than some raiders come badly timed to the wrong feast. Here was the iron hand of the Oathsworn, who had fought dragons and half-woman, half-horse steppe horrors and who had Burned Men fighting for them.

For all that, Crowbone and others all agreed later, the Galgeddil horsemen had ridden the great swell of it bravely enough, ridden it right to the top and looked down on their own deaths – and then swooped down, screaming.

'Hold,' Crowbone yelled, which was all he had time for before the shriekers crashed on the shieldwall like a raging wave on a rock dyke.

They were too new to the saddle, came in too fast and too loose, desperate with fear; the horses veered or reared for the riders could not press them home, so that those who did not fall off could only throw their long lances, which clattered off the implacable wall of ring-mailed men like angry dogs clawing at a door.

Murrough's skill and strength took one loop of the long axe in a downward cut straight through the neck of a horse, then the upward scythe of it took the falling rider and sheared the head and part of a shoulder off him. The Irisher stood like a rock as the headless pair ploughed a bloody furrow through the sand to his left, spraying gore and grit. The other riders, looking only for escape, spilled right and left away from him, heading round the flanks.

Crowbone had been waiting for that, standing calm behind the shieldwall and watching, like a good jarl should; when he saw them stumbling sideways, he sent men left and right from the back rank. He was so intent on that he missed white cloak, urging the shoulder of his mount into Rovald, barrelling him aside.

It was only the desperate howling of the white-cloaked Lord, screaming courage into himself as he bore down, that snapped Crowbone's head round. An eyeblink later something slammed hard on the side of his shield, half throwing him sideways and whirling stars into him; he knew it was the toppling Rovald even as he heard the grunting man fall. No, he thought, in a strange quiet place in his head that was all the more mad for the stillness there. Not killed in a woman's dress. I will never live the shame of it down.

Crowbone hardly knew he did it, he dropped in a crouch so low that he felt his arse brush the stiff grass and sand, half spun on one foot and scythed the legs from the horse, even as the rider's longsword hissed a silver arc over his head, a backward cut that snicked trailing hairs from the horse-plume of his fancy helmet.

The horse shrieked, a high, thin sound, one fetlock cracked, the other severed almost entirely. It drove nose first into the sand, throwing up a bow wave, its screams swallowing the hoarse bellow of the rider as he was hurled to the ground.

Crowbone was up and moving even before the rider had stopped rolling. The Lord Duegald, tangled in his blood-streaked white cloak, staggered to his feet in a spray of wet sand to find a tall, beardless youth standing over him, his odd eyes glaring like burning glass. He had time to wonder why the man wore what appeared to be a dress.

The Galgeddil lord had a long-nosed face, neat with trimmed beard and bewildered blue eyes. Somewhere, a mother loved that face, but Crowbone, shaking with anger and fear, snarled it all out on the long nose and blue eyes in a furious flurry of wet-sounding chops.

When he surfaced from this, it was all over. A few horsemen were bolting for it, riderless mounts following after. A horse hirpled, one leg skewed. A man dragged himself, coughing and cursing, until Kaup, grinning, dragged his head back by the sand-and-blood-crusted hair and slit the terrified screams out of his throat.

The aftermath saw men retching, or panting, open-mouthed with disbelief and mad exultation that they had survived. Some did this after every fight and no-one thought the worse of them for it; the unaffected considered it booty-luck, since they were hunting, unopposed, in crotches, under armpits and down boots for hidden valuables, paddling in blood and all unconcerned. There was a rich choke of spilled shite and new blood.

Staggering a little, Crowbone went to the dead lord's horse, which was flailing sand and screaming, and cut the life out of it in two weary strokes. The ending of the screams was like balm.

'Good fight,' said a voice and Crowbone turned to see the great grinning face of Murrough wandering towards him, hook-bitted axe over one shoulder, tossing a fat purse in the other. He looked at the dead man in the blood-soaked white cloak and nodded admiration.

'I thought he had you – but you fooled him entirely,' he added. Crowbone kept his lips sewed on the fact that he had thought the man had him, too. Mar loped up and searched the lord swiftly, came up with hacksilver and trinkets and handed that and Murrough's fat purse to Crowbone, looked at the sword briefly and left it alone.

That was all a good sign, Crowbone thought. Not that Mar

knew how matters worked in the Oathsworn – that they shared all, though looted weapons and ring-coats were the jarl's to give or keep – but that he did it easily enough. Of course, everyone hid a little, running the risk that they might be found out and pay the price for it, which began with losing all you had and greeting the Oathsworn's other true friend, pain.

Crowbone tried not to look at Mar, or the ruin of the Galgeddil lord's face, fought to look smooth as a blue-glass cup as he turned away to bawl at Kaetilmund to leave off plundering and get to the ship.

He picked up the lord's sword; it was a solid Frankish blade fitted with down-curved iron quillons and a fat three-lobed pommel above a braided leather grip. Basic and workmanlike, it was not the ornate sword of a little lordling, but one used by a fighting man; still a fearsomely expensive item all the same, since it had one purpose only and that was killing people. A luxury, then, to folk who used blades for chopping wood, or fish, or chickens. Beyond that, though, it was the mark of a warrior and increased in worth because of it; men without one watched Crowbone as he hefted it, hoping they had been noticed enough to warrant the gift of such a blade.

They tallied the losses as well as the gain – a man dead and four hurt, one almost certain to lose his hand. The dead man was curled on himself, skewered on a spear, the splintered haft showing ash so white it was almost too bright to look at. His face, half-turned to the last dying light he had ever seen, held only slack jawed astonishment that made him look stupid, which he had not been in life; Crowbone remembered him, shooting wit like arrows and laughing with the joy of what he was and who he was with.

'Fastarr,' said a voice and Crowbone turned to see Mar looking at the dead man. He pulled his helmet off, ran a hand through the sweat-damp iron tangle of his hair.

'His name,' he explained. 'Fastarr, by-named Skumr. A boy

we picked up in Jutland when we were the Red Brothers. Said he had seen fighting, but I did not believe him. He wanted to go far-faering, all the same, and was pleasant company.'

Crowbone stared. He had never heard his name and that shook him a little, for he knew it was an important matter to know the names of men prepared to die for you. He felt a jolt run through him, like a blow badly blocked, when he realised he had never spoken to this boy, whose by-name, Skumr, meant 'brown gull' and was a name given to one who chattered as noisily as that bird.

'Well, now he is *farlami*,' Mar declared. 'So also is Kari Ragnvaldrsson, I am thinking.'

Faring-lamed – a term used as a wry joke as much as a small comfort of words. Not dead, just *farlami*, unable to go further on this journey.

When Crowbone went to him, Kari was pale with blood-loss, cradling his smashed hand, which was wrapped in the tail of his own tunic. His sword hand, too. Crowbone offered him thanks and promised him wealth enough and then told him he was done with the Oathsworn and that he would be left on Mann when he found someone to stand in his stead, his oath fulfilled.

Crowbone turned from the stricken look on Kari's face, knowing the man would have given the other hand to stay, but he was spared the awkwardness of argument by the arrival of Rovald, nursing his shoulder and spitting sand.

'You have not had a good day of it,' Crowbone pointed out and Rovald, knowing that he had failed to protect his jarl when he was bundled aside like old washing, flushed a little and went tight-lipped, which at least kept him from saying something stupidly dangerous.

Instead, he nodded to where a lone figure moved steadily towards them, almost seeming to glide because his feet were hidden by the flap of his long robe.

It was brave of this Domnall, Crowbone thought, to

plooter through the gore-muddy sand towards snarlers filled with victory and blood-fire. He said as much aloud, so folk would get the point of it; the snarlers grinned their wolf grins, cleaned their clotted weapons in the sand, ignored the priest and hefted their dead and wounded off towards the Shadow.

'You have slain the Lord Duegald,' Domnall said and his face was pale. He clasped his hands together and bent his head to pray.

'Once,' he heard a voice say, 'a Raven was overtaken by a Fox and caught. Raven said to Fox: "Please, pray first before you kill me, as the Christmann does." This was the time when beasts had voices, you understand.'

Domnall, astonished, opened his eyes and stared at Crowbone, who stood with his legs slightly apart and his silly woman's dress tucked up into his belt at the front, so that it looked as if he wore baggy, misshapen breeks. The priest saw that those odd-coloured eyes were dull, like misted beads.

'Fox asked: "In what manner does he pray? Tell me."

'"He folds his hands in praying," said Raven and Fox sat up and folded his paws as best he could, which meant letting go of Raven. "You ought not to look about you as you do. You had better shut your eyes," added Raven and Fox did so. Raven flew away, screeching, into a high tree.

'"Pray away, fool," he said and Fox sat, speechless, because he had been outdone.'

Domnall stared. Crowbone blinked and shifted, then smiled at the priest.

'Pray away, fool. When you open them, your prayers and your prey will both be gone and all this will be a dream.'

'God is not mocked,' Domnall said sternly and Crowbone laughed as he turned away, hefting his sword on to one shoulder.

'Of course he is, priest,' he called out as he went. 'His son was sent to promise an end to wicked folk. Odin promised an end to the ice giants. I see no ice giants, priest – but the world is full of wicked men.'

Domnall could still hear the laughter as the swaggering youth reached the tideline and was hauled up the strakes of the Shadow by willing hands.

The embers whirling round their ears from the dying fires of the borg, the people of the White House crept out from hiding to stand at the side of Domnall the priest while the black ship unleashed itself from the land. The blood-red mourn of sail sped it away after the *knarr*, the plumes of ash and smoke trailing over them both like curled wolf tails.

SIX

Holmtun, Isle of Mann, a day later . . .

THE WITCH-QUEEN'S CREW

THE wind hissed out of the dark, thick with sea-salt and fear, for it was a raider's wind, one that could drive dragon-ships straight down the throat of the town and folk huddled, seeing them out there in the dark. The three men moved closer to the flattening flames of the brazier; the youngest stared over his shoulder at the comfort of the gate they guarded.

'A raw night,' said a voice and men turned to stare at the cloaked man who limped up. The nearest to the visitor was an old man whose hair wisped like white smoke in the dark and he half-lowered the point of his suspicious spear a little. Next to him, a man with a timber leg struggled to get off the log he squatted on. The boy, his face bright with firelight, squinted at the newcomer, who was no more than a dark figure, blooded here and there by the flames.

Erling came up, slow and easy, then flourished a leather flask out from under the cloak and unstoppered it.

'As well you have me, then, to take the chill off,' he grunted and passed it over. 'Thought you lot could use it. Done this meself an' no-one cares, do they?'

The old man hesitated, then laid the spear down and took the flask, tilted it and swallowed.

'You have the right of it friend,' he said, hoarse with the spirit's grip on his throat. He passed it to the timber-leg, who raised it in a grinning salute to Erling before swallowing.

'You with the masons, then?' asked the youth and Erling nodded.

'If your lot would fix the yett,' the old man grumbled, 'we would be in the dry and warm.'

He got the flask back and held it a longer time at his lips before handing it back to Erling. He hefted it for a grinning moment, then handed it to the boy.

'Your ma will flay you,' the old man declared and the boy bristled.

'Old enough to stand here with my arse frozen,' he said, trying to be gruff. 'Old enough to hold a spear.'

'Aye, right enough,' Timber-Leg added bitterly. 'If the raiders come, old enough to die at this gate, too – so old enough to drink.'

'They say the Witch-Queen's son is out there,' the old man added softly.

'With some sort of shapechanger,' the boy added, eyes moist and bright with drink that choked him and which he would not admit did just that. The course of it in his blood added to the raw thrill of stories brought back by Ogmund's men.

'They say he can kill in an eyeblink. Maelle saw it happen when Ulf died.'

Timber-Leg snorted.

'Shapechanger my arse,' he spat bitterly. 'Not that one is needed here – all the good men are gone to Olaf's army at Dyfflin, save for Ogmund. Him and a handful in a fortress with a broken gate. And us. Old, crippled and over-young – what are we likely to do against sea-raiders?'

'Not much for your part,' answered the boy scornfully, 'but I have two good legs and can use a spear.'

'Enough,' snapped the old man angrily. 'Ghile-beg here has seen fighting which you have not. It is more than likely that if the raiders come, you will not be dancing this time next year.'

He turned to Erling and seemed surprised to find the flask still in his hand. He raised it in toast and drank, then smacked his lips and scowled back at the boy.

'No more for you. You are already at the moment when rudeness seems wit.'

Erling laughed and shook his head in mock sorrow.

'If the Witch-Queen comes, with her son and the shape-changer,' he declared, 'it might be better to be gone away. But that is unlikely. After all – what would bring them to Holmtun that is worth the taking?'

The old man spat angrily in the flames.

'Some prisoner,' he declared. 'Dragged into the borg to be put to the question by Ogmund.'

'He should have taken him to Olaf in Dyfflin,' Timber-Leg declared, 'but wants to wave answers at the king and the jarl, to show his cleverness.'

'Aye,' said Erling, stretching a little so that the cloak slackened round his body. A shadow flitted like an owl in flight and only he noticed it. 'This is as I had heard it and so it is a sore struggle of task you have, lads, and no mistake. You seem brave boys, all the same, and we have shared drink this night, so it is all a right pity.'

The old man held the flask up to his lips and realised it was empty as he lowered it.

'Pity?' he demanded owlishly, handing the empty flask back to Erling. 'What is a pity – other than that this fine flask is empty?'

He handed the empty flask back to Erling, who took it with one hand and came up with the other full of bright, winking steel.

'This is,' he said and gave three quick, sharp blows into the old man's ribs, catching the body close to him so that the shocked eyes, rheum-bright and bewildered stared into his own. The last breath tickled the hairs in Erling's nose.

'And he is,' he added with a nod to Timber-Leg, holding the old man in the crook of one arm before letting him slide to the cobbles. Timber-Leg whirled as the dark figure spirited out of the blackness behind them; he had time to see an angel's face, bloody with firelight, before a great scythe of light stole his sight forever.

The boy whimpered and backed away, the horror robbing his throat of sound. Od came out of the darkness towards him, his head cocked to one side like a bird studying a beetle. He waved the sword to make the boy twitch and dance.

'Do not play with him,' Erling ordered sharply and Od gave a little shrug and struck like an adder.

Erling whistled and now the dark spilled out men, Gudrod striding at their head over the unguarded raising-bridge, through the broken yett and over the three bodies and blood, into the borg of Holmtun.

In the deep of the place, Ogmund stood slick with sweat before the hanging figure of Hoskuld, the trader's naked body dark with streaks of blood and shit. Ogmund was thinking he should have called Murchadh down to do the heavy work with the whip and hot iron. He did not like the burning feeling he had down one arm, nor the rasp when he tried to breathe – but the lure of winning for himself the information everyone sought was too strong. It was an advantage to have this place empty of fighting men save for his own ship's crew.

Old, am I, he thought savagely and hefted the whip. He wondered if this trader had, as he claimed, told all he knew. A limping priest and a written message held by the monks – he glanced sideways at the document he'd had fetched from the monastery. The monks had squealed a bit at that, he had heard. The original had been sealed and marked for a Jarl

Orm, as the trader had said – so that was real enough but might be anything, since Ogmund could not read it. He did not know of any jarl called Orm.

'You have more to say,' he crooned to the bloody dangle that was Hoskuld and took a deep breath as he raised the whip, wincing at the stitch in his side. 'I will have it.'

There was a clattering on the stairs and he turned with annoyance; he wanted no-one around when the trader vomited up all he knew.

'Murchadh, I told you . . .'

It was not Murchadh. It was the Witch-Queen's son, with the terrible, beautiful youth behind him.

He had time only to discover how old and slow he truly was before the angelic youth blurred the life from him with a handful of bright steel, cold and silvered as a winter dawn.

North and west of Mann, not long afterwards . . .

CROWBONE'S CREW

The sea Mann sits in is a black-souled, scawmy water that can turn vicious out of a clear blue sky. Like a woman with a smile, Stick-Starer said, who has one hand behind her back with an iron skillet in it and a deal of stored-up argument.

The two ships had tacked and twisted a painful way south from Hvitrann – Crowbone did not want to row the Shadow off and leave the *knarr* behind again – a long muscle-ache of hauling the sail up and down until the palm-welts burst. Men did not complain, all the same, for they were aware that they had burned out a borg and slain a Galgeddil lord; putting distance between them and the bodies on the shingle was well worth some blisters and ache.

'I wish we had Finn's weather hat,' Kaetilmund roared out when the first wind squalled out on them, hard on the berthing

130

side, swirling like the tongue of a lip-licking cat, so that the Shadow heeled and staggered with it.

Those who knew about Finn's reputedly magical headgear laughed, but Crowbone stayed grim; he did not like the white-faced, fork-tailed Ran-sparrows he had seen earlier, whipping through the wave spume, low and fast as arrows.

'St Peter's birds,' Gorm declared, seeing Crowbone watch them.

'Because they seem to walk on water, like Christ as witnessed by that holy man once,' he explained. Crowbone did not care what the Christ-followers called them; he only knew the Ran birds spoke of storm. Besides, he did not want to speak to Gorm, or the others now – he had what he wanted from Halk, the Orkney steersman, who made it clear he was too new to Hoskuld's crew to care about them much.

'Hoskuld had three gold coins from this priest he met in Holmtun,' Halk told Crowbone, the wind that took them from under the smoke of Hvitrann whipping the hair away from his round, thick face. 'One took the priest and ship to Olaf in Dyfflin, as you know. A second took him to Sand Vik, where they found me to steer for them.'

He broke off and grinned ruefully.

'If I had known . . .' he began and Crowbone's stare silenced him as surely as if he had clapped a hand across his mouth. It was clear the prince did not care much what Halk thought, clearer still that he cared less for the regret Halk felt. The steersman wondered if he had made a mistake in allying himself to this prince, for he felt the eyes of Gorm and the others on him from the far end of the boat and the blue-brown gimlets of Crowbone from this end; now he knew how the iron felt between hammer and anvil.

'The third,' he went on, feeling the spit dry in his mouth under the odd-eyed stare, 'took the priest across to Torridun, where he was left. We then went back to Mann where Hoskuld took the writing for Orm. Then on to the Baltic, charged with finding Orm Bear-Slayer and telling him of matters.'

'Torridun?' demanded Crowbone and had the answer – the last old fortress-town of the Painted Folk who had once been strong in the north, before the *vik*-raiders from Norway ended them and let the kings of Alba reduce them further. Torfness, some knew it as, because the folk there found grass sods that burned like wood. Why would a monk be plootering in the ruins of that place?

He asked Halk, who shrugged.

'Not ruined entirely – traders from Norway still go there. Besides, he is a priest,' he corrected. 'Not a monk.'

'They are all the same,' Crowbone declared, waving a dismissive hand and Halk, politely enough, Crowbone noted, put the matter to rights. A priest was more of a Christ-follower than a monk. Anyone could become a monk, but a priest was trained by others of his kind to talk to their god personally.

'He was a hard man, this Drostan,' Halk ended. 'A skelf has more meat, yet he was wiry for all that – and the foot must have pained him a great deal, judging by the limp he had, but he never made a sound on matters. Not that you could have understood it much, between his lack of teeth and his way of speaking. Saxlander, Gorm said. From Hammaburg.'

The hackles rose on Crowbone's neck.

'We have to run with the wind,' Stick-Starer yelled, whirling Crowbone to the sound of his voice. The wind keened and he saw the rain sheet between him and the *knarr*; he fretted like the spume-ragged tops of the waves, wanting to keep the *knarr* in sight.

He was vaguely aware of it, as if, like the *alfar*, it was truly visible only out of the corner of the eye. His mind was back on the winter steppe, the Great White, where he huddled in the lee of Orm's armpit under an upturned cart as the howling wind scoured snow over the enemies who had kidnapped them. They had been led by a priest from Hammaburg called Martin, a man with a mouthful of ruined teeth, who had lost his shoe trying to kick out at Orm before vanishing into the shrieking whiteness, staggering towards Kiev, four days away.

Much later, Crowbone had heard how this Martin had been picked up and carted to Kiev. In return for them saving his life, he had told the ruler there, Yaropolk, all he knew of Orm and the men out on the steppe hunting all the silver of the world. He had lived, too, Crowbone had heard – though it had cost him a foot and he limped badly.

Martin. Orm's bane. The one who had set the Oathsworn on the path of silver riches, in the days when Einar was jarl.

The dark grew; things sparked in it and Thor rumbled out a laugh.

'Third reef,' bellowed Stick-Starer and men sprang to the walrus-hide ropes. Mar blinked rain from his lashes and saw the grim jut of Crowbone's jaw; the *knarr* could no longer be seen, yet the boy, shaven face pebbled with water, stared stubbornly at where it had been, as if he could reel it in with the force of his odd eyes.

Nothing, Mar thought, would surprise me about this prince – yet the world was reduced to grey and black, as if it sat on them like a gull on eggs. Then the searing light split it with a flash that left the jagged print of it on the back of his eyeballs and the stone in Mar's belly sank, cold and deep.

'Not even Finn's Weatherhat will find a safe harbour now,' Onund roared and even through the tearing wind the bitterness in his voice was gall to Crowbone. The waves had no rhyme to them, torn and ragged by the wind before they could take shape or order. They hurtled at the Shadow and a sheet of water creamed down the length of her, the spray horizontal as braced spears.

Yet they all saw Crowbone, still as the prow beast, standing with one hand on a line and the wind whipping his braids on either side of his face, staring straight ahead as the Shadow plunged into the long dark, the scowl on him darker yet.

They thought he was raging at being separated from the

knarr, or furious at the storm itself. They were wrong. Crowbone's head was full of a name which told him almost everything he needed to know.

Martin.

Run with the wind, Thorgeir had said, for that is what the Shadow will do. Bergfinn had no better option, so that is what they did. It was a good *knarr*, even laden as it was, coursing up the great glassy swells, cutting through the white spume-mane, planing down the far side. It was built for this, after all, more so than a *drakkar*.

After a while, with the sail reefed to the last knot, enough only to keep them steering, men curled their bodies a little less; they would ride the storm out and, with the luck of whatever gods they followed, perhaps meet the Shadow when the last clouds blew themselves to rags.

Thorgeir began to ease the thought that had padded blackly after him since he and Bergfinn had been sent back to this *knarr* – that the boat was their doom, a wyrd woven in wood by the Norns. He looked to where the wrapped body of Fastarr Skumr rolled in the wet, waiting a decent burning; next to it, Kari Ragnvaldrsson hugged his shattered hand and his misery, facing nothing better than a purse of hacksilver and an uncertain future no matter where they reached.

Cripples and the dead, Thorgeir brooded. Not the best crew, but fitting for such a ship as this.

The wyrd of it cracked open not long after when the steering oar collar snapped for the second time.

Torvold, a fair smith in his day, could do nothing with his forge-built muscle. He should have let the steerboard go, but without it they were all doomed, so he dared not and the weight of it dragged him over the side even as men, their screams torn away by the howl of wind, sprang too late to help him.

The Swift-Gliding balked, whirled like a stung stallion, no

more use than a wood chip in a flood. Bergfinn had time to look at Thorgeir, to see his answering, flat-eyed gaze, all hope sucked from it as he watched the Norn curse come at them, woven now in water.

Then the great black-glass curl of sea fell on them like a cliff.

Later . . .

Vigfuss Drosbo looked, but could not see Crowbone in the deck huddle; he wondered if the prince was looking for birds to guide them, then realised that, sensibly, they were all on shore with a head under one wing. He saw Kaup, clinging to the mast with one hand, his mask of a face twisted with terror; he did not like a sea storm, it seemed. No sane man did, though the way of it, as Vigfuss said to the Burned Man, was to keep bailing and not think hard on anything.

It was day, Stick-Starer said, though you would be hard put to know it, but Mar and Kaetilmund staggered down the length of the deck, handing out a rising-meal of wet bread with most of the mould removed. There were some of the old crab claws too, so that Rovald, grinning and dripping, declared that he would at least get to eat them before their kin ate him.

Crowbone blinked out of his head, where a storm raged almost as bad as the one sweeping the Shadow.

Martin was the Drostan Orm had told him of, that was clear. If there had been a real Drostan to begin with, that one was dead and gone. Martin was a venom-spider and Crowbone remembered him, remembered the way the Saxlander priest had slit the throat of Bleikr, the beautiful dog Vladimir had given him. It would not, Crowbone thought, be much of a step to slitting the throat of an inno-cent monk called Drostan.

That whirling wind of possibilities, lashed with the confused sleet of what Martin was plotting, was bad enough. What was worse, what was the shrieking tempest of it all, was the matter of Orm in it. What had he been told? Had he told Crowbone all he knew?

And the great crushing wave of it – could Orm be trusted? It had come to him that he had, perhaps, misjudged Orm, dismissed him as a little jarl. It had come to him that this might not be the truth of matters, that Orm had ambitions and silver enough to raise men and ships – and use the Bloodaxe for his own ends. His hackles rose as his stomach fell away at the thought of Orm standing against him.

Yet all that had happened pointed to it like a good hound scaring up game; Orm had sent him with Oathsworn, supposedly to guard and help him, but probably to spy as he tripped all the traps set by Martin for those chasing the secret of this Bloodaxe. Then Orm would snatch it at the last, was perhaps close by even now. The thought turned him left and right to search, burned him with the treachery in it.

The worst of the real storm was gone, Crowbone realised when he surfaced from all this, and he said as much as he eased the stiff wet of himself. Nearby, Berto sat and stared at the deck with unseeing eyes, while the yellow bitch lay, head on paws and eyes pools of wet misery as deep as the ones that sluiced the length of her and down the rest of the boat. Stick-Starer glanced at the sky while the wind tried to tear his beard out by the roots, then shook his head.

'We are in the mouth of it,' he said. 'We are running hard with the wind and it will get much worse than this before we see the last of this weather.'

'There is cheer for you,' grunted Murrough and Onund, coming from checking the mast and steerboard and how much water was shipped, looked at Gjallandi and said: 'A tale would be good while we throw water out of the ship.'

136

'Not one about the sea, all the same,' added Murrough, scooping water over the side with his eating bowl. He nudged Berto, who seemed to wake from a dream and took another bowl up listlessly.

'Or dogs,' added Vandrad Sygni, as the yellow bitch, staggering in the swells, shook water out of itself all over him.

'You can stop a dog from barking and howling by turning one of your shoes upside down,' declared Murrough and then stared, a crab claw almost at his mouth, when he felt eyes on him.

'What?' he said.

'When did you know so much about dogs?' demanded Kaetilmund, shaking a cask to see how much drinking water was left in it.

'We of the Ui Neill know everything about good hounds,' the big Irishman boasted. 'The health of childer will always be better if you allow them to play with dogs. If you see a dog rolling in the grass, you should expect good luck or news.'

'Or expect it to be covered in its own shit,' Kaetilmund countered.

'Good news?' demanded Vigfuss Drosbo, looking at the yellow bitch. 'Does it work if the beast rolls on ship planking?'

'No,' answered Murrough with a grin, 'but it is good luck to allow strange dogs to follow you home. And wherever else we are going, we are going to my home.'

'Never give a pig away,' Gorm offered, huddled with the others of Hoskuld's men, who were doing nothing much at all. 'I had that from my old da, before I took to the sea. He said it was a curse from the old time, but most who heard it thought it only sensible trading.'

'No help, even if we had a pig,' Gjallandi noted pompously. 'Maybe, though, it would take your place at the bailing. Time you sleekit seals did something for your bread and water.'

Since he was wrapped imperiously in his wet cloak and doing nothing much himself at the time, this brought laughter

– but the idea was sound and Hoskuld's crew were handed buckets and bowls. Crowbone saw that Halk had moved to help Rovald at the steering oar.

'Since you do not bail,' Crowbone declared bitterly to Gjallandi, 'it would be good to have those tales now.' And he threw more water over the side, with a flourish to show that he was also working, prince or no.

'As you command, my prince,' Gjallandi answered wryly, though it was clear he had no stomach for the thought. Crowbone narrowed his eyes a little and stopped throwing water.

'I am bound by the Odin oath, same as you,' he said pointedly, 'but do not press too hard on me keeping to it and not harming you at all.'

Gjallandi felt his mouth dry up, which made it the only dry place on that ship. He began to gather his thoughts, but Crowbone's odd eyes had turned to soapstone.

'A great bear, who was the king of a great forest, once announced to his subjects that he wanted someone to tell stories one after another without ceasing,' he said and Gjallandi closed his mouth on his own tale.

'If they failed to find somebody who could so amuse him, he promised, he would put them all to death.'

The men had all stopped and Onund kicked first one, then another, into starting bailing again.

'Well,' Crowbone said, settling back on his haunches, 'everyone knew the old saying "The king kills when he wills", so the animals were in great alarm.

'The Fox said, "Fear not; I shall save you all. Tell the king the storyteller is ready to come to court when ordered." So the animals did so and the Fox bowed respectfully, and stood before the Bear King, who ordered him to begin. "Before I do so," said the Fox, "I would like to know what your majesty means by a story."'

'Something Gjallandi does not tell,' bawled a man from

down the deck; Bodvar, Crowbone remembered, by-named Svarti – Black – because of his nature rather than his looks. Gjallandi's scowl was soot after that.

'The Bear King was puzzled by this,' Crowbone went on, ignoring the pair of them. '"Why," he said, "a narrative containing some interesting event or fact." The Fox grinned. "Just so," he said and began: "There was a fisherman who went to sea with a huge net, and spread it far and wide. A great many fish got into it. Just as the fisherman was about to draw the net the coils snapped. A great opening was made. First one fish escaped." Here the Fox stopped.'

'Just as well,' muttered Onund, 'since a tale about the sea is not so welcome.'

Crowbone ignored him, too. '"What then?" demanded the Bear King. "Then two escaped," answered the Fox.

'"What then?" demanded the impatient Bear. "Then three escaped," said the Fox. Thus, as often as the Bear asked, the Fox increased the number by one, and said as many escaped. The Bear grew annoyed and growled loudly. "Why, you are telling me nothing new!" he bellowed.

'"I wish your majesty will not forget your royal word," said the Fox. "Each event occurred by itself, and each lot that escaped was different from the rest."

'The Bear King showed his fangs. "Where is the wonder in all this?" he demanded.

'"Why, your majesty, what can be more wonderful than for fish to escape in lots, each exceeding the other by one?" said the Fox. "I am bound by my word," said the Bear King, gnashing his fangs and flexing his great claws, "or else I would see your carcass stretched on the ground."

'The Fox, in a whisper to the rest of the animals, said: "If rulers are not bound by their own word, few or no matters can bind them. Even oaths to Odin."'

The wind was loudest on the ship for a long moment, then Gjallandi cleared his throat.

'The Lay of Baldur,' he began and Onund whacked him on the shoulder.

'Shut up and bail,' he growled. 'There are too many fish in the boat and not all of them are escaped from that story.'

South of Hy (Iona), some days later . . .

THE WITCH-QUEEN'S CREW

The sea creamed and smoked where it was not black as a slice of night and the spray smoked in Erling's face, so that he turned away and let the raggles of his hair flail one cheek for a moment.

Od, unmoved by anything other than keeping his blade dry, grinned back at him from a pearled face; he sat alone, for Gudrod's crew would not go near him if he could be avoided. They did not do this with any sneering, for the last thing they wanted was to annoy the beautiful boy, so they busied themselves with little tasks that kept them from sitting near him.

There were enough tasks to go round, Erling decided moodily, since the wind was thrawn in the rigging lines, singing like a harp while the waves hit the unmoved dragon-beast with a shuddering power that broke them into shards and smoke.

Standing up in this, watching the horizon, was Gudrod, one hand on a rigging line, one just touching the sealskin pouch where the letter they had taken from Holmtun was snugged up, warm and dry with his other precious treasure, the cloth nine-squares and bone counters of 'tafl.

One is as unreadable to me as the other, Erling thought bitterly, remembering the sighs and sneers of Gudrod over his playing. That left his mood as black as the sky behind them, where clouds, massive as bulls, were silvered by flickers of light.

'We have to make for land,' Hadd screamed out. Gudrod

140

did not need his shipmaster to tell him, though he suspected they had skipped under the worst of the storm, which was roaring and stamping closer to Mann. Still, they had a wind coming out of the east which wanted to push them west and contrary currents slamming waves into them from the north. The thought of running with the wind turned his bowels to water, for he had heard of others who had done this and missed Ireland entirely, never to be heard from again.

'Hy,' he roared back and Hadd left the mastfish and stumbled to his side, where he did not have to bellow his fears for the others to hear. Hy was not far off but a small island, hard to approach at the best of times, never mind at night in a storm. Difficult landing on an open beach where a mistake would rip the bottom off.

'The wind is wrong and the wave with it,' he said, his mouth fish-breath close to Gudrod's ear. 'It will be a hard row.'

Gudrod looked at his men and knew they needed something to shove fire into them, something more than muscle. He was the Witch-Queen's son and he had been around his ma long enough to have learned a few things. He nodded to Erling, then to the miserable, bound figure of Hoskuld.

It was a right shame, he thought to himself, stepping up to the prow, an iron-headed axe in each out-thrust hand, bellowing out old chants to Aegir and Ran and Thor, for he had hoped to bring Hoskuld all the way back to his mother, who would know if the old trader had anything left worth telling.

Still, there was the writing in Latin-runes, which probably told all there was to know and he planned to sail into Hy and get the monks there to read it. He threw the axes over the side for Thor's consideration, then drew his seax and turned to Hoskuld, whose face was stiff with fear, for there was too much sailing-salt in his blood for him not to know what would happen.

He wanted to tell Gudrod of the three gold coins sewn in the hem of his tunic but stitched his lips thin on that, for he knew Gudrod would then get the coins and would still use the knife.

The spray pearled on the silver of the blade and Hoskuld looked at it, then at Gudrod's set face. Then he spat, though the gesture was lost a little when the wind sprayed it back in his own beard. Gudrod laid one hand gently on the old man's wind-whipped hair, feeling the flinch in the man then.

Hoskuld's eyes grew wide and panicked as a hare; Gudrod felt him shake then, heard him squeal, but the words were whipped away by the wind – something about his tunic. He gripped, pulled the throat up and sliced. The men howled as the blood flashed, whipping away in red ropes by the wind. Hoskuld, like an old anchor stone, toppled over the side and was gone; the crew scrambled to their rowing places.

An hour later, the wind died and the sea settled to a long, slow, black heave, like a sated wolf breathing in its sleep.

The Manx Sea, at the same moment . . .

CROWBONE'S CREW

'We are turning,' Stick-Starer screamed and it was not a request. Onund, his hair and beard all to one side and stiff as a hackle, bellowed something back at him, but the wind ripped it away. They traded mouthings while the rain and wind tore and spat; Crowbone saw, in the blue-sparked dark, the tight, grim faces of men, wet with the sweat of fear as much as spray and rain.

'We have lost the shore,' Onund bellowed, forcing himself close to Crowbone's ear. 'He is guessing where it is.'

Now Crowbone was afraid. They had seen the land in the last of what passed for day, a silver sliver of light below a

142

great black glower of thunderclouds, and started to row for it. Then the grey mirk had sheeted down on them, the wind drove it sideways like a sleeting of arrows and they had lost sight of that thin, dark lifeline. Stick-Starer had raised the sail a notch and they ran on with the wind, hoping it did not plough them into unseen rocks as they slanted towards where the land had been.

They needed ship-luck and wave-luck. The deck felt pulpy to Crowbone and he fancied he could feel the Shadow wallow, fat with shipped water; he felt sick at the thought of being plunged into that madly shifting black maw and, at the same time, almost welcomed it, for he had dived in it daily in his ringmail, threshing and choking, training himself to slither out of the stuff underwater. That had been in quiet shallows, all the same, where he could recover the byrnie.

Then the yellow bitch barked. The roar and hiss of the wind chopped the sound off with a vicious abruptness, but the dog stood on splayed, staggering legs, stiff-ruffed and shaking with every bark, as if its whole body was forcing them out.

Berto went to it, turned and pointed out into the dark. In the next flare of blue-white, the curve of shingle between thick forests etched itself on the back of all eyes and a delighted Onund thumped Stick-Starer on the shoulder, hard enough to spurt water.

He sprang to the steersman, already helped by Halk and two others, while men fought the sail back on to the spar, gripped the oars and started to pull; laboriously, the Shadow turned, wallowingly and rocking like a sick cow, the rowers hauling and grunting. One fell sideways and men hauled him away; Rovald slid to the bench and began to pull, while others hunkered, waiting to relieve those who collapsed.

There was a long time of wind and rain and cursing. The Shadow plunged and bucked, tried to spin, was flung forward, then sucked back.

Finally it staggered to a sudden stop, throwing everyone

flat. The sea grabbed it and sucked it out again, then flung it back to the shore, this time hard enough that everyone heard the harsh grating and the sudden crack. Onund howled into the wind and rain, wolfing out his pain and outrage at what was happening to the ship, as if it was his own bones breaking and not planks, but the sudden tilt of the deck flung everyone sideways, some of them completely out of the ship.

Then there was a longer time of struggling in knee-deep water that slapped and sucked folk off their feet as they staggered to the shingle, hefting precious sea-chests. Kaetilmund and Stick-Starer fought through the surf and heaved lines ashore, looking for good fastenings.

Finally, safe ashore and looking back, Crowbone saw that the storm was growing and spat salt water as the crew gathered slowly beside him, slipping their sea-chests down and rubbing the rain and spray off their faces.

'Cracked like an egg,' roared Onund against the whine and howl of the wind and did not need to say more; the Shadow lay canted on the shingle and sand, the white of splintered wood bright on her.

'As well we made it to the shore,' Stick-Starer yelled back. 'Now we need shelter.'

'At least someone has found a mate,' Murrough bawled and stabbed his axe towards the yellow bitch, then stumped off up the rain-hissed beach, laughing.

Everyone turned; a brindle hound circled the yellow bitch, the pair of them sniffing each other's arse while men chuckled.

'Well,' said Kaetilmund to Berto, 'there was me thinking your yellow bitch was as magic as Finn's Weatherhat, or Crowbone himself – yet it was all because she is as prick-struck as a weasel in heat.'

'Different magic, same effect,' muttered Rovald. 'What I want to know is – who owns the other dog?'

'I fancy the light will tell us,' Gorm growled and pointed

to where the faint yellow glow of the lantern bobbed and swayed.

The owner was a cloak-wrapped figure looking for his dog and cursing it for having run off on such a foul night. Instead of his dog he came on a pack of wolves and, screaming, dropped the lantern and fled into the dark.

'Fuck,' said Vigfuss Drosbo with some disgust. 'All we want is a bit of shelter.'

'And some food,' added a voice.

'Ale would be good,' said Vandrad Sygni. 'And a woman or two.'

'And all the gold and silver they have,' Murrough finished, making everyone laugh as the rain dripped down their necks.

It was not hard to find where the man had come from – a huddle of buildings shut tight save for one back door of the main steading, left banging in the wind; the owners had fled into the storm night. Murrough stepped inside and found the fire in the hearth and a cauldron bubbling; a little salty, but that could as well be kale as the owners having gobbed in it before they left. As good a stew as you could hope to find in Ireland, he announced after tasting it.

'If we are in Ireland,' Crowbone growled back, with a pointed look at Stick-Starer, who shrugged.

'Storms run us where the gods wish,' he answered, ducking under Crowbone's black look and into the warmth and shelter. One by one, men crowded in, grateful to be out of the wind and rain, dumping sea-chests and shaking themselves like dogs.

Crowbone sent Kaetilmund off to explore the other outbuildings; when he came back, he announced that the place had storerooms, a brewhouse, a decent cookhouse with a bread oven, a byre with plough oxen contentedly chewing – and the building Crowbone had been most concerned about, a stable.

'Four wee ponies, five stalls,' Kaetilmund said and Murrough spat into the hearthfire.

'So they have sent word somewhere,' he growled, then helped himself to the stew.

Crowbone went to the door and looked out; the wind was rising and the rain pelting. Blue-white light rippled, the sky cracked and he could not see the sea from here, though he knew it would be lashing itself. He did not think a messenger would make good time to any warriors, nor they back to this place – and no man would want to drape himself with metal when Thor hurled his Hammer. He turned back to the fire and said so and Gjallandi shrugged.

'Unless there is a borg close by,' he pointed out. 'Where would the folk from this place be running to, after all?'

Murrough snorted.

'Anywhere. Too many women and weans to risk putting up a fight. They will find what shelter they can and spread the word of us for miles . . . gods curse it, boy, get your wet serk and breeks off or you will die.'

This last was directed at Berto, who was shivering near the fire in his wet clothes while men stripped and tried to find space to dry their clothes. The Wend eyed the big Irishman with a jaundiced look.

'When the same sort of men as we found in Galgeddil arrive here,' he piped back, 'I would rather be dressed and wet than have to face them bare-arsed.'

Which made a few laugh – and even more decide to get dressed again.

Crowbone looked to where Hoskuld's crew hugged themselves in wet misery – Halk was apart from them now – and looked pointedly at Gorm.

'How good are your trading skills?' he asked and had back a wary stare. 'Let us suppose they are great and we manage to persuade the people of this place that we mean no harm. Let us suppose that, if they had not run off, you might have helped in this and that, as a result, they generously agree to providing a good eating horse in exchange for, say, four new slaves. Seems a shame to wait for all this to work itself out, so we shall take the horse now.'

'I am no thrall, to be bought and sold,' Gorm exclaimed. 'It is against the law to sell a decent freeman as a thrall, never mind a Christian.'

Crowbone cocked his head to one side and curled his lip, having waited for this moment to let Gorm and the others of Hoskuld's crew know where they stood.

'I am the law,' he answered. 'And no decent Christian, as you pointed out before. You are thralls now, whatever you were before.'

Kaetilmund, on his way back to the stables with two others and a throat-slitting knife, laughed at the look on Gorm's face – but the Christians, Mar noted, kept their eyes on the floor.

They spit-roasted the best of the pony and had shelter, food and warmth in a storm, which was enough for everyone to feel content. Lolling in the steading, with a good hearthfire and watchers posted in case folk crept up, they listened to the storm whine and shriek, so that it was generally agreed only madmen would come to a war in this. The only fighting was between those jostling for drying space or the last of the horse and, apart from growls and scowls, nothing much came of it.

The wind heightened during the night and only the yellow dog slept soundly, for strong winds made men restless, as did the lurking possibility of armed men arriving. So men checked edges and helmet thonging in preference to sleep.

Gjallandi came to Crowbone after a little while, squatting beside him and nodding to where Berto sat, shivering a little and staring into the flames.

'I am thinking death sits hard on that boy,' he said softly. 'It occurs to me that the man he killed in Hvitrann was his first.'

Crowbone looked, then nodded and Gjallandi moved away. After a moment, Crowbone moved quietly to the side of the little Wend, who jerked from the flames as if stung.

'It is a hard matter to kill a man,' Crowbone said and Berto's deep brown eyes seemed luminous as moonlit pools when he looked in them. He remembered his first killing; Klerkon, the raider who had taken him and his mother and his foster-father. His mother and foster-father dead, Crowbone had been freed from his privy-shackling by Orm who, though he did not know who Crowbone was, had treated him kindly. More than kindly – in Novgorod, he had sent him off with Thorgunna to buy clothes and other necessities, part of which had been a little axe, for the nine-year-old Crowbone had argued that he was a warrior and so needed a weapon.

In the main square of Novgorod, he had seen Klerkon with Orm and Finn and the others – Martin had been there, too. Crowbone did not even see them clearly, did not know then that they had been arguing about momentous events. He simply saw Klerkon.

He remembered the feelings then – a sudden, savage exultation that had taken him across the square with a hop and a skip, for he was too small to reach high, that took him up into the face of Klerkon, burying the axe in the man's forehead.

It had gone in like a knife on an egg, he remembered as he told this to Berto. He did not tell how that feeling had come back to him night after night for a long time, bringing a strange sick itch to the palm of the hand that had held the axe. He did not need to, for Berto saw it all in the clouded eyes and, suddenly, laid a hand along Crowbone's wrist.

That stirred the prince from his darkness and he shivered a little, then rheumed some gruff into his voice, for he was supposed to be consoling Berto, not the other way round.

'Later,' he added, 'I killed Kveldulf, the man who killed my mother, in much the same way, but I did not have dreams about him.'

Berto had eyes like the yellow dog when Crowbone glanced at him and it made him uncomfortable – reminded him, in fact, of the Khazar girl he had first lain with and he said so, trying to change the subject. Berto's cheeks flamed and his eyes grew round.

'You have had many women?' he asked and Crowbone considered the matter.

'The first was the Khazar girl. Vladimir and I called her Bench because she always did it on her hands and knees.'

Those nearest laughed and Berto's eyes grew even larger and rounder, so it was clear to all of them there that the Wend youth had never humped in his life.

'I was eleven,' Crowbone went on, 'which folk tell me was late in starting.'

'You made up for it,' Kaetilmund growled morosely. 'There was the Dane girl we took in a raid and you would not share.'

'Sigrid,' Crowbone said slowly, remembering. 'She died of the flux not long after, so no-one had much joy of her.'

'Then there was the famous twenty,' Kaetilmund declared. 'Last year, when we went to Polotsk to get Vladimir the bride who spurned him.'

Crowbone stayed silent, for the memories of that brief and bloody little campaign were locked in the black sea-chest inside his head and he did not want to drag them out.

'The Prince of Polotsk,' Kaetilmund explained to a droop-mouthed Berto, 'objected to his daughter marrying Prince Vladimir – so we all went to his fortress, killed him and took her. We took twenty Polotsk girls, too and little Olaf here had them all before we sold them. It is a wonder he could stand up, never mind find the strength to whack Vladimir's brother between the eyes with an axe.'

Men roared with laughter and Crowbone shifted, feeling Berto's eyes on him and not liking to look, for he felt hot and uncomfortable under the gaze and did not know why. So he grew serious as a reef, talked about shieldwalls and large battles.

'You have never been in any battles,' he said to Berto, 'nor have we had much chance to show how we form Burh and shieldwalls for practice, then we fend off Murrough's pretend berserk lunges and Kaetilmund's shield kicks.'

'Have you been in battles, then?' asked Berto and Crowbone wondered if the boy was as innocent as his eyes said he was, for the question had only made Crowbone aware of what he did not know.

'One or two,' he said, then rubbed his beard ruefully. 'Not big ones,' he admitted.

'I have,' growled Murrough, passing by and hearing this. He squatted without asking, which made Crowbone scowl, but Murrough only grinned at him, then turned to Berto.

'You have a bow, I see. Learn to use it, for it is easier to kill a man at distance than when you are looking into his eyes,' he said. 'If you have ringmail you will stand in the front line – The Lost. That's the place of honour, where the best warriors belong. Others, usually the called-out men, the *fyrd*, fall in behind them with their spears and leather jerkins and old war hats.'

Lifting a piece of horse on a stick and blowing on it he went on, 'You saw us do that against that Galgeddil horse lord.' He tested the horse for heat, then tasted it, smacking his lips. 'Oh, for some of that *limon* Finn got out of Serkland,' he said, dreamy with remembering. Then he became aware of Berto, patiently waiting. He sighed.

'Well, here there is no *fyrd*, for we are all Chosen Men – the Oathsworn,' he went on, beaming. 'Our fame is great and jarls want us on their side when they fear even their own house warriors will flee. The *fyrd*, of course, are men who take up arms when their families or land is threatened. They are farmers first and fighting men second, unlike us.'

He sucked the meat while the fire swirled a little in a draught, the reek catching his eyes and making him curse. Crowbone still scowling at this intrusion said nothing, was acutely conscious of Berto's hand still on his wrist. Berto was patient and still as old stone, though there was a tremble in the underneath of him that Crowbone could feel, like a fly-twitched horse.

'For all that, it is necessary to have second and even third ranks, spear-armed,' Murrough went on. 'In the front rank all you have to do is stand and not get killed – harder than it sounds. You cannot do much fighting, for there is hardly room to lift an elbow and all you are there to do is protect the men behind you, whose spears will be stabbing past your ears and doing the real work.'

'No fighting?' Rovald said, leaning forward to get meat and then having to slap the ends of his burning hair. 'It is The Lost who win such battles.'

'In the end, of course,' admitted Murrough and took up his axe, which was rarely far from a hand, 'for there is only one way to find room to fight – you push into them, step by step until they break apart. Then you fight them to ruin. In pairs, which is why we practise that, too.'

Mar, who had been paired with Murrough, nodded and grinned across at his partner, who raised his beard-bladed axe to him. Berto already knew that Murrough used it to hook shields to one side, while Mar did the killing of the exposed man.

'This axe trick is used by the Irishers,' Murrough went, grinning and looking the hook-bitted weapon over like a man does a willing girl. 'The Dal Cais of this Brian Boru fellow perfected it, and much as it pains me to admit it, folk call these axes after them.'

'Mark you, that trick is fine when you are moving forward,' added Halfdan. 'The hardest matter is to step back a pace or two and still keep the line.'

'Aye,' admitted Murrough. 'It is bad enough being in The Lost with no-one else in front of you and the enemy howling down – the second and third ranks seem pleasant places then. But stepping back is hard.'

'Why would you?' Berto demanded and those who knew chuckled. Because war is hard work, he learned from a dozen throats. An hour of struggling and sliding and yelling and stabbing seems like a whole day and actual edge-swinging leaves you on your knees and gasping in half of that.

Murrough's understanding was that men whose world is war will last the pace – farmers with spears and axes will not, but even fame-laden warriors such as the Oathsworn would need to step back and take a breath or two eventually. It was possible to feed fresh men into the fight, exchanging one rank for another, but few had the Roman skill of this and did not use it much for fear of the chaos it caused.

All this talk did nothing to send men to sleep and Berto eventually got up and went into the dark looking for the yellow bitch, leaving Crowbone feeling the heat of his touch on his wrist and confused by the loss of it. Halfdan joked that the Wend was jealous of the brindle hound, now vanished.

'I wonder how the *knarr* is faring,' Onund muttered and Crowbone saw Gorm's head come up at that.

'Sunk entire,' Stick-Starer declared moodily. 'We will find them strewn all over the shingle come morning.'

'You are a hard man, Stick-Starer,' Kaetilmund answered, shaking his head. 'That is no wish to put on sailors.'

'Go down to the shore and hail them if you are so concerned,' Crowbone told him and Kaetilmund waggled his head from side to side in a non-commital way. Vigfuss Drosbo stuck his bluff, square face into the conversation and announced he would go if Stick-Starer would, since he had left his own porridge pot on board the *knarr* and was missing it now. They talked round it until they wore the subject to a nub, but did not go all the same.

'Aye, it is hard life at sea,' Murrough declared, stretching languidly in the fire heat. He farted and took the rough edge of tongues from those nearest him as his due for it.

'What would you know of it?' scoffed Stick-Starer. 'You Irishers plooter in the shallows in a skin bowl, so you do.'

'I have sailed,' Murrough spat back indignantly. 'I have seen the smoke-spray where the sea pours off the edge of the world.'

'The world is round, you oaf,' Onund rumbled. 'As any sailing man will tell you.'

'And how do you know this?' demanded Halfdan – and a few others, Crowbone noted, stirring interestedly from half-sleep. 'Are there not *duergar* at the four corners of the world, holding up the sky? Four corners, note. Of a square. Even I know this of our gods and I am not a learned man.'

'It is a disc,' said Stick-Starer. 'Surrounding the World Tree. That ocean you see is the one that separates us from Utgard, the void of all matters.'

'The world is curved like a round ball – how else do you account for the masts of ships showing over the horizon before the hull?' answered Onund, sitting like a lopsided hill by the fire.

'Sailing uphill now are we?' jeered Halfdan and Onund, who could not quite find an answer to that, hunched and said nothing. Stick-Starer simply spat a hiss into the fire.

'The world is round,' Gjallandi told them sonorously, 'for Odin and the gods of Asgard decreed it so to spoil the desires of High Kings. No matter how far they go in conquering, they will only end up staring at the dungheap in their own back yard.'

There was laughter at that, contented and easy; someone broke up a bench for firewood and the wind shouldered the steading so that the rafter-bones of it groaned; draughts fluttered the flames and, if Crowbone shut his eyes, longing painted the inside of his eyelids with Vladimir's fortress in Novgorod when he was fourteen years old and clasped with the comfort of being warm and safe while the world raged.

Novgorod, he noted to himself. Not Orm's hall at Hestreng, where he had also spent storm-lashed nights in warm comfort.

He did not like to admit to himself, but was aware of this being because of the revelation that the monk they sought was Martin.

Martin, who had sent word to Orm. Now Crowbone had to consider the possibility that Orm had not told all he knew of the matter for good reasons of gain and felt sick at that thought. The closest Crowbone had come to a father had not been Uncle Sigurd when he had been alive – it had been Orm, with his tales of when he was a boy, with nothing more worrying than having his fringe cut or his ears washed. Crowbone, who had never had any similar experiences, hugged Orm's childhood to himself, from scaling slick, wet-black cliffs for gull eggs, to perching on the muscled rump of the fierce stud stallion in its stall.

For all that, Crowbone did not want to become Orm. He looked round at the growling, snoring, whispering, farting men, all beards and grim fierceness; he was still in Orm's hall and here Orm's family. This is not for me, Crowbone thought. Men are weapons and tools, to be used to make kingdoms. Then that serpent-thought coiled in on him again – perhaps Orm has also worked this out and, like me, realised that fame alone lasts only as long as the last stone with your name carved on it.

He thought of Grima of the Red Brothers, fameless under his lonely pile of stones on a strange shore, and shivered.

SEVEN

The coast of Ireland, a day later . . .

CROWBONE'S CREW

CROWBONE woke to find Berto cradled in the hook of one arm, a warmth that was welcome and a strange, disturbing softness that was not, that made him unlatch himself and move away, pretending to check on the weather.

The wind had backed, was blowing inshore and had been for some time, for the whole place was palled in spindrift, sucked off the creaming shore and flung landward like quivering snow. But the storm was gone, no more than hollow puffs and sighs and the dull rumour of it in the sea.

There was no sign of the *knarr*.

Vigfuss Drosbo and Svenke Klak found this out when they left together into the pewter of the day, the one anxious for his porridge pot, the other frantic with the remembering of his ringmail, rolled in sheepskin and stowed under the corpse of Skumr.

Now they came back, stumbling up, wild-haired and wildeyed, with the news that there was a hole in the world where all their plunder should be.

'Sunk entire,' Stick-Starer declared, with some relish, as though he had seen it and told everyone just that.

'There is no wreckage,' Svenke answered hopefully, sick with the knowledge that his ringmail was probably gone forever. That and the view of the Shadow in daylight made men hunch into the spattering rain, gloomy as the grey day itself.

Crowbone saw that the Shadow was done and did not need Onund to look at him and shake a mournful head – the straked planks along one side of the prow were splintered in a great gash the length of a man and as wide as a forearm.

They would have to carry their gear and Crowbone's resolve on not raiding this place, wherever it was, now vanished; they needed ponies and carts if there were any and he sent men scurrying for them, while Onund and Kaetilmund wrestled the prow beast off and started to fasten it on a spear; on or off the ship, the power of the prow could still battle the spirits of the land.

Drosbo sat with his chins drooped at the thought of his missing pot and Svenke stood with the look of a ram which has just butted a wall. Folk patted his shoulder, for ringmail was as fabulous as a dragon egg and as hard to come by – especially for the likes of Svenke, whose by-name, Klak, meant peg and had been handed to him because he was so broad across the shoulder and narrow in the hip that he looked like one.

'Borrow the prince's,' Rovald said daringly and everyone laughed; Crowbone acknowledged them with a wry wave of one hand, then hauled out the offending ringmail. It had been boiled in whale oil, which made it almost black and helped proof it against the rot – but it hung like a shed snakeskin, streaked red and with rings dropping from it. Which was the result of Crowbone training himself to swim in the sea with it and men who prized the craft and work of it as much as the expense, shook their heads at the ruin. Svenke Klak's gaze was bitter on a man who could treat ringmail so badly.

'Perhaps we will find a smith who can move a few links in one we take as a prize,' Kaetilmund soothed and Svenke nodded miserably.

'He may get the chance soon,' panted Halfdan, coming up at a hard trot. 'Riders are coming – lots of them.'

It was not the place Crowbone would have chosen for a fight, this shingle beach slathered in sea foam, but men came spilling up in knots, half-dressed for war and aware that all their sea-chest possessions were still in the steading.

'Ach,' Murrough yelled out, hearing them mumble and fret, 'I had a good pair of *naal-bind* socks in my chest, only darned twice and hardly a hole in them. Now I will have to go and buy for new.'

Men left off their grumbles and a few laughed, shamed and sheepish, hardened raiding men who knew that you should be able to leave anything behind in an eyeblink, for it was sometimes the way of the wave and war that a good sea-chest vanished. Yet there was a mutter, about how all the plunder from one place was gone and now it looked as if the rest was lost, too. Poor raiding luck from this new jarl.

Crowbone heard it. Fridrek, he thought, still breathing through his mouth since his nose was broken. He felt the rage surge in him then, and wanted to stop Fridrek breathing entirely – but he knew what to do instead.

'We have not even thrown a few sparks off an enemy blade,' he bellowed out. 'We are not turned and burned yet.'

So they laughed and formed up, shields casual and ready by their sides. But when the men came up, they made everyone blink; Crowbone felt his face go stiff with the sight of them.

They were not horsemen, just men on horses and they had wisely climbed off them and sorted themselves out into a long thick thread of shields and helmets and spears. Their leader rode a little *fyrd* pony, was slathered in ringmail cut for riding and coming down over his thighs; off the horse it would drag at his ankles.

He had a decorated helmet with a brass boar crest and mail all round the front so that only his eyes showed, like a dog peering from a kennel. He rode forward a little and peeled off the helmet, revealing a flushed face, black hair bound back and ragging in the wind and a chin shaved save for a long moustache. Slightly behind him, a boy looked on from the back of his own horse, curious and unafraid.

'More driftwood washed up?' the man said in heavily accented Norse, fighting the mouth of the pony so that slaver flew. Eighty men, Crowbone counted and felt his own men shift slightly, for even if they could not tally beyond fingers, they knew when they were outnumbered.

His tongue felt like old wood, but Crowbone forced himself to be light and easy, as relaxed as if he sat at his own hearth-fire with a horn in one hand and a woman in the other.

'You have found some driftwood already?' he asked and the horseman frowned a little at that, cursing as the pony tried to dance him round in a circle.

'Aye,' he answered and waved a hand. Men came forward carrying a limp form and laid it down alongside the pony, which snorted and stamped at the smell of death.

'One less Dyfflin raider,' the horseman snarled and Crowbone stepped forward. It was Kari, puffed with water, his shattered hand still stuck in his tunic belt. Men groaned when they saw it, for the fate of the *knarr* was now confirmed.

'By all the gods of Ireland,' bellowed a voice which snapped heads round. Murrough stepped forward, his big hooked axe held in front of him. 'You dare call me a Dyfflin raider? Who are you to insult a son of the Ui Neill then?'

Crowbone flared with anger that someone should have crashed into his speaking without a by-your-leave – yet he also saw the horseman's head snap up and his eyebrows go even further than that. Then Murrough went off into Irish, a great scathing, snarling dragon-spit of words which left the horseman lashed and even more flushed, his lips thin as wires.

'Your Chosen Man reminds me of my manners,' he said eventually, stiff and painful. 'Congalach macFlann, macCongalaig, macDuin macCernaig. I serve Gilla Mo Chonna macFogartach macCiarmac, ri Deiscert Breg.'

He broke off and indicated the boy behind him, who kicked his horse forward and rose up a little in the stirrups to announce, in a shrill voice, that he was Maelan macCongalach, macFlann and so on.

None of which made the least sense to Crowbone, but he knew the Irishers were reciting their lineage and that they were father and son. Not that it meant much, since every ragged Irisher was as proud as a king, even if he had no arse in his breeks, and every one was rich with names if nothing else. Still, he had no idea who Gilla Mo was but did not show it, for he knew how to behave like a prince. Vladimir had taught him that.

'Olaf Trygvasson, of the Yngling line of Harald Fairhair, king of Norway and a prince in my own right,' he declared. 'And no friend to the Norse of Dyfflin.'

'So this Murrough macMael fellow says,' Congalach replied. 'You are part of the Oathsworn of Jarl Orm, the White Bear Slayer.'

Crowbone glanced at Murrough with narrowed eyes, wondering what else the Irisher had said, but only had a broad grin in reply. Behind him, Kaetilmund grunted as if kicked.

'Oh fuck,' he muttered. 'Now we have trouble – they know us.'

Crowbone merely inclined his head and the horseman cuffed the head-tossing pony on one ear.

'I have heard of those men,' Congalach declared, frowning. 'I am told they are not Christians.'

'The Oathsworn have been prime-signed,' Crowbone replied, which was no lie for they had all been once; Crowbone had the tales of it from Finn. 'I myself have just come from the chapel of St Ninian at Hvitrann.'

Leaving a deal of dead and a Galgeddil lord's family weeping – but there was still no lie in it, thought Crowbone, though he felt the heat of black stares on his back from the likes of Onund and Kaetilmund and all the other firm pagans. He willed their teeth together.

Congalach smiled.

'Then you are welcome,' he said, 'in the lands of the Ui Neill.'

'God bless the Ui Neill,' Murrough added cheerfully and made the sign of the cross on his breast, over the Thor Hammer neatly hidden beneath his tunic.

'*Amén*,' Crowbone lied smartly.

The island of Hy (Iona), around the same time . . .

THE WITCH-QUEEN'S CREW

'I believed you to be Christians,' said the abbot and Gudrod acknowledged him with a slight ironic bow, which flitted up the stone walls and flickered, wavering, as the wind threatened the fish-oil lamps.

'As Christian as you are,' he replied and the lash of it was not lost on the abbot, who had barred the door of the monastery when the ship had first appeared, afraid of the sleek of it and not consoled enough by the friendly removal of the dragon-prow to offer Christian charity. The door, which had been briefly opened, was shut and barred once more for the abbot was Frankish and from the eastern borders of that place, where no-one was to be trusted.

It had taken Od's toying with some of the monks who had stayed outside the monastery, cowering or praying in their beehive huts, to get the door opened again, by which time Gudrod was rain-soaked and bad-tempered as a wet cat. He waved the written parchment under the abbot's nose and demanded he read it in a decent tongue but all he got was a babble of Frankish prayers. It came as no surprise to Erling that the abbot soon found himself strung by the ankles above his own altar, but what amazed him was the passive courage of the other monks, who simply knelt and started to pray. One or two rose up, shouting, 'Saint Blaithmac', then subsided to prayer again.

'Who is this Blaithmac?' Od demanded.

Erling did not know, so he asked and, eventually, a whey-faced priest told him in stumblingly poor Norse – a monk, martyred by raiders for refusing to give up the shrine of Columba on the island of Hy a hundred years ago at least.

'So he is dead?' asked Od and Erling nodded, which made the youth shrug; a god who would not protect his own from death was not much of a god – though the house these folk had built for him was interesting. Stone and solid as a fortress.

Erling pointed out that the priests seemed to be made of the same stuff as the saint, for Od had killed three already and the abbot was still refusing to read anything to help pagans and murderers. He continued babbling prayers in his own tongue.

'Remember also the signs of old burnings on the way up here,' Erling pointed out as they stood in the flickering half-dark, waiting for Gudrod's next move. 'This Hy place has been scorched before. My da's da probably did it.'

Laughter flitted round the stone columns, so that the monks shut their eyes and prayed harder, trying not to notice the skull-grins from the shadowed men lurking beyond the light and angry at having been left so long out in the wind and rain.

'*Fater unser, thu thar bist in himile, si geheilagot thin namo . . .*' the abbot panted, the drool running up his own nose. Erling sighed; it did not appear to him that this one was about to do as was demanded of him and he said as much. Gudrod's eyebrows braided and he backhanded the abbot twice, then glared at him, sucking his knuckles as the Christmann swung like a bad bell.

'Do you play *hnefatafl*?' he asked suddenly and the abbot, swaying and bleeding, only moaned. Gudrod sighed.

'I thought not. If you did, you would have known that the king is surrounded in this game and it would be as well to give in.'

The abbot started a gasping call for God to visit plagues on the pagan and died so suddenly, when Gudrod's temper snapped, that even the monks were surprised. The abbot's throat was opened by a seax in mid-rant, the priest's last curse a hiss of blood-mist that Gudrod had to wipe off the writing.

'Well,' muttered Erling with pointed sarcasm, 'do I pick another and find out if he can read?'

Gudrod, well aware that he had acted hastily, bent and wiped the seax clean on the abbot's robes while the blood pooled out under the man's head like a black, spreading shadow in the lamp light.

'No need,' said a voice and a figure stepped into the light and stood to let Gudrod and Erling look him up and down.

Indistinguishable in his dress from any of the other priests, he was as different from them in bearing as donkey from stallion; tall, hair neatly cropped and tonsured, eyes clear and unafraid. Lips, Gudrod thought to himself, thin and bloodless as wires and an arrogant tilt to the chin.

'Who?' he demanded.

'Mugron,' the man declared.

Proud, Gudrod thought. Knows his worth. Here is a man who wants to be the next abbot of Hy. Better still, here was a priest who spoke decent Norse and could read the Latin.

He thrust the parchment at him.

'In return for this, a peaceful departure in the morning – you will have shelter and food for the night,' Mugron said. 'No-one else killed, nothing burned, nothing taken.'

Gudrod's smile was twisted.

'Do you play *hnefatafl*?' he asked and the priest frowned.

'Possibly. I play *skáktafl* which I learned in Rome.'

Gudrod had heard of *skáktafl*, the Shah's Table, an invention of Musselmen and a game with more pieces and lined up like opposing armies – but Shah was just the Serklander's name for a king, and any game of kings was one Gudrod wanted to play. So he smiled.

'You have the word of a Christian on matters,' he answered, while the blood of the abbot patted in large, wet drops to the stones. There was the briefest of hesitations, then the priest started to read.

Cnobha (Knowth), Kingdom of Brega in Ireland,
days later . . .

CROWBONE'S CREW

They skliffed over worn stone slabs, clack-clacking in salt-stained boots, skidding in the scowl-dark of the place, which was all tall shadows broken by the dazzle of torchlight so that Crowbone could not get a true impression of it.

They walked through skeins of men in the long hundreds, sorting themselves out so that the whole of that fortress writhed like a cut snake. Then, suddenly, they were at a door and the men in the lead, swathed in shoulder-fastened cloaks of muted check, stood to one side to let their king go through.

The king half turned then, to where Crowbone and Gjallandi and Murrough followed, rearing to a stop with the surprise of facing him. His eyebrows, like snow on lintels, had closed to make one iced line and his long moustaches, the colour of old walrus teeth, trembled almost as much as his belly when he spoke.

'Watch your words,' he growled. 'This is Mael Sechnaill himself in here and he is judge. I have offered my hand to you on the strength of this Ui Neill man here and would not like to find I had misplaced it.'

He paused, then hitched up the great gold pin that fastened his cloak to the bulk of him.

'Prince,' he added, in such a scathing way that Crowbone took a step forward until Gjallandi's hand gripped his forearm and stopped him. The anger in him burned his belly, all the same, as he stepped after the king of Brega, Gilla Mo Chonna. Gjallandi caught Murrough's eye as the Irisher stepped up and was not made easier by the wild grin he got back.

They moved into the bright of the place, blazed with torches. Crowbone was surprised to see a floor of stone slabs that bounced the light back, so that the place seemed like the inside of a great bowl of red gold; he became aware of the salt streaks on his clothes, the tarnish on his pin and neckring.

He half-turned once to the other two, convinced the three of them were griming a trail on the floor, like slugs on a gold plate – then his laugh, half-shamed, died on his lips at the sight of the guards he had forgotten were behind them like pillars, long ring-coats jingling and dragging round their calves, faces blanked by helmet metal. It reminded him that his men were snugged up in the warm, but not part of the feast and kept away from the High King's army until matters were resolved.

The dark gable of the place soared above Crowbone and the noise and smell of food was a blow to the senses. Ahead on the High Seat sat a figure, his dark hair bound back by a braided thong of gold threads, his face wreathed in smoky torchlight as he spoke from one side of him to the other with all the lesser kings – Mael Sechnaill, High King of the Irishers.

He turned as Gilla Mo stepped up and, smiling, waved the king of Brega to the seat beside him. This was Gilla Mo's hall and that was his High Seat, but he acknowledged Mael Sechnaill as his better and bowed, then sat – on his left, Crowbone noted, not at his right hand, which was reserved for what seemed to be a blind man.

In a moment, though, Gilla Mo had his white hair close to

the High King's ear, while Crowbone stood, aware of the looks and the muttered questions, the faces turning like hog snouts to see who was coming to share the trough.

Crowbone could guess some of what the fat king of Brega told – how a band of Norse claiming to be part of the famed Oathsworn and led by a self-styled Prince of Norway had wrecked themselves on the shore near Ath Na Gassan, the Ford of Paths. On how they claimed to be Christians and one of them had announced himself as an Ui Neill called Murrough macMael, so Brega had offered them hospitality and brought them to the High King.

A fair walk it had been, too, Crowbone thought bitterly – they rode and we tramped. After a few hours of forested hills, humping their own sea-chests on their backs, Crowbone had refused to go further until this was resolved. In the end, reluctantly, Congalach had relented and the sea-chests had been taken on the front of the ponies; it had gone some way to quelling the black scowls directed at Crowbone from his own men, who thought his luck was poor.

On the way, Murrough had tried to find out more about these men of Brega and what they did, but beyond the mention of Mael Sechnaill's army being at Cnobha, Murrough found out nothing much.

'He is mannered enough,' he whispered to Crowbone one rest-halt, 'but this Congalach speaks a lot and tells nothing. I only know that the army goes to Tara and his men took seven years to train for war.'

'I know that we are prisoners, for all we have our weapons,' muttered Kaetilmund and grim faces growled agreement to that. Crowbone laughed as easily as he could make it.

'As long as we have edge and hand, we are not prisoners,' he told them. 'We are war, waiting to be woven.'

Standing in front of the High King, all the same, Crowbone did not doubt that he had his feet firmly planted in a kennel of dogs who eyed him like a strayed wolf, so he pretended to ignore the stares and squints, looking instead at the richness of the hall.

There were wall hangings – a winged youth or a woman, in blue and green; a bearded man who seemed to be dead or sleeping and others, their colour faded by dark and smoke but some with the gold head-circles that Christ figures had. Real gold wire, too, Crowbone noted.

'Murrough macMael.'

The voice cut through the noise and stilled it at once. The High King raised a hand and flapped it at them to come forward and Murrough, grinning, swaggered out. Gjallandi and Crowbone hesitated a moment and felt the body heat of the guards closing in behind them, forcing them forward. Congalach strode out in front and to one side.

'Kneel!' he ordered and both Murrough and Gjallandi went down on one knee.

'Kneel before the Ard Ri,' Congalach bellowed. 'And the king of Brega. And all the kings of Ireland.'

Crowbone saw the cat's arse purse to the Brega king's mouth then and thought – aha, here is a man who does not like being an afterthought on the left hand of a High King. Then he felt the hard wolf eyes of all that other nobility raking him, so that he clenched hard on the bowels that threatened to turn to water and tilted his chin.

'Never bow the knee, me,' he declared and Congalach moved, two clacking steps, with one hand poised to grip Crowbone's shoulder and force him down; then the odd eyes turned on him and he felt himself stop in mid-stride.

'Lay that on me, Irisher, and suffer for it,' Crowbone declared, then raked the assembly with a single sweeping glance. 'Know this – you think we are prisoned here with you, but it is you who are trapped with us.'

'In the name of Christ's heaven,' cracked out a voice and you could taste the dark scowl in it. 'What does it matter? The man is a prince of Norway, after all, who does not need to bow even to the High King of Ireland. If we find that to be less than true, all the same, we will take his measure anew. If only to allow for the length of his burial hole.'

Congalach swallowed and the muscles in his jaw worked before he drew back. Mael Sechnaill rose, moved to the edge of the High Seat dais and stepped confidently off it. Suddenly, there was a stir at the back of him as men parted to let a figure through; it was the blind man from Mael Sechnaill's right-hand seat and Crowbone stared at him.

He was old, with a face seamed and soft-skinned as an old purse, his eyes blind-white as boiled eggs. He was wearing a long kirtle of check and Irisher-laced shoes, with a blue cloak fastened round his waist and thrown over one shoulder, fastened with a pin which winked silver.

'This is Meartach, my *Ollumh*,' the High King said with a smile. 'He has no eyes but he sees a great deal.'

Crowbone heard Gjallandi move slightly at the announcement and remembered that an *Ollumh* was some sort of superior skald for the Irish; small wonder our own skald is concerned, Crowbone thought, since he might have to prove his worth in front of an expert.

Meartach came shuffling up, close enough for Crowbone to see the napped white hair, fine as a dusting of snow on his pink scalp, the lines and grooves of the man's face. The *Ollumh* reached out both hands and Crowbone drew back from him, which made the old man laugh like the rattle of old bones.

'Have no fear, Prince of Norway. What can an old man do?'

'Odin seems an old man,' Crowbone answered uneasily, letting fingers trace his face; they were warm and dry as lizard skin, smelled of meat and old dust. 'One-Eye, however, is dangerous to let close to you, even as a friend. And a king may do what he pleases in his own hall.'

This brought a chuckle.

'Is he your god, this Odin?' Meartach asked, moving on to

pass his fingers over the grim smile that was Murrough, trembling like a horse at the start of a fight.

'Not in this place,' Crowbone answered and the High King laughed.

'I thought Christ had reached the ears of the Oathsworn,' he said.

'The White Christ is everywhere,' Crowbone admitted and had back a nod and wry twist of grin, while Meartach hovered around Gjallandi, making noises in the back of his throat, something between a cat purr and an expression of surprise.

Then he shuffled back to the platform and sat on the right of the High Seat, which Crowbone saw made the Brega king scowl.

'A prince he is, for sure,' Meartach announced, which brought a brief murmur, a moth-wing of sound racing round the smoky hall. 'There is more there, but it is shrouded and I cannot tell of it.'

Mael Sechnaill seemed surprised and impressed, stroked his chin and then went back to sit down.

'The others?'

'A warrior, the big man,' Meartach declared. 'The other has song in him, but not as much as he would like.'

There were laughs at this and the scowl of pride it brought to the bristling Gjallandi. Crowbone was impressed, but it was tempered with the thought that the *Ollumh* had not said anything that could not have been gleaned from matters already known.

It was, all the same, enough. The High King waved one generous hand at the benches opposite him.

'In which case, Prince Olaf – welcome to this hall. You also, skald – and you, Murrough macMael.'

They climbed onto benches and food arrived – salmon and other fish, coal-roasted pork and fine venison in great slabs on a platter of flatbread. Women brought ale and Crowbone felt the heat of their bodies as they poured for him; it had been a time since he had taken a woman.

'I was hoping you would not claim kinship, Murrough macMael,' the High King said with a smile, 'since I am over young to have sired something the size of you and not known it.'

Folk laughed and Murrough grinned, meat juice running down his beard.

'The Mael I am sired from is as far from your High Seat as the worm from the moon – a simple farming man from down *Inis Sibhtonn* way.'

This brought mutterings, for that was in the lands of the Dal Cais and, though they were also Ui Neill, Crowbone knew the rivalry between south and north was considerable.

'I should have known from that axe,' Gilla Mo chimed and then had to explain it all to the High King. Crowbone chewed meat and bread and watched the level of his ale cup closely.

'Do you not bless your meat?'

The speaker was small-mouthed, long-fingered and had hair the colour of faded red gold, rippled the way sand does when the tide goes out. He looked truculent as a rooting pig as he stared at Crowbone, who matched it as cool as he could manage.

'Do you?' he countered, feigning astonishment.

'Of course,' the man snapped back, though bewilderment made his voice tremble.

'Why?' Crowbone asked. 'Are you afraid of being poisoned by it?'

The man opened and closed his mouth, for any answer to this mired him in a swamp he did not want to put a foot in; Crowbone saw Meartach's tooth-free mouth gaping in a silent laugh.

'Seems to me you are no Christian at all,' the man persisted. 'It appears to me that you are as pagan as the amulet you wear under your shirt.'

'This?' Crowbone replied and pulled out his Thor Hammer.

'Neck money, no more. There is at least four ounces in it of good burned silver – enough to buy you some better taunts than you are trying here. Perhaps I should lend it to you?'

Neighbours laughed and one of them was the High King. The red-haired man scowled and glanced sideways, to where the king of Brega sat, bland and unsmiling. Aha, thought Crowbone, so that is the way of it – you are looking to impress your fat old lord.

'I have taunt enough for you, heathen,' the man eventually sneered, which was so poor that Crowbone almost sighed.

'I doubt it,' he declared mildly, 'considering that I frightened off a great troll with taunts once.'

The man opened and closed his mouth; Murrough, grinning, picked up the head of his salmon and mimicked the look with his fingers on the fish's mouth; folk roared and some beat the table.

'I had heard of the Oathsworn wonders,' the High King declared, loud enough for his voice to carry over the burr and buzz of the hall and bring it to silence. 'Did this troll-scaring take place on the hunt for that fabled hoard of silver?'

'There or thereabouts,' Crowbone declared, off-hand. 'There was a range of hills, but the name of the place escapes me entire. A troll called Glyrnna – Cat's Eye – lived there and I happened upon it by chance.'

'The luck that wrecked you here holds true, then,' snarled the red-haired man, seeing his chance at a sally. Crowbone almost pitied him.

'Perhaps so – it was worse even than I knew, since Glyrnna was a troll-woman and they are worse than the men of their kind, for sure. Yet that same luck brings me here to the High King's table, same as you.'

That brought more laughter and then Mael Sechnaill signalled for Crowbone to go on; somewhere, a woman shrieked and then giggled, only to be shushed – the story was more interesting than any fumbling in dark corners.

'Mark you,' Crowbone continued and Gjallandi saw his eyes, flat and glassed as a summer sea, with almost no colour in either of them save what the torchlight threw, 'I do not deny that my breeks were not entirely clean after hearing her bellow. "Who comes there?" demanded the troll, stood standing there with a large flint stone in one fist and the same look on her face as Murrough here is giving that slice of fish.'

Murrough paused, a portion of the same fish bulging out his cheeks.

'So I told this Glyrnna who I was,' added Crowbone while the laughs burred round the benches, 'but it did not seem to impress her much. "If you come up here I will squeeze you into fragments," she yells at me and crushed the stone between her fingers into fine sand as she did so. "Then I will squeeze water out of you as I do out of this stone," I answered, taking a new-made cheese from my bag and squeezing it so that the whey ran between my fingers to the ground.'

There were cheers at this and groans, too, for it was an old story-telling device. Crowbone grinned and flapped one hand.

'Aye, aye,' he went on, 'you may scoff, but that old trick still works, as you can see. However, it did not make this troll any colder. "Are you not afraid?" she asked and I told her plain enough. "Not of you," I said and there was more lie in that than truth. "Then let us fight," says this Glyrnna, which was not what I wanted to be hearing, so I rattled around in my thought-cage and came up with – a taunting, I told her. A good taunt, as you all know, will get anger and anger always gives cause to fight.'

'Well, this troll racked her head so hard over it I could hear the thoughts grinding round the inside of her skull. "Very well," she says and thinking herself cunning, declares that she will go first. "Speak on," says I and she takes a deep breath.'

The silence was as thick as smoke in the pause Crowbone gave, screwing up his face like a desperately-thinking troll. Then he roared out.

'"Your ma was a crooked nose hobgoblin,"' he bellowed and then shrugged apologetically. 'That was her best. I was as sorry as you for having to hear it.'

'What was your reply?' demanded a voice and Crowbone spread his hands.

'I strung my bow and nocked an arrow,' he said. 'Did I mention I had such? No matter – I have it now. Once the arrow was drawn, I yelled to her: "You are uglier than a bucket of sheep grease and armpits," then shot her just under the ribs, so that she squealed. A man would have been dead from it, but the troll-woman just tried to pull it out and demanded to know what had hit her.

'I told her plain enough – a taunt, though there was more lie than truth in that. "Why does it stick so fast?" the troll demanded of me and pulled the arrow out with as big a slab of meat on the hook of it than sits on the king of Brega's plate.'

There was a deal of laughing at this and the expression on Gilla Mo's face, eating knife half-way to his mouth.

'I told her why it stuck,' Crowbone went on into the hush that followed. 'Because a good taunt takes root. "Have you more of such?" inquires she. "Here," says I, "have another. Your old ma was so stupid she tried killing a bird by throwing it from the top of a cliff." I shot another arrow, this one into her eye. I did not mean it, I confess freely, for I am not good with a bow and was aiming at her foot at the time.

'She shrieked a deal and then asked if I was angry enough to fight, so I told her I had a few more taunts yet, at which she shrieked even more loudly and told me to walk where I will, though it would be an obligation on her if I would do it somewhere other than this hill.

'And so she ran off.'

The laughter and table thumping lasted a long time and even the High King had to stand up and raise his hands in the end, for the sound of his voice alone was not working.

'A good tale,' he declared, beaming greasily. 'Enough to earn the Hero's Portion at this feast, for I doubt any will better the beating of a troll with a taunt.'

The roars confirmed it and a brace of women brought the meat, the musk-sweat smell and bobblings under their kirtles tightening Crowbone's groin as they looked slyly at him; one winked.

'Now I am convinced of the tale of how the Oathsworn gained all the silver of the world,' added Mael Sechnaill, resuming his seat.

'With such riches,' Gilla Mo retorted savagely, 'why would such a man set forth with only a small company so far from home?'

'Odin promised us all the silver of the world,' Crowbone answered. 'He did not promise we could keep it.'

The chuckle was from Meartach, like a wind through red leaves.

'So it is with pagan gods,' he declared piously. 'No doubt that is one reason you found the way to Christ's path.'

'No doubt of it at all,' Murrough broke in, grinning.

'Now one of you three has earned his meat in my hall this night,' Gilla Mo declared and Crowbone heard the slight stress on the 'my hall' of what he said. 'There are kings from all over Ireland looking you over – what can you bring to this feasting fit for a High King, skald?'

Gjallandi cleared his throat and stood, one hand clenched in a fist over his heart. Then he gave them the tale of Brisingamen, which was clever.

Brisingamen was the true name of it, though Tears Of The Sun was another and both were equally shunned by the mouths of men. It was a necklace, crafted by the four *duergar* Brising brothers in their dark hall and so desired by the goddess Freyja that she was prepared to play the slut with them all to possess it. Or perhaps it possessed her.

A good *scop* could earn the best place by a fire, choice

meats and a good circle of armring for telling the tale of it – but it was not often trotted out, for it was dangerous and depended on the audience.

For a Christian household, with women and bairns listening, it was a hint, a shadow of the lusts in it, enough to leave the weans round-eyed and the women stuffing their head-squares in their mouths to quell squeals of delighted horror.

In a hall still true to the old gods, it was a brave *scop* who told it and, if he did, he transformed Freyja's lust into a pious sacrifice, like Odin hanging on the World Tree, or giving his eye to Mimir for a drink from the Well of Wisdom – the glittering-eyed women lurking in the dark of the hall would not hear otherwise of the Sorceress Queen, mistress of the magic and mystery of *seidr*. If he was brave and clever enough not to offend, a *scop* would leave that place wealthy and arrive at the next without becoming grey-faced and coughing, or vomiting blood, or drooling mad.

For a hall of feasting men with women spilling in their laps, however, it was perfect, with the meat of it provided by what the four black dwarves, stunted in every way but one, did with the luscious goddess in the sweaty dark. At the close, the approving roars brought a beam to the red-flushed face of Gjallandi and he bowed.

'Well told,' the High King declared, then looked at Murrough, who blinked a bit. 'What of you, Irisher – what do you bring to a High King's feast?'

Crowbone knew it even before Murrough opened his mouth, had felt the wyrd of it in every whirring wing he had seen all the way from the shore to this place. The words, of course, condemned them all to the same enterprise.

'Why sure,' said Murrough, his face bright with grease and grin, 'my axe and the arm that wields it, against your honour's enemies.'

EIGHT

Ireland, some time later . . .

CROWBONE'S CREW

THERE was a little wind that fretted this way and that, a hound fresh released from the lead. It slithered and snaked through trees and grass like the invisible water which found its way between neck and tunic and, if he could have seen any wet at all, Crowbone would have cursed it.

There was no rain, only a white, thick, soaking milk-mirr that even the little wind could not do more than shift a little, like a spurtle in a pot of porridge. It reduced the world to the length of a poor spear-throw and made tracking almost impossible; if it had not been for Kaup and the yellow bitch, Crowbone thought, we would not be on any heading that made sense.

That fuelled the slow-stoked anger in him, flared to life the moment he had been told that Gorm and the three others of Hoskuld's crew had fled. That Halk was with them did not help, while the news that Fridrek and four others of the Oathsworn crew had also gone with them was a breath of forge bellows to his rage.

'Well,' Gilla Mo said when he heard of it, 'it is bad enough that your thralls are running round loose in my land without half your own warriors gone with them, waving their blades and frightening folk.'

He perched on his High Seat in the brindle morning of his hall, where the smoke swirled greasily grey and people still farted and snored. He drew his cloak more snugly round him against the damp, kicked his own thralls into blowing life into the pitfire embers and so clearly enjoyed seeing Crowbone smoulder in front of him that he prolonged the whole business of giving his permission to pursue them.

'Take what men you think you need,' he went on, peering under the bar of his scowl, 'but make one of them that blue man you have. My folk are no strangers to blue men, since they are common enough on the Dyfflin slave blocks, but the sight of one as dark as he and treated like a true man and a warrior is unnerving to them. I do not want trouble over it.'

He eased his buttocks on the seat and savoured the last few moments of Crowbone squirming.

'Congalach will go with you,' he added. 'There is no need to thank me for the help. You have two days only – have this resolved and be back with the army to march to Tara.'

Crowbone could only offer a curt bow and clack his way over the flagged stones out into the rainwashed day, where the clouds scudded as fast as his beating heart. Old arse, he thought viciously, who only sits in his own High Seat because Mael Sechnaill is sleeping in his bedspace.

Tracking after Fridrek and Gorm had not improved his mood, for it had been a long, slow stumble through the tired yellow light of a dying day, questing here and there after the trail like a bat among moths.

They came on a line of slow cattle, the drovers wisely hiding until they knew who came up on them, stepping out suddenly from behind trees to stand, packbags on their backs, while Congalach shot Irish at them and had it fired back in measure. Eventually, he turned to Crowbone.

'Two handfuls of men passed them a quarter-day ago,' he said. 'They tried driving off a beast or two, but were bad at it and gave up. They have one of their number with a bow and the shafts for it.'

'That will be Lief Svarti,' Mar said. 'He is as good with that weapon as he is with his little-headed axe, so we should be wary.'

Crowbone almost asked why the drovers had not fought back, then thought better of it; they were not fighting men and the cattle were not their own, but belonged to Gilla Mo and were meant for feeding his army.

'What's ahead?' he asked Congalach and had a squint look and a shrug in return; the man was fretting over his son, Maelan, who had wanted to come with them and had been refused. Crowbone knew already that Congalach found it hard to refuse his boy anything. Besides that, Congalach had been sent to shepherd these Norse and did not care for the task.

'Not much,' Congalach growled. 'The Boinne, which we do not wish to cross, for that will take us too close to the Dyfflin Norse. We are out in front of the whole army here.'

Crowbone heard the annoyance in his voice and offered the man his two-coloured stare, seeing the truculent twist to Congalach's jaw and the rain pearling off his black moustaches.

'Then that is where they are going,' he said, seeing it clearly. 'They are Norse themselves and will arrive with news that will make Olaf Irish-Shoes smile.'

'What news?' demanded Congalach, blowing rain off his moustaches.

'Numbers,' Crowbone explained patiently. 'That and how the High King has drovers with cattle, which means he has prepared not only for a fight at Tara but for a siege at Dyfflin.'

Congalach was impressed despite himself, but pretended scepticism; he knew numbers only as others did – a handful, some, many and, finally, enough to run away from.

'What can folk like those know of numbers?' he snorted and Crowbone sighed, wiping the drops that ran round the rim of his helmet and down the nasal.

'Gorm and his men are traders,' he answered patiently, 'who can tally in at least three tongues. Unlike your Irishers, they can do it without the need to take their boots off and use their toes. Olaf Irish-Shoes is a king, so he knows the worth of this. I am a prince, so I do also.'

You are nothing much at all, so you do not understand it, was what was not said, though Congalach felt the lash of it and hunched bristling, though he could find nothing to say as they rode. He saw the Burned Man and the yellow dog questing ahead and thought them as ugly a brace of animals as any he had seen. Then the light turned to pewter and, finally, to white.

'We should seek shelter out of this,' Congalach declared suddenly, reining sideways into the face of Crowbone's pony, so that it shied away and tossed its head high and hard enough to almost hit Crowbone in the face.

'You seek it,' Crowbone replied sourly and jerked the reins hard, turning the pony off after the faint shape of the yellow bitch, a small sun in the white. He saw a figure ahead and thought it was Berto, since he and the dog were never far from one another; behind, he heard Congalach spit out some Irish and knew it for a curse.

Something snaked through the white, a little blur, fast as a whirring bird. Congalach gave a sharp cry and fell; men yelled and milled uncertainly.

Crowbone was bewildered, heard the yellow bitch baying, saw it contract its whole body as if to squeeze the yelping howls out of it. A second bird whirred, struck his helmet and rang his head like a bell, so that he jerked hard away from it.

The pony reared and almost flung him off. Arrows, he thought. Lief Svarti . . .

He was a sack on a horse and he knew it. When the pony lost reason and bolted, all he could do was hang on grimly, jouncing on the saddle. He went past two figures, panting and seemingly locked together; one was Berto – then they were gone behind him into the mist and he half-turned to try and see, almost pitched off and clung round the pony's neck as it sped off.

It seemed a lifetime and a half to Crowbone but the ride ended as he had known it would – the pony came to something it could not go through or over and simply veered sideways, pitching Crowbone off. He crashed into something which splintered under him, hit the ground hard enough to drive the air out, rolled over and over, feeling the sword batter down the length of him, the hilt gouge his ribs.

There was a moment when he knew he had just woken, but had no idea if he had been out of it for a minute, an hour, or longer, for the world was still white and his body ached so much he thought the pony might have galloped back and forth on him for malice.

It was nowhere to be seen, though something loomed out of the pearling mist. He was lying at the foot of it and, as he started to climb to his knees, wincing and checking for bits broken, he saw it was a great stone cross with a ring round the join of it, one of those Christ runestones, worked with panels showing scenes from their sagas. Every inch of it was covered and there was a little steading house carved right on the top, a representation in stone of one of those boxes Christmenn kept their saint bones in.

Under him he saw wood, new-white where it had broken and realised he had crashed through a rough fence and rolled to the foot of the cross; he looked up at it and wondered if this was an omen.

'I would not move at all were I you,' hissed a voice and Crowbone jerked, which he realised in the next second had been the wrong thing to do; the steel felt wet and cold against his neck. His helmet, he saw, was some feet away and the ties on it had snapped.

'I will be after slitting you, so I will,' the voice said and this time Crowbone got control of himself. It was a slight voice and he squinted sideways to see the hand that held the steel; a small fist, white round the knuckles with gripping.

'You are holding that too tight,' Crowbone offered politely. 'For if someone did this . . .'

He rolled and whipped one hand up, cupping the little fist in his own and squeezing. There was a sharp cry and then Crowbone had the knife in one hand and the front of a tunic in the other.

It was a boy, with a snub nose, a shock of flame hair and a face as red as the arse of a sunburned pig. He glared back at Crowbone, rubbing his hand, truculent rather than afraid.

'Who are you, then, who sticks a knife at the throat of a prince of Norway?' Crowbone demanded and the boy wriggled a little until he saw the grip on his tunic front was not about to slacken.

'Echthigern mac Óengusso,' he said, then added defiantly. 'My da is lector here.'

'Odin's arse,' Crowbone snarled. 'Do you folk have no easy names to call yourself? And where is here? And what is a lector?'

The boy told him, his voice slightly strained until Crowbone eased the pressure on his throat a little. Mainistir Buite was the place, a monastery where Echthigern's da read the tracts and lessons – lector, Crowbone was told, was the Latin that meant 'reader'.

'Will you kill me?' demanded the boy at the end of this and Crowbone cocked his head a little at him and grinned.

'Why for would I?' he asked and the boy blinked once or twice, suddenly seeing the odd-coloured eyes for the first time and not liking them much.

'Because the rest of your heathen Dane kin are in the

church,' he answered bleakly, then his lip trembled. 'My da is there.'

Crowbone let the boy go and he sank, rubbing his throat and looking up into Crowbone's face.

'No kin of mine,' Crowbone said. 'I am here with King Gilla Mo's men to hunt them down, so you can show me where they are.'

'You fight for Brega?' the boy declared, grinning and hopeful. 'But you are a Dane.'

'Not all Norse are Danes, boy,' Crowbone answered climbing to his feet and fetching his helmet. He winced as he tested various muscles. 'Not all Norse care for the Dyfflin king, either.'

The running figure took them both by surprise; the boy yelled and Crowbone whirled, cursing and trying to drag out his sword. The figure burst forward, a dark stain out of the mist, stumbled over the ruins of the fence and then skidded to fall at Crowbone's feet.

Crowbone looked down and saw the white, frightened face of Berto looking up.

'Bowman . . .' Berto panted and, at that moment, a second figure pounded like a shadow from the mist. Lief, Crowbone thought wildly and half-crouched, sword up.

Lief was half-stumbling and screaming, which was a surprise to everyone, for it was clear he had been chasing Berto and now seemed to be running away from something else. Then the yellow bitch hurled itself into the huddle at the foot of the stone cross, a brass dagger of snarls and teeth. Lief went down, the jaws ripping and shaking the forearm he put up to keep them from his neck; he was flung this way and that like a rat.

'Call him off,' Crowbone ordered hoarsely and Berto struggled up and started making kissing sounds. The yellow bitch, jaws locked, merely hauled the screaming Lief towards the little Wend.

'Odin's hairy arse!' Crowbone exploded and whacked the snarling curl of yellow with the flat of the sword, hard enough to knock the animal sideways – but it held grimly on. The Irish boy moved swiftly then, past Berto with his pathetically flapping hands and kisses, to the rear of the fight. He paused, grabbed the bitch's tail and shoved two fingers hard into the softness under it.

The bitch, outraged, opened its jaws and howled, allowing Lief to scrabble away. The boy let go and leaped away as the bitch whirled to snap at him, but Crowbone kicked it hard, so that it tumbled over and over and got up shakily, the fight knocked from it. Berto moved to it while Crowbone grabbed Lief and hauled him up to his knees. Blood sprayed from him.

'You shot at me, you hole,' he spat, but Lief's eyes were rolling and one look at the stripped red-meat remains of his right forearm told Crowbone that Lief would not be shooting any more bows, even if he survived. Crowbone let him flop, an empty sack, back to the ground.

'Are you hurt?' he demanded of Berto, who shook his head, eyes wide with shock and his face as white as the mist. The yellow bitch looked back at Crowbone with reproachful eyes.

'He tried to shoot you and we fought,' Berto managed to explain. 'He was stronger and I had to run for it. Then Yellow here chased him as he chased me.'

The Irish boy cleaned his fingers on the wet grass and Crowbone nodded to him.

'Good trick, that.'

'Sure, we have hounds ourselves and they are always quarrelling,' he answered levelly. 'Can we go and help my da now?'

'Lead on,' Crowbone ordered and the boy looked at the moaning Lief pointedly. Crowbone sighed; it made sense not to leave anyone in their rear, even one as hurt as Lief. He crossed to the man, remembering the tall, rangy figure laughing round a fire somewhere, hauling on a line during the storm.

He was a handsome man with a neat, grey beard and the giggle of a girl when he was drunk.

Lief had lost his helmet but still wore the padded linen arming cap, as like the headsquare of a woman as to be funny on a bearded man. He was not laughing now, all the same, though he stopped moaning as Crowbone knelt and his black eyes, pools of misery already, grew bright with the fear of what was to come.

'You are a prince,' he gasped, the slaver wild on his lips. 'It is princely to grant mercy.'

'Once,' Crowbone said dreamily, 'in place far from here, do not ask me where, a woodsman entered a wood with his axe on his shoulder. The trees were alarmed, and addressed him thus: "Ah, lord, will you not let us live happily some little time longer?" It was the time in the world when trees had voices, you understand.'

'The concern of these trees I can understand,' Lief panted, hoping to prolong the tale. The blood was seeping from the forearm and the pain almost blinding; he could see the white of bone in it and did not want to look more closely. Crowbone ignored him.

'The woodsman,' he went on, 'said he was willing to do so. "However," he added, "as often as I see this axe, I am tempted to come to the wood, and do my work in it. So I am not so much to blame as this axe blade." "Don't blame the axe bit," answered the trees. "We know that the handle of the axe, which is a piece of the branch of a tree in this very wood, is more to blame than the iron; for it is that which helps you to destroy its kindred."

'The woodsman spat on his hands and hefted the trees' worst fear. "You are quite right," he said. "There is no foe so bitter as a renegade." And he set to chopping.'

Lief tried to swallow, but his mouth was dry.

'Have you another?' he started to say, but the bright flash of the blade made his eyes squint and the tug at his throat seemed to steal the words from his mouth. He saw Crowbone's hand come down to cover his eyes and heard his voice.

'Tell Hel – not yet, but soon.'

Crowbone climbed to his feet and saw the Irish boy looking at him, wary as the yellow bitch. Berto knelt beside Lief and covered his face with the arming cap; he seemed to be praying, Christ-fashion.

'Do you tell stories to all you kill?' the Irish boy asked and Crowbone merely smiled and settled his helmet snugly on his head.

'Remind me never to ask you for one,' the boy muttered.

'What is your name again?' Crowbone demanded and the boy scowled.

'Echthigern mac Óengusso,' the boy answered sullenly.

'Eck,' Crowbone declared firmly. 'Lead on.'

A wind got up and shredded the mist to witch hair, so that the body they would have stumbled over was easily seen, right at the door of the dark gable end that was the church. Crowbone was distracted, concentrating so hard on the church, marvelling at the tall building of wood and half-stone and why folk would go to all the trouble of it when they did not live in it most of the time. It was as useless as the tower, a tall, slender stone prick rearing up not far off – the height of a couple of ship masts and all it did was hold a bell.

'Christ and all his saints preserve us!' the Irish boy burst out, crossing himself at the sight of the rag-doll shape at the door.

'For ever and ever,' Berto repeated without thinking and Crowbone shot him a glance; he had not known the Wend was so hot for the Christ that he knew the responses – but the body shoved that from his mind.

It was Gorm, his head lopsided and smashed in like an egg, the blood spreading in a dark lake underneath him, right down to his knees.

'One less,' he grunted and looked at the door, which lay slightly open. A postern, the boy called it, used for daily coming and going while the big main door was used only for letting in folk to glory in their god.

He started forward, but Berto, as if released from a bow, suddenly darted in front of him and in through the door. There was a high-pitched squeal, a scuffling and, with a curse, Crowbone ducked inside, blinking in the dark. He heard a rustle, felt the breath of movement and half-turned, just as someone yelled.

The blow crashed on him, rattling his whole head almost off his neck and the world exploded in bright light and then a great well of darkness, which he fell into.

Túnsberg in Vestfold, Norway, on the first day of little snows . . .

MARTIN

He knew they were watching him, so he minded his manners and, when he smiled at the little girl whose doll he was repairing, he did it with his lips stitched so his ruined mouth would not frighten her to screams. It felt strange to his cheeks, all the same and he did not do it again.

The hall of Haakon Jarl, King of Norway, was bright and bustling, though folk avoided where the priest sat, both for the look of him and for what he was. Martin knew that Haakon Jarl had broken with his supposed overlord, Harald Bluetooth of the Danes, and it was said he did it because Bluetooth had forced Christ priests on him while he was visiting Denmark. The tales had it that Haakon had pitched them into the sea and forced them to swim home, so there was danger in coming so openly to his hall wearing a cross.

The truth, of course, was a matter of princes, Martin mused

185

to himself, while he fiddled out the broken straws that fastened the doll's leg to the body. Haakon now ruled Norway in his own right and dared Bluetooth to do something about it. Bluetooth looked to be daring just that and so there would be red war between them – Eirik's axe would be a powerful attraction for fighting men and was not a prize Haakon could overlook.

The thought made Martin smile, just as a thrall woman brought meat and bread and ale for him; she shoved it across and left, hurriedly.

He gave the doll to the girl and she looked solemnly at him for a moment or two and clutched it tightly to her.

'You are very ugly,' she said and a man laughed close by, making Martin twist to see, a movement that spasmed pain through his foot.

'Such reward for your labours,' said the man, shifting into a bench opposite. Martin saw his russet and green tunic, his friendly, open smile and shock of dark hair. He envied the man his neatly trimmed – and curled, he saw – beard and, most of all, his teeth. Almost to spite himself, he took a large portion of meat which he knew he could only suck, a noisy and messy business.

'I trust kings are kinder,' he growled. He knew this man and, for all he had his hair and beard still, he was a thrall. He was also Haakon's friend and what he said might just as well come from the jarl's mouth, while what he heard went straight in the jarl's ear.

'You have news for me, Tormod Kark?' he asked, mushing his gums round the meat in a deliberately repellent fashion. The thrall did not flinch at all.

'The king finds it strange that a Christ priest should come all the way from Hammaburg to tell him he knows the way to Eirik's Bloodaxe, a rich prize for what you folk call heathens.'

That was straight out, a flat blade of a statement banged

on a wooden bench. Martin spat out the sucked gobbet and wiped his fingers down his front; his smile was greasy and blackened.

'I am a long time gone from Hammaburg,' he said, 'but Haakon Sigurdsson knows this, for I came in a trading ship from Torridun in the north of Alba and, before that, from Orkney.'

He leaned forward a little and now Tormod Kark did flinch, drawing back a little and touching the silver amulet band round his left wrist as a protection against spells. Martin saw that but kept the sneer to himself. He had stirred up all the hornets who sought the Bloodaxe and now needed the one with the biggest sting, to make sure he and God received the reward for such cunning.

'The Witch-Queen and her last son,' he said, 'plus Olaf, Tryggve's son, and Orm Bear-Slayer of the Oathsworn. All Haakon's enemies, lured by me out into the wilds of the Finnmark after this axe, to be slain by him and the prize taken. All you need do is provide the ships and the men to take me there and guard me while the axe is recovered from where I know it lies. Then you kill them all and we come home.'

Tormod Kark blinked a little. This limp-footed little ruin of a man did not look like any of the shaved, tonsured Christ priests the jarl had pitched into the sea, but he claimed the role and wore a battered cross. There was also something about him – Haakon had already agreed to provide ships and men, but he would not speak directly to the little priest because he worried what magic the man had and whether even his breath was a curse. It could be, Tormod thought bitterly, if the smell is anything to go by.

Tormod, of course, had pointed out to Haakon that, if this ragged-arse priest really knew the way to Eirik's famed axe, he had already promised all the others the same. Haakon merely smiled; this was the game of kings, as well constructed as a spiderweb and with much the same purpose – all you had to do was pick your way safely to the prize at the centre of it.

He said as much and Tormod bowed, thinking to himself that the real trick was to pick your way out again with the riches. He said nothing all the same, just smiled, the same way he now smiled at the priest.

'Your reward for this gift?' Tormod asked, with the air of one who has already sold himself and thinks all the world is the same. Martin looked sourly at him.

'A stick,' he answered, which made Tormod blink.

'A stick?'

'An old spear. Orm will have it, or know where it is. Do not kill him until I have my stick.'

Tormod swallowed, for he wondered if the priest was working some subtle magic, as Haakon had feared. He wondered if this spear-stick was part of it.

'We will consider it,' Tormod said and rose, easy and white-toothed. He spread his hands. 'Meanwhile, I offer you the hospitality of the hall of Norway's king.'

'No gift from a thrall, who owns nothing, not even his own name,' Martin said viciously, which brought the blood surging to Tormod's face. 'Thank the king for it from me, all the same. Tell him not to take too long in the considering, for the year turns.'

Tormod swept off, trailing a chill cloak of indignity; Martin went back to sucking noisily on his meat, mainly because it kept folk from sitting near him and that suited him well enough.

It would be endless day in the north now, but they were shortening fast and soon Bjarmaland and the Finnmark would be cloaked in long night and ice.

Dark and cold, Martin thought. Like revenge.

Mainistir Buite (Monasterboice), Ireland, around the same time . . .

CROWBONE'S CREW

'You were lucky,' said the voice and Crowbone tried to see the face that belonged to it, but his eyes would not open entirely and the little they did would not permit focus; the light was blinding. A woman, he noted, with the part of his thought-cage that was not thundered with pain.

'You were,' echoed another voice, deeper and stronger. A man, then.

'It was as well the girl squealed when she did,' the woman went on, 'for it made you more wary and Óengusso's blow was badly struck.'

'It was, so it was,' echoed the man and the woman sighed.

'Óengusso, go away. You are not helping here – drink this, young Olaf.'

'I just wished to make sure the wee prince was not too dunted,' the man answered, while Crowbone felt the bowl click against his teeth and a slightly bitter liquid filled his mouth. He swallowed and then felt warm breath, smelling of rosemary, close to his mouth, then his ear. The woman sang, whisper-soft and seeming nonsense, but Crowbone knew *seidr* when he heard it and the hairs on his arms rose. He felt her draw away from him and the voice of her was so familiar that her name was on the end of his tongue.

'He will be finer than new linen,' the woman replied firmly. 'I have sung the charms of mugwyrt, plantain, lamb's cress, cock's-spur grass, camomile, nettle, crab-apple, chervil and fennel into his mouth and ears.'

'In the name of God, I hope,' the man said and Crowbone knew him for a monk by the tone. Suddenly, with a rush as warm as strong wine, he knew the woman, too, had heard that voice a hundred times when he could not see the face, as she sat behind him and combed his hair. Before that she had salved his scabbed, badly shaved head the day Orm had rescued him from his tether by the privy on Svartey.

'Thorgunna,' he said and opened his eyes into the great smiling sun of her face. Then the other face swam into view and ruined the moment.

Óengusso had eyes like a pig, tiny and blue, fringed with straw lashes. He was big and fat-bellied, too, yet there was muscle under the monk's garb and quiver of him, which Crowbone had to acknowledge when he saw his helmet, held out to him by apologetic hands.

'Sure, I am sorry for it,' Óengusso said, watching Crowbone slowly sit up and swing his legs over the side of the pallet bed. He sat for a moment until the world settled, then took the helmet from the Irish monk; the left side of it was dented, the little plume-holder battered.

'We could not get it more straighter, sure,' Óengusso offered, seeing Crowbone's silence as accusing. In fact, Crowbone was wondering what the side of his head was like if the helmet had been this bad; if the throb and ache of it was anything to go by, it was crushed and his left ear was almost certainly missing.

'No, no,' Óengusso said when Crowbone said as much. 'Hardly a dunt on you. A good helmet that.'

Crowbone said nothing else, for he was trying to stand up and the floor would not help him. It swayed like a ship side on to a swell and, eventually, Óengusso thrust out an arm for Crowbone to grip. It felt, he thought, like a bar of iron and he knew now where the strength that all but flattened his head had come from.

He held it for a long moment, staring at the hanging on the wall until the bird on it stopped flying round in circles and stayed fixed on the blue square.

'The dove of peace,' Óengusso explained, seeing him look and thinking he was puzzling on it, 'returning to Noah's marvellous boat with a twig to prove that the Flood was ended and God had spared Mankind.'

'We do the same,' Crowbone managed to say, 'though we use ravens to find land.'

'I thank you for my son,' Óengusso said and Crowbone looked at him. This would be the lector.

'You are a singular Christ-follower,' he managed, trying to keep the sickness from bokking up in him. 'Not many of your kind hit so hard.'

Except here, he discovered a day later, when he had recovered somewhat. There were many hard-hitting monks here, it seemed, for all the renegades had been laid out and six were dead of crushed skulls. The only casualty had been one monk with his thumb flattened – carelessly getting it between skull and hammer – and Congalach with an arrow through his forearm, though it was his pride that truly smarted.

It must have come as a shock to Gorm and Fridrek, two of the dead, to find wolves when they sought mice, Crowbone thought. He asked if that had been the way of it when Óengusso brought him broth and the monk pursed his fleshy lips and frowned.

'A person who would distress thee more, thou shalt not admit him to thee, but at once give him thy benediction should he deserve it,' he said piously. 'As the blessed Coluim would have it. Or thereabouts. So we gave them benediction.'

'With what – a forge hammer?'

'The holy cross,' Óengusso replied blandly and fished it out from under his thick, rough tunic; Crowbone blanched, for it was as big as any forge hammer, suspended on a thick braided cord, the ends of the crosspiece capped with black iron, dented and streaked.

'I had this from owld Brother Conchobar, who had it himself from one who knew it to have been wielded by Abbot Cathal of Ferns,' Óengusso went on beatifically. 'That was a wheen of years ago, when the monastery of Taghmon, assisted by

Cathal mac Dunlainge, king of Ui Chennselaig at the time, made bloody war on the monastery of Ferns, in which four hundred were killed. Cathal made himself vice-abbot of Ferns after the victory.'

He went on, while Crowbone stood, mazed and wary of the room, which was still not as steady as he would have liked. It was a long litany of head-bashing, attack and counter-attack between Clocnamoise, Birr, Durrow, Drumbo, Taghmon and a score of other Irish monasteries. By the time Crowbone had finished the broth, he was reeling with Óengusso's tales and had made up his mind that raiding Irish monasteries was not a sensible or easy occupation; if he wanted silver for ships and men he would look elsewhere than the Christmenn of Ireland.

He was relieved when the monk tucked the Christ amulet back inside his tunic, but impressed; this was the first time he had come on Christ priests who would fight and who sired sons with no shame, though Orm had told him of a Brother John whom he had met and travelled with. He had been Irish, too, Crowbone recalled.

'You should not be on your feet.'

The voice brought both of them round and Crowbone smiled. Thorgunna stepped forward, neat in a sea-grey dress fastened with a loop of braided leather and wearing a white headsquare – it was a strange garb for her to be seen in, for Crowbone had usually seen her in brighter clothing and with more silver hanging off her, while the headsquare had not been part of her dress at all.

'It is the way Christian women wear it,' she answered, seeing his look. 'If they are married.'

'You are still married, then . . .' Crowbone moved slowly towards her and took her hands in his own. 'If so, there is a husband looking for you.'

'You have seen him recently?'

Her voice, he thought, held only an echo of eagerness and he was sorry to hear so little.

'Aye, not so long since. He seeks word of you, though he is in Gardariki lands at present. Conspiring with Vladimir, possibly.'

She heard the bitter bite of that and studied him a little. How he had grown – fine and tall and true. As fine and tall as any son she had hoped to have . . .

Crowbone saw the sudden flick of her head and the brightness in her eye, thought it was about Orm and was confused – apathy and now tears?

'You have quarrelled with Orm,' she said and he blinked a bit, wondering how she had reached out and grabbed that idea from the air. Before he could think, his mouth answered.

'I am certain he has betrayed me.'

There. He could scarcely believe he had said it at all, but when it was out, he knew it had tumbled from his heart. Óengusso, not part of this and bewildered, shuffled his feet and looked from one to the other, as if it was a blow-for-blow *holmgang* fight.

Thorgunna showed no surprise; Crowbone had never been able to keep his heart stopped up when she asked and she was pleased that growing up with the games kings play had not robbed him of it. Not yet, at least.

'Why do you believe this?' she asked and the dam in him split, spilling the whole tale of it through the cracks until, at the end, he had to sit down again. He felt better, all the same.

Thorgunna tasted the wormwood in it, saw his wavering pride and uncertain strength. Olaf Tryggvason knew what a king should be and would try to make himself one, she thought sadly, but it would eat the best of what made him a man.

'I never liked this Martin,' she said eventually. 'Sleekit. Anything he was involved with always was rancid as old cod. You think he killed this Drostan?'

Crowbone nodded, too numb even to speak.

'You are after thinking that he sent word to Orm, then went round all the others – Dyfflin and Orkney and the like – to set a trap?'

Again he nodded.

'You believe Orm knew it was Martin who sent word? That he sent you without telling you of this because he desires this silly axe for himself?'

It was the sick heart of what Crowbone believed and she saw it in his eyes. For a time, she did not say anything at all and, eventually, Crowbone regained some strength, so she went on.

'The matter of Eirik's axe is certainly true,' Thorgunna said, 'otherwise there would be nothing to tempt Dyfflin or Orkney at all. Martin will be promising them a dazzle of prizes. Olaf Irish-Shoes needs men and the axe will also make him feel he has one more triumph over his old enemy, Eirik. Gunnhild in Orkney – well, you know more of that. She wants you as much as she wants her man's old axe.'

'I had worked this much out,' he answered and she raised an eyebrow.

'Had you now? This cleverness did not give you cause for an easy sleep, or ease the worry of what Orm's part in all this was.'

He acknowledged it with a flap of one hand and Thorgunna sucked in a deep breath until her prow-built breast threatened the seams of her dress.

'Ask yourself what Martin truly wants,' she said simply. 'Ask yourself what Orm truly wants.'

Crowbone blinked a bit, but his mind was smoke and mirrors, so he smiled wanly at her and risked standing up.

'Orm wants you, lady,' he said and she laughed, a bitter, sad affair that reminded Crowbone of blowing red leaves and claw-branched trees.

'Aye, may be,' she said simply and then waved one hand. 'He has his faults in that regard – he is always saying how he hates faring here and there, yet he was away more often than home. He loves his gods and his men more than he loves me.'

'Come back to Hestreng and see,' Crowbone said, but she shook her head.

'I will never go back to Hestreng.'

'Somewhere else, then,' Crowbone answered, remembering why she would hate Hestreng, where the malformed mite she had given birth to had been left on a stone, put into the care of the gods. Crowbone had stood with Orm and others round that stone, had seen the tears in Orm's eyes and said as much.

'Aye, aye,' Thorgunna said. 'If tears would undo the gods of Asgard, then I had enough to drown them all. They are unmoved; I am done with Asgard and Hestreng and the Oathsworn. If it means I am also done with my man, then so be it.'

She stopped and sighed, then held up her hands.

'I miss my sister Thordis and cousin Ingrid, though,' she added, 'not least because no-one here can sew me into my sleeves, or unpick them again at night.'

'So you are one of Christ's women?' Crowbone said and could not quite keep the sneer from his voice. She looked sharply at him, then smiled.

'A nun? Not me. I am not about to climb off my knees to Odin just to get back on them to Jesus.'

Óengusso shook his head in sorrow and made the sign of the cross at her, but Thorgunna patted him lightly on one arm.

'I am a Veiled Woman,' she said. 'Permitted to remain alongside priests and monks, provided I do not molest them or turn them from their ways. This is possible here in Ireland, less so elsewhere. I am happy here.'

'Useful, too,' said Óengusso. 'Who knew that wearing the bone from a cod on your head takes away belly ache before she came? Or the Nine Herb Charm she worked on your head?'

Crowbone looked at her sideways.

'Seidr?' he replied. 'You always said that magic neither worked for you or against you.'

195

'God love us all,' Óengusso exclaimed, crossing himself.

'For ever and ever,' Thorgunna responded, then smiled at Crowbone.

'Old healing is hardly *seidr*,' she said. 'Not like you and those birds.'

Óengusso looked frantically from one to the other and Crowbone stared at him from under a single brow, his odd eyes glowering.

'One crow, sorrow, two crows, mirth, three crows, a wedding, four crows, birth,' he said, then winked at the astounded monk. 'See what women bring down on your house?'

Óengusso crossed himself again and then frowned, seeing he was mocked.

'You should not be so hard on women, boy,' he said firmly. 'Sure, was it not one who kept my benediction from breaking the egg of your head entire?'

'What woman?' Crowbone demanded, puzzled and Thorgunna looked at him and laughed, seeing the truth of it.

'The one you have clearly imagined to be a boy for some time,' she said. Then, into his open-mouthed disbelief, she added:

'The Wend you call Berto. Her real name is Bergliot.'

NINE

Mainistir Buite (Monasterboice), Ireland, not long after . . .

CROWBONE'S CREW

SHE walked beside Thorgunna in to where Crowbone stood
– still a little pale, she thought, with a lurch. She was wearing
a dress for the first time in months and the catch of it round
her knees felt strange.

'You kept the secret cleverly,' Crowbone said, his face stiff.
He had had some time of lying about recovering to recall all
the clues he had missed about her, from her unnerving softness to the way she had avoided taking off her wet clothes
on the night of the storm.

The strangeness of her was like something seen through
rippled water – the face was familiar, like a round owl, the
dark hair was down to her ears and raggedly cut, the eyes
big and soft. Yet now it all belonged to a girl and not the
youth he had thought and the dress she wore, even if it was
made for Thorgunna and too large, only accentuated the
curves everyone had failed to notice.

'I wore a few tunics,' she answered in a small voice, hearing
the flat, bitter tone of his own. It would be the shared

197

man-moments, she thought, when he told of how many women he had taken. 'To hide the shape of me.'

Small wonder, Crowbone thought, looking her over. How in the name of Odin's hairy arse had she hid those breasts from all of them? Those hips? She saw him stare and grinned, the old grin when she was one of the crew and not a woman.

'You see what you want to see,' she declared. 'I had to hold in my business until landfall a lot of the time. Once or twice I could not and did it in my breeks, but folk just thought me smelly. Like all boys.'

She saw her error in the grim reef of his face and the smile wavered like a faint flame in a wind, then was lost entire.

'Aye, you hid it well,' Crowbone said, remembering all the little moments, feeling his face flame at some of them. It explained how he had felt, at least – which was a relief; those moments when his groin had tightened had been for a girl after all. Still, he did not understand how his body had known even if his mind had not and it was more than a little disturbing.

'Did Grima know?' he asked, sitting down. 'Bergliot – is that the name now?'

She saw the strain in him then and made a move; the odd-coloured eyes stopped her like two fists in the chest and she stepped back a little way.

'Stick to Berto,' she said, a little more harshly than she had intended. 'It is easier.'

'Hardly,' he answered wearily. 'Those days are gone.'

'Do not judge too harshly,' Thorgunna said softly and he looked at her, sitting quietly with her hands folded in her lap and then shook his head.

'I have problems enough with the men who follow me,' he said. 'They think my luck is flowing from me – they may be right. Now one they thought a comrade turns out to be a cuckoo in the nest.'

'A cuckoo who saved your life,' Thorgunna pointed out,

but Bergliot saw the truculent flex of Crowbone's jaw and the centre of her sagged.

'Grima knew,' she answered and left it perched there like a crow on a branch. She saw him work through it, his head tilted and thoughtful, as if he was a bird with a beakful of snail and a stone in front of it.

'He did not touch you,' he said slowly, weaving it as he spoke. 'Made out that you were a boy of no worth . . .'

'He stumbled on me during a raid,' she replied flatly. 'Just him alone. He thought I was someone else, then realised I was not.'

'Still of worth,' Crowbone mused. 'Grima would have tupped you in an eyeblink and flung the remains of you to the others – save that you had value. Made you dress like a boy and keep the secret of it absolute, because he no longer trusted any of them.'

'A bad matter,' Thorgunna flung out, 'when trust is shattered. Who is the betrayer then, little Olaf?'

He looked sharply at her, then back to Bergliot.

'You went over the side after him,' he rasped. 'Why?'

'Balle would have killed me,' she answered simply.

'And who are you, then?'

She shrugged and the tremble in her was obvious.

'Bergliot. No more. Grima thought I was Geira, but I was only her handmaiden and he knew he had missed the greater prize. His men would have scorned his battleluck, he knew, and would take out their annoyance on me. But I was Geira's friend, too, so that she would pay to have me back and Grima saw that.'

'Geira?' Crowbone asked and Thorgunna put her arm round the girl's shoulders and drew her away.

'Geira,' she said. 'Eldest daughter of Burisliev, King of Wendland, and a queen in her own right.'

A queen's close friend. Close enough, Crowbone thought, to be worth something, one way or another and he said as much later, when he went to the men waiting uneasily in the church outbuildings, taking Bergliot with him.

They had already heard the tale of it; some could not look her in the eye as she stood there, wrapped in a warm, fur-trimmed cloak – another gift from Thorgunna, who had not, Crowbone thought wryly, left Hestreng too distraught to forget possessions entirely. Most of the old crew who had been with Grima would not even look this new Bergliot in the face. A few – the Oathsworn gifted from Orm, Crowbone noted – were easier about it.

'This explains why you are not good with a pole lathe or an axe,' Kaetilmund declared with a smile.

'Just so,' she answered with brittle brightness. 'Does this mean you will stop calling me No-Toes?'

Kaetilmund scrubbed his beard with wry embarrassment while Stick-Starer and Halfdan chuckled and nudged him. For a moment, she felt the old warmth, then saw the men's faces as they looked at Crowbone. More was revealed there than the surprise she had presented them with.

Crowbone saw it also, the blank stones of their stares, and had to heave himself up against the crush of it. Well, he thought to himself, if they cannot be made to love me, they can be made to fear, which is the way princes and kings must think.

'Where are the prisoners?' he asked and Mar stepped forward, his helmet dangling from his beltline and a spear in his hand. Behind came Kaup and Murrough shepherding a shuffling group whose sorrow and fear came off them like stink and, behind that, he saw Congalach, bound hand cradled in the crook of the other and his eyes wet with pain and misery.

Eight of them, Crowbone saw – Halk was there, sorrowed as a whipped dog, pleading with every look, though he knew there was no hope. And Fridrek, all sullen and twisted mouth.

He looked them over for as long as it took for Óengusso to come up, his arm across his son's shoulder, then he turned to the lector.

'What would you do with them?' he asked. 'Since it was you they offended last.'

'Sure I would hang them,' Óengusso said and there was a stir among the men.

'No Christ mercy, then?' Crowbone demanded harshly. 'Some of them are Christ baptised.'

Óengusso laced his hands together, while his snub-nosed piglet of a son gazed adoringly up at him.

'A mind prepared for red martyrdom, a mind prepared for white martyrdom,' he said sonorously. 'Rules Eight and Nine. Fervour in singing the office for the dead, as if every faithful dead was a particular friend of thine – Rule Twelve.'

'That is not what the blessed Columba had in mind when he made the Rules,' Mar declared bitterly. 'I am sure of that.'

'They broke the oath,' Crowbone pointed out and Kaetilmund studied him for a moment, trying to work out if the odd-eyed boy spoke of the Oathsworn's oath or the oath he knew others had sworn personally to the prince. He was still no wiser when Kaup started dragging the men away.

Halk babbled and pleaded, but Fridrek, half-stumbling, flung curses back at them over his shoulder and men who had known him a long time shifted and shuffled.

'If you have a mind to allow it,' Crowbone said, 'I would like that dove flag you have.'

Óengusso blinked, then smiled and nodded, sending his son scampering to get it, then went off on his own; not long after they heard his great bell of a voice and the singing chants of the monks. They waited in the dripping day, while the bast ropes creaked and scoured the tree branches, hauling their kicking burdens high into the air.

When the dead had stopped swaying, Crowbone said his farewells to Thorgunna, who stood like a cloaked shadow in the shelter of the church, the great tower hunching itself into the sky over her shoulder.

'What would you have me tell Orm if I meet him?' Crowbone asked and she flicked a little smile on her cheeks, made old and withered in the harsh daylight, he saw suddenly, like the last winter apple in the barrel.

'That you are sorry you did not hold to the Oath,' she answered and the slap of that made him take a step back.

'I meant about yourself,' he answered, which was as good as admitting the truth of what she said, though he only realised this much later. 'Shall I tell him where you are?'

'You will or you won't,' she answered sadly, which left him no wiser. Then she dragged her woollens tighter round her and looked up at the sky.

'I am leaving,' she said, shivering a little, as if a wind had kissed her neck. Crowbone did not know whether she meant now, or this place entirely.

'I am gone,' she whispered, her eyes black as an iced sea and turned away; the bleakness she left was more of a desert than before.

As he marched out of the place, conscious of the men filtering along behind him, sullen as rainclouds, Crowbone turned to the woman he had known as Berto and held out the blue flag.

'Here,' he said, vicious as a slap. 'You are a woman now. Sew this in the way I tell you.'

Teamhair, the Hill of Tara, some weeks later . . .

CROWBONE'S CREW

There were horns blaring and the great reek of warriors, giving off so much heat that the air above the armies wavered like water. Irishers trotted past near Crowbone, one of them fumbling to try and fasten his rolled cloak over his right shoulder to leave his arms free; he had a leather helmet half-tilted over one eye and a long spear that smacked the shoulder of the man behind, who cursed him in a long spit of Irish.

'Here – I have sewn it.'

She held out the tall spear, the furled cloth held tight to it with her fist, then let it go and flutter free; someone made a noise between jeer and cheer and Crowbone glanced up at it. A cloud-blue square with a white eagle on it, though there were those who thought the wings were strange. Not surprising, since it started life as a dove.

'You have sewn it well,' he said, which was the truth – the silly twig was unpicked and the thread saved had been used to curve the beak and add some talons. It was not, as Onund said pointedly, the Oathsworn banner, which was Odin's *valknut*, but Crowbone merely asked Onund if he could sew one in a hurry and, if not, then this one would do, for Prince Olaf needed a banner.

'Can I carry it?' Bergliot asked, her face tilted and defiant.

She had done it well, as he had to admit. Now she stood there, in the middle of a stinking, bustling, roaring army about to dive headfirst into blood and slaughter, holding it on a long spear and asking her question. Men paused in what they were doing to hear the answer.

'No,' Crowbone said, though he could not help the leap in him at her courage. 'You cannot carry the banner. That is work for a man, which you are not. Now take off those breeks and pull your dress down – we are at war here.'

Kaetilmund laughed at the scowl on her face, then plucked the banner from her hand and raised it high; the shouts were half-hearted at best and Crowbone saw Congalach striding up, his Irishmen at his back and Maelan trotting at his side in his own little fitted suit of ringmail.

'I hope they fight better than they cheer, Norseman,' he growled at Crowbone, then went off laughing to the side of Gilla Mo, raising his sword high so that his own men burst their throats with his name – Congalach, son of Flann, lord of Gaileanga.

'Thinks well of himself, that one,' said someone close – Bryti his name was and Crowbone was pleased to have remembered it.

'So he should,' Murrough said, slapping Bryti hard on the back, so that the rain spurted out of the wool cloak, 'for he is a prince of the Ui Neill and so worth ten of you.'

'Princes,' snapped Onund and then spat pointedly, so that Kaetilmund chuckled. Crowbone said nothing, pretending that this was just the way of all Icelanders, but he burned inside, so that his belly hurt and the battered side of his head felt like ice.

'Well,' Halfdan declared, rolling his own cloak round his shoulders like a ruff, giving him better protection there and freeing up both arms, 'he is a dead prince of the Ui Neill. He should have listened to his da – everyone else did.'

Folk laughed. The argument between Congalach and his old father Flann had been loud; the old man had wanted Congalach to stay out of things because the arrow wound meant he had no proper grip in his sword hand. He did not want his grandson in it, either, claiming the boy was too young at twelve.

Congalach had all but whined that neither would be left out of this, a great battle and the only one they might ever be involved in. Now he was striding off with his sword lashed tight in his fist and his son dogging his heels like a small shadow.

'Things are moving,' Murrough said and looked inquiringly at Crowbone, who took a breath and then ordered everyone to form up, sliding the wet helmet on as he did so. It felt strange, with the old fitted comfort of it battered out and where it now touched, the new bruising seemed colder than before, as if there was ice there.

They went into a two-rank line in the rear of Gilla Mo's

Chosen – at least it was that, Crowbone thought sourly, and not in the back of a bunch of horny-handed Irish farmers. The Irishers turned half round and muttered about having northmen at their back; one looked up at the flag and squinted a bit, then laughed and said something to his neighbour.

Murrough growled and spat Irish back at them, then turned to Crowbone, beaming.

'That dung-smeared cow's hole there said our flag looked more like a shot pigeon than an eagle, so I told him it was no eagle at all, but a stooping hawk.'

A Stooping Hawk. Crowbone liked the idea and resolved to tell Gjallandi of it when this stushie was done with – there was no point in looking for the skald in this, for he took care to keep away from such events, being no fighter of any note or inclination.

Horns made farting sounds close by. The men nearest to Crowbone rolled their neck muscles, fitted helmets more snugly, touched amulets, crossed themselves; a few glanced at him, their faces pebbled with rain and one even smiled. Crowbone wondered if they would fight for him.

'Rain is an amusement when it is hissing from the gutters and you are in the dry and warm looking out,' Halfdan said moodily and folk laughed, saying he was going soft. Kaetilmund called out that Halfdan was thinking he wanted to be back in the warm with Bergliot. The name and the memory of her – of him, who was now her – brought a silence that the rain lisped through while they moved, half-stumbling over tussocks and ruts. Crowbone did not know where they were when they eventually stopped, panting like blown bulls. Horns blared again.

Apart from Murrough, not even the grimmest of them could smile into a rain that came down like stones, stung the face, sluiced down ringmail and seeped through to wool and neck. Crowbone's boots were sodden with it, his braids dripping and he wondered blackly if Ireland had any other weather.

'Call this rain?' Murrough demanded, grinning and happy as a hog in a wallow.

'Only you and him do not seem to care,' Halfdan answered and jerked water off his beard indicating the stone figure nearby. 'Who are you thinking it is, eh, Crowbone?'

Crowbone did not know. It was weathered and bird-splashed stone, half the height of a true man, a youth with a scabbed dog caught by the ruff in one hand and the other arm raised, holding a dripping slather of slimed weed from the stump of a wrist. The face, worn and speckled, had an expression of bewilderment, not helped by the lack of nose.

'Ask Murrough,' he grunted, but the big man only grinned and shrugged, blowing rain off his nose.

'Who knows? Cuchulain maybe. This is Teamhair – the place is thick with this sort of stuff.'

Teamhair, Hill of Tara, High Seat of Kings. The place where Ireland's overlord was hailed by all the lesser kings, Crowbone had been told. A place of pillars and monuments, of course – and known to both sides. An easy place to arrange to meet in battle without all the tedious business of marching about seeking one another out.

A good place to play the game of kings, the true choosers of the slain.

'Archers!'

The warning came from the front and shields went up as shoulders went down. There was a pattering, as if the rain had hardened. Something whumped into the chewed grass near Crowbone's foot, but it was no arrow – a stone, Crowbone thought. No, a smooth lump of lead.

'Slings,' Murrough spat. 'By The Dagda, but I hate them folk worse than I hate archers.'

There was a loud whanging sound and everyone jerked their necks in, then peered round. Bryti, his hand shaking, pulled off his helmet and looked at the dent in it.

'By the gods of all Ireland,' Murrough said into the man's

dazed look of wonder. 'You have enough luck there to be Ui Neill.'

Bryti fingered the place where the lead shot had struck and looked up, grinning. The next stone took him in the jaw with a wet smack that tumbled him backwards, spewing blood and teeth. Murrough frowned, watching him choke and die, quivering like a terrified rabbit.

'Well – perhaps not Ui Neill after all,' he said, glancing at the straw-doll tangle of limbs. 'Keep your shields up lads.'

'Remind me again,' Mar said grimly and he did so to be heard by Crowbone above all, 'why we are here, good men of the north fighting Norsemen for the Irish?'

'Something concerning an axe,' roared a voice Crowbone did not know and the rage bokked up in him, so that the struck side of his head throbbed and he bellowed the cords of his throat raw.

'Because it is my wyrd. I am Olaf, Prince of Norway who will one day be king and if you are wise you will all remember that.'

Then he slung his shield on his back and took a spear in either hand as they moved forward. Kaetilmund fell in on his right, the banner in one hand and a sword in the other, while Rovald fell in on the left, the only one with a shield up and charged with, somehow, protecting them both.

It had stopped raining, but the ground was churning under so many feet and the sharp smell of turned earth and torn wet grass was enough to make the heart leap, for it was the smell of life and death.

Horns bayed like staghounds and men stumbled over the rough ground, up to where the Chosen of Gilla Mo swarmed into a copse of trees and stood beneath the branches; Crowbone and his men joined them, feeling the drips spatter.

Crowbone looked at Kaetilmund, saw the drawn-back snarl of his lips and knew, if he looked to the other side, he would see Rovald the same. His own skin felt tight and the corners of his mouth gummy; his head ached and where the helmet touched still felt as if an icicle had been slid into his skull.

A brown bird whirred in to land on a branch above his head. It was exhausted from having been beaten from cover to bush by thousands of tramping feet, the swish of long grass on calves, the leather creaks and frantic shouts. Crowbone watched it closely as it perched on a branch and looked back at him with a bright black eye; he shivered at the wyrd of it.

Somewhere ahead there was a huge shout and a great thundering crack, as if a giant door had been slammed shut – the shieldwalls coming together. Now there was a stirring and the faint shrieks and bellows where the lines struggled in a ruck, but Crowbone could see nothing at all.

There was a deep roaring from the left, where the Leinster men forged forward, roaring out that they had come to free their king, held hostage by Olaf Cuarans in Dyfflin: they were determined to let him hear them from his prison.

Suddenly, Crowbone saw Gilla Mo's banner raise up and go down – once, twice, three times.

'Move – fight in pairs. Keep together . . .'

If the Chosen Men were going in forward it either meant the battle was already won, or in the balance. Crowbone loped along, peering ahead as the solid ranks melted apart in front of him – a chase then, the battle won on this part of the field at least.

Others sensed it, heads went back and the great wolf howl of the Oathsworn rolled out, followed by the shouting of their name. The blue banner cracked in the wind and men started to tumble over bodies, seeing the backs of fleeing men and fevered by the sight, as cats are with running mice.

Crowbone stumbled to his knees over a body and started to lever himself up using one of his spears; then he paused at the sight of the little shape, unnaturally still and face down.

'Are you hurt?' panted Kaetilmund coming up to him, Rovald pounding desperately along behind him. Crowbone did not answer, merely stuck the butt of his spear under the small frame and rolled it over.

Maelan, his youthful face a fretwork of blood and bone where a blade had punched him. Even his own da would not recognise him.

Not that it mattered much – two steps further on was his da, who was past recognising anyone. Congalach lay on his back, staring at the sky, his sword still lashed to one hand, the other clutching the burst rings of the mail on his belly and the tarn of his own lost blood thick and dark around him.

'Ah, shite,' Murrough said as he came up and saw them. 'A bad day for the Ui Neill and Gaileanga – are them the ones that did this?'

Crowbone looked to where Murrough pointed his hooked axe and saw the tight group of men moving backwards steadily, shields up and protecting a man in their midst. Beside him, like a great tree in a field of long grass, was a bareheaded giant with a mass of tow-coloured hair.

'Christ's bones,' muttered Mar, 'he is even bigger than yourself, Murrough macMael.'

'So he has further to fall,' Murrough answered, though he butted the axe and leaned on it thoughtfully – but Crowbone was already waving them forward, for he knew the sight of a lord and his picked guards when he saw it and wanted them at his feet, for his glory as a prince.

Kaup set out to unnerve them, capering in front like some great dancing *draugr* but Crowbone saw at once that these were better men, for they only hunched behind their shields a little more at the sight of a black warrior, gripped their weapons tighter and dared their enemies to come on them.

So Crowbone sent them, surprised that his men went, howling and roaring. The lines smacked; men hacked and slashed at each other, bellowing curses and screaming. A gap opened and Kaup fell back out of it, blood pouring from a wound on his thigh and his mouth large and wide with the shock. The tow-haired giant burst out of it like a boar from a thicket, clattering his way through the hole.

Rovald sprang forward and the giant's shield swept him up and off his feet, flinging him back to gouge a trail through the muddy grass. Murrough roared, the great axe scything and the blade of it smacked the shield and staggered the giant, so that he had to let it go. He waved a sword wildly and backed off through the gap before it closed, away from the bright bit of the hooked axe. Murrough pointed it at him as he went, bellowing challenges.

'Step back, step back!'

Crowbone heard the man in the rear call this, while the giant yelled out a repeat of it until the men stepped back, away from the fighting. Some of Crowbone's men followed up, but most stood where they were, panting and sobbing, no breath left to shout now. The lines slid apart, them leaving their dead and groaning wounded; Svenke Klak stabbed one viciously in the groin as he tried to crawl away and the man curled round the spear like a pinned beetle, coiling and uncoiling in a writhe of agony until he died.

Crowbone stepped forward, Kaetilmund to one side of him, the banner whipping above his head. Rovald was being helped up and holding his chest, whey-faced, gasping and shamed that, yet again, he had failed to protect his jarl. Crowbone offered him a brief look and went on, the scorn slathered on him; it was clear the gods had stolen Rovald's battle luck and he would not be Crowbone's shield man after this.

The lord of the Dyfflin men stepped out and looked at the fluttering banner.

'I do not know it,' one called out, 'but I am after thinking it looks like the dove of peace.'

'Exactly the opposite,' Crowbone answered. 'The Stooping Hawk of Prince Olaf, son of Tryggve, of the Yngling line of

Norway's kings. No dove and no peace for you unless you beg for it.'

The man had a beard so pale it looked like clotted cream on his chin and his helmet was worked with brass or gold. He had blue eyes and a way of carrying himself that was so close to arrogance as to be a brother.

'You say?' he answered. 'Well, I am Raghnall, Olaf's son, wyrded to be lord of the Dyfflin Norse when my father dies, which will not be soon, I hope. This giant with me is Thord Vargeisa.'

Vargeisa. An interesting name, Crowbone thought. It meant Wolf-Ember and was a dangerous name to have, but the man who owned it carried it lightly enough on his ring-mailed frame. His face was smothered with faded yellow hair, though the skin which could be seen looked to have been ploughed over and his eyes were small and set so deep they were merely tiny lights in twin caves.

'Oathsworn, you called out,' he rumbled. 'You do not look much, in rotting ringmail as you are. Are you true Oathsworn, or just liars? If you are, show me this Finn I have heard of, who fears nothing.'

'Oathsworn we are,' Crowbone replied firmly, 'though neither Finn nor Jarl Orm Bear-Slayer are here – you need not be grateful for it, all the same, for the ones who are here are mine, the Oathsworn of Jarl Orm's friend, Prince Olaf. I can show you some of their heroes – Murrough, who chewed the shield from your arm with his axe is one. Or myself, better known as Crowbone. Do not concern yourself much about the state of my ringmail, for I will certainly have yours by the end of this fight.'

They had heard of his name by the looks they exchanged and the sun of it swelled him with a fierce fire. Crowbone looked up at the sky, then to right and left, where men ran, or knelt plundering bodies.

'This day is lost. The Irish are in the right and left of you, at the behind and the front of you. If you do not give in, you will have to run and you will all die. If you stand and fight, you will all die.'

Raghnall spat and twisted out a grin.

'There is another ending to this tale,' he answered. 'We can kill you renegades and go our way.'

'Not possible,' Crowbone declared, shaking his head. Raghnall let out a bark of laughter, shaking his own head, but with admiration.

'A stripling you may be,' he said, 'but you have the balls of a man, for sure. However, I am the lion here.'

'You never saw a lion,' Crowbone countered quietly. 'I have. Once, in the days when animals spoke, such a beast went for a walk with his friend, the Fox. Lion began to boast and talk big about his strength. Fox had, perhaps, given him cause for it, because by nature he was a flatterer. But now that Lion began to assume so many airs, said he, "See here, Lion, I will show you an animal that is still more powerful than you are."

'They walked along, Fox leading the way, and met first a little boy. "Is this the stronger animal?" asked Lion. "No," answered Fox, "he must still become one."

'After a while they found an old man walking with bowed head and supporting his bent figure with a stick. "Is this the wonderful stronger beast?" asked Lion. "No," answered the Fox, "but he has been."

'Continuing their walk a short distance they came across a young hunter, in the prime of youth and accompanied by some of his dogs. "There you have him now, O king of beasts," said Fox. "Pit your strength against his, and if you win, then truly you are the strength of the earth." Then Fox wisely made for the shelter of nearby rocks to see how matters would turn out.'

'Is this a long tale?' demanded Raghnall, 'for I am growing thirsty and have some good ale back in Dyfflin.'

'You will never drink it,' Crowbone declared, then cocked

his head and went on with the tale. The yellow-haired giant stood, silent and droop-lipped as a bairn, listening.

'Growling, growling, Lion strode forward to meet the man,' Crowbone said, 'but when he came close the dogs rushed him. He, however, paid but little attention to them, pushed and separated them on all sides with a few sweeps of his front paws. They bowled away, beating a hasty retreat toward the man, who pulled out a bow and shot an arrow, hitting Lion just behind the shoulder, but still the king of beasts came forward. The hunter pulled out his steel knife then and gave him a few good jabs. Lion retreated, followed by the flying arrows of the hunter, up to where Fox hid, watching. "Well, are you strongest now?" asked Fox.

'The Lion shook his maned head, blood pouring from his wounds. "No, Fox," he answered. "Let that beast there keep the name and welcome. In the first place he had about ten of his bodyguard storm me. I really did not bother myself much about them, but when I attempted to turn him to chaff, he spat sharpness at me, which took root and burned. When I tried to pull him to the ground he jerked out one of his ribs with which he gave me some very ugly wounds, so bad that I had to get away, chased by more burning roots. No, Fox, give him the name."

'So saying,' Crowbone finished, 'the Lion slunk off and admitted his lesser quality.'

'A good tale you tell,' Raghnall admitted, 'and I see why you have done so – more Irish are coming to help you now.'

'I do not need them,' Crowbone answered as Raghnall backed off. The giant blinked once or twice and grinned a great uneven tombstone cave at him.

'You have a pretty mouth,' he said. 'With it and your cheeks I will make a purse.'

'You look like a troll-woman I knew,' Crowbone yelled out as the giant trotted after Raghnall. 'Her name was Cat's Eye and I sent her running with just a few sharp words.'

Men who had heard the story roared their approval. Raghnall's Chosen set their shields with a slap and moved swiftly forward, eager to finish the business and escape. Crowbone's men met them with a roar and a crash. Men struggled, locked boss to boss, faces within kissing distance behind shields, blades stabbing and thrusting and hacking.

Kaup felt the shadow fall on him and looked up at Crowbone looking down. The pain in his thigh was a deep, distant throb now and he felt light-headed, wanting only to lie back and look at the silver-streaked pewter of the sky.

Crowbone looked at the rent in the Burned Man's breeks, saw the purple flesh parted like a lipless mouth, high up inside his thigh; his boots were half-a-foot length from the man, yet he squelched in Kaup's blood. Red he saw, as anyone else's.

'A bad wound,' Kaup heard Crowbone say, felt rather than saw the man squat beside him. 'Too high up to tie off and blood pouring from it. If you have a god, Burned Man, I think it is time to pray to him.'

Kaup wanted to reply but felt too weary even to speak. He thought of his home and the far away of it brought a choke into his throat, for he knew he was dying and wondered if God minded him having fought for heathens. He made a dismissive wave of one hand, as if to say that he had suffered worse and would get through this, too, but all Crowbone saw was the fingers of one hand flutter briefly.

He straightened, sighing; he had liked the Burned Man.

Rovald hirpled up, his face the colour of old narwhal horn and wheezing a little.

'You keep falling over when you should be shielding me,' Crowbone said, but the joke of it was lost on Rovald, who only felt the shame of having failed twice.

The Irish arrived, but they were farmers with spears, looking for plunder now that the battle was clearly won and did not want to get in a new and dangerous fight, so they hung about the edges, or slunk away to search bodies. The great battle, or what was left of it, was now lost and everywhere Crowbone looked he saw dead, or shrieking, groaning wounded and the only ones moving swiftly were the plunderers, flitting like flies from body to body.

But in this part of Tara the clatter and clash and grunt went on. Men shrieked and went down. Mar staggered out from the pack, clutching his cheek and cursing, then saw Kaup and gave a great cry, stumbling to where the Burned Man lay.

'The battle is not yet done,' Crowbone said and Mar looked up at him, misery and flaring anger in his eyes.

'He is already dead,' Crowbone pointed out gently and Mar blinked, nodded wearily and climbed to his feet to get back in the fight. Just then, the end came.

Raghnall's men broke, like a quarry stone chisel-hit in the sweet spot; the Oathsworn surged forward after them, howling their triumph. The giant, roaring and flailing, sent men scattering on either side and Murrough closed on him with a great bellow of his own, but was shouldered off his feet as the giant forged forward, straight at Crowbone, sword up and the slaver trailing from his mouth.

Crowbone's first spear took the giant in the thigh, a slicing stroke that opened a great tearing mouth that trailed gore as the giant ran. The second shunked into Wolf-Ember's side, bursting rings apart and biting deep, but the giant simply tore it out in the next step and hurled it back.

It smacked Rovald as he hirpled desperately forward, went through the shield and into his ring-mailed body hard enough to make him grunt and tumble backwards. Wolf-Ember kept coming and Kaetilmund dropped the point of the spear and thrust it, banner and all, so that the cloth of it furled round the giant's head, blinding him.

Crowbone had his sword out now and stepped once, twice, spun to avoid the blundering flails of the giant and cut just once. His stroke frayed one end of the banner and went into the back of the giant's neck, so that he arched and howled, falling like a crashing oak. Blood flushed up the length of the blue banner, even as Kaetilmund wrenched it away.

It was then that Crowbone realised that Wolf-Ember had been forging a path for Raghnall to reach him.

The son of Olaf Irish-Shoes had the eyes of a mad rat in a blocked tunnel and a fistful of vengeful steel. When he saw Wolf-Ember go down, he gave a great howl and a savage leap into the air, both hands on the shaft of an axe.

Crowbone saw it in a fixed flash, watched his doom come down on him and marvelled at it, for this was the way he had himself killed both Klerkon and Kveldulf. The gods' jokes are seldom funny, but you can always hear them laugh if you listen, he thought.

Two blurs passed him. One was yellow and low to the ground, a fast snarling bitch who ploughed into the shins of the leaping Raghnall. The second was faster still, a bird-whirr of sound that stirred the wind on Crowbone's cheek and took Raghnall in the throat, snapping his head back.

The heir to Dyfflin crashed to the feet of Crowbone, the yellow bitch's jaws locked in his leg as it snarled and wrenched. The axe wyrded for Crowbone's skull spun harmlessly over his head and skittered through the bloody mud.

There was no resistance from Raghnall, not even a sound, for the arrow that had taken him in the throat had ripped the voice and the life from him in one. His eyes were wide with surprise and his mouth worked once or twice then froze; after that the only movement from him came because the yellow bitch was jerking him to and fro and growling deep in the back of her throat.

'Leave off,' Crowbone snarled and the hound let go and slithered backwards on her belly, bloody jaws on her paws, tail moving uncertainly. Crowbone was only mildly surprised that the animal had obeyed him, but his mind was elsewhere. It was on what he hoped he would find when he turned his head – his legs, he knew, were not up to the task of moving at all from the shock. He hoped he would find Vandrad Sygni, nocking another arrow and grinning at him.

It was as bad as he had thought. No Vandrad Sygni – but back across the slope they had come down, over all the dead and groaning wounded, all the way back to the copse of trees – Odin's arse, a hundred long paces or more – a small figure perched in a branch and waved her bow at him. Crowbone knew for certain it would be the same branch where the exhausted bird had sat, staring at him with a prophetic black eye.

'By The Dagda,' said Murrough admiringly, hefting his axe and testing the distance between its edge and Raghnall's neck, 'that wee woman of yours can shoot, Crowbone.'

Tmutorokan on the Dark Sea, that same day . . .

ORM

The walkway planks were hot beneath their boots and the resin smell from the sun-cracked roofs was as rich as the cackle of strange tongues. There was a stir in the crowd at the woman who was offered; anyone with a trader's eye would admire the skill of the dealer.

A long fall of linen the colour of old slate covered the figure but it was clearly a woman who tugged slightly at the end of the thin line fastened carefully round sheepskin cuffs to her wrists, so the rope would not bruise the flesh.

The dealer, a Khazar Jew smiling the last of his teeth at the crowd, hauled a ratty fur hat off his head in a glorious bow, then pulled the veil away with a flourish; she stood before them naked, unable to crouch or use her tethered arms to hide herself. In the end, she stood in a slight curl, halfway between shame and defiance.

They were enthusiastic, the crowd, even though the day was hot. Orm caught Finn's eye and the slave-master turned the docile merchandise this way and that with a practised hand as he called out to the crowd in Greek, which was the tongue of traders.

'This one is a certified virgin. A captive princess from the far regions beyond the Khazar Sea, you can see from her shy ways that she has never known the hand of a man.'

You had to admire him, Orm thought to himself. She had almost certainly been humped full of at least one bairn and by a horny-handed farmer, since she was as much a captive princess as Finn was. Nor did she come from beyond the Khazar Sea and had clearly been told to fasten her mouth or it would be worse for her – whoever bought her would be surprised at the amount of Slav she knew.

The dealer took his fingers, heavy with bright-stoned rings, and grimed them through the woman's thick, dark hair. In the crowd, the Arabs and Jews, rivals in anything and everything that could be bought and sold, shifted expectantly.

'This incredible shade of night is her hair's natural colour,' he said, then took her firmly by the chin and raised her face up. 'And this has had no help from dye pots.'

He turned and leered a little as he stroked the hand down one naked, flinching flank.

'These delicate white curves speak for themselves. This is a rich ornament, worthy of any bek or jarl or sheikh. It is only due to chance and my own financial misfortune that such a rare creature is being offered at all, for I was keeping her for the Basileus in the Great City himself. I am stabbing myself in the heart to offer this to you.'

Someone would, this day or the next, if this slave trader kept lying at this level, Finn whispered out of the corner of his mouth. Orm agreed – but not before he had, hopefully, told where to find Takoub and his brother in this reeking trade town of the Khazars.

Tmutorokan was what was left to the Khazars after Sviatoslav's Kievans broke them. Once, it had belonged to the

Great City and probably would again, unless the Kievans got to it first, and it sat on the Dark Sea like a boil, pus-filled with crooked traders and hard men looking for work. It had buildings of brick with tiled roofs, more of wood – and, in the heat of summer, most of the Khazars sensibly took to living in tents, which sprouted like evil, coloured mushrooms on every spare piece of ground.

The place festered with everything else, too – bad drink, worse women and men prepared to do anything for money, even to telling the truth now and then. This time, it took only the sparkling spin of a whole silver coin to brighten the slave dealer's day and point them in the right direction; they left, feeling the eyes of the Slav woman, hopeful as a hungry dog.

Takoub's slave hold was a rough square of sharp-pointed timbers. The gate was merely a circle cut in timbers, which was woodworking skill in itself. In the arch at the top, in a semi-circle, was a spatter of sharpened staves pointing downward and, set across the entrance so that anyone had to step or stumble between them, was a second set of stumps, the ends dark with stains which might just have been old paint. The whole matter had been designed to look like a mouth, gaping open to swallow any who went in and the effect of it was such that it needed only a brace of bored guards, who lolled and leaned.

'Let me guess,' Finn said, strolling up to the guards, 'you can get in on foot only, but not out at all. Am I right?'

They looked back at him with eyes unmoving as boulders, a pair of sweating men in leather with spears and long knives. If they had any humour it was in a locked chest in a deep cellar.

'If you are selling or buying,' one said, after a long pause filled with the reedy cries of hucksters, 'you can come and go as you please. If you are bought and sold, you never leave through this gate, only enter.'

'Which are you?' the other asked, after looking Finn up and down. His voice was heavy with greasy dislike.

'Tell Takoub that Orm Trader is here,' he said. 'Also known as Bear-Slayer. Tell him the Oathsworn are at his gates.'

The guards stared back blankly and one squinted, eyeing the pair up and down. They saw a jut-jawed northman with a black and salt beard plaited and ringed with silver, hard eyes and a worn-hilted blade in a scuffed sheath. They saw the man with him, younger by some years, with missing fingers, a scar across his forehead and lines at the corner of eyes that had stared at horrors few men ever looked at.

Seeing no overt sign of wealth the guard sneered.

'You have heard of the Oathsworn?' Finn demanded, his chin thrust out.

'Aye,' answered the guard. 'Slayers of dragons and witches, or so I have heard children tell it.'

'For men who found all the silver in the world,' the other chirped, 'you have clearly buried far too much of it and bought far too little.'

'You should not scoff,' Finn said to him, stepping closer and squinting sideways at him, 'with a nose like that.'

The guard raised an eyebrow and touched his neb reassuringly, then scowled.

'What is wrong with my nose?' he demanded.

Finn's right fist smashed it. Blood flew out, the guard flew back with a yelp and landed in the dust, throwing up a cloud of it and rolling over, groaning. The other one, taken by surprise, tried to grab his spear and back away at the same time, only succeeding in dropping the weapon. There was shouting and a deal of screaming from the man with the bloodied nose; Orm could sympathise, for he had had that done to him in the past and remembered the considerable pain.

The clamour had an effect; more men appeared led by a sword-waver, which showed that he had more rank than the

220

others. Before matters could boil over, Orm told him who they were and the captain glanced at the disarmed gate guard, the one sitting dripping blood and then back to Orm.

'Pick up your spear,' he ordered the gate guard, with the sort of lip curl that promised the man a deal of pain later for such carelessness.

'Wait,' he said to Orm – though politely – and turned to go and find Takoub. Then he turned back, almost apologetically.

'There would have been less trouble over this had you tried the gate on the far side. This is the Eater of Hope, where only slaves enter and through which no-one leaves.'

'I said so,' Finn declared to Orm, grinning. Orm shook his head in mock sorrow.

'This place will make me remember to pay more attention to your wisdom,' he replied wryly. 'And save on noses.'

It was not, in the end, what they would most remember of the place. What they remembered most, when they came to the tale of it later, was the smell – the tented room was cloyed with it, a swirl of strong, spiced perfumes that hazed the still, hot air inside the canopy and, for all its muslin thickness, it had only managed to reduce the stink of rot to a faint thread.

Orm saw two men, one standing, the other swallowed by cushions and swathed in silk that had been drooped over his head and draped round his face, so that only the eyes showed, dark and shifting like rats in a hole.

The standing man stepped forward. He was big, had once been muscled but was running to fat, had once worn expensive silk but had stained and ragged it to near worthlessness. He had grimy hands and put one of them on a jewel-hilted dagger stuck carelessly in a sash-belt.

'I say we kill them now,' he growled and looked right and left into the shadows, to reassure himself that his hidden men were near. 'We have removed their weapons and they will never be more in our power.'

'You may have removed the weapons you can see,' said the silk-wrapped man, 'but this is the Oathsworn. That is Finn, who has at least one blade hidden about him. That is Orm, slayer of white bears and dragons and so favoured by his north god that he was led to all the silver of the world.'

It was rheum-thick, that voice, black with rot and Orm did not recognise it, or him, until the man leaned forward, his breath hissing painfully.

'Is that boy still with you?' he asked. 'The one who axed Klerkon in the square in Novgorod?'

Takoub. It was Takoub the slave dealer and life had not been good to him.

'Crowbone,' Orm answered, recovering from his shock. 'He stuck another axe into Klerkon's right-hand man not long after. Same style – smack between the eyes. Then he did the same to Yaropolk, brother to Prince Vladimir of Kiev.'

'He has grown a little,' Finn added, grinning. 'He does not have to jump up so far.'

There was a hiss and Takoub slumped limply on his cushions.

'I dream of that boy,' he said. 'I dream he comes, sent by you for what happened to those of the Oathsworn I took as slaves and sold.'

This was blunt and clearly the other man thought so, too, for he growled and spun round to face Takoub.

'Enough, brother – we can sweeten your dreams with their death, here and now.'

'Barjik,' said the whisper-thin voice. 'Go and do something elsewhere.'

Barjik glared at his brother, then at Orm and Finn and finally rammed his scowl between them and went out, the wind of him trailing the rot and perfume over them like a lover's fingers.

Takoub forced himself upright, a process of grunts and pain, then slowly unwrapped the silk from his head. Even Finn gasped.

222

It was worm-pale and eaten, that face. The nose was a collapsed ruin of wet blackness, the lips smeared with blotches, the cheeks looked as if rats had gnawed them and one eye was a shrieking agony of yellow pus. The rot was inside his throat too and made his voice a whispering rasp.

'The Alexandrine disease,' Takoub said. 'There is no cure.'

'Scale,' Orm answered, then said it in Greek – *lepros*.

'I am punished,' Takoub said, 'whether by your god or someone else's is of little matter. But my own god has brought you here to give me some relief.'

'Aye,' Finn said before Orm could speak. 'I could find my hidden blade and give you relief, right enough.'

There was a sound like wings falling and it took Orm a moment to realise that it was laughter.

'I cling to what is left of my life, pain and all,' Takoub answered. 'It would be less bitter if sleep was the balm it is supposed to be.'

'You want me to help with your sleep?' Orm asked, bemused by all this.

'My dreams,' he hissed. 'We are traders. I will trade for a lack of dreams. I have what you seek.'

'You want this as a blood-price,' Orm said, realising the path this was on. 'You want to be told that I will not send Crowbone to you, armed with a little axe for what you did to my men.'

There was a rustling, like roaches in straw, as Takoub shuddered and nodded. Strange, Orm was thinking, how sickness and the nearness of death took some people's minds. Here was Takoub, rank and cunning as a hunting stoat in his day, fearful of the boy he had seen once in the square in Novgorod. So fearful he was seriously bargaining for forgiveness and peaceful sleep, now more precious to him than silver or jewels. He was not to know, he thought, that the Oathsworn he had sold had turned on their former oarmates and had been killed for it.

Fleetingly, Orm wondered where Crowbone was and if he had uncovered the weft of matters concerning Eirik's Bloodaxe – by now he would have uncovered who Drostan really was and what he had written. If he had had the clever to ask, he would have known it as soon as he fell to questioning Hoskuld, who had not been keen to keep quiet until Crowbone put the right questions in his mouth.

'Why keep the boy in darkness?' he had asked and Orm told him – because he has been fed silver and men and ship like *skyr* off a silver spoon. If he wants to make his own name, let him use his own cleverness.

Privately, Orm thought the whole business with the axe was foolish – but Martin was in it and that made it dangerous. If the boy held true to his course and the Oath he would be in Mann and know everything. If he decided to scorn Hoskuld and go off on his own, then he would have a harder lesson, though Orm never doubted that the notable man-boy was alive.

Then he corrected himself; not man-boy any longer but full grown. It was foolish to hold the old memory of an odd-eyed youth not yet into the power of himself. Orm wondered if he was still holding to the Oath he had sworn.

They would all find out soon enough.

Takoub rheumed out a wheezing cough. Orm had no interest in pursuing the slave dealer, with or without Crowbone, but Takoub did not know that, so Orm made this worthless coin ring true and paid for the bargain with it.

Takoub sighed, rang a little bell and someone slithered in to the rancid cloy of the place, a wrapped bundle in his hands, which he handed to Orm. Orm twitched a corner of the wrapping back and saw the old veneer of it, the nub end of black iron; it was the holy spear Martin sought so desperately, the one he had lost in the steppe. Orm nodded; he had given up wondering how Takoub had come into possession of it, or if he believed it was what was claimed. All he cared about now was that Martin had written that he wanted it, in return for the Bloodaxe which he seemed confident of lifting; Orm did not doubt that Martin had set all the dogs at one another's throats and thought to sneak off with the prize while they fought. Well, even if he did, he would come, at the end of it all, to trade with Orm Bear-Slayer.

'It is done,' Takoub said, 'we part satisfied.'

For a shuddering moment, Orm thought he would spit on his rotting hand and offer it for the slap of a trader handshake. So did Finn, who chuckled.

'Best not,' he said. 'Hard to find the bits that fall off in all those swaddlings.'

'Sweet dreams,' he added as they turned to leave. 'You should know that it is not the living you should bother with. It is the ones who were balls-cut and died because you sold them to the Serklanders. Their *fetch* are coming for you, Takoub.'

Outside the walls of Dyfflin, not long after . . .

CROWBONE'S CREW

You can always tell the beaten, Crowbone thought, for they take a deal of interest in the ground. Neither do they walk like men but shuffle like thralls.

He watched as they moved slowly, with their necks pulled in as far as they could get them, mud-spattered, bloody and, when they did look, it was with a fleeting gaze and eyes that were pools of shame.

'Our own kind,' Kaetilmund growled moodily, stirring the embers of the fire and watching the northmen prisoners on their way to be thralls of the Irish. Folk stirred and muttered; no-one liked to see northmen humbled, as Halfdan pointed out.

'Unless it is by other northmen,' Crowbone answered with a whip in his tone. 'Anyway – these are men like us, hired to fight. Like us. The Oathsworn, who beat them hollow and reaped the rewards of it.'

No-one spoke, for the rewards of it were mixed. Three days after the battle, everyone had sorted out their plunder and Crowbone had been lavish, so that four swords had been given out as well as Raghnall's brass-dagged ringmail, handed to Svenke Klak, who now strutted like a dunghill cock in it. True to his promise, Crowbone had Wolf-Ember's mail, but it was too large even for Murrough.

On the other hand, they had howed up eight men, including Kaup. Sixteen more were wounded, but only one would not recover from it – Rovald lay coughing blood up and Gjallandi said that the giant's spear throw, though it had not gone through the ringmail, had broken something in Rovald's chest. It did not help, Crowbone thought moodily, that the men know it was my spear.

'The Oathsworn.'

It was a dragon growl, thick with the bitter rheum of hate and Crowbone did not need to look round to know who it was.

'The Oath is broken,' Mar rasped, the scar on his face like a badly-done hem, for Gjallandi was poor with a needle. 'Even by your own heathen rites, it is broken.'

'The ones who broke it paid for it,' Crowbone answered sharply. 'And you gave your oath also to me, Mar. Twice oathed, twice cursed if you break it.'

It was not the time to give out such a warning, Onund thought, when he saw Mar's eyes flare like the fire coals. Besides, there were too many oaths flying about here for the Icelander's comfort and he saw that the gods of the White Christ and Asgard faced each other like two snarling shield-walls. No good would come it, for men would have to choose where they stood in the end.

'You should have let me stitch that,' the girl said, stepping under their rough awning and into the firelight. She knelt by

Mar and turned his cheek to see the scar better, but he shied his chin away from her. Her hand drooped like a willow branch, but only for a moment.

Then the head of her came up in a defiant tilt, the same way it had when she strolled down from her perch in the tree and smiled sweetly at Crowbone. The yellow bitch had loped from her side and sat, tongue lolling, close to Crowbone, looking at him, the tail moving a little.

'You could have had my head off,' Crowbone had growled and her smile grew more honeyed still at that. She went and plucked her arrow from the ground where Murrough had left it after his axe work.

'Instead, it is Raghnall's head which is off,' Bergliot had answered and nothing more had been said between them from then until now.

Raghnall's head had been severed and delivered to the High King, though Crowbone had heard nothing from it and that made him frown. He needed praise and the salt of gold to keep these muttering dogs at bay.

Murrough paused in cleaning the stubborn remains of Raghnall from his axe and looked up at the girl, smiling.

'Come and sit by me, girl,' he said amiably and the tension slid away slowly into the dark. Bergliot graciously accepted a seat beside Murrough and a bowl of whatever had been in the pot, while Crowbone tried not to scowl; he was not sure whether Murrough was being bland or clever in what was surely wooing, but he did not like it – liked the fact of that even less.

She looked too fine, Crowbone thought, her black hair like a river of pitch above the *brat* thrown round her shoulders and fastened with a fine pin. All plunder, he knew, given to her by various of those round the fire, who had thought of her in the middle of all that blood and guddling in bodies for loot. The thought of what they wanted in return made Crowbone burn deeper inside than any rage he had known.

Just then, another figure appeared, making heads turn. It was a tall man, with a cloak thrown over one shoulder and a spear he held like a staff; Crowbone had seen him before, standing behind Gilla Mo at Cnobha and filling his cup whenever it emptied.

'The High King asks for you,' the man said politely enough and with a little bow to it.

'Aha,' said Svenke, still basking in the glow of his ringmail, 'more rewards for our brave efforts.'

'Just so,' Mar spat. 'Perhaps he will give us some of those new thralls he has marched by us.'

'You are just annoyed because you did not get an iron Irish sark like Svenke here,' Murrough said as Crowbone levered himself to his feet, stiff after the battle and the sitting.

'Come with me,' he said to Murrough, who grinned with delight at the idea, 'in case I need the Irish tongue.'

He broke off his walking after the messenger to look down at Mar, who kept his eyes fixed on the fire.

'If the High King does offer me a thrall or two,' he said, the promise of gold reward from Mael Sechnaill lending him new resolve, 'I will ask for a black one for you, to replace the one you lost. Meanwhile, while I am gone, improve your mood, for your face is putting the fire out.'

It was a vicious slap, particularly about Kaup and he felt the twin embers of Mar's hate burn his shoulderblades, but did not look back as they moved through the dark, where other fires glowed and men, blood-dyed with the light, looked up as he passed.

One or two acknowledged him with a brief 'heya' or a wave and Crowbone knew Gjallandi had been busy spreading the saga of Crowbone's fight with Raghnall. He was sure there was no mention of a woman in it, all the same.

To the right of where they picked a way through the flow-ering field of fires, was the dark earth and rampart wall of Dyfflin, now under siege. Crowbone knew Mael Sechnaill had no *val-slöngva,* the war-slings the Romans of Constantinople called *ballista* and, without them, the Irish would have to storm the walls or starve out the defenders. He knew the harbour was open and, though the Irish had taken some ships in a lesser trade harbour just outside the walls to the south, they did not have enough vessels to blockade the place.

So it would be over the walls, he thought to himself. He had the sick feeling in his bowels that this was really what Mael Sechnaill wanted to see him about – the Oathsworn, leading the way over the walls of Dyfflin. Crowbone did not think any of his men would follow him if he ordered it and would have been away with them if he could – but he had come into this mess because he needed to know what Olaf Irish-Shoes had found out from Hoskuld. He needed Hoskuld. If any of them still lived, they lived in Dyfflin.

The High King had a grand tent, a maze of poles and lines and as big as a steading, striped like a sail. Outside it was a fire in a brazier and guards who grinned at the messenger and stood with their spears butted under a tall pole which held the head of Raghnall.

Inside was all guttering lamps and harp music, a contrast with the dark that left Crowbone and Murrough blinking. There were, when either of them could see, benches filled with the lesser kings and their entourage, clustered round a raised wooden dais where the High King himself sat, listening to his harper, the blind *Ollumh* Meartach, who stopped playing a heartbeat before the messenger rapped a bench with his spear.

'Prince Olaf of Norway and Murrough macMael.'

The High King looked up and there were a few cheers from those who had warmed to Crowbone and the Oathsworn after the day's fighting. Mael Sechnaill grinned; even Gilla Mo looked pleased, though that was shown only by his lack of scowl.

'Your *val-haukr* showed its talons today,' Mael Sechnaill declared with a grin and Crowbone frowned at that – *val-haukr*

229

meant 'carrion-hawk' in the Norse and he did not care for that description of his new banner. Wisely he said nothing.

'Mark you,' Mael Sechnaill went on, 'there are folk here who would not, perhaps, agree with you.'

Bewildered, Crowbone looked cautiously around as he walked to the ushered place at table. Then a short, stocky man stood up, his blue tunic trimmed with red and a deal of silver sparkling at his throat and wrist. He offered Crowbone a stiff bow, as did another barrel of a man next to him and a woman, young and pretty in a long-nosed way with her dress cut tight and low, designed to have the effect it had on Crowbone's groin. Not worn for him, he noticed. For Mael Sechnaill.

'This is Glúniairn, son of Amlaib,' said Mael Sechnaill and the stocky man bowed a little.

'The other is his brother, Sitric,' the High King went on, bland as milk. 'This is Queen Gormflaeth.'

Crowbone reeled but managed not to gawp or make a sound. Murrough was not so good and let out a ripping curse, which he covered with a fit of coughing. The pair sat down, stiff-faced, grim as wet cliffs while Crowbone reined in the plunge of his thoughts.

Olaf's queen and his two sons – Odin's bones, half-brothers to the man whose head was stuck on a spear outside . . .

'Prince,' he said eventually, for he knew that Glúniairn was the Irish way of saying Jarnkne, Iron Knee, just as Amlaib was how they mush-mouthed Olaf, but he did not know if the man liked to be known only by his by-name. Mael Sechnaill chuckled.

'King Glúniairn it is, since his da has given up his High Seat and taken himself off,' the High King said and turned, all sweet innocence, to the glowering Iron Knee. 'Where was it, now?'

'Hy,' Sitric growled before his brother could speak and had back a squinted glare for it. 'The death of Raghnall and the day's ills broke him entire. He has took himself to the monastery at Hy and left us to deal with the mess of it.'

His voice was bitter, the words sludge in his mouth and Crowbone saw the mess and how the brothers and the wife had to deal with it. Olaf's eldest son was here to make peace, to beg for the High Seat his da had disowned, though it meant being under the rule of the High King of Ireland. The quivering cleavage of their stepmother, Gormflaeth, was the seal on it.

He should have been leaping for joy at not having to go over the walls of the place, but Crowbone only had one thought, even as he asked polite bland questions that revealed Hoskuld was not held by Dyfflin's Danes and that Olaf Irish-Shoes was gone.

He could do nothing but brood on it, all the same, while the hall roared and reeked. Folk drank until it came down their nose and then spewed most of it up and started in to drinking more. There was boasting and shouting, arm-wrestling and some frantic humping, not limited to the shadowed corners either. A few fights broke out, bones were flung, benches overturned and, at one point, a pole was split, so that the High King himself, red-faced and greasy-chopped, launched himself into the affray, cursing those who were destroying his fine tent.

In short, it was as satisfying an Irish victory feast as any seen in the land, according to Murrough, shortly before his nose sank into a puddle of drink and he started in to snoring.

Crowbone had sipped, watching the two brothers and their stepmother, who were equally light on their drink. At the end of the roaring and struggling round the pitfire, the High King staggered out of the ruck, his arm round the shoulders of a man whose long straight hair, streaked a little with grey as if a gull had shat on him, was plastered to a streaming face with eyes like a mad owl.

'Dómnall Claen mac Lorcán,' the High King declared blearily. 'Sure, it is good to have you back among us, so it is.'

'Good,' agreed the man, who clearly wanted to say more but had little control of either legs or lips, for he slipped and sat, then giggled a little. His eyes rolled and he sank back on the reeking straw and snored.

'Behold,' Mael Sechnaill declared, waving one paw at the fallen figure, then clawing his way back to his High Seat, 'the king of Leinster.'

He sat down and gasped, blinking and grinning at the two brothers. Then he leered at Gormflaeth.

'You should . . . know him well. He was your guest for some time.'

'A year or two,' Iron Knee admitted, his face wooden as the table he leaned on. 'His freedom is part of the agreement making peace between us.'

'Jus' so,' Mael Sechnaill said, nodding. He belched, then he looked slyly at Gormflaeth and Crowbone realised the High King was not nearly as deep in drink as he appeared.

'My dear,' Mael Sechnaill said, his words grime on her skin. 'Patience. I have one more kingly act to perform, then you and I can discuss other parts of the agreement of peace.'

Gormflaeth had the grace to flush a little, but she also wriggled in her dress, so that the cleavage deepened. Mael Sechnaill cleared his throat and blinked.

'Reward,' he said and though he spoke to Crowbone, he was unable to stop staring at what was on show. 'Suitable. For your part in the victory. State your . . . what do you want?'

'As many men as will follow me,' Crowbone said, 'rather than stay as thralls to the Irish.'

Mael Sechnaill blinked away from Gormflaeth to Crowbone, then he sat back and laughed.

'No gold? Silver?'

Crowbone was tempted, but he had the riding of this horse now and he knew what he had to do. He had seen the shuffling prisoners and knew them for what they were – hired men, not about to stand and die for old Olaf Irish-Shoes; they would be looking for a way out of their predicament.

Mael Sechnaill saw it too, stood up and held out his hand for Gormflaeth to take.

'As many as will follow you,' he said to Crowbone, 'as long as it is out of Ireland and out of Dyfflin. How you do that is your affair but if you are here after a week, matters will alter. I do not want the likes of you with a bunch of sword-wavers at your back plootering about Ireland causing trouble.'

He went off, towing Gormflaeth in his wake, pausing only to turn a snoring body out of her path with one elegant toe. Crowbone watched the brothers watching their stepma whore herself to the High King of Ireland.

'You should have taken the gold,' Sitric said eventually, looking sourly at Crowbone. 'The best of Dyfflin's fighting men died on Tara – but you will have no shortage of offers from those nithings who gave up. They were not worth the hire.

'You will only lose them again,' he added, taking a sudden, deep swallow from his cup. There was a burst of singing, loud and enthusiastic, but it was not the bad key that made Sitric slam the soapstone beaker down so that froth leaped out.

'Fucking Irish,' he muttered. 'Time we were gone from this feast, brother – they have started in to bad singing.'

'You only waited for me,' Crowbone said, 'so let us now get to the meat of the matter.'

Iron Knee's head came up at that and his blue-sky eyes clashed with Crowbone's stare.

'I will not lose the crew I pick,' Crowbone said, 'for I will be gone from Ireland and Dyfflin within the week. Is that not so, Jarnkne?'

'Magic them all wings, will you?' Sitric sneered. 'I have heard the tales of you, boy, such an event will be interesting to watch.'

Crowbone kept his eyes on Iron Knee.

'Ships,' he said. 'Not wings. You will give me ships. The High King will give me men.'

Sitric glowered, waiting for his brother's cutting comment. When none came he looked uneasy.

'Four,' Iron Knee said eventually, then found his mouth so dry he had to grab up his own cup and drain it. 'Good *drakkar* all of them. You will fill them easily enough from those hired men who do not want to end up thralls to the Irish.'

Sitric's eyebrows went to his hairline and he stared for a moment, then exploded upright.

'Are you fucking crazed?' he demanded. 'This is the louse who killed our brother. Who was part of the army that ruined us almost out of Dyfflin entirely. Ships . . . four . . .'

'Will you do it?' Iron Knee said to Crowbone, ignoring his spluttering brother. 'If you do not, I will know and I will not rest until you are dead in the foulest way I can dream. I dream very foul these days, Prince of Norway.'

Crowbone merely nodded.

'In three days, then,' Iron Knee declared, suddenly standing up. Bewildered, still working his mouth wetly, Sitric stared from one to the other.

'Do what?' he growled. 'What is he to do?'

'Come,' Iron Knee said to his brother, smiling gently. 'Time for us to go home to Dyfflin, where I will explain the game of kings to you, who may one day need the knowing of it.'

Crowbone sat for a time, listening to the mourn of voices, the odd squeal and distant sigh. The king of Leinster stirred, woke up, bokked to one side, then rolled over and fell blissfully asleep; the smell of ale vomit slithered to Crowbone's nose, as apt a stinking seal on what had just been concluded as any.

The victory at Tara had opened up all doors for Mael Sechnaill, who got the Dyfflin Norse broken and contrite, the king of Leinster owing him life and freedom and Olaf's queen as a wife, which made him overlord of Dyfflin as well.

Iron Knee got the crown of Dyfflin, even if he had to bend

the knee to the High King. Sitric got an education in the game of kings.

For it all to work, though – for Iron Knee to be confirmed truly as Dyfflin's king, for Gormflaeth to stay a queen and for Mael Sechnaill, good Christian that he was, to take her as a wife – a father and a husband and an old king had to die.

Men and ships, Crowbone thought. Enough of a price for the murder of Olaf Irish-Shoes, once he had told all he knew.

Sand Vik, Orkney, middle of Haustmánuður (double-month – October) . . .

THE WITCH-QUEEN'S CREW

Outside was cold and bright with sun, but the hall was dim, grey-smoked, dappled here and there where the light broke in through the open doors. Thralls chattered cheerfully, sweeping out the long beaten earth floor with birch brooms brought at great expense from Norway, scrubbing benches and tables; the sharp catch of ash and old rushes and white lye made Erling clear his throat.

'The days are even, light and dark balanced,' she said in her husk whisper voice and Erling wondered how Gunnhild knew this, since she never seemed to venture out. Even now, while the hall bustled and flared with life and thrall work-songs, she had closeted them in her private sleeping place, shaped like the prow of a dragon-ship and right into the dark of the place.

'From now,' she went on, 'night will eat the light.'

Erling watched what he could see of Gudrod, which was only the dim gleam of a cheekbone, the bright glint of an eye as he turned; he could not see Od at all, but the boy was there all the same, close by, his breath a mist from the shadows like grey-blue smoke.

'All the more reason to hurry. The monk-scratching reveals the place,' Gudrod said, his bass rumble annoyed because this place was so lacking light that he could not set up a 'tafl board. The growl of him seemed to come up through Erling's boots in the smallness of the room; once she had ruled all Norway and then the lands round Jorvik, now Gunnhild, Mother of Kings, barely had space to stretch out, small though she was.

'Hurry,' she answered and it was scorn-sharp. Erling saw her face, then, as she leaned into the faint light of the stinking fish-oil lamp high in the wall sconce, saw the strange beauty of it, as if seen through a spiderweb – saw the eyes that raked her last son with disbelief at his stupidity.

Gudrod leaned into it, as he had done since all his brothers had gone under to treachery and blade. Mother of Kings, he thought bitterly, except the last of her sons is not one. Not that she was much of a mother – he had seen others, listened to men talk of their ma and knew the difference between what they knew and what he had suffered.

'You do not hurry to this place,' she said, sliding back into the dark. 'This is a Sami place, deep in the Finnmark. Of course they would take the Bloodaxe back – they gave it in the first place.'

Her voice had grown sealskin soft and dreamy, which made the hairs on Erling's arm stand like bristles. He heard Gudrod shift and grunt a little and knew he did not care for it much either; the air in the room grew thick, from too many people breathing it – or *seidr*, Erling did not know which.

'Is she working magic?' demanded a voice, in the sort of bad whisper that almost made Erling cry out. Od leaned forward, his beautiful face frown-creased; Erling felt like whimpering as Gunnhild put her face back into the light and laughed, but only with her voice, for her mask did not change at all.

'You are curious, lovely boy,' she answered. 'That is good.

You are like Odin's own raven for the knowing of matters – but take care, for even ravens can be caught and plucked.'

Od opened his mouth and Erling moved swiftly to clamp his wrist so hard that Od stopped and looked down at the grip, puzzled. Gunnhild sank back into the darkness, with a sound like bats flying out of a dark hole; laughter, Erling realised.

'Eirik did not win Odin's Daughter,' she said suddenly. 'It was gifted to him, by me, as were all his sons and I cannot say whether birthing any one was harder than what I did to get that Bloodaxe from the Sami. I had it from them, from the two brothers, who should have returned it to the goddess but gave it to me instead . . . It was gifted before to other kings, all of the Yngling line. It was made by the smiths of the Sami and to them it has again returned.'

She trailed off and Erling paused, remembered the tales of her, of how she had gone as a young girl to learn from two Sami wizards. There were lascivious, tongue-on-lip rumours of what she had done until Eirik had come for her, though no man had ever mentioned it to her face – or his. Like Freyja and the *duergar* necklace-makers, he thought to himself, she fucked the prize right out of them.

'I am wondering who took it back to them. Not those two Sami brothers, who were well dead by then. Was it Svein, the King's Key, who carried it? If not, he knew who it was who took it to her. I remember Svein. He did not like me.'

Her voice was a dreaming rasp and Erling went cold at the idea that she might see into his thought-cage and almost leaped up there and then to leave. Gudrod's voice, strangely, lashed him to the bench.

'No man likes you,' he said to his mother, which was harsh and bold. 'Does it matter? We know where the axe is now. All we have to do is get it and use it to put me on a throne. That is what you want, is it not, mother?'

Gunnhild made a ticking sound with tongue and teeth.

'Let me tell you of the Yngling kings,' she said, her voice slow and circling as mist tendrils. 'They all had Odin's Daughter and the only one who died old was Aun.'

Gudrod said nothing, while sullen rolled off him in waves, tangible as heat. Erling cleared his throat.

'The others?' he asked, knowing the answer but hoping for better news.

'One fell in vat of mead and drowned,' she said. 'Fjölne. He went to see Frodi in Zealand and a great feast had been prepared. Frodi had a large house where he stored a huge vessel full of very strong mead. Above the vessel there was an opening in the ceiling so that mead might be poured into it by men standing in the loft. After the banquet, King Fjölne was taken to stay the night in an adjoining loft, but he rose in the night and stumbled through the wrong door to fall into the great vat and drown in mead.'

Od clapped his hands and laughed with delight until Erling hit him on the shoulder and shushed him. Gunnhild never seemed to notice.

'King Swegde then took the High Seat and the axe, but a black *duergar* lured him into the runestone which sat on his land and he was never seen again,' she went on, weaving the words, thick as tapestry. 'Then there was Vanlande, who annoyed a Sami woman called Driva. Great with power was Driva and Vanlande died, even though he was days away from her.'

The admiration her voice shivered Erling and his tongue stuck to the roof of his mouth, so that he could not even swallow.

'There were many others, murdered by plots from vengeful wives taken by force, or dragged out by the folk they ruled when drought or famine showed they had failed – King Dag had a hayfork through his eyes from a work-thrall over a quarrel regarding a sparrow, of all things. Alric and Eric, two brothers and great horsemen, quarrelled over Odin's Daughter and beat each other to death with the iron bits of their bridles. King Jorund was hanged by Gylog of Halogaland when the axe betrayed him and he lost a battle. Egil was gored to death by a bull which had been wyrded for sacrifice by that axe, but escaped.'

She stopped. There was silence, where the distant thread of thrall song was like a lifeline back to the light of the world.

'They all accepted the Bloodaxe,' she added dreamily, 'and it made them kings, then betrayed them in the end, for they were not worthy of it. Not even my Eirik.'

'King Aun,' Od said, a slapped stone in the still pool of that dark dreaming place, so that Erling and Gudrod both shifted with the surprise of it. Gunnhild's moth-chuckle rustled.

'Wise, beautiful boy,' she crooned. 'Yes – King Aun grew old with the axe. No warrior that king and one less worthy to hold Odin's Daughter cannot be dreamed. Yet he was cunning and made a trade with Loki, giving that one – who is now the Devil the Christ-followers fear – the sacrifice of a son in return for a bite of Audun's apples. Those fruits keep the gods young and a single chew gave Aun ten years of life. Nine of his ten sons were spilled on an altar stone by Odin's Daughter, but the last killed the *godi* with it and escaped, so Aun died, drooling like an infant, fed with a spoon and hated by all who were near him.'

'I am taking five ships,' Gudrod rasped when this was done. 'I will sail before the winter ice closes Bjarmaland.'

We might make it there, Erling thought to himself mournfully, but the ice will close and we may never make it back. All for a blade on a pole that gave no good of itself to the owner.

'Six ships,' Gunnhild replied. 'You are taking me.'

There was silence for a long heartbeat, then Gudrod sighed.

'It is long and cold and dangerous,' he said. 'We will have to overwinter in the north, with luck in Gjesvaer, which is a miserable hole at the best of times. Haakon of Norway may also be searching for this prize, for I am believing this monk went to Norway. You will also have half a year of darkness to endure.'

A long dark, Erling thought, was no threat to the likes of Gunnhild. She shifted and brought her face slithering back into the dim light. Her eyes seemed to be no more than sockets in a skull and, for a heart-crushing moment, Erling thought she had read his mind.

'This priest is trying a cunning plan,' Gunnhild said, her voice sharp as a ship's adze. 'Speaking of monks – you did not kill the one on Hy, did you? The one who read for you.'

Gudrod blinked and shifted, then spread his hands.

'I would have had to slaughter them all . . .' he began and his mother made that disapproving ticking sound, which was shout enough to silence him.

'Then the next man along will know what the monk wrote,' she pointed out and sat back into the dark, a long sigh sounding like her last breath. 'It will be Tryggve's son.'

'That boy,' she added, her voice darker than the black. 'That cursed son of Astrid. You should have killed him when you killed his father and been done with the brood.'

'He was not even born,' Gudrod said, his voice rising and she hissed at him, as like a snake as to make Erling shrink away.

'Then you should have killed the mother.'

Even the thrall singing had stopped. Erling looked longingly at where he thought the door was, the way back to light and the world of men.

'You play the game of kings well on cloth, my son,' Gunnhild sneered, 'but not in life. The Sami have Odin's Daughter and you will need me to get it from them.'

No-one spoke; the seconds scraped past like claws on slate until Gunnhild sighed.

'Go away,' she said suddenly. 'I need to work.'

Erling scampered from the place, needing no other

instruction and not even wanting to dwell on what work she was doing. Outside, he sucked in the salt air and the sparkle of the sea.

Od was last out, ambling easily, the sword swinging nakedly from the ring at his belt. He stopped and yawned, then looked at Gudrod, who stood with lowered eyebrows, scowling out to sea but not looking at it.

'Why do you want this axe?' the boy demanded. 'All it brings is death to those not worthy. If your da was not worthy, what makes you think that you are?'

Erling groaned silently to himself; the boy was always asking such questions and there was no way to learn him out of it. Gudrod stirred and turned slowly.

'My mother,' he said.

Od pursed his lips, looked back at where they had come from and nodded.

TEN

Isle of Hy (Iona), not long after . . .

CROWBONE'S CREW

THEY splashed ashore at the Port of the Coracle, which was nothing much more than a good shingle bay, whooping with the stinging cold of the water. Crowbone went with a strong party up to the highest point, no more than a bump; Murrough said it was called *Carn-Cul-ri-Eiriin* – the Hill With Its Back To Ireland – where the wind caught them like a blow, stinging tears to the eyes.

'The Colm Cille fellow was a priest and prince,' the big man explained. 'A man for the killing, it was said, who grew sick of it and himself and sought a cure from his god. He was told he would not find the peace of his god unless he went to a place where he could not see Ireland.'

As clever a way of getting rid of a rival as any, Crowbone mused. More fool Columba.

'He searched a long time,' Murrough went on cheerfully, 'until he found this place. Even from up here, the highest point around, you cannot see Ireland, so Colm Cille was happy and this became a place favoured by the White Christ god.'

'Not favoured enough,' growled a big man, his arms full of water-skins, 'for we are never done coming here and robbing them.'

'And you a good Christian man, too,' chided Murrough, laughing. 'Or so you told us when you joined.'

Atli, Crowbone remembered, frowning with the force of it. His name is Atli and folk call him Skammi, which means Short. It is a joke, for he is exactly the opposite of a small man – but his brother is bigger, so say those who know the pair of them. Crowbone was pleased to have remembered all this, for there were four ships and some two hundred men spilling ashore, starting fires and sorting themselves out. He swelled with it, the thought of all those men oathed to him.

That had brought scowls and growls from the likes of Kaetilmund and Onund, but Crowbone had told them that it was better to find out the strength of these new men before getting them to swear the Odin Oath. After all, he reasoned, they were escaping thralldom in Ireland and so might say anything. It was a wonder the lie did not rot the teeth from his head, but his smile stayed bright and fixed while, one after another, the new men came and placed their hands in his.

Flouting that Odin Oath bothered him, all the same, like an insect bite that itched and festered. It was a powerful Oath and no good had come from defying it – but Crowbone, when he thought of Odin at all, fancied that One-Eye had no power over him, just as he had no power over the weaving Norns. Those three sisters, blind and in the dark, were what held the threads of Crowbone's destiny, he was sure of that – so far, they wove true and Eirik's axe, Odin's Daughter, was a bright weft in it.

With that axe, Crowbone knew, he would be the chooser of the slain – not second on the Oathsworn's boat, but first on his own. He was certain Odin himself was woven into the thread of that, yet Asgard's jarl had power and a temper – his son was Thor, after all, who had inherited his red-haired fury from his da, for sure.

243

The surf was white against the dark shingle and men had moved up and over into the shelter of rocks. Fires flared. Men chattered and grunted, looked at the cloud-scudded moon and the sea beyond the surf, judged for rain, grumbled that it was cold. The sea was grey black, the waves rolling like old whales; folk made noises about going to the distant buildings, marked by pallid lights.

Crowbone looked for gulls and saw none; they were all nestling in the rocks and bleached driftwood and he knew rain was coming. This, the south part of the island, was the best spot to be when the wind drove the sea in according to Stick-Starer, who was happy that he had managed to get them safely here at all.

Crowbone moved among the men, settling them like storm-twitched cattle. He knew these men already, dirty swords who required plunder to keep them contented as fed wolves. The island monastery had been raided so often, he told them, that there was nothing much left to take, not even food. If it rained, they would all crowd into the beehive cells of the monks and the stone and wood buildings, though there would be precious little comfort in it.

'Soon,' he went on, 'there will be wealth enough for all.'

They hoomed at him and went back to cooking or admiring their new weapons, liberally given by their rescuer, the young, confident youth who claimed to be a prince. Onund watched him stride through them, the corroded dags of his mail shedding rings as he walked, the coin-weighted braids of his hair flailing in the gusting wind; in the dark, he looked as if he had climbed out of some old grave mound and the Icelander shivered.

'Aye,' said a voice in his ear, making him take a surprised step sideways, hand on his hilt – but it was only Kaetilmund.

'Orm was right about that boy, when he worried about him coming into the main of his years,' he said, low and slow and Onund nodded. They went back to their own fire, where the old Oathsworn sat and listened to Rovald wheezing out the last of his life, wondering whether they should stay or make their own way back to find Orm, even though he had made them promise to keep Crowbone safe. It was clear to them, at least, that Crowbone did not trust any of the old Oathsworn, was braiding his doom with every new man he ordered bound to himself alone.

Crowbone came up not long after, but not to find out how Rovald was – the truth was that he had almost forgotten the man now and counted him already dead. Rovald had, he reasoned, failed to protect his lord three times, so what had happened to him was what was wyrded for him after his battle luck had clearly vanished.

He fetched Gjallandi, looked briefly at Bergliot sitting in the middle of the Oathsworn and smiling, then turned away, heading towards the monastery. He had seen Mar and others not far away and knew that he had several crews here, not one. Still, he had enough power to quell any of them individually, even the Oathsworn if they decided to try and exert themselves. He could gather one group against the other – the Christ-followers against the pagans or the other way around, or the new men from Ireland against those firm with the Oath. No matter who started in to snarling, Crowbone already knew how to play the game of kings with some skill.

He took Murrough, then added Atli and four others of the new men, enough to be a guard, not enough to be a threat, then moved through the tussocked dark to the buildings beyond. The wind ragged back their cloaks, blowing hard and bringing the boom of the sea as it crashed on the shore.

Seachd bliadhna 'n blr'ath
Thig muir air Eirinn re aon tr'ath
'S thar Ile ghuirm ghlais
Ach sn'amhaidh I Choluim Chl'eirich

Crowbone was heartily sick of the sound of Irish, which was as like a clearing of the throat as made no difference.

That and the mourn of them made him want to slap Murrough, but he wisely kept that to himself and, instead, asked what poetry that was.

'A prophecy,' Murrough replied, hefting the axe on his shoulder, 'to do with this place. Seven years after the Day of Judgement, the ocean will sweep over Ireland and elsewhere. Only this place, *I Chaluim Chille* – the isle of Colm Cille – will float above the waves.'

'Would you listen to it?' demanded a voice from the dark, one Crowbone did not yet know well enough. 'The arrogance of these Christ folk takes the breath from you. Day of Judgement, indeed – the Doom of all Powers sucks away all, even the gods.'

They reached the monastery door then and Crowbone nudged Murrough, who hammered on it with the butt of his axe. A slat opened.

'Olaf, Prince of Norway,' Crowbone announced. 'Open the door.'

'*Caelum, non animum mutant, qui trans mare currunt*,' said the shadowed face, which meant nothing to Crowbone. He turned to Gjallandi, who shrugged.

'They change the sky, but not their souls, who hasten across the sea,' he translated.

'Haste is right,' Crowbone said, feeling annoyed at being thwarted by a door-warden, 'if you do not open the door in your next breath, it will be your last breath.'

'*Melius frangi quam flecti*,' said the voice and Gjallandi sighed.

'It is better to break than to bend,' he declared and Crowbone, racing past reasoned argument, kicked the door with his foot, though he might just as easily have booted a stone.

'Enough priest tongue,' he yelled. 'I know you speak Norse well enough. Open up – I am seeking Olaf Cuarans, once king of Dyfflin.'

'*Abiit, excessit, evasit, erupit*,' said the voice mournfully and Gjallandi, primed and ready, simply repeated it so that everyone could understand.

'He has left, absconded, escaped and disappeared,' the skald said, then shrugged as if apologising and was about to say more, but Crowbone's snarl cut him viciously off. He nodded at Murrough, who spat on his palms, hefted the axe and swung it. The boom echoed distantly and chips flew. The slat slammed shut.

The second swing of the axe drummed out another long echo and more chips flew. Murrough paused then, frowning and examining the edge.

'There are iron nails in this door,' he declared. 'It will do no good to the edge of my axe.'

Crowbone fought his rage, though his mind shrieked to visit bloody horrors on Murrough and Gjallandi and everyone around him. For a moment the edges of his vision turned red, then curled back and vanished.

The door slat opened.

'Forgive Brother Malcolm,' said a voice in good Norse. 'He is a good man from Alba, but a little afraid, as are we all. Nor is he entirely full in his senses.'

'Open the door,' Crowbone replied sullenly. 'We mean you no harm. I want only to speak with Olaf Cuarans.'

'You have several hundred men,' the voice replied, smooth and polite. 'We have nothing of value and, if you take what food we have left, we will die of starvation.'

'We want nothing that you possess,' Crowbone replied, more patient now. 'Only a word with your head monk and some few more with Olaf.'

There was a pause, then the slat shut. A moment later came the sound of a heavy beam being lifted off and the door opened to reveal a tall figure, neatly dressed in robes, shaved and with the tonsure of his head bouncing back the lantern-light held in the swaying hand of a small hunched man with the eyes and face of a rat.

'I am Abbot Mugron,' the tall man said and smiled, though the effect was spoiled when his nervous top lip, thin as a wire, stuck to his dry teeth.

'Olaf, Prince of Norway,' Crowbone declared, then introduced the others.

'*Est autem fides credere quod nondum vides; cuius fidei merces est videre quod credis,*' Mugron declared with forced beaming. 'As the blessed Augustine said.'

Then he added, because he knew this prince would not have understood: 'Faith is to believe what you do not see; the reward of this faith is to see what you believe.'

'I want to see the king of Dyfflin,' Crowbone declared shoving past the priest. 'I have faith in that, for sure.'

Gjallandi, who thought that rudeness was not princely or helpful, sighed and followed, with the others piling through. Atli gave the rat-faced brother his blackest scowl on the way past.

They clacked across the worn slabs to the rear of the shadowed place, into a forest of shadows where monks shifted, their voices humming in prayer. Crowbone wondered how they could live like this, huddling in the half-dark like fearful sheep each time a ship was sighted off their shores. A cowled figure scuttled away as they approached and Mugron, hands folded inside his sleeves, frowned and paused at a door.

'I understand Brother Olaf has given up the world,' he said and, for a moment, Murrough thought the monk spoke of this prince, then realised his mistake and laughed. Mugron, misunderstanding, raised his eyebrows, but Crowbone merely shrugged.

'Brother Amlaibh,' Mugron corrected. 'The men who brought him said he had renounced throne and world in favour of God. Two of his men have stayed on, though they have not yet embraced God in total.'

'Do they still embrace weapons in total?' demanded Crowbone and Mugron inclined his head politely, frowning.

'They yet retain the marks of their status as guardians of the king of Dyfflin,' Mugron said, his voice stiff with disapproval, 'even though such a personage does not exist here, only an old and sick man who has come, at last, to the fold of Christ.'

Crowbone looked back at Murrough and the others; then, hard as whetstones, they went through the door.

The room was bright enough for them to see that it was furnished well; Olaf Irish-Shoes had clearly not come to his White Christ empty-handed. The man himself sat in a good chair, as like a High Seat as next of kin, wrapped in a fur-collared blue cloak and with his feet stuffed, not in Irish sandals, but in sealskin slippers. His hair was trimmed to the ears and the ring-hung braids of his beard had been shorn, but the face that scowled at them was red as a wean's fresh-skelpt backside, the eyes in it boarlike and annoyed.

There were others – two monks, one tall and blond, the other small and dark, fussing with a basin and cloths round the outstretched arm of the slumped Olaf. Two others, in coloured tunics and silver, bearded and long-haired, stood on either side of his seat and stepped forward, swords out.

'Lord Olaf,' Mugron began and Crowbone whirled on him.

'Prince,' he spat back and Mugron recoiled a little, then smiled.

'I was talking to our brother in Christ, lord of Dyfflin,' he explained greasily and Crowbone blinked, annoyed at his mistake. Anger made him rash.

'No longer,' he snarled. 'Another has that High Seat and name now. Tell those dogs to lose the steel.'

'I know who claims the seat,' Olaf Irish-Shoes spat back, his face turning blue-purple and his breath wheezing. 'My treacherous son, not fit to lick the arse of his brother, who died . . .'

He broke off then and slumped back, his face deep blue. The Chosen Man nearest to him looked anxiously at him, then flicked his eyes back to Crowbone and the others, his hand clenching and unclenching on the sword hilt.

'Are you well, lord?' he asked Olaf Irish-Shoes over his shoulder, at which Murrough laughed.

'Of course he is not well, you arse,' he bellowed. 'He has a face like a bag of blood and two monks sticking his arms with blades – are you blind?'

'We were in the process of bleeding him,' said the yellow-haired monk and Mugron frowned.

'Again? Is that wise?'

'He is choleric, lord abbot,' the monk replied, but Crowbone interrupted him, harsh as thrown gravel.

'You and you,' he said to the armed men, 'throw those blades down. I will not say this again.'

'*Dum inter homines sumus, colamus humanitatem,*' Mugron said nervously and Atli turned to Gjallandi.

'I hope that he is telling them to be sensible,' he growled and the skald, nervously backing away from the glinting steel, shook his head, then nodded, confused.

'In a manner of speaking,' he began. 'Something like being among humans and so being humane.'

'Speak Norse,' Crowbone declared to Mugron, then nodded to the two men. 'Kill them.'

Mugron started to protest; the dark monk shrieked and the yellow-haired one sprang back. Olaf himself struggled weakly, his blue cloak falling open to show his white underserk – the basin of his own blood flew up and crashed on him.

It took moments – for all that the men were fine fighters, they were outnumbered and taken by surprise a little. Even Murrough was, for he had not expected the prince to be so bloody, so the fight was a mad flail of blades and ugly blood trails.

Mugron knelt and babbled, the dark monk with him; the abbot was clearly shocked by this and Crowbone was pleased. Now he knows what he has let in his door, he thought and he turned to Gjallandi.

'*Oderint, dum metuant*,' he said, saying it carefully so as to get it right; it was the only Latin he knew, gleaned from an inscription on some weathered monument in the Great City. Let them hate as long as they fear. Gjallandi knew it at once – an Old Roman emperor had said it first and the skald licked dry lips at the drawn-back snarl of lip that came with it. That Old Roman ruler had been a madman, but Gjallandi said nothing on that.

Olaf struggled upright, his belly plastered to the blood-drenched serk, but his eyes wild and angry.

'Hoskuld,' Crowbone said. 'Where is he? And the monk that was with him. I know you know.'

Olaf stared at the bodies, the blood pooling, gleaming viscous in the flickering torchlight.

'Magnus,' he said and looked at Crowbone. 'I have known Magnus from when he was a bairn. My Magnus . . .'

'Not yours now,' Crowbone said. 'Hel has him and will have you if I am not happy with your answers – shut that priest's fucking babble!'

The last was bellowed as he spun to where Mugron chanted; there was a meaty smack and Atli sucked the knuckles of one hand, grinning, while Mugron climbed unsteadily on to one elbow and wiped his mouth, then gazed, incredulous, at the blood on his fingers. Murrough leaned thoughtfully on his axe; he did not like what he was seeing here at all.

'Hoskuld,' Crowbone repeated and Olaf blinked once, then twice and seemed to see the odd-eyed youth for the first time. 'Eirik's axe.'

'Hoskuld?' he repeated. 'How would I know? Ogmund had him and lost him to Gunnhild's son and some Grendel of a boy he has in train. Eirik's axe is a story for bairns,' said Olaf scornfully. 'Such as yourself.'

It took an effort not to cut the old man down, especially when four or five questions later Crowbone realised, with a sinking stone in his belly, that Olaf Irish-Shoes knew nothing

251

at all and Hoskuld was either gone to Gunnhild or dead. He looked at the proud old man and wondered; he had to be sure.

'Fetch those hangings,' he said and men leaped to obey; not Murrough, he saw from the corner of one eye and ignored it. When they started to string Olaf up by his bound ankles, using the stripped hangings as rope over a beam, the Irisher cleared his throat.

'I'm thinking this is not right or clever,' he said and Crowbone turned, his odd eyes seeming to bounce the light, so that those who saw it drew back a little. Murrough was suddenly aware of the iron stink of blood, smothering air from the room.

'Orm has done it,' Crowbone replied, which was true and Murrough had to admit it. All the same, Orm had strung folk up with some sense to it – but Murrough did not say this, though he managed to meet the odd-eyed stare until Crowbone grew tired of the game and looked at the slowly swinging Olaf. His blood-soaked serk had drooped over his face, revealing spindle shanks, stained underclothes and thin, veined legs; when Murrough lifted the serk to look, he saw the old man's face was turning bluish red.

'You are certain there is nothing more to tell me?' Crowbone demanded and Olaf, swinging and wheezing, merely glowered at him. Then he shook a little and foamed at the mouth – the yellow-haired monk moved swiftly towards him, but not as fast as Crowbone's voice.

'Stay,' he snapped and the monk stopped, stared with cool grey-blue eyes and went on to the side of the dangling man, ignoring Crowbone completely. Finally, he looked up into Crowbone's blazing face.

'Cut him down,' he said. 'Or else he will die.'

'Let him speak the truth.'

'He cannot speak at all. Cut him down.'

Murrough decided it, the axe scything briefly through the

252

air and so close to Crowbone that, for the flicker of an eyelid, he thought he was the target – but the blade sheared through the cloth strips and Olaf Cuarans collapsed in a soggy heap, his heels drumming. Crowbone glared at Murrough, but decided to let the moment pass. He would remember it all the same.

The dark-haired monk started to babble in Latin and Gjallandi, gnawing his knuckles at all he had seen, blinked out of the horror that was no part of the hero-sagas he told and into the moment, into what the monk was wailing.

'A letter,' he said and Crowbone turned.

'A letter,' Gjallandi repeated, pointing to the dark-haired monk. 'That one wants the abbot to tell what was in it, before everyone dies.'

'What is a letter?' Atli demanded and Gjallandi started to tell him, but Crowbone snarled him to silence and rounded on Mugron. Behind him, the yellow-haired monk knelt by Olaf and muttered prayers.

'What letter?' he demanded and Mugron stirred from his prayers and unfolded his hands. He laid his hand gently on the shoulder of the dark-haired monk kneeling beside him and wearily climbed to his feet.

'There was such a message,' he said, 'which dealt with the matters you seek. It was brought by Gudrod, who claimed to be the son of Gunnhild, the Witch-Queen. It was written by a monk in Latin and I translated it for this Gudrod, who went his way.'

He paused and blinked a little, as if to get the horror out of his eyes.

'We played a game,' he said. 'On a cloth with little counters. The game of kings. Do you play?'

Crowbone wondered if the blow had addled the abbot and leaned his face forward a little.

'I play,' he growled, 'but not on cloth with counters – you remember that writing-message. Tell it to me.'

'So you can then kill me? All of us?'

Crowbone shook his head impatiently.

'No, no – only those two sword-dogs had to die. Have I harmed a monk yet? Well – apart from a wee dunt to your teeth, that is. I will hear what you have to say and go, taking nothing and doing no harm.'

'*Dum excusare credis, accusas*,' Mugron declared bitterly and Crowbone whirled to Gjallandi, who had been whispering about the nature of letters to Atli and had missed it. For a moment, the skald felt the world tilt and disappear beneath his feet at the sight of Crowbone's fist of a face, waiting furiously to be informed.

'When you believe you are excusing yourself, you are accusing yourself.'

The yellow-haired monk rose slowly, as if his knees pained him.

'St Jerome,' he added, then made the sign of the cross over the rasp-breathing Olaf.

'He will die, this night or the next,' he said accusingly to Crowbone. 'For no reason at all.'

For four ships and crews, Crowbone thought and felt the wyrd of the moment – he had killed Olaf Cuarans, as he had agreed and had not as much as nicked him with a blade, so could be accused of nothing. Not that it would bother him, he persuaded himself.

'He was Olaf Irish-Shoes,' Crowbone replied harshly. 'For some that is reason enough. He is even an affront to your god, for he was a pagan all his life and now seeks to crawl into your Christ *valholl* through a hole in the wall.'

'God will not be mocked,' Mugron answered stiffly and Crowbone laughed, a sound with no mirth in it at all, it seemed to Gjallandi.

'Your god opens himself to mockery,' he answered, then pointed to the dark-haired monk, whose eyes went big and round.

'You – your name?'

It took him three attempts, but he managed to tell the terrible youth that his name was Notker.

'He is from Ringelheim in the Empire,' said the yellow-haired monk. 'As am I. My name is Adalbert.'

Crowbone looked from one to the other, then at Mugron.

'Here is what I propose,' he said, seeing the weave of it unfold gloriously as he spoke. 'You, Notker, and you, Adalbert, will argue why your god cannot exist. Mugron, your abbot – being holier than you and so worth the pair of you – will argue why he does. If Mugron loses he tells me the content of the letter – and you pair die. If the two of you win, I leave in peace, with nothing.'

'The Lord is not a wager,' Mugron spluttered, then sighed. 'I will tell you what is in the letter.'

Gjallandi saw Crowbone's face and knew the truth.

'*Post festum*,' he said sadly. '*Periculum in mora.*'

'What?' demanded a man behind Atli, but Gjallandi just shook his head; there was no point in telling everyone that Mugron had come too late for this feast, that Crowbone had turned on to a new tack and was driven by some Loki wind along it.

Murrough cleared his throat and this time he spat a gob on the bloody floor, as pointed a gesture of disgust as he dared make. He knew Crowbone had marked it, but the youth did not comment. Instead, he nodded to the man behind Atli, the one who had spoken up against Christ priests on the way in.

'What are you called?' he asked and the man, pleased to be singled out, heaved out his chest and told everyone that he was Styr Thorgeistsson from Paviken in Gotland. Crowbone nodded, picked up the bloody sword that had belonged to Magnus and handed it to the delighted man.

'Make that pair begin,' he ordered.

Grinning, Styr poked Notker in the ribs with his new weapon and the monk whimpered, then began praying frantically in Latin, his voice rising until Adalbert, still calm, laid a hand on the man's arm. Notker subsided, panting; the front of his robe darkened and his shoes got wet.

Atli and the others chuckled, for it was reasonable entertainment when there was little drink and no women, but Murrough stared at the floor. Orm had strung folk up when he needed them to talk, dragging out his little 'truth knife' to whittle pieces off them until they told all they knew. That was for good reasons of gain. This was a sick thing, which you could see in Crowbone's too-bright eyes.

Notker started and everyone knew he was doomed right from the start if left to himself. He was devout enough – he had come to this place all the way from Saxland and you had to be mad for your god to do that – but his Norse was stuttering and he was too afraid, Murrough thought. Adalbert silenced him gently with a hand on his shoulder.

Mugron was no better, Crowbone marked, disappointed suddenly. He had hoped for some moment, a flash of insight or understanding, a sign from some god somewhere. But Mugron was not it – there must be a God, he babbled, for if there was no God, there was no Judgement and that was surely unfair. And if there was no God, how could he, Mugron, be a priest and abbot?

Atli and the others beat their thighs at that, trading comments on how the abbot would look with a second smile. Murrough looked at the two dead men and the dying Olaf Irish-Shoes, whose great belly no longer trembled with his breathing; the stink of blood was choking.

Notker fell to his knees, all tears and snot and prayer, but Adalbert turned to Crowbone, calm as the mirror-water in a fjord and cleared his throat.

'I will restrict my arguments to three,' he declared in a firm, clear voice. 'I could easily adduce more, but three will do.'

Everybody fell silent, for this was new. Here was a monk, calmly announcing he had more than three ways to denounce his faith and his White Christ god. Atli laughed and declared that this was even better than seeing stumbling Styr try to walk oars. Styr offered back a scouring brow.

Adalbert stepped forward suddenly and slapped Styr's shield, back-slung to leave his hands free. Styr grunted angrily and raised a meaty fist, but Crowbone merely leashed him with a blue-brown stare. Adalbert, ignoring all this, held up his first finger.

'A shield, which you all have, has been made by someone. The very fact of it reveals such a thing as a shieldmaker. So the existence of the cosmos and all of nature, the flow of time and the greatness of the heavens, require a prior cause and a creator, one that does not move or change and is not confined, but infinite.'

He paused, looking round at the gape-mouthed and those who had a dim idea of what he meant. Gjallandi shifted slightly. '*Parturient montes, nascetur ridiculus mus*,' he said. Adalbert bowed.

Atli growled. 'Fucking Latin – what does he say?'

'Mountains labour and only a silly mouse is born,' Gjallandi told him, which left him none the wiser.

'It is a quote by an Old Roman called Horace about verses and really means something about a lot of work and nothing to show for it,' Gjallandi declaimed and Crowbone rounded smoothly on him, that beacon stare silencing him, too.

'If you know your Horace, perhaps you also know your Aristotle,' Adalbert continued, folding his hands and bowing graciously to Gjallandi. 'If so, you will recall that he said that this Unmoved Mover was God. In short, if there is a shield-maker to make shields then there must be a God to make trees and the sea, raiders who come out of it and poor monks from the isle of St Columba the Blessed.'

This everyone understood and they nodded admiringly. Atli threw back his head and howled like a wolf, which made Styr laugh. Adalbert held up his second finger.

'It has been argued,' he said, 'that no God exists because He could not allow such bad things to happen in the world – such things as this, for example. Evil events. In truth, the opposite is true.'

'*Aliquando bonus dormitat Homerus,*' Gjallandi intoned.

'There you go again, you fat-lipped arse,' roared Atli, exasperated. 'If the monk can speak fucking Norse, why can't you?'

Gjallandi scowled, but Atli glowered right back.

'He said,' Gjallandi offered, before things forged up to melting, 'that sometimes even good Homer sleeps.'

'Who the fuck is this Homer and what has he to do with any of this?' growled Styr, scrubbing his head.

'A better way of saying it is "you cannot win every time". I am thinking the priest is losing,' Gjallandi explained.

'Why not say that, then?' grumbled Atli. 'Not that it is a secret, as anyone can see.'

He then glared at Adalbert. 'What does this Aristotle Homer have to say on cutting your own throat? You are supposed to be arguing that your god does not exist. Good arguments you have – but you are charging the wrong way.'

Even Crowbone laughed and Adalbert inclined his head as Mugron declared desperately, breaking from Latin to Irish in his passion, about how Adalbert would die a martyr.

'The very existence, the utter conception of evil requires the existence and the concept of good, likewise the freedom of the individual will to choose between the two,' Adalbert went on, seemingly unmoved. 'Only God could confer such freedom on us, his creations – otherwise we should be bound by the necessity of being, like the sheep or the ox. The fact that we know we have such choice, such free will, thus shows not only a divine presence but also that a spark of His divinity lives in us, in our immortal souls.'

'My head hurts with this,' moaned Styr.

'You are a dead man,' Crowbone declared, puzzled, 'unless

your third argument is good enough to undo all that you have said so far.'

Adalbert held up his third finger. There was a silence, save for the wheeze of Olaf's breathing; even Notker and Mugron held their breath.

'If there is no God,' Adalbert said, voice like a bell, 'then you, Prince of Norway, would not have to be struggling so much against Him.'

There was a hoot of laughter, then another and Atli clapped Adalbert on the back, grinning. For a moment it made Crowbone as mad-angry as a smouldering bag of cats – but he suddenly saw it, how the wolves and bears that were Atli and Styr liked the spirit of this Adalbert. Even Murrough was grinning, thumping the butt of his axe on the floor. Mugron, he saw, was bow-headed, hands clasped in silent prayer; Notker was slumped on the floor, as if all his bones had deserted him, the hem of his robe mopping up the pools of blood.

Still, Crowbone thought, slightly bewildered, Adalbert had argued badly. He was supposed to disprove the existence of his god and had done the opposite. He and Notker were the ones who should die. He said so, though his voice was weak with confusion – that last proof of Adalbert's had had a barb to it. Still, the silence that followed was thick enough to grasp.

'On the contrary,' Adalbert said quietly into the middle of it. 'No-one should die. For the proposition we had to put has lost – yet it is clear that your men have voted me to live. Under the terms you set for this game all of us have won.'

Right there is why law-makers will rule the world, Crowbone thought – if they live long enough. The monk dazzled him, all the same, so much that he laughed with delight and stroked his coming beard with wry confusion; this was the game of kings, right enough, but played in a strange and excitingly different way.

'Now I will make you a proposition,' Adalbert declared.

'Mugron will tell you the content of the letter and you will take it and leave quietly, harming no-one. But I will come with you.'

Mugron's head came up at that. Crowbone cocked his own and stared at the monk, who thought he resembled a curious bird.

'Why would you?' he asked softly and Adalbert smiled.

'To bring you to God,' answered the priest. '*Probae etsi in segetem sunt deteriorem datae fruges, tamen ipsae suaptae enitent*. A good seed, planted even in poor soil, will bear rich fruit by its own nature.'

Crowbone laughed, the hackles on his neck stiff with the wyrd of it all. Was this the sign he looked for?

'At the least, you can teach me this Latin tongue,' he declared, 'so that I know when Gjallandi lies to me.'

The skald's face was stone and Crowbone's good-natured smile died away at the sight. Mugron unsteepled his fingers and looked up at Adalbert.

'You do not need to make this sacrifice,' he declared piously, but Adalbert's returning gaze was cool, grey as an iced sea.

'You did as much when Gudrod strung up your predecessor,' he declared and there was iron in his voice. 'I merely did it before an abbot died.'

Mugron flinched and bowed his head.

'*Pulvis et umbra sumus*,' he said and, in unison, Adalbert and Gjallandi translated: 'We are dust and shadow.' They stopped and looked at each other, one cool, the other glaring.

Crowbone laughed with delight as the abbot closed his eyes so that the letter was as clear as if it was before him. Then he started to speak.

Later, when Murrough came up to the fire, Kaetilmund raised a questioning eyebrow.

'Do not ask,' Murrough said, shaking his head and the Swede was stunned by the elf-struck bleakness of Murrough's eyes.

THE WITCH-QUEEN'S CREW

Men blew on their numbed fingers and huddled close to the snow-frosted ground, where the mist fingered them with icy talons. The sky was still blue, scudding with white clouds and the great rolling white expanse they had just come up folded away behind them. If Erling squinted, he could just make out the ships, slithered half up out of the grue of ice that wanted to be the Tana River.

'Jiebmaluokta,' Gunnhild said, her breath smoking out from under the veil she wore, a contrivance of silk that showed only her eyes, old as a whale's. She turned her whole upper body, swathed in a white-furred cloak of grey-blue trimmed with red; another swaddled her legs so that only the sealskin toes of her boots peeped out and she had hands thrust in a great muff of white fox. The chair she sat in like a throne had poles thrust through it and the four men who carried her now knelt at each one, panting like dogs.

'What?' her son replied, distracted. This place was already cold and the guide, a Sami supposedly friendly, had disappeared. Gudrod did not like that much.

'Bay of Seals,' Gunnhild answered dreamily, 'in the tongue of the Sami.'

Erling, vicious with hate for her and afraid she might know, thought bitterly that she was the only one enjoying all this. Well, apart from Od, who crouched like an adoring hound, staring up into the veiled face, wrapped in a wolfskin she had given him. Erling did not like the way the boy fawned on her.

Gudrod did not much care what this place was called. When they had heaved six ships into Gjesvaer, old Kol Hallson had welcomed them well enough, but pleaded to go lightly on his stores.

'Haakon Jarl's men have already eaten me out of half the

winter,' he moaned. 'Now there is you – what is so interesting here that brings both Gudrod Eiriksson and the king of Norway's men to Finnmark so late in the year?'

He had been warily respectful when Gunnhild was brought in to the fire all the same and did not stint on his stores after that, though it seemed to consist of whale and walrus and salmon. Gudrod learned that eight ships of the king of Norway had come to Gjesvaer two weeks ago, led by Haakon's Chosen, Hromund Haraldson and including the king's favourite, the thrall Tormod. There was also a Christ priest, Kol recalled, whom no-one liked the look of.

'Is there to be war up here, then?' he asked, alarmed. Gudrod soothed him, for though the steading was small, with almost no men and only three ships, it was the only decent shelter for days in any direction.

Kol lent them Olet, a broad-faced Sami who traded seal and walrus with him. He had, he confessed, offered the man to Hromund and Tormod, but they had refused, because the Christ priest said so. The priest knew the way, Kol said, clearly curious to know where the priest and everyone else seemed to be going. It was clear to Gudrod that this Christ priest was the Drostan everyone had heard of, though he was puzzled why the letter had been written by a priest called Martin and sent to Jarl Orm of the Oathsworn.

Another contender for the prize, Gudrod thought moodily and was not about to tell the Sami guide where they were headed before they left, which was two days later. He did not need Kol adding his interest to the crowd chasing the Bloodaxe.

Kol and the Sami guide made it clear, however, that chasing anything in Finnmark was beyond foolish – it was late in the year for plootering about up the Tana; the long night was closing in and the day scarcely a flicker.

Now Olet the Sami had vanished and Gudrod was hunched like a stunted tree among the rocks, two hundred men shivering around him and the mist trailing hag-hair over them.

Somewhere ahead and heading for the prize was Haakon Jarl's crew and the mad Christ priest, but Gunnhild was certain that they would not get the goddess to part with it. That needed her, she claimed, though Gudrod saw that no-one was happy hearing the word 'goddess'; such magic did not sit well with them.

There was a movement off to one side and men tensed, weapons up; Olet wraithed up, his gait odd, as if he was trying to avoid leaving anything like a mark and the odd furrows and holes he shuffled into existence in the snow seemed to lack any destiny and collapsed as soon as he had passed.

He slid out like a tendril of the mist and moved through the knots of men to Gudrod's side, where he took a knee and wiped his face, thick with bear grease against the cold.

'Nothing,' he said. 'Up ahead are some trees and a little hunting hut. There are reindeer everywhere, those big-horned ones, females fat against the winter. Someone will be watching over them.'

Gudrod did not doubt it; he had felt eyes on him for some time and the place was not helpful – grey rock patched greenish red with lichen, cut with gullies and sudden drops where water was turning to porridge, studded with icing tarns, stuck with little wizened trees like claws, clotted with early snow. He stood up and waved scouts ahead, to right and to left, then started forward, his presence dragging everyone else.

Erling rose up, stiff and cold. If he had known what Gudrod was thinking, he would have agreed and added in the reindeer, which scared him shitless, since they could hardly be seen at all except at the last and stood and stared instead of running off like sensible beasts. The fact that he was afraid of them did not help his mood.

After a toiling climb, they came to the hut, a low affair of stone, the roof a wither of old summer growth and branches. Beyond, a line of stunted grey trees hung with a witch-hair of frost-covered lichen, twisted themselves to the skyline; in the summer, Erling thought, they would be bright and there would be cloudberry bushes too . . .

Gudrod grunted, as if the sight had slotted something into place and now the whole cunning tiling was clear. In fact, he was now thinking it was time to give this up for the day, for plootering about in the sleet and mist as the dark grew was not sensible. Yet the night already seemed interminable.

'Did you see Hrapp? Kjallak?' he asked, naming the leaders of the scouts he had sent out, but Olet shook his head.

'Well,' said Erling, looking at him. 'There is the hut. At least we can shelter from the cold in it.'

There were some two hundred men here; twenty under Hrapp scouted to the east, a similar group under Kjallak to the west, while Olet alone skulked out in front. There were more men back with the ships and Erling, turning to look, swore he could see the red flower of their fires and envied them.

Gudrod did not like the hut, for the mist was closing in and they were going to be stuck there for the night, which was not a prospect with much flavour in it. He said as much, turning to his mother, and Gunnhild, snapping like an annoying dog at the men who were lurching her too much, glared embers through her veil and said: 'Well, you are the man for the leading here – so lead.'

He hated her and feared her, yet he had seen her power, knew it well. She wanted him a king and he had thought he had wanted that, too, like all his brothers – but all his brothers were dead.

'I am after getting cold here,' Erling said pointedly and Gudrod blinked out of the thinking and into his scowl, then nodded. He signalled; men moved forward.

They were creeping-soft, as cautious as rats approaching that hut, along the length of the stream which slid past it, heavy with ice. It started to snow, fine as querned flour.

'Look lads,' said Ozur Rik, pointing with his spear. They

followed it, shaking sweat and meltwater from their eyes to see the reindeer skins pegged out on a wooden frame. They were only half-frozen, newly flayed, a simple domestic task that showed the place had been occupied only recently – perhaps still was.

'A proper cured one of those would be warm,' a man growled.

'The hut,' Gudrod reminded them, more harsh than he had intended and men hunched hastily under his frown. From somewhere in the misted trees came a coughing bark; those who had heard it before knew it as one of the reindeer, but most thought it was a loose hound.

'Hold the dog,' a man called Myrkjartan shouted, which caused chuckles, for it was the traditional greeting you gave to announce to a hov that you were no threat, even though you were arriving as a stranger.

Then all the animals of the stunted wood rose up on their hind legs and howled down on them out of the misted trees.

The Borg, Moray, at the same time . . .

CROWBONE'S CREW

The snow lay clumped on the sand, packed and powdered where the water had not melted it away; pools crackled with ice, luminous in a world of eldritch moonlight almost clear as day. The world seemed filled with the flicker of *alfar*, those hidden beings at the edge of vision, so that folk spoke in low voices or even whispers, touching iron for warding as they banked up fires and made their shelters.

To the left, Crowbone saw the bulk of the fort that gave the place its name, perched on a headland reached by a narrow neck. It had many names – Torridun, in the days when Sigurd of Orkney had come and pillaged it. Torfness, too, after the way the people who lived here cut up turves that burned like wood or coals.

Borg – fortress – was the best name for it all the same, thought Crowbone. In the years between Sigurd and now, the place had recovered itself. Three walls now stretched across the narrow neck and a great semi-circle of rampart behind that, all oak and iron and stone, so that the Bull Kings who claimed Moray could strut and trade.

Strange folk, for the most part, who spoke like the Irish and wore tunics and breeks woven in a pattern of squares – when they wore breeks at all – and with a fringing along the bottom. It kept the damp from sucking up from the hem, Bergliot said to those who marvelled at it, which was a sensible thing, especially for the long skirts of the women.

Adalbert said the Old Romans had called them *pictii*, meaning Painted People and so called because they had skin-marked their faces in blue. They named them with reverence, all the same, for these *pictii* were one of the few folk the Old Romans failed to conquer – but that was then and this was now.

They were sensible folk, Murrough thought, but they had had their day, the Bull Kings of the north, with their skin-markings and their strutting nobles and their endless chipping away on stones. Worse than the Norse, the Irisher thought to himself, for stone marks no-one but themselves could properly read and understand.

Scores of those stones lined the road up to the gate of the place and Crowbone was aware of the effect, knew it for what it was – another piece in the game of kings. Look at us, the stones demanded. Look at us, see the power and time it took to make and raise us. Only a great people can do this. We are choosers of the slain.

Yet three stones had started to lean drunkenly to one side, the foundations eroded, and Crowbone knew these people's greatness was the same. Sooner rather than later, the Norse of Orkney would come and take the entire of Moray, if only to keep the Albans of the south from doing the same.

Meanwhile, though, there were declarations of peaceful intent to be made and gifts to be given to appease the haughty nobles of the place with their silly, fringed, wool tunics and Irish shoes. Of course, the nobles were sensible enough to keep the scores of Norse outside their fortress, camped on the great curve of bay between the borg and the town. The town was prepared to sigh with relief that the Norse were not about to rampage through them – and, once they learned that the men had good weight silver about them, flocked out to invite them in.

Crowbone was happy, all in all, as he sat down to feast with the nobles of Borg, for he had learned that Martin had been here and left for Norway and Haakon Jarl. The letter to Orm had been flat and cold, scarcely surprising since they were far from friends, yet it revealed what Martin wanted and where he was headed to get the Bloodaxe.

Now Crowbone knew, though had turned all the words of it over in his head as if examining suspect coin and still could not work out whether Orm was playing him false or not. He could not be sure that Hoskuld had not been charged to tell him of the letter when the time was right – like a bairn at learning, Crowbone thought bitterly. Yet Hoskuld had tried to run from him – though Crowbone was nagged with the idea that he might have caused that himself with his harshness.

Yet he was content. His men were in shelters on a cold beach, but they were used to colder still and he had handed them out buckets of silver, so that there was warmth and comfort to be had for a price in the town.

The silver had come from Orkney and the glow of it, the sheer surprise of it, still made Crowbone smile.

From Hy they had sailed for Orkney and come ashore at Sand Vik, storming through the creaming surf and forming up for a fight, Crowbone's heart thundering as it never had before at the prospect of taking on the Witch-Queen, bane of his life – except that no enemy force appeared. Crowbone was confused by this, uncertain of whether to plough on to the hall and its huddle of buildings and did the worst thing possible – nothing at all. In the end, just as he cursed his uncertainty and made his mind up, Stick-Starer called out that riders were coming.

A fistful of men stopped a long bowshot away and dismounted. A man held the little stiff-maned ponies and the rest trudged towards them, one holding up a white shield.

'They want to talk,' Mar declared, which was so obvious that Crowbone scoured him with a glance that made him flush. He called out Murrough and Kaetilmund, with the Stooping Hawk snapping out behind him as he walked. He indicated to Gjallandi to join them, because the man was a skald and he wanted this remembered – and the priest, Adalbert, still getting his land-legs back and whey-faced from bokking up his dinner as an offering to the goddess Ran.

There were four Orkneymen in all, all ring-mailed and armed. One carried the raven banner – the *hrafnsmerki* – and Crowbone marked him; it was said that the banner had been made by Gunnhild, or one of her kind and that it made sure of victory, even as it guaranteed the death of the man who carried it.

The man, stern and spade-bearded, met Crowbone's gaze coolly enough, but had the flat, grey eyes of the hopeless; later, Murrough wondered what made a man take the pole of that banner in his hand and Kaetilmund said a woman was at the bottom of it, needing money and driving the fool to fame. Crowbone did not answer, but he knew the truth; the man's jarl, to whom the banner-bearer had oathed away his own reason, had chosen him as the slain.

One other was there to defend the banner and he held high the white shield of peace. The other two were chieftains, for sure, in their best war gear of brass-dagged long coats of rings and fancy silver-ended swords – one older and one young, built like a barrel of ale.

'I am Arnfinn Thorfinsson,' the older one said, peeling off his helmet to let the grey-streaked hair be ruffled by the sea breeze. 'This is Sigurd, son of my brother Hlodvir and brought here for the learning in it.'

Crowbone nodded. Sigurd was older than Crowbone by two or three years, no more, and one day would be a ruler of Orkney – if his father lived and his uncles let him. Crowbone searched the boy's face for a sign, a mark, anything that revealed why he had been picked for greatness and not another. There was nothing but his red-flushed cheeks and a lopsided half-grin.

'Olaf,' he said, before the silence grew insulting, 'son of Tryggve. I am a true prince of Norway and the rightful king.'

'Just so,' Arnfinn declared. 'I had heard this. You have come for my wife's mother, of course and her son, the last of the brood. Did you know he was the one who killed your father? He tells of it often, for it was the first man he cut down in a fight and he is very proud that it was a king who blooded him.'

Crowbone raised an eyebrow. Was the man deliberately trying to provoke? Yet Arnfinn's face was bland, almost cheerful.

'Gunnhild and her son are gone, with a wheen of my men. Good riddance I say, even if it means I have fewer men than I would like if it comes to a fight. My wife is of the same mind, for she is nothing like her mother at all.'

Crowbone saw it then, a flare like flint and steel sparking in his head. Gunnhild and Gudrod had gone, following the instructions in the monk-message and taking a lot of Arnfinn's men with them, so that Orkney was only lightly defended. Arnfinn wanted to deal and Crowbone had an idea what he wanted thrown into the trade.

When he realised what the offer was, the force of it took his breath away. Arnfinn hauled out buckets of silver and offered supplies for Crowbone and all he seemingly wanted was for Crowbone's men to go away without a fight. All they took in exchange was the body of Rovald, who had wheezed his last and was to be decently howed up.

'Just like that,' Gjallandi declared into the delight of men loading the stuff on the ships. 'With no fighting at all, only the threat of it. Young Crowbone here did not as much as wave his sword and all of Orkney handed him its riches.'

The knowledge that silver could be had for the threat stayed with them all the way to Borg and sat beside Crowbone on the Bull Kings' feast bench as men roared and boasted and threw bones at each other. Crowbone smiled and nodded, but kept his counsel.

It did no harm for the men to think that Arnfinn and the rest of Orkney had handed out silver out of fear, but the truth was another piece in the game of kings, a truth arranged in private in the dim dark of the hall; if Gunnhild and Gudrod came back from this axe hunt, Arnfinn would be a man disappointed in the true prince of Norway. It was ceasing to surprise Crowbone, the way folk were prepared to pay to be rid of the unwanted.

When sufficient honour to each other had been done, Crowbone and the others he had brought – Kaetilmund, Onund and Murrough, who were the captains of his other three ships – thanked their drunken *pictii* hosts, wrapped themselves in their cloaks and walked out of the gate and back down the avenue of Bull stones, round to the curve of bay and bright red fire-flowers there.

'One day,' Murrough said, looking back at the bulk of the fort, 'better men will make these strutters bow the knee.'

'You are only annoyed because they say a man who fights with an axe is no man at all,' Onund chided and Murrough chuckled in the dark.

'Nor do they fight with the bow,' he added and shook his head. 'It is a wonder they have endured this long, what with all that and their silly little square shields and their tunics you could play 'tafl on.'

Crowbone was only happy to be leaving them entirely, though he notched the place in the tally stick of his head; one day, when Norway was his, this would be a good stepping stone for the rest of the north of Alba.

Back at the camp, music filtered, strange and fine in the night, as someone plucked strings in a delicate, leaping lilt. Men shuffled in a stamping jig, while others kept time beating hands on thighs and laughing; flames danced shadows and the smell of cooking was a comfort wafted on the cold wash of night air.

Crowbone came into the middle of them, grinning and getting chaffered about him deigning to join them from his richer revels; he acknowledged it with a good-natured wave and came up to the fire and the player. It was Bergliot, who smiled at him but did not stop her fast fingering of the instrument.

It was a *gusli*, which one of the Slavs from Kiev had brought with him, a five-stringed affair called *krylovidnye* which meant 'shaped like a wing'. There was another type, bigger and shaped like a helmet and with more string, but this was a good travelling instrument and Bergliot played it well. When she finished, he graciously said so and she flashed flame-dyed teeth across the fire at him.

'Shall I play you something?' she demanded sweetly. 'A wee cradlesong, perhaps, like your ma no doubt did for you to sugar your dreams.'

'My ma never played such,' he answered, harsh as a crow's laugh. 'Thralls were not allowed instruments and I was usually chained to the privy, so there was nothing much that could sweeten my dreams save revenge on those who did it to us.'

There was silence at that, both from those who knew the

tale of Crowbone's past and those finding out about it for the first time. Everyone now knew that the reason they had gone to Orkney was to visit that revenge on Gunnhild. Still, that and the pursuit of an axe now seemed better business with silver weighing the purses tucked under armpits or between their balls and, besides, this so-called prince of Norway had plucked most of them from ruin in Dyfflin.

Bergliot went still and quiet, her eyes bright in the firelight and so close to tears, it seemed to Crowbone, that he felt ashamed at having been so snarling.

'She did tell me stories, though,' he added lamely and the tension slid away from the fire. Bergliot wavered up a smile.

'Long ago in Lord Novgorod the Great, lived a young musician,' Crowbone said suddenly and there was a wind of sighing as those closest leaned in to hear better. 'Every day, a rich merchant or noble would send a messenger to this man's door, calling him to play at a feast. The musician would grab his twelve-string *gusli* and rush to the banquet hall and make them dance. The host would pass him a few small coins and let him eat his fill from the leftovers – on such as he was given did the musician live.'

'My life entirely,' said the owner of the *gusli* sadly, a man called Hrolfr, and those who knew him laughed.

'Then you will know this man's friends,' Crowbone went on, 'who would often ask how he could survive on so little. "It's not so bad," the man would reply. "I go to a different feast each day, play the music I love and watch it set a whole room dancing."'

Crowbone paused. 'Now that I think of it, I am sure – more than sure – that his name was Hrolfr.'

People laughed at that and clapped the man from Novgorod on the back, he beaming back at them. Crowbone saw Bergliot, her eyes round and bright as an owl.

'Yet,' Crowbone went on as more men filtered quietly in, attracted by the news that a story was being told, 'sometimes

Hrolfr was lonely. The maidens who danced gaily to his music at the feasts would often smile at him and more than one had set his heart on fire. But they were rich and he lived on thrown coins and leftovers and not one of them would think of being his.

'One lonely evening, Hrolfr walked sadly beyond the city walls and down along the broad River Volkhov. He came to his favourite spot on the bank and set his *gusli* on his lap. "My lovely River Volkhov," he said with a sigh. "If only you were a woman, I'd marry you and live with you here in the city I love."'

'It is true,' Hrolfr burst out. 'Is there another city such as Lord Novgorod the Great in all the world? Is there any better place to be?'

'Silent is a better place to be,' growled Stick-Starer from the shadows and Hrolfr, prepared to argue the point, was patted and soothed to be quiet.

'Hrolfr played and the notes of his *gusli* floated over the Volkhov,' Crowbone continued. 'All at once a large shape rose from the water and Hrolfr yelled with fear. Before him stood a huge man, with a crown crusted with jewels like barnacles, with a great neck veil of pearls and, under it, a flowing mane of seaweed hair. "Musician," said the man, "behold Aegir, King of the Waters. To this river I have come to visit one of my daughters, the Princess Volkhova. Your sweet music reached us on the river bottom, where it pleased us greatly." It was all Hrolfr could do to stammer his thanks.

'The King said that he would soon return to his own palace and that he wanted Hrolfr to play there at a feast. "Gladly," said Hrolfr. "But where is it? And how do I get there?" The King laughed. "Why, under the sea, of course. You will find your way – but meanwhile, you need not wait for your reward." The king dropped a large fish at Hrolfr's feet. A fish with golden scales, which turned to solid gold as it stiffened and died.

'Hrolfr was astounded, but the King waved a dismissive hand. "Say no more," he said. "Music is worth far more than gold. If the world was fair, you would have your fill of riches and no rose would have thorns." And with a splash, he sank in the river and was gone.'

'Heya!' bellowed a voice. 'I am from Novgorod and all I ever got from the Volkhov was a chill.'

'You cannot play as much as a bone flute, Wermund, so that is hardly a surprise,' yelled a reply and people ordered them to whisht. Crowbone waited, then went on.

'Hrolfr sold the golden fish to an astonished merchant, then left Novgorod that very day on a ship, down the Volkhov, across Lake Ladoga and into the Baltic Sea. As it sped above the deep water, he peered over the rail. "The sea is big enough to swallow whales," he murmured. "How can I ever find the palace?" Just then, the ship shuddered to a halt. The wind filled the sails, yet the ship stood still, as if a giant hand had grasped it. The sailors grew afraid.'

'I know these sailors,' Adalbert interrupted. '*Illi robur et aes triplex circa pectus erat, qui fragilem truci commisit pelago ratem primus.*'

'No, no,' Crowbone shouted as Adalbert opened his mouth to translate. 'Let me. As hard as – something – wood, I think – and three bronzes once is . . . the heart of him who . . . who . . . who . . .'

'Is there an owl in this story?' demanded Stick-Starer.

'Or does it go on in the tongue of Christ priests?' added Kaetilmund. 'If so, I will need help with it.'

'Not bad,' Adalbert admitted, ignoring them all, 'but it should be: *As hard as oak and three times bronze was the heart of him who first committed a fragile vessel to the keeping of wild waves.* Horatius.'

'Was this Horatius on the ship then?' bawled Hrolfr. 'What happened to me?'

Crowbone held up his hands and smiled. Adalbert sat,

stunned by the speed at which the youth was mastering the Latin that had taken the monk years to perfect.

'The sailors prayed for their lives,' Crowbone went on. '"Do not be troubled," called Hrolfr. "I know the one he seeks." And clutching his *gusli*, he climbed the railing and, before any could lay hold of him, jumped into the waves.'

'Not likely,' Stick-Starer declared, outraged and men laughed. Crowbone, ignoring them, continued.

'Down sank Hrolfr, down all the way to the sea floor, where he saw, in the dim light, a white stone borg, big as the one to our left. He passed through a coral gate, only now beginning to marvel at how he was alive and breathing like a fish. As he reached the huge wall doors, they swung open to reveal a giant hall. The elegant room was filled with guests and thralls, all of them from under the oceans. Herring and cod and sand eels and sea scorpions, crabs and lobsters, starfish and squid, giant sturgeon and a brace of whales.

'Standing among the guests were dozens of maidens – river nymphs, the Sea King's daughters. On a great High Seat at the end of the hall sat Aegir and his Queen, Ran, her hair green as wrack and waving in the eddies. "You're just in time," called the King. "Let the dance begin."'

Crowbone paused and the listeners shifted and grunted in their eagerness for him to go on. He took a breath.

'Soon the whole sea floor cavorted. The river maidens leaped and spun and the King himself joined the dance, robe swirling like rippling sand, his hair streaming like weed. Above, though Hrolfr did not know it, the waves lashed and broke on the shore; ships were whirled like wood chips. By the end of the night, Hrolfr's fingers were raw and the King well pleased – so much so that he wanted to marry Hrolfr to one of his daughters and keep him beneath the sea. "Your Greatness," said Hrolfr carefully. "This is not my home. I love my city of Novgorod."'

'Just as well,' Wermund interrupted, nudging the real Hrolfr

275

hard in the back. 'Your ale would always be salty and watered down there, for sure.'

'But the King insisted and the one he chose was the Princess Volkhova,' Crowbone said, not even hearing Wermund. 'She stepped forward, her eyes shining like river pearls. She had thrilled to the music Hrolfr had played on the shore, she announced, and now she had him as husband.'

'Hrolfr marvelled at the beauty of the princess, but Queen Ran leaned over so that her wrack-green hair hung close to his cheek and said softly: "If you but once kiss or embrace her, you can never return to your city again."'

'That night, Hrolfr lay beside his bride on a bed of seaweed and sand and fine-crushed pearls – and each time he thought of her loveliness, the Queen's words came back to him and his arms lay frozen at his sides.'

'Aye, there's the lie of this tale, right there,' growled Murrough from the back, his voice thick with bitter irony and yet no-one laughed, hanging on the lips of their young jarl.

'When Hrolfr awoke the next morning,' Crowbone said, 'he felt sunlight on his face, opened his eyes and saw beside him . . . not the Princess but the River Volkhov. He was back in Lord Novgorod the Great. "My home," said Hrolfr and he wept.'

Crowbone stopped, confused by the sudden rush of memories, of his mother's voice, of the privy chain and Orm looking down on him on the day he had released him, standing in Klerkon's winter-steading with the light dappling through the withy.

'For joy at his return,' he faltered. 'Or sadness at his loss.'

'Or both,' said Bergliot, smiling.

She came to him later, of course, as he knew she would, silent and drifting as seaweed through the cold dark, while Hrolfr played cradlesongs for the men and heard the tale of himself repeated back and forth as if it had been true.

'Will you wake by the Volkhov?' she said, sliding the length of her body against his, hot as if it had come from the forge, the fork between her legs hotter still as she moulded it to his thigh.

'Nei. Drowned in the deep,' he said, reaching for her and she laughed, low in her throat.

Later, snugged in the harbour of his arms, she asked what had happened to the story-Hrolfr and Crowbone told her – he became a merchant, and in time, the richest man in Novgorod, married a fine young woman and had strong sons, at whose weddings he played the *gusli*.

He was happy, Crowbone told her, yet sometimes on a quiet evening he would walk out to the river and send his music over the water. Sometimes a lovely head would rise from the river to listen. Or perhaps it was just moonshadow on the Volkhov.

She slept, her cheek resting on his shoulder and he could feel her breathe like the sea on a shore, feel the suck and sigh of her and he stayed as still as possible all night, trying not to disturb her, trying to keep her close and afraid that he might succeed.

ELEVEN

Finnmark, near Surman Suuhun, the Jul feast . . .

MARTIN

THE scouts came in as the snow thickened and started to swirl, cutting the iron-grey tumble of mountains to dim shadows. They had seen nothing, they said to Hromund, but had shot a reindeer. They pointedly tried not to speak directly to Tormod at all, for he was a thrall and Tormod, used to it, merely listened and spoke quietly to Hromund when they were standing apart from others.

'Nothing?' Tormod said in a voice that dripped bile. Hromund scrubbed his nit-cropped hair, which gave him his by-name, Bursta-Kollr – Bristle Scalp.

'Eindride is a good man,' he said stubbornly, while the good man himself laboured with others to string the buck up by the heel tendons. 'A master bowman, too.'

'I see he shoots well,' Tormod answered patiently, 'which must mean he has good eyes. Yet he has seen no sign of the enemy?'

'Other than the one I shot earlier,' growled a voice, so close to Tormod's ear that he smelled the rank breath and saw the smoke of it, which made him spring back, startled. Eindride grinned out of the ice-spattered matting of his beard.

'I meant no disrespect,' Tormod declared and Eindride looked at him, as if seeing him for the first time.

'If I thought that,' he answered, 'I would beat you, thrall-born.'

Tormod's face flamed; he knew Eindride was a rich *bondi* in Óðinssalr in the Trondelag, probably the oldest farm in the world, yet the thrall did not like to be reminded of his true status for he was Haakon's wisest advisor and opened his mouth to say so.

'Has he spoken yet?' Hromund demanded, before matters welled up. Eindride shrugged and looked over to where the Sami hung, like the buck from a frozen tree branch, by his heel tendons. Eindride had brought him into the shivering camp like a hunting prize from the last scout he had done.

'Ask the Christ priest,' he answered bitterly, then spat and swaggered away to oversee the butchering of the buck. Tormod watched them tie off the bowels, draw out the guts, belly, liver, spleen, gall, lungs and heart. Rumps and hams, ribs and loin were all neatly cut out and wrapped, yet there was still much left on the carcass. Men ate the cooling liver, chewing with relish and grinning with blood on their teeth. It was the Jul feast and they had been drinking *minni* toasts with the last of their strong ale.

The king's thrall swallowed his anger. Nearby hung the Sami, swinging like the buck and yet able to see what was being done to it – which was, no doubt, part of the Christ priest's plan.

Hromund, frowning, went over to where Martin hovered, hunched and hirpling back and forth from his crude sail shelter to a fire. A dark dwarf, the Chosen Man thought miserably. This was the place for such matters, for sure, a place of the *jötnar*, those blood-thirsting giants who were enemies of Asgard's gods and kept at bay only by the threat of Thor's own Hammer.

Not for the first time, he wondered at the sense of this untimely journey through the high mountains in search of . . . what? A legend? Yet, he thought to himself, if it were true, if the Bloodaxe of Eirik was somewhere in these mountains, then the one who possessed it had power. You take Odin's Daughter to wife and you got One-Eye as your in-law – Hromund shivered at that thought. He would make you king, as the saga told it, then one day turn the axe on you, laughing.

The Sami groaned and swung. There were raw festering marks on him, blackened at the edges – crosses, Hromund saw and he felt his mouth fill with saliva and spat it out.

Martin saw it as he returned the iron cross to the flames and curled his lip. Hromund, of course, was a heathen, like all of them in Norway, so he did not see the benefit of God. The Sami did and Martin smiled at what the man had already babbled – in Norse as Martin had surmised would be so when the man was brought in, shot through the thigh by Eindride. He had never seen the guide he had refused from old Jarl Kol, but he had known at once that this Sami was the one.

A hunter and trader, for sure, this Sami who wore good north wool and knew Norse well enough, even if he knew nothing about axes, which Martin had suspected when he had the man strung up. He had learned since that the man's name was Olet and that he had been sent, as Martin had thought, by Jarl Kol with the men from Orkney – with the Witch-Queen Gunnhild, he said. She has power, he said, enough to face the goddess of the mountain. He also knew the place Martin sought and, in the end, confirmed it, whimpering.

Surman Suuhun. Their heathen way of saying 'the mouth of death'. Each time a holy cross was placed on his flesh, red-heated from the fire, fierce with the power of God, the man gasped out, screaming, '*Surman Suuhun.*'

'And the enemy?' Hromund asked after Martin had explained all this, wiping his hands on the uneven, ragged dags of his robe.

'What enemy?' Martin retorted scathingly. 'There are so many Norway men here that these mountain hunters are no threat. Gudrod and the Witch have got ahead of us, all the same – though all that means is that they do all the fighting.'

Hromund scowled at the implied slur on his leadership and was about to bark back when the Sami grunted. They both turned, astonished to see that he grinned bloodily, a horror made worse by his face being upside down.

'She will take you all,' he slurred through the blood of his own bitten lip. 'Ajatar's handmaiden.'

'Who is Ajatar?' Martin demanded at once, for he had never heard Gunnhild called that before. An arrow struck the Sami as he swung, took him in the back and came out through his front in a gout of blood, with heart meat snagged on it. He arched for the last time and screamed.

Hromund and Martin pitched to the snow-covered ground, yelling; men scattered like chickens and there was shouting; someone screamed. Then silence.

By the time men had gone out of the camp to look, Hromund knew it was pointless; no-one would be found, a fact which Tormod stated, his voice a sneer at Eindride, who flushed. The bowman knew he and his men had missed the hidden Sami and marvelled at that – even on this almost bare landscape of tumbled rock and lichen and gnarled, twisted trees, he had not seen them.

Yet he cut the arrow from the dead Olet and studied it, as if it would provide some clue, while the snow whirled in and around them like white bees. A slender shaft, blackened with pitch, fletched with owl feathers. A short arrow, so the bows were wood and sinew, not powerful, but enough, all the same, to kill a man with no protection – or even with if they were shot true.

Eindride had no doubt these bowmen could shoot true. He picked up the bow the dead Sami hunter had been using and saw that it could easily have shot this arrow, noted the soft fur puffs round the string below the bow tips to muffle the sound of the release. Pitch-blackened arrows used on a bow that shot them silently – night hunters, too, then.

'They do not want us to get to where we want to go,' Hromund said, as men went back to cooking and making what shelters they could against the snow. Martin, blinking flakes from his eyelashes, grinned his black grin.

'Up is where we go,' he said and pointed to the tallest of the mountains, now no more than a shade in the white whirl. 'Up and fast, to get there just as the Witch finds out that God will not let her have the prize.'

Hromund knew where he pointed, for they had been seeing it for days, the great grim fang of it. He shivered and not just with the cold; the smell of cooking deer mingled with the charred stink of the cross-burned Sami and, suddenly, Haakon's Chosen Man had no appetite. Worse than that, the mountain they were heading for smoked, a plume curling from the side of it like the tail of a snow wolf.

The drum started to sound like a distant woodpecker, insistent as a racing heartbeat. When the *juoiggus* chanting came with it, he felt sick and more afraid than he had ever been in his life.

Finnmark, the same day . . .

CROWBONE'S CREW

The snow eased, started to fall in smaller and smaller flakes, until it was fine as emperor salt, sifting through the short day into long cold nights dark as raven wings save for the faint flickers of green moving like skeins of yarn far to the north.

Fox fires, Svenke Klak declared and those who had been in the high north before agreed. They heralded plague and pest some said, though Onund grunted like a rutting deer at that.

'All it means,' he said, 'is that a cold is coming that will freeze fire. I had that from Finn Horsehead, who fears nothing.'

Kaetilmund had heard Finn say that once, but it was no comfort, as he whispered to Murrough when they were close together, drip-nosed by fires that never seemed to get them warm.

'We have little provision for this,' he muttered, which was only the truth and men knew it, giving the prince harsh glances when they thought he could not see – yet marvelling at how he sat, seemingly unaware of the cold, wrapped in a dirty-white cloak that was too small for him, with a furred collar patched and mangy.

Those who knew told them the cloak had been his first present from Vladimir of Kiev and he had been nine, so it was old, yet precious. He had had it when he, Vladimir, Orm and all the rest of the Oathsworn went into the Great White, the winter steppe, to hunt out Atil's treasure. Small wonder the youth did not feel the cold, after that.

Crowbone was freezing, but would not show it, not even to Bergliot. He had not wanted to bring her further than Gjesvaer, but she would not be left and Crowbone did not trust Kol Hallson. The old jarl had had more than enough of visitors and Crowbone had come late to the feast, it seemed, for Haakon Jarl's men, followed by Gunnhild and Gudrod, had all chewed their way through his winter stores.

'Now there is you,' he declared and was surly because, though he had heard of Crowbone and the Oathsworn even this far north, he thought the youth arrogant and with no claim to the title of prince at all. Worse than all that was the thought of what was happening in the Sami lands to have brought all these folk and whether there was profit in it that he was missing out on.

'I have nothing left to give you,' he said and Crowbone, who had been polite in the hope that Bergliot could be left, lost his temper with the old man, sitting on his High Seat with his great moustaches and his belly and his bowl-cut hair. He looked like a walrus with a bird's nest upturned on its head, Crowbone thought and made the mistake of saying so.

It had not been entirely wise, as Stick-Starer and Onund and Kaetilmund and all the others had pointed out when they were forced back to their ships empty-handed – Mar simply scowled – until Crowbone bellowed at them to leave him be.

So they did, in a sullen, cold silence, all the way here – which was not even the best harbour for ships. That was taken by many longships belonging to Haakon Jarl and they had scudded past them like a rat looking for a drain, then approached the next seeming safe berth with caution, half-expecting to find the Witch-Queen's crew. Crowbone did not know whether to be happy that they were nowhere to be seen, or unhappy to think of them lurking a short sail down the coast.

Stick-Starer and a handful were left with the ships and the rest went on towards the mountains; the only one who kept close to Crowbone now was Bergliot, which did not help for it was clear what was going on between him and the woman and men denied the same sweetness and warmth drew their brows down and muttered together with Mar.

'Not, mind you,' Mar was forced to admit, bringing bitter laughs from the growlers, 'that I think I could water my colt there, for I remember her too much as Berto and that has a diminishing effect.'

They struggled into the mountains and came upon spoor almost at once – a snapped boot toggle, a broken horn spoon – that told them they were on the right trail, following northmen, though they did not know who. Others had questions on the subject.

'Following them to where?' Mar demanded as they huddled into the long night. 'For what? For an axe? There is no plunder in this for us – only for this prince we have tied ourselves to.'

He said this to the men from Ireland, all the same, not to

his former Red Brothers, or to the old Oathsworn, for he could not be sure that they would listen kindly to him.

Then Vandrad Sygni loped in through the snow with an arrow in one hand and a tunic in the other, neither of them his. The tunic was old and patched and had been blue once, but it was clotted with frozen blood now. The arrow was strange, black and fletched with owl feathers. Crowbone, sitting with the yellow dog and grateful as much for the friendship as the heat, looked at the archer's face and silently followed him back to where he had found these treasures.

He led them to a small clearing in the tumble of rocks, patched with snow and lichen. Men gathered round, looking nervously right and left when they could tear their eyes from what had been done.

'Killed by arrows,' Kaetilmund said. 'Howed up in rocks, as was proper – then some whoresons dug them up.'

'For the weapons,' said a man called Thorgils, one of the old Red Brothers. 'They did that out in the Khazar lands, too, so that we had to break spears and swords and burn the bodies.'

There were twenty bodies and all of them blue-white and bloodless, gashes like lipless mouths, frozen with hands on their breasts, though the fingers had been broken to prise good blades from them.

'Who are they?' Crowbone asked and a voice answered, thick and savagely bitter: 'Norsemen. Like us.'

Crowbone knew it was Mar and ignored it; soon enough, he would have to deal with Iron Beard, but this was not the place.

Onund straightened stiffly from one body and held out his hand; folk craned to see. It was a little ship with a dragon-prow, a neck ornament moulded from pewter and torn from its leather thong. Those who knew the style nodded.

'Orkney made,' Onund confirmed and Crowbone stroked his hoar-frosted beard. So Gunnhild and her last son had run into trouble – the thought was warming, though he kept the smile to himself.

It grew colder when they came on more of the same. By the time they had tallied past a hundred, men were working saliva into dry mouths and wondering why they were ploughing on along the same bloody furrow.

The last in this rimed knot of tragedy consisted of thirty-two dead and none of them had been howed up, just left to lie along either bank of a frozen stream, fringed with dwarven, snow-laden pines. Men hauled out weapons and crouched a little, like dogs expecting a kick – unburied bodies meant the survivors, if any, had fled and left them, which meant the attackers were still about.

Then, sudden as a hand-clap, the demons of the mountains came howling out at them in a shower of arrows and throwing spears and a mad, leaping charge. One minute men were turning this way and that, looking at the snow-shrouded tree line, the next, the world was full of shrieking horror.

'Form! Form!' bawled Kaetilmund, but some men broke and ran, yelling, sliding, tumbling over and over and cracking themselves on the iced rocks. Those left turned to fight, hard-eyed and snarling, grim as cliffs, sliding towards Crowbone and Kaetilmund like filings to a lodestone.

They took the first rush of spears and arrows clattering on their shields, then lifted their hoared eyebrows and saw the furred faces, ears and whiskers and fanged muzzles. Lesser men would have had trouble – the ones who ran, or wallowed in confusion, died for it – but even the ones who kept facing to the front felt their bowels opening. Dry-mouthed, they had to force themselves to stay rooted at the sight of animals risen on their hindlegs and snarling.

It was Bergliot who ended it. She nocked and shot as the howlers started moving down on the huddled band. The arrow took one of the beasts in the face and there was a yelp of pain; the beast muzzle seemed to come apart and the body fell the other way, a tangle of limbs with a flat face, bloodied and unbearded and undeniably Sami.

'They are men!' roared Murrough and, even those whose minds were numbed by the surprise and shock of it were so honed with war that their limbs knew what to do. Arms brought shields and edges up; legs moved and men slid so swiftly together that shoulders were bruised in the clash. Others, too slow to reach the shieldwall, stumbled into fighting pairs.

They are men. The roar went up, a fire that leaped from head to head. They are men and so could die.

There was a skidding moment or two, then, as the enemy felt the new resistance. They were not beasts, as Bergliot had revealed, but men in furs and masks made from the heads and muzzles of animals – wolf and fox and bear, the snarling jowled heads fitted over their own, the little ears sticking up, the withered muzzles bared with loosened fangs; from inside, he saw white eyes gleam.

A few black arrows flew, shot by unseen archers from behind the others; one shaft whirred over the front rank and hit the helmet of a man next to Onund with a clang that rattled him sideways, then it spun off, skittering dangerously over the iced rocks. The beast-men roared up enough courage to hurl themselves on the shieldwall.

Crowbone had his shield on his back, which he realised was foolish, but it was too late to swing it free. He dragged out his sword as the Sami crashed like a wave on the wall of linden shields, then washed round the flanks, shrieking and screaming; a northman spun backwards and landed on his arse, most of his face punched in with a spear – Hrolfr, the *gusli* player, Crowbone saw dully.

The one who did it gave a fighting roar out of the depths of his bobbing bear mask, a great black and brown affair with puckered eye pits. He hefted the bloody spear – then hurled it through the gap at Crowbone.

No shield – I look like an easy mark, Crowbone thought with snow-crisp clarity as the spear came at him, flexing and spinning, the gore spuming off the iron tip, which grew larger and larger. He saw the pitted head of it, the notched edge as he twisted sideways to let it half pass him. He watched his hand come up, though it looked like it belonged to someone else – then he snatched the spear in a fist, reversed it and hurled it back, all in an eyeblink.

A bad throw, he thought as the spear spun from his hand; I must work on that left, it is weaker than the right. It carved to the right of the bear mask and the man howled with surprise and fear, his eyes following the spear as it clattered to the ground, as if it was a snake about to coil and spring at him.

The real danger stepped in close to him, close enough to see the weathered yellow fangs and old leather lips of the bear jaw, to see the Sami's sweat and charcoal streaked face deep in the maw of it, the eyes wide and white. Then Crowbone stuck him under the right ribs with the sword, once, twice, three times, hard enough for the round, blunt point to rip him off his feet, on the last blow the beast-man falling away, groaning.

Another turned this way and that, wild and uncertain, so Crowbone closed with him quickly, before he could gather courage and sense round him like a cloak on a cold day. He was larger than the rest of them, Crowbone noted, though still a half-head shorter than any of us. He had the mask of a fox, with the russet ears perked up on his head – more immediately, Crowbone saw that the man carried a good Norse sword and an axe, but by the time Foxmask had worked out what was happening and which one to use, Crowbone had slashed a second mouth for him.

The man fell backwards on his arse, making guh-guh sounds and the blood slicked the haft of the sword, so that it slithered out of Crowbone's hand as he spun, looking for another to fight.

Weaponless, he crouched and looked wildly around – the yellow dog sped past him, boring in hard and snarling on another of the masked Sami, barging him off his feet and scrabbling to get at the man's throat. Eventually, Svenke killed the man and stopped him screaming, which was a relief for everyone; by then the Sami's forearms were shredded by the yellow bitch's fangs.

They had no belly for it, these little mountain men. A shower of spears and arrows and the sight of them in their beast masks and furs had always worked before, sending Gunnhild's Orkneymen running and shrieking to be easily cut down.

We are different, Crowbone exulted and howled it out until the cords of his neck hurt, as different from what the Sami had faced before as lambs to wolves.

'You are Olaf's men,' he screamed and the warriors bellowed agreement, slashed and carved their beast-masked enemy until they fled, yelping, back up into the misted tree-line. Those chasing them stopped, panting and retching, hands on knees and sweating in the iced air; breath and steam smoked as if the place burned.

Crowbone stumbled over to collect his sword, half-dazedly wiping it clean with snow, while the man whose throat he had slit choked on his own blood, his hands empty of Norse-forged weapons now, grasping like claws as if trying to swim to the surface of water.

'You have blood on you,' Murrough noted.

'His,' Crowbone answered, jerking his chin at the gargler.

'That was a wee dunt,' Murrough said cheerfully, looking round. 'Now these creatures know who they fight – that was a fine trick with the spear, all the same. Is it hard to learn?'

This was said loud enough for others to hear and they growled out agreements; those who had not seen it were told of their young prince's hand skill while they poked among the dead. Crowbone spoke soft to Murrough, not wanting to ruin what he had made, but pointing out their own dead and silently sending him to find out the tally for this day.

He was back soon enough – Hrolfr was dead, as well as a Jutlander called Lief and a Saxlander called Taks. Mar and Vandrad Sygni were missing. Crowbone did not know much about Lief save that he played 'tafl well but Taks did good leatherwork and everyone would miss his shoe repairs. Hrolfr, though, was a loss that brought something sharp into Crowbone's throat, remembering the skill of the man's playing. Vandrad and Mar were more of a worry, all the same – they were two of the three best trackers and the third had four legs.

'Aye, well,' said Kaetilmund moodily, scrubbing the rain off his face. 'They ran – I think Mar went off and Vandrad went after him in anger. Odin's bones, though, matters could have been worse.'

'Just so,' agreed Murrough, lumbering past. 'It might have been snowing as well – for the love of all the gods, man, will you just die and give us all peace.'

This last was spat to the choker still struggling to breathe and Murrough's big Dal Cais axe rose and fell, cutting the last breath out of the man.

'What now?' demanded Kaetilmund.

Crowbone told him – hunt for Gudrod and Gunnhild. Search the bodies for a big man with the look of a fancy jarl about him and an old woman, he told them and they pawed their way through the corpses while Bergliot, her dress looped up through her belt and breeks on for the warmth, helped others prepare a fire from the little that was available to burn, grinning at Crowbone until he answered it.

Later, the men sat with bellies full trying to ignore the stiffening dead nearby, nudging each other when they saw Bergliot clump up on her too-big turnshoes and throw herself next to Crowbone, forcing him to offer her the shelter of his cloak. Crowbone, aware of the scowls and nudges, tried to ignore them; the dog came up, muzzle bloody, tongue lolling and permitted itself to be patted warily.

'I cannot keep calling this animal Yellow,' he said to Bergliot. 'I will call her Vigi – Stronghold – instead.'

'No matter what you call her,' she replied sternly, 'she will answer only to me.'

It was the truth, but Crowbone did not like to hear it and decided, as the cold dark drifted down on them, to put matters on the straight between them. He took a deep breath.

'Listen,' he began. 'I have no home to give you, nor time to find you safety. I am awaited beyond the mountains and the truth is that I don't know but that it is my death waiting. The best I can do for you is ask Murrough, or Kaetilmund or the priest to make sure you get to safety – though there is no surety of anyone living through this. Is there anywhere you could go before the winter sets in hard?'

He felt her stiffen beside him, turn from warmth and limpid length to a log.

'There is nowhere I can go, not before, not after winter. What would you have me do, prince? Would you have me a bed slave and no more?'

Crowbone looked at the fire until his eyeballs seared. She was, he realised, the first woman to come to him willingly and that was what was colouring matters here, so that he could not simply up and walk away. That and the fact that there was nowhere for her to go that did not mean her death.

'There is nowhere I can go. I shall be here, or dead,' she said, as if reading his mind, which snapped his head up to look at her.

'Woman, listen to me,' he said. 'I am a prince who intends to be king in Norway. I do not need a wife and if I did . . .'

He stopped, seeing the mire he was plootering into the middle of, but it was too late. She pushed herself away from him.

'If you did,' she said slowly, 'it would not be the likes of me. The princess, not her friend, is that the fact of it?'

It was so completely the fact of it that Crowbone could not answer and, eventually, she stood up and looked down at him.

'Prince,' she said, soft and gentle and all the more scathing because of it. 'King who would be – yet not kingly enough to be kind and even offer to take me home.'

She turned and started to walk away, paused and looked back.

'A boy,' she said. 'I see only a boy, who cannot even find it in him to thank me for saving his life.'

It was the truth, but he did not like to hear it from her and watched as she went to the other side of the fire and sat, so that her image wavered through the flames. He was aware of men silently watching this and his anger seemed to flare with the sputtering fire.

'Once,' he said suddenly, 'Thor had two sons on a mortal woman. Two young thunder-gods who grew to red-headed manhood in the way boys do, then fell violently in love with the same woman, as boys do. Said one of them to the other, in a joking way: "I will become a flea, so as to be able to hop into her bosom." Said the other: "I will become a louse, so as to be able to stay always in her fud."'

'It is only your lice that let you know you still live,' Adalbert interrupted, seeing the glares between Crowbone and Bergliot. Crowbone ignored the priest.

'Thor heard this and fumed,' he went on. 'And he roared: "Are those your wishes? You shall be taken at your word. Be slaves to a woman all your lives, then." He turned them into flea and louse, which is why we have them today and why, whenever there is a thunderstorm, fleas jump out of all sorts of places where there were none to be seen before and your crotch lice itch more than they usually do.'

Men chuckled but most realised why the story had been told in the first place and stitched their lips shut until the silence was broken only by the whine of wind and the stutter of flame. Then Kaetilmund reported that they had searched all the dead, but there was no man or woman like the ones they sought.

'Now,' Crowbone told him, 'we go on.'

When the dawn came up, whey-faced and chill, they sorted themselves out, bound up cuts and ground on into a long, cold climb, carrying their dead and leaving the Sami and the old Orkney dead, though Adalbert grimmed about that.

No-one else did, for they did not want to each be burdened with a cold-stiffed stranger, though there were no mutters about stumbling along weighed with their own comrades; no-one wanted to be left as one of those blue-white corpses when their turn came and everyone agreed they would burn their own men when they had got far enough away from that killing ground and into some decent trees.

They did, though it took most of the long night, thawing out enough stunted, twisted pine, which popped and spat out ice in three great dead-fires. Even they could not keep the dour away from the dark beyond the flames, shrouded by trees that seemed to close on them. Crowbone sat by himself now, for the yellow dog lay with Bergliot and though both were only across the width of a mean fire, it might have been the other side of the world itself.

Adalbert muttered prayers, which brought one or two glances from the good Odin and Thor men, so Gjallandi intoned prayers to Odin in his sonorous voice, so that all heads turned. At the end, knowing he had done well, he smiled a triumphant, knowing smile with his great lips and inclined his head in a gracious bow.

'One of my many accomplishments,' he declared. 'Together with reading and writing runes, at which I am a master as much as I am at the *drápa* and *flokkr*. At the first, I can delight with the *dróttkvæði* and the *Lausavísur*. With the second, I am able to make tears with my *nidvisur*.'

'I have heard weeping when you speak, for sure,' Halfdan interrupted savagely, 'but the only time I heard people listen intently was when you gave us a *mansongr*.'

That raised a weak chuckle despite the mood, for Gjallandi's boasts about courtly verse in its various forms and his ability to make decent *nidvisur* – flytings of scorn – were all true enough, but his *mansongr*, the filthy verses he made for the delight of hard men, were best of all.

Crowbone turned to Adalbert then and said suddenly: '*Illi robur et aes triplex circa pectus erat, qui fragilem truci commisit pelago ratem primus.*'

Those who remembered the priest saying this on the beach at Torfness ages since nudged each other at this feat of memory and the priest himself acknowledged it with a murmur of praise and no corrections. Crowbone beamed.

'Now,' said a man unseen in the shadows. 'If you could pluck this axe up as easily as you learn the Christ tongue, we would all be thankful – do we know where it lies?'

'As to that,' Gjallandi declared, before Crowbone could snap back, 'you should have paid more attention to those Sami at Kol's steading. They speak of this axe and say it might be the Sampo, hidden in a mountain.'

'Now I know this,' Onund declared, 'I know even less than before – what is a Sampo, then? You are rich in *seidr*, Crowbone – I have seen and felt it – do you know?'

Crowbone was pleased at the reference to his powers, but he had never heard of a Sampo and admitted it, then looked expectantly at Gjallandi. The skald sat and composed himself neatly by the ice-grumbling fire; folk sighed, seeing the preliminaries of a performance.

It was long and involved, as good sagas are, but the gist of it seemed to be that some Sami smith of note was forced to make a Sampo, a great work of magic, in return for a bride. Then a sorceress stole it and, in the struggle to get it back, this Sampo was lost.

'But what is it?' Halfdan demanded and he was only the first of a clamour. Gjallandi shrugged.

'No-one knows,' he answered. 'Some say it was the World Tree itself, which is obvious nonsense. Others say it was the ever-grinding quernstone that made flour, salt or gold from thin air. Others have it that it was a strange device that the Greeks call *horoscopium* for reading what the Norns will weave in the actions of stars. I have heard also that it is a Bloodaxe – Odin's Daughter – from the time when the young AllFather still had both his eyes.'

There was silence for a time, while eyes glittered in the half-dark bright with new interest.

'I like the gold-milling one best,' said Tuke, who was small and round, with a beard as bristled as a badger's arse, so that folk called him Duergar, meaning Black Dwarf.

'I am standing beside you there,' agreed Murrough.

'I favour the axe,' Halfdan added, 'for I am hoping it is the one which makes our Crowbone into a king and lets us all become rich.'

Folk laughed. Adalbert cleared his throat.

'Cornucopia,' he said and eyes turned to him until he felt the scorn in them and raised his head into the heat of it.

'A Greek horn from the Godless times,' he said, 'which poured out whatever your heart desired and never grew less for it. Seems to me this Sampo is whatever folk wish it to be – and that is the work of the Devil, who tried to persuade Christ himself to all the world's power.'

'And was refused,' declared one of the Christmenn passion-ately, then crossed himself; Crowbone was surprised to see that it was Wermund, one of the Kiev Slavs. There was a pause, split by the crackle and roar of the fire; somewhere, snow loosened by the heat slithered from the trees and men glanced round, to make sure the sentries were alert.

'He turned down all the power of the world?' Crowbone demanded and then shrugged into Adalbert's stern nod.

'He had a lot to learn about the game of kings, then.'

'There is no game,' Adalbert answered flatly, 'for God spake that the world should be governed by kings and princes.'

'Did he now?' Crowbone said, staring levelly at the priest with his odd eyes. 'So was it your God that appointed who rules the Northlands? To stand against Haakon is to stand against the White Christ?'

Adalbert frowned a little and folded his hands in his sleeves.

'Just so – and not so. Haakon is a heathen. Those unanointed who stand against an anointed king are not on the side of good Christians, only of the Aesir,' he decreed. 'All the baptised kings and princes will shun such a man – will join in war against him.'

Crowbone's eyes narrowed, but Adalbert did not flinch.

'You are brave, priest,' he answered slowly, 'but not invulnerable.'

Adalbert waved a dismissive hand. 'We can sit here calling each other names until Heimdall blows his horn, as you people say, but it will not change matters. You want to be king in Norway, but that will never be until you embrace Christ. Look at Haakon – he is a heathen and the world lines up to topple him.'

'Haakon is still king in Norway,' Crowbone responded. 'He threw your kind into the sea.'

'Is he the true king, then?' answered Adalbert. 'Or are you, as you claim? Christ will decide, not the gods of the Aesir. Nor any cursed axe.'

Finnmark, the mountain of Surman Suuhun . . .

MARTIN

No-one wanted to go in that smoking cleft in the dripping grey stones. There was a hot wind from it that seemed to pause every now and then before whining out of the cleft in a gout of white smoke and the stink of rotten eggs.

'Surtr,' muttered one of the men and Hromund glanced uneasily round, then up, blinking in the snow which had been falling steadily all night and into the short, leaden day. The rest of the peak hunched over them, capped with snow, misted in a sinister shroud. He did not like to admit it, but the man had the right of it here – this was a place of Surtr, the fire *jötunn*, and all his kin spawned from Ymir's armpit. No place for men; he shivered.

Martin saw it, knew it was not the cold and curled his lip back on his black stumps; this was where the axe was and he had expected no help. This was where Sueno had known it would be, hissing it out as he clutched Drostan's rough wool sleeve, demanding promises that the astonished and frightened monk agreed to.

Afterwards, Martin had sternly told the trembling, bewildered Drostan that he had placed his soul in peril by listening to such heathen blasphemy at all, never mind making promises. And, when the monk knelt, eyes squeezed shut to receive absolution from Martin, the *clerk regular*, Martin had given him it, with a stone. He had absolved Drostan so fiercely that he had crushed one of his own fingers, but he scarcely felt that among so many of the pains he bore.

The reek swirled round him, stinging his eyes and he saw the faces of the Norway men waver and blur, as if under water, then looked at the cleft in the rock, so like the unclean part of a woman's body. Such a pagan, blasphemous item – what else would it be but in one of the entrances to Hell itself, reeking with the stink of the Pit?

'Who will come?' he demanded, knowing none of them would, for they were followers of false gods and their hearts knew it even if their heads did not. They did not have the power of God to keep Satan's imps away – Martin did not doubt for a moment that he would meet the denizens of hell and slaves of the Fallen Angel inside that hole in the mountain.

The wind sighed out of the gash and men backed away from it, crouching down. Hromund looked round and saw that none of them would go; he wanted to say that he would, but had persuasive arguments with himself that his place was outside, with his men.

Eindride saw the scornful look on the priest's face and felt anger surge in him, stoked it with more indignation that this twisted, hirpling follower of a coward's godlet would dare the place while good northers squatted and looked at the ice and rocks rather than each other.

As good as courage, it welled up and burned the words out of him.

'I will go.'

Men offered up 'heya' to the courage of the archer – then blinked in astonishment as Tormod shouldered through them.

'You have a wee son at home – I will go instead.'

He and Eindride looked at each other and the archer smiled at what had not been said – a thrall would not be much missed, even a king's favourite. He turned to Hromund.

'If things go badly,' he said, 'you will see that my wife and son are safe?'

Hromund nodded and Eindride split his ice-clotted beard with a grin that burst blood on to his cold-chapped lips, then clapped Tormod on the back.

'Together, then,' he said.

Two men, not about to be outdone by a thrall, king's favourite or not, sprang up and announced their names – Kjartan and Arnkel – and their intention not to be shamed. The rest, too afraid even to worry about the shame, offered up no sound at all.

Martin, staff in his cold gnarled hands, shuffled towards the dark opening; the more practical Tormod organised torches, food and water.

'*Gloria Patri, et Fili, et Spiritui Sancto*,' Martin intoned at the entrance, raising the staff up as if to strike down an enemy.

'*Sicut erat in principio, et nunc et semper, et in saeccula saeculorum, Amén.*'

Eindride gave a sound, half way between cough and grunt, then pushed the priest scornfully to one side and strode into the maw of the place, one hand clutching the Thor amulet at his throat. Martin hirpled after him. Kjartan licked spit on to his lips, Arnkel took a deep breath and they both ducked after Martin, as if plunging under freezing water. At the entrance, Tormod turned once and met Hromund's eyes, smiled wryly and then was gone.

Hromund and the men sat for a moment, as if waiting for something cataclysmic, but nothing happened at all. The smoke stopped pouring from the hole, the wind in it moaned a little, there was a pause, then it began again. From somewhere came a distant rumble, as if a storm brewed and Hromund shifted.

'Make fires and a camp,' he ordered, cramped and stiff with cold. 'We will wait here.'

He did not say how long they would wait and the scores of rimed men did not want to ask. They did not have long, as it turned out, for the short day was sliding to death when Gudrod's men wolfed out of the shadows, led by a Tyr-howling boy.

Not far inside, pausing to tie cloths round their mouths to help them breathe in the foul reek of the place, Martin and the others heard the shrieks and crouched. Kjartan whimpered, sure that the Sami animal-men were coming; Tormod snarled him to silence and they waited, blinking in the guttering light of the torch, the sweat stinging their eyes. Nothing changed.

Martin grew impatient, wanting to move on, but no-one shifted and the reek swirled round them. Nothing changed.

Except . . .

'Someone is coming,' Eindride said and they all turned to where the faint iced light from the entrance had been a comfort, a thread leading back to the world of men.

Now, they saw the red-gold of a bobbing torch and Eindride nocked an arrow, growling. Martin crouched, wary as a rat and looking over his shoulder; there was screaming down there, a moaning shriek that shaved the skin from the back of his neck.

Then a voice from behind the red-gold torch whispered out like the wings of bats. A woman's voice, old and soft as sealskin.

'My son bids me tell you that it would be better if you turned over your King piece. You have lost this game.'

TWELVE

Finnmark, the mountain of Surman Suuhun . . .

THE WITCH-QUEEN'S CREW

WHEN she thought of ravens at all, which was not often or with any regard, she thought always of the white one. They said the worst winters were when AllFather let loose the third of his ravens, the white one. While his black brothers, Thought and Memory, stuck their heads under one hunched wing, the white raven trailed frosted pinfeathers over the world, teased clouds with talons, drawing out the long, slow tumble of soft white, silent as sleep that fell on high peaks, was razored by thin crags, sifted softly into the deep soul of the world.

Once, long ago, beyond this place, she had been a girl in a fire-warmed home who looked out to a world softening to curves of drifting landscape, looked out in wonder at how the world could come to such a whispering end. She was young and hugged herself then, wishing for warmer winds and the kiss of sun on her skin.

It was not to be. She had been brought here not much later and ever since the only world that existed was the one of short, blazing-passionate summers and long winters full of dancing night fires that skeined the dark with green and red.

There had been travellers, the curious and brave who tried to seek her out. The ones who came for riches seldom arrived, but those who sought wisdom were allowed and sometimes stayed long enough to tell her their own secrets and some of the workings of the world beyond the fire mountain. There had even been two Greeks and a Serkland Arab who all professed to know the secrets of snow and other matters, speaking loftily of winds and tides and clouds.

Once, she had travelled out of the mountain, out of the Finnmark, hoping to learn more of this strange new god, the Christ. In the cut of cold, folk struggled to badly-heated eggshells of stone where Christ prayers smoked; some who shivered there secretly went home to bind their hearth with an older invoking. Those she smiled at, for there was hope for them – then she came home to the smouldering mountain and left them to their world.

Yet she envied all of them, for they all crouched by fires, succoured by the light as much as the heat, sharing a hope as old as dark that the flames would not fail. It was no longer a part of her life, to be with them, to have ones she loved and who loved her.

So here she was at the end of days, pushed by obligation and if any saw her they fastened their lips on it. Ajatar's handmaiden, they called her, which made her smile. It had pained her, that name from her own Sami folk, but she knew what made them liken her to the favourite of a goddess of pestilence and disease, who could strike you with a look and who suckled serpents. They reflected their own twists of ugly suspicion on her, making her monstrous.

Yet even some of them came to her, struggling up the fire mountain for the power they believed she had. Wise woman some called her and she liked that name, though it was plain and there was pride enough left in her to resent it; all women were wise, long before her age and certainly by it, for they had learned the feel of the world. Younger folk were not for listening and so missed a deal of life, for you fished more meat out of that cauldron by just looking and remembering.

It was all about Hugin and Munin, the black brothers of the white raven, all about Thinking and Remembering and there was enough of the norther in her to appreciate that. The north god, AllFather, knew this, had learned this through hanging pain and spear-thrust, nine nights on the World Tree for the whisper of runes, the mystery she knew well as a result.

Those northers who feared her called her a silly auld wummin, only half believing it was true, hoping that she was diminished by them making her seem small. Some, who knew a little better, called her 'cunning' and that never bothered her, although she doubted it meant what they thought. She did not mind the scathing *wyrd-rider* either and was as likely to tell folk that she had wyrd needed riding as 'farewell' when she had decided to close the door on herself.

Only a few called her by her true name, a name older even than the dancing lights that split the long north dark. *Spaekona*. Witch-Queen. It was the name they used when they came with heads lowered and eyes resting everywhere but on her own, twisting their hands in their lap and looking for daftness they should not be seeking.

She did not hear it from those who wanted a leech wort release from pain, or root potion to help with a sad loss, or relief from the sickness of the long dark. She only heard it from those wanting to snare an unwilling man, or curse a rival, or lose a bairn. When she refused them, that was when they hissed '*spaekona*' under their breath and for those whose hate made them bold, she had her hunters, with their skin cloaks and spears. Those hunters knew her true worth, knew she belonged to the north mountains and them and understood the wordless bargain that went back before the first handsealed contract, beyond even the blood oath.

Now they watched her closely, hunkered round fires that were near yet far enough away and wearing the full masks of the beasts they killed, though she only half understood why. She did not mind being worshipped for it was the least due to her, latest in a long line who were chosen for this. Last in a long line, she thought suddenly, unless a new goddess is found to learn from me.

The one who had gone before her – she could not remember her name now – had sent men to her village and stolen her, such was her desperation. There had been a long time of fear and hate, then a moment when she saw what was being taught to her and, finally, a too-brief time when the pair of them worked in tandem. Then, suddenly, she was alone with the burden of waiting, for the axe and her own successor, the first to be returned to the stone kist until someone brave came to claim it, the second to sit at her fire and begin the task of shouldering the burden of all the long years of old knowing. So it had always been, so it would always be.

Well, the first had come, passed hand to hand through blood and danger, for the axe had claimed its cursed victims – she remembered being told that the axe had failed to return only once, when a true *spaekona*, a full-cunning woman of the north had tricked the Sami carrying it into revealing their powers and those of the Bloodaxe. That *spaekona* had given it to her husband, for the power in it and hoped to pass it to all of her sons in turn – but the curse of the axe tainted all her sons, according to the man who had last brought it back to the fire mountain.

Svein he had called himself, a man bitter with defeat and death, she had seen, twisted from his faith by the betrayal of that axe. His king and master had commanded him to take it here, he said. He did not want his sons to get it, she learned, even the worst of them, for none were worthy and all would be betrayed, like him. She had watched this Svein stumble off and thought it likely he would die in the Finnmark cold, for he was so uncaring of life.

The second had not come and she was beginning to wonder if it would ever happen. There was always the raid on a village – but she remembered the fear and the hate of it and balked at doing it.

Now, she thought, it might be too late. There were many folk plootering over her fire mountain to claim the Bloodaxe and her hunters had suffered for it. It had come to her, just recently, that perhaps she was the last of her kind and the thought troubled her.

She found a nice spot by the clawed hand of tree, while the wind hissed down the bowl of the valley and drew the reeking white smoke out of the entrance to it. She knew the swirl of it sucked the smoke from the strange hot, bubbling pits in the Cleft, then roared it out through the mountain beyond, as if the place breathed.

She had made fires here before and liked the place, for it reminded the air about true cold. It took a hard winter to make this sheltered, eldritch-heated valley clog with snow and she was used to the warmth, so that stepping out beyond it ached her bones these days; she preferred to wait until folk came to her.

She found her ring of old stones, coned a few sticks together and sparked up a fire. Her hunting men settled down to watch. They were hurting and sick and too many of them had died and she was sorry she had asked them to. They thought they had been fighting to keep the northers away from this place, the home of their wise-woman goddess and that they were failing; they did not know that they were meant to fail if one wyrd was to prove a success.

The soft flames spilled red-gold into another long night of white and bruise-blue. A good fat moon, crisp air and a warm hue dancing in a hearth. Grandma was another name she didn't mind, though only children, the ache of her lost heart, called her that. She had not seen one for some time, but remembered how they had liked her stories, in the days when she had gone abroad more.

She liked to tell stories to herself – at least, that is what she said when she caught herself mumbling into the straggles of her hair. Sometimes she let the fur-masks listen, but even those hunters preferred to creep away, ducking away from an old-young, shapeless, mumbling woman hung about with odd weavings and difference.

She knew one or two stopped to listen and would have been surprised at the few, the very few, who wondered if what she muttered needed some other name than 'story' – but they only wondered that sort of thing when they could not hear it being told.

While they were listening they felt lifted up into a cloud of dusted age, where there was nevertheless something firm and strong, like finding a good pass through the mountains. There were some who said she spoke of their own home, but long ago, where their people must have lived forever. No-one who listened went away unmoved and some were woken to wondering who the stories were for.

Now, though, the Sami beast-warriors saw that she just seemed to be humming to herself, and kicking snow off the old hearth, talking life back into it, like a bitch mouths and licks the litter's failing runt. The hunters sat silent and waiting.

The man came quiet out of the cleft, but the hunters knew and their beast-masked heads came up; others followed the man. The hunters glanced at their goddess, but she showed no alarm and they took the hint, lowered their weapons and waited.

She watched the group coming towards her – a litter on poles, with a man at each corner, another man hirpling painfully, and one with a bow, some more behind. The hirpling man had a robe which might have been any colour but now was mainly stain, dagged and torn round the hem where it straggled in strips. He carried a staff in one hand, had a face like a long stretch of bad road and one foot was bare. Twisted and crippled, that foot, but not so dead that it never felt the bite of stone or cold, but the eyes in him were even more dead than that and the dangling cross made her catch her breath.

A Christ priest. Here. Did he come to claim the axe? The thought stunned her, almost crushed her with the wyrd of it – then the litter was set down and she sensed the *seidr* from it, even before the figure was helped out, moved slowly towards her.

Old, she thought. An old power, this, and one to be feared. Still, she did as she was supposed to do. She nodded at the curved roots opposite and watched as her visitor sat down. The wind sighed and the fire hissed and the Old Power looked at the hunters and they looked back at her, hackles ruffed as dogs, for they sensed what she was. She looked round at the place, at the lack of snow, and the warmth compared with what was on the other side of the rock walls and nodded.

Then, finally, she turned and looked into the sere, ageless face of the woman opposite.

'Goddess, is it?' she said, in a voice made harsh by design. The woman nodded briefly, trying to look through the spiderweb-silk veil and seeing only the glitter of old ice eyes.

'Aye, so they call you now. They have power, the Sami, but no common sense.'

She stopped, sucked in breath and muttered.

'Still, no reason to be discourteous,' Gunnhild added. 'I have come for the Bloodaxe,' Gunnhild said. 'I had it before, when your . . . predecessor . . . was here, though I did not ask politely then. I had it then for my husband. Now I take it for my son.'

All her trepidation about old power vanished and the Sami goddess laughed with the sheer delight of this funny little veiled woman who thought the Sami had no common sense, yet came for the axe that had killed her husband and all her sons but one.

CROWBONE'S CREW

The masked Sami would not stop. They were harried from rock to treeline, into clumped stands of pine and out on to the bare tumble of snow-draped rocks and still they would not go away. Crowbone wondered what hand guided them, for he knew there was a leader driving them. There seemed, to most, to be no sense in the losses they took, but Crowbone knew the game of kings well and the King Player's best defence was to hurl his warriors at the enemy. The Orkneymen had died in winnowed droves and now Crowbone's men did, too.

They found Mar spreadeagled on a rock, his insides laid out in some ritual. Gjallandi thought that a Sami wizard had done it, but the why remained a mystery. Crowbone sat back on his heels and looked at the iron-tangle of the man's beard, the frosted eyes. Because he had broken that Oath he had taken so lightly? He looked to where Onund and Kaetilmund stood, accusing-grim, but they said nothing and, eventually, he broke their gaze.

'We should give this axe foolishness up,' growled Klaenger, a tall, rangy man with a nose red-raw with cold. 'It is clear the folk here do not want us to have Odin's Daughter.'

Crowbone knew that the man and Mar had been friends and saw a few agreeing nods from others. He looked up, to where the grey-green rocks piled ever higher, right up to the mountain fang where the white smoke plumed.

'Look behind you,' he said to Klaenger, who jumped and did so. When he saw nothing threatening, he turned back, scowling and wary.

'Do you see the sea?' Crowbone demanded. 'Our ships?'

Klaenger's lip drooped sullenly.

'Look ahead,' Crowbone offered and it was no longer for Klaenger, but for all the men. 'There is the mountain where our quest ends. Which is easier to get to now?'

Men scuffed the ground with what was left of their boots and said nothing – the mountain was easy enough to navigate to, but no-one knew what terrors lay in it. But they went on. When the dog found Vandrad Sygni not long after, no-one even grunted.

It was clear that he was dead from the way his head lolled brokenly to one side. His eyes had been dug out with his own horn spoon, which had been left beside him. The strange, loose, sideways turn of his feet showed where he had been hamstrung; as a message it was as subtle as a slap on the forehead – your best tracker cannot see us, cannot move quietly enough, is no match for us.

They were attacked again not far ahead, a sudden rush as short and vicious as the day itself – a shower of black-shafted arrows and a howling of beast-masked men. Almost in a heartbeat it was over and, again, they left more dead than they caused.

Yet one of those they killed was Vigfuss Drosbo and another Thorgils, who had taken an arrow in the armpit, straight up the short sleeve of his ringmail. They are whittling us away, Crowbone thought, desperate and weary, like flakes from a lathed bowl.

It was then that Murrough, cleaning his axe beside a body, announced that he was sure he had killed this one the day before.

'They all look the same,' Kaetilmund growled in savage answer, trying to warn the Irisher off such a topic with his eyes. 'Slit-eyed, flat-faced fucks with stolen weapons.'

No-one laughed, all the same and the idea persisted that they were killing the same men over and over again.

The next short day saw no sign of live men at all, but the yellow dog spoored out more dead, some from under fresh snow. One was a Sami and he had been burned with crosses and shot with a black-fletched arrow, then hung from a tree like a gralloched deer. That was clearly the work of Martin and Crowbone scowled and squinted at the snow glare, as if he could hook the monk to him with his odd eyes.

'Perhaps not exactly in that order,' Kaetilmund argued, frowning, 'but all of those matters took place here.'

The other was a snow-buried norther and Gjallandi was sure this one was a Norwegian, though he could not be certain. He could be certain the man had died because an arrow had gone into his kidneys. Most of the rest did not care, one way or the other, for they had found the remains of a deer hanging in a nearby tree and there was a lot left on it, even if it was hard as stone.

Crowbone looked at the growing dark and felt the cold stone slide into his bowels; the days were so short, the nights long and fired by red and green lights, so that the mountain never seemed to get closer. They were danger-close to failing – yet he could feel the nearness of that axe, like heat.

Men started fires with old twigs and branches dug from under the snow, lichen plucked from rocks at the start of the day and dried out down boots or inside tunics. Stacked into small cones, sparked into life by flint, steel and gentling breath, fire budded, then blossomed.

The men thawed out the meat enough to cut, stuck it on strong twigs or even their knives, careless of the soot blacking the metal. Men on watch stamped and looked at the fires enviously, licked their lips as the white fat slowly began to broil and sputter; meat and smoke smells eddied up and away into the maw of the night.

Crowbone closed his eyes, swathed in the too-small white cloak, but those nearest him were never sure if he slept or not.

'What are you after thinking?' asked a voice and Bergliot swam into his waking vision, holding out a sharpened branch which speared meat. A rush of saliva drowned his reply and he held the stick with one hand, biting into the meat, then sliding his eating knife along to slice the mouthful free with a casual pass.

Crowbone never answered and she, thinking her attempt to mend fences had been spurned, did not ask again, merely huddled nearby and ached for the lee of his body. Crowbone never noticed; he was thinking that the dead Sami, whoever he had been, had been handled badly and that the Christ priest had done it. It was Martin, for sure – once before Crowbone had seen this cross-burning work of his, done on the back of the addled Short Eldgrim to try and get him to tell what he knew. That was when Crowbone had made a mistake and quit Orm in favour of Prince Vladimir.

He remembered it well enough, for Vladimir had been too young, not yet enough of a prince and matters got out of hand – Thorgunna's first husband died and Thorgunna herself had been kicked in the belly, hard enough to ruin a child out of her. The same man who had done it to his mother, Crowbone remembered – Kveldulf, who had paid for it later.

For a moment Crowbone remembered the utter hopeless-ness, recalled his tears and snot as he huddled beside Thorgunna, stacked like a log in the boat Vladimir planned to use to sail down to the Black Sea and away from Orm and the Oathsworn.

He had wept like a cracked heart, for his mother, whose face he could not remember, for Thorgunna who had been like one to him and for himself, alone and abandoned and afraid. Poor Thorgunna, Crowbone thought, to have lost two men and two bairns.

Orm had stolen the boat and Thorgunna, dragged him out into the light and, Crowbone remembered, could have killed him but did not. He had taken him almost as a son. And married Thorgunna, too, later.

Yet Orm had been treacherous now, Crowbone was sure of it. The Oathsworn he had taken – Onund and Kaetilmund and the others – had not been been chosen by him, he remem-bered, but by Orm, sent to make sure Crowbone tripped all the traps Martin had made. Orm wants the prize, he thought bitterly, using me like some stupid young hunting dog.

Yet Orm does not know me, Crowbone thought. I will not be surrounded in this game; I am no fawning hound, to be sent out to spring snares.

As if it had heard, the yellow bitch nosed hopefully and he flung it the gristle of his meal, which it snapped up. Bergliot, smiling, tossed it some better chunks and men laughed. There was a murmur of soft talk.

As if they were not freezing on a bare mountain with all oaths in tatters, chasing a madness and fighting beast-men to do it, Kaetilmund thought. He murmured as much, quietly, to Onund, adding: 'Perhaps Orm has not judged this well.'

Onund grunted his bear grunt, which could mean anything.

When the light struggled reluctantly back, they moved on, with mountains in every direction save the way they had come, which was a long, winding trail back down through the scree and pine and rocks. A river ran through it, frozen to milk-white, iced rills curling round and over the rocks and narrowing until it ended at the foot of a cliff.

Halfdan looked up, squinting at the white glare of it.

'In summer,' he said wistfully, 'this would be a pleasant place of sounding water and wildflowers, birds and good air. A man could take some refuge from the heat of the sun in the pool here.'

It was a good vision, yet as forlorn as a flower in that place and he had back harshness for fetching it up.

'Even in summer the water would be freezing,' Onund pointed out, 'while the insects would drive you out of your thought-cage entire. I have seen elk running off the top of cliffs because the insects plagued them to blind madness.'

'You would not want to bathe in it now,' Tuke added, lumbering past and cackling. Halfdan looked up and could only agree; the river was frozen like an immense hall hanging, stopped still in the middle of falling down the rocks and layered in folds like white stone. He turned as something black flitted and stared at a raven, the first bird he had seen for some time.

Crowbone stopped, too, the hackles on him stiff as hog bristle. It had gobbets of meat hanging red in its beak and shouldered into the depths of a dead, stunted pine at the foot of the falls, a tree now a splintered and frost-sparkled larder for the bird.

'Steady,' he said, low and soft. 'That bird's beak tells a whole saga.'

Kaetilmund saw it at once – fresh meat, unfrozen. A recent kill. He nodded and sent men on ahead; they began to climb the treacherously rimed trail alongside the waterfall, Crowbone, last to start up it, watching the raven as it watched him with its cold unwinking black eye. Only when it took its full beak into the depths of the tree did Crowbone blink back to the now of matters and start to climb; he was surprised to see the yellow dog at his heels.

At the top was a flat area through which the little stream flowed when it was not a ribbon of ice. There were hardly any rocks for a long way round, making it a good place to camp – which is why the men who had got there first had done so.

Crowbone arrived to find men panting hard, shoulder to shoulder and the breath rising from them like spray from a blowhole. Kaetilmund looked round, saw him and simply jerked his chin out in front. There were dead beast-men dotted here and there, stiff but not yet frozen; the raven's feast. Beyond the scattered dead stood men, shields up and weapons ready.

They are iron-grim, these men, Crowbone thought. Faces like bruises, eyes red-rimmed and not looking at you so much as through you to somewhere distant, while the meltwater from their smoking breath ran off their helmets and refroze on their beards. They were stained and bloodied and coldly desperate, their hands on hilt and shaft flexing and clenching. Crowbone half turned, realising they were no different at all from the men at his own back.

'How many of them, are you thinking?' Onund asked, craning to see. A stone's worth, said Gjallandi, though he was prepared to revise that upwards a few times, aiming it at men who tallied laboriously from one to twenty – *ein, tveir, þrír* – then took a stone from a pile and started again.

Crowbone heard a voice claim three stones' worth, but that was from Tuke, who came from somewhere north of Jorvik and counted in some eldritch way – *yan, tan, tethera* – and did not do it well, even with his boots off.

'There are enough,' Kaetilmund claimed and the air grew thick and heavy with frosted fear. Crowbone pushed his way to the front and spread his empty hands wide. There was a pause, a stir as if a bird fluttered in the bush of them, then a man stepped from safety and stood looking at Crowbone.

He was middling old, though the cold had crippled his face to that of an old man, a rough, greying beard frozen to it like lichen to a rock and a nose that seemed to spread across what remained of his face. Crowbone knew him as if he had been a brother, had followed the name from Hy to Orkney to here – Erling Flatnose; he felt the ice-spear in his head stab viciously, so that one eye shut and he winced with the pain of it.

Erling watched the boy curiously, saw the sudden twist, the flicker of pain and wondered at it – or if he had seen it at all, for it was gone in an eyeblink. It left a sharp face, coin-weighted yellow braids dangling on either side and the dusting of a good beard rising to meet them. Average height, not any sign of special on him at all and wearing ringmail that a dead man would scorn from the grave.

Yet the eyes Gudrod had warned him about gripped him, one blue, one brown; he felt them on his face like the trail of cold fingers and it made him shiver.

'Here we are, then, son of Tryggve,' he declared, attempting to get matters walking on the trail he wanted. 'Seeking the same, fighting the same. It seems to me that the Sami are watching us and will laugh to see us carve each other up.'

'No need for it,' agreed Crowbone, so amiable and quick that Erling was confused. 'There are other ways to settle matters. Where is Gudrod and that mother of his?'

'Gone, with the axe you seek, of course. I will be following them once matters are done with here.'

Crowbone laughed and stood, hip-shot, though he trembled and hoped it did not show.

'So,' he said thoughtfully, 'Gudrod has left you here to . . . what? Kill me? Die for him? For a man with the Bloodaxe of victory, he seems strangely reluctant to face me in person. Perhaps he fears the curse of it.'

Erling shifted slightly, for the thought had entered him also.

'He plays the game of kings,' he answered, shrugging. 'To win it, you get your king to safety.'

Crowbone flung back his head and laughed with what he hoped sounded like genuine delight.

'Only if you play it on a cloth of nine squares,' he answered. 'There are other ways to win – but if that is what you intend, then matters are simple here and only one needs to die.'

Erling nodded, for he had been told to expect this.

'Were you thinking only two need risk themselves? Yourself being one of them? What does the winner gain?'

'Everything,' Crowbone said, wondering at the ease with which Erling had helped steer this course. 'The winner agrees that his oath-men go their own way unharmed. Those that wish and are acceptable may even join with the winner.'

Onund gave a barking growl at that and Erling heard it, flicked his eyes briefly to the hunchback, then back to Crowbone's face.

'It seems not all your oath-men agree,' he answered.

A prince should always strive to be good, Crowbone thought, but if necessary he should be capable of evil.

'Some are oathed to me, others have taken an Odin Oath to each other. Those whom we do not trust, we can kill,' he harshed out, loud enough for all those behind to hear it. 'For we are choosers of the slain, you and me. I am thinking it will not matter to you which ones I take a mistrust to, since you will be dead.'

Erling laughed.

'Agreed,' he said and it came to Crowbone, too late, that Erling would not be the one he would fight, as he had thought. Even as the spit dried in his mouth, he saw the man turn and raise a hand. Everyone watched the youth step out, gliding as if on bone skates, the sword in a ring at his belt.

'This is Od,' Erling said. 'Od, this is Olaf Tryggvasson, called Crowbone. Kill him.'

The youth flicked the sword out of his belt-ring with one hand as Crowbone drew his own blade; men made yells of encouragement as he fell into a fighting crouch, watching the youth called Od, who made no movement at all save for the tilt of his head as he studied Crowbone.

Crowbone saw the face in the slow heartbeats that ticked away. Beautiful as a girl, it was, untouched by the weather or the world and, for a moment, Crowbone felt a sharp pang deep in him and wanted the boy to go away, to keep his face untroubled and unblemished.

Od saw the eyes of the man he would kill, blue and brown, and thought they were pretty, like agate stones he had found once on a beach. He smiled; they would be good on a sacrifice to Tyr and the god would be pleased. Above them was a domed helmet with a plume of white horsehair braiding its way out of the top and he thought he might like that – then he frowned.

'It has a dent in it,' he said and Crowbone, puzzled, did

316

not understand him at first, thought it some ploy and watched him warily.

'Your war hat,' the boy said, waving the sword in the general direction of Crowbone's head. 'It has a dent in it.'

'So will your head,' Crowbone croaked out, 'since you do not wear one at all.'

Od smiled brightly at that and shook his head.

'I never get hurt,' he declared proudly. 'Tyr protects me.'

The boy moved then and Crowbone almost squealed with the terrible speed of him – but he got his sword in the way and Od's blade skittered off it with a high, thin tang. Then the boy was whirling, sure-footed, across the frozen stream, skipping like a flung stone.

He did it again and Crowbone fended it off again, though he felt the sick certainty that he could not hit this youth, who seemed like smoke. Onund thought so, too, and looked at Kaetilmund and they nodded – whatever happened, the Oathsworn would not become Gudrod's men.

The third whirl of the sword was another high slash and Crowbone turned it yet again and this time managed a half-hearted slash of his own, but Od was already turning, almost strolling, back into striking range.

Then Crowbone saw it, saw that the fourth would come in like the others, but it would be feint, for he would whip it low and up, hoping to get under Crowbone's defence and cut up into the armpit.

It came, the high cut, a whirr like a bird wing and Crowbone held back – when the feint slice came in, his sword met it with a resounding ring of steel and, when Crowbone had shaken the sting of sweat from his eyes, he saw that Od was frowning.

Men were yelling on both sides, screaming at their men to finish it. Erling was only aware of them as a noise, like insect whine, for he was watching Od. He had seen the move, seen the strange-eyed boy counter it and the frown on Od's face;

317

for the first time he felt a worm of unease creep into his belly, for Od had never taken so long to finish a man.

It was the game of kings, thought Crowbone, only faster and using steel. He felt better for knowing it, for the game of kings was his game; he smiled.

When Od skipped in again, Crowbone sucked the breath from those watching – he flipped his sword from right to left hand and Od, just as he started to cut, found himself open all along one side and desperately changed his mind. His feet skidded a little and Crowbone, exultant, slashed at him.

There was another clash of iron and the boy reeled away, his beautiful face twisted, pale and ugly with fear and hate now. This had never happened before. He had never been made to do this before, to feel this way.

Crowbone heard the rasp of his own breath in his ears, felt the sick hopelessness. He should have had him, there and then – by all the gods, this Od was fast. Perhaps he really was beloved of Tyr One-Hand. Perhaps Gunnhild's *seidr* magic was still strong and, somewhere far away, she worked it in the muttering dark.

Od came in, all anger and blinding speed, so that Crowbone backed away, a foot skidded on the ice and he went down on one knee and the helmet, badly fastened, slid off and clattered away; men howled and roared as Od closed in and started to hack, madly, blind with fury.

Erling shoved to the front, roaring with anger. 'No, no – kill him, Od. Kill him now.'

But the boy was using brute strength and no finesse. A sliver to the right or left and Crowbone, sword held up and across him, would have been cut to the bloody core – but Od slammed his sword against Crowbone's blade again and again, as if trying to drive it down into Crowbone's own pale, upturned face.

There was a sudden sharp bell of sound and everything stopped. No-one spoke, or even seemed to breathe; Od stared at the shattered nub of his sword blade while the main length of it spun lazily through the air. When it landed, with a soft tinkle that skidded it along the frozen stream, time and noise began all over again.

Crowbone hurled himself upright. He had this chance, this one chance and Od, stunned and squealing, backed away. Crowbone tried once, twice, three times to carve his blade into the body of the boy, but, even with the broken remnants of his sword, Od's hand-speed glissaded the danger away from him.

Panting, sobbing for breath, Crowbone paused briefly and launched a new attack. Od half-turned, dropped to one heel and flung the broken blade at Crowbone's face, making him shy sideways and lose his concentration. Something whacked his sword hand and he felt the fingers go numb and uncurl, heard the blade ringing on the ice. Erling's men bellowed out hoarse cheers.

Crowbone closed with the boy, before he could get away and find a new weapon; he was stronger and taller, yet the fight had sucked at him and they both locked together, straining for advantage, feet skidding on the ice and snow. There was an axe snugged in the belt at the small of Crowbone's back but there was no way he could get to it quickly, even when he freed one hand.

It had irritated Crowbone since he had started to wear it, but he had had the idea from Finn and the nail in his boot. Crowbone, since he had strapped the dagger sheath to the outside of his left ankle, wondered how Finn stood the rubbing and annoyance – and he did not even have a sheath to ease matters. More than a few times, Crowbone had thought of taking the contraption off; now he prayed to Odin for the wisdom the god had clearly provided.

His hand drew it out, a long, thin, sliver of steel only slightly shorter than the length of his forearm. He got it up and round, saw Od's eyes widen with shock when he saw it and felt the great surge of triumph that comes with the certainty of victory – then the world exploded in red mist and pain.

He stumbled back, blinded by tears, desperately dashed them and the blood from his nose, cracked by Od's forehead. He saw the boy, smiling, standing hip-shot and easy and with the dagger dangling loosely in one hand; he had not even felt the boy pluck it from his hand.

Here it comes then, he thought numbly. Somewhere, the Norns' weave had gone awry, for this was clearly not what Olaf Tryggvasson had seen of his own future – but it was happening. The snips were closing on his thread.

He lunged, the boy skipped away, smiling, while people jeered.

'Freyja's tits, boy – fucking kill him!' screamed Erling and Od, frowning, struck like a snake. Crowbone saw the wink of it, the cold, shining stab of it and then the length was in his shoulder, right in, driving the rot-brown metal rings into his flesh, spearing through them and the sweating skin and the raw meat until it grated on the bone; he screamed – though there was no pain yet – at the violation of the iron in his flesh.

Od slid, skate smooth, behind him, keeping one hand on the dagger, putting the other round Crowbone's pale, sweating forehead; Erling tensed and dared not speak, for the pair were close to the edge of the waterfall now, not on the frozen spill, but to the right of it, where the rocks were just as slick with ice spray.

Crowbone felt the wash of pain, then, the hot, sick surge of it and his legs almost buckled. Behind him, Od crooned and stroked his hair, sweat-plastered to his forehead. At the same time, he worked the dagger into the wound a little more, a slow circle, so that Crowbone could feel it in great red billows of pain.

He heard Od chuckle, a wet, sick sound. He felt the heat of the boy behind him, the groin heat and the hardness and the revulsion blasted the pain away in a white light. Od's chin was down on his shoulder, his breath hot under Crowbone's ear and Crowbone took one hand and placed it over Od's, the one holding the knife, just as the boy began to intone his dedication to Tyr.

Od stopped and frowned, for he had been about to cut Crowbone's throat, but he laughed instead, for now Crowbone seemed to be trying to prevent him moving the dagger out of the wound. It would keep it from his throat, but Od did not mind a little more play; when Crowbone's second hand came up and covered the first, he grew even more eager for the idea. He did not understand it, but the pleasure of it seemed to suck the breath from him and he wanted desperately to press himself tight against Crowbone.

Three hands clasped on the hilt, they stood for a moment, their mingled breath smoking, cooling and pearling. Men fell silent, not understanding what was happening, why one did not kill the other and there was unease at it.

Then Crowbone roared and thrust with all his strength. The dagger went through, right to the grind of the hilt on the ringmail of his shoulder under the bone and out the other side, into Od's neck. The pain tore the feet out from under Crowbone, sent him blind and retching to his knees – but Od staggered and clutched himself.

Erling saw it then, the dagger through from one side of Crowbone to the other, saw Od grab his neck and scream. No great jet of blood, Erling saw with a leap of relief. Not a dangerous cut then – but he saw the boy take his hand away and look at it, then search for Erling across the distance between them, his fine, girl's face twisted with shock and fear, the blood clear on his fingertips.

He has never been injured, Erling realised. Tyr has failed him . . .

He was about to call out for him to stay, to wait. Od reeled, panicking and Erling saw the boy's eyes roll up into his head, one foot slither out from under him and he yelled, seeing the inevitable. With a sharp cry and a slither like the rushing of wind, Od vanished over the edge; there was a crash and a shrill screaming that ripped through everyone, so that some crouched and put their hands over their ears. Then silence.

Surfacing, with a whoop as if he had plunged into cold water. Breaching like a whale from an ocean of dark into blinding agony that made him roar.

'Easy, easy,' Bergliot soothed, while she seared lances into him and men held him down. He saw her, fingers and bone needle bloody, hooking another rusted iron ring out of the wound and flicking it away like a tick from a dog. The cold chewed on the stripped bare shoulder, the rest of him swaddled in a cloak, his hauberk and tunic both removed.

There was a flurry of movement behind Crowbone that drew all their heads round; men milled, uncertain and uneasy about what to do next as Erling came up, with Onund and Kaetilmund, the three of them carrying the body of Od. They had scambled down scree and snow to the foot of the frozen falls, Crowbone realised, while Gjallandi and Bergliot had been busy with his shoulder, howling more agony into him with their attempts at healing. Who did they now stand with, he wondered?

Kaetilmund saw Crowbone's stare and ignored it, for his mind and eyes were still full of Od in the raven tree. When he and Onund and the tallow-faced Erling had skidded and slithered to the foot of the waterfall, they saw Od spread-eagled across the splintered remains of the dead, stunted pine, skewered through arms and legs and body.

The worst was the branch which had gone up under his chin, needled through his tongue and come out of his mouth. The force of him landing had snapped it, so that his ruined face lolled sideways, staring at them with eyes like a fresh-kicked dog. On a rock nearby, the disapproving raven glared at them, black and unwinking.

Getting him off had been a hard, panting struggle of cracking ice-hard branches, but they managed it and lugged him back up the side of the falls again. Onund, sucking air into his searing lungs, lowered the feet of the boy and straightened into the eyes of Crowbone.

'Is he dead?'

Erling, his face twisted still with the shock of it, heard Crowbone's question and the truth of it crashed like a wave, so that he grunted and almost buckled to his knees. The boy was dead. Od was gone.

When no-one answered, Crowbone shoved folk away from him and struggled up, weaving, hoping his knees would not buckle. The earth heaved like a ship in a swell.

'As well,' Crowbone said to Erling. 'That boy was wrong in his head.'

Erling gave a hoarse, high shrill of sound and Crowbone, gasping with the pain it caused him, hauled out the axe stuck down his belt in the small of his back. Onund and Kaetilmund had grabbed the struggling Erling, were forcing him to his knees, the great hunchback cooing at him as if he was soothing a restive horse.

'You need to guard your mouth, Crowbone,' Kaetilmund said bitterly.

'You mistake me for someone who cares about a man trying to kill me,' Crowbone spat back. He stepped forward to where Erling, his eyes raving and wild, struggled and kicked, held tight by the two men.

For a moment he stood, while Erling, his mouth covered by Onund's massive hand, hoarsed out screams between the fingers and lurched, fighting to get to Crowbone now that his target was close.

'In the name of the gods,' Kaetilmund panted, 'move away at least.'

Crowbone looked at them each in turn and shook his head. He could not believe that Erling was still alive and wondered why these, his men, had allowed it. His shoulder burned and the side of his head had that cold icicle driven in it. In a movement, quick as a snake strike, he brought up the butt of the hand-axe and slapped Erling in the forehead, then grunted and cursed with the pain it seared through his shoulder and into his whole body.

Erling slumped like a sack, then stirred and blinked.

'Let him go,' Crowbone ordered and Kaetilmund and Onund did so; Erling fell to his knees and started to retch.

'Behave yourself,' Crowbone said to him, 'or I will use the blade.'

Then he looked at Onund and Kaetilmund.

'This one should be dead. He wanted to attack the jarl you are oathed to protect – yet all you did was struggle with him.'

'Which oath?' asked Onund savagely. 'The one all Oathsworn give to Odin? Or the one you had others swear to you alone?'

Crowbone ignored him, looked round at Erling's tight-faced men while their leader wiped his mouth and climbed to his feet.

'Who among you is a shipmaster?' Crowbone demanded and, after a series of shuffles and looking from one to the other, a man stepped forward, small and ice-grimmed, his eyes like wary beasts in the thicket of his face.

'I am Ulfar Arnkelsson,' he declared. 'I know the stars and the waves, rarely make a mistake in runes and am a shipmaster of note. I can ski a little . . .'

'I am not looking to hire you,' Crowbone snarled and the man's teeth clicked together.

'You should be wondering why you are all alive,' Crowbone told him and the men at his back, 'so I shall tell you. You will take the body of Od back to Gudrod in Orkney. You will take those men stupid enough to pass up the chance of riches with me and had better hope there are enough of them to crew a ship, for you will get no more.'

Ulfar glanced over Crowbone's shoulder, to where Erling stood like a weary ox.

'No,' said Crowbone softly, shrugging the cloak free and leaving himself naked to the waist, though he felt no cold. 'Do not look to Flatnose, for his day is done.'

He turned then and struck, knowing the distance between them to the last finger-width. The axe split Erling's head sideways under the hairline so hard that the man's feet shot out from under him. He hit the ice of the frozen riverbank with a crash, blood and yellow gleet spilling from his head, cracked like an eggshell. If he made a sound, or knew what had hit him, he gave no last sign of it.

There was a howl of outrage and the Orkneymen stirred like a broken byke; weapons came up, shields clattered.

'Mother of God,' whispered Adalbert, but Onund roared him down.

'Odin's holy arse, boy – what are you?'

Crowbone fixed him with his odd-eyed stare as his own men fell into fighting crouches, weapons ready.

'A prince,' he rasped back, 'who knows the game of kings enough not to leave a threat at his back.'

There was sense in it, enough so that Kaetilmund, sick at the ease with which Crowbone had killed Erling, flicked a worried gaze at Onund. The Icelander's face was thunderous, his neck drawn in and his hump towering up like the mountain itself.

'The gods have given up on you, boy prince,' he snarled. 'And so have I.'

Crowbone tensed. He had half-expected it, but the actual moment of it was crushing. Behind, he heard confusion and angry voices, knew that men were drawing apart, the Oathsworn sliding towards Onund and Kaetilmund. Across the way, the Orkneymen were looking at one another and spotting a chance, while Erling and Od bled sluggish tarns on to the scuffed ice.

The cold air grew thick with fear and tension, the shouting rose up like the smoke of their panting breath. Kaetilmund blinked once or twice, looked at the furled Stooping Hawk banner he carried, then flung it at Crowbone's feet and stepped back; Crowbone's men growled and the yellow bitch, picking up on the thick angry air, whined uneasily, not knowing who was the enemy.

Then a voice cut through it like the whirl of Crowbone's hand-axe.

'I have come just in time, it seems.'

There was silence. Orm Bear-Slayer stepped up over the edge of the falls trail and men spilled up after him, springing eager and weapons ready. One was Finn.

'By the Hammer,' he said, with a look towards Crowbone that mingled disgust and admiration, 'you have not learned the lesson of axe and head, have you, boy?'

THIRTEEN

Finnmark, the mountain of Surman Suuhun, days later . . .

CROWBONE'S CREW

THERE was not one among them who liked the place, though only one admitted it openly, scowling up at the slick, grey-green rocks and the dark cleft spilling out white smoke which stank.

'It has always been my belief,' Murrough grunted, glancing uneasily at the dark split and the white vapour, 'that such a place is the home of a dragon.'

It raised hackles on everyone at once, for the suck and roar of it, with the hot, smoking breath that went with it, certainly looked as much like the breathing of a great, scaled wyrm as any had imagined. Finn, of course, merely grinned, heady with delight at having found warmth and only slightly annoyed by the smell.

'What do you know of dragons?' he countered, while the Irisher glowered back at him. 'You come from a country where there are not even snakes, let alone a decent-sized wyrm.'

'Regardless,' Murrough muttered. 'A hole in a wall of rock with stinking hot smoke coming from it is not a welcoming place.'

'Dwarves,' agreed Tuke. 'If not wyrm, then a *jötunn*, for sure, perhaps even Surt himself.'

Then he grinned.

'Or a *duergar*, forging up some marvellous blade.'

Since he looked so much like one, folk made warding signs, not entirely certain he was not planning to introduce them to his kin.

'Cursed, so it is,' Murrough added with relish and everyone nodded and agreed that this was almost certainly the case. Finn, festooned with bundles, stopped adjusting himself and stared at the Irisher, clearly impressed.

'A wyrm,' declared one of the Orkneymen who had come with them, 'for that stink is its fire-breath, waiting to happen.'

Onund Hnufa gave his usual preliminary grunt and heads turned as he forced his huge, deformed shoulder – as big, it seemed, as the cliff towering over them – into the pack.

'By the Hammer,' he growled, then spat derisively. 'Gather up your skirts and listen to me, you fuds. I am from Mork in Iceland. I have lived a deal of my life with Hekla on one side and Katla on the other, two great mountains only reached across a field of black rock where nothing grows at all. There is this same stink and same white smoke almost all the while from those places – at night I have seen the red glow off them. Folk who live there assure me this is because the World Wyrm itself has his slumbering head right beneath our feet. Yet I have never, ever, in all my life, seen anything that resembled a single scale.'

No-one spoke, for Onund was fearsome when he scathed. In the end, only Murrough dared.

'Well then. Not Jörmungandr's head, as Onund tells us that is in Iceland. His arse, probably, judging by the smell.'

'Ha,' scoffed Halfdan, 'that is Finn, suffering from his own cooking.'

Finn, who was reeking most of the time, beamed and that

brought some chuckles. They were forced, all the same; no-one cared for this place and they had struggled up to it over fresh snow, studded with bits and pieces of men's life – and the men themselves.

They had found helmets, a scrag-end of fur, a broken spear – a hand. They dug out the bodies at first, saw them frozen as wooden dolls and soon realised there were so many it would take them forever.

'Haakon's men,' Orm declared. 'Gudrod's Orkeneyers also. They fought and here is where Gudrod won his victory.'

Crowbone knew he was wondering if the priest, Martin, was among them, for he was not with anyone else. Unless he was alone, of course. It would not surprise Crowbone to find that Martin had come to this place alone, where scores of men had clearly failed.

'So Erling spoke true,' he answered, bitter with thought that Gudrod had won.

'The curse of the axe,' growled Klaenger and men looked from one to the other, unsure of matters and bitter that they had come all this way after having been told the truth by Erling after all. Orm saw it; he knew the Oathsworn could be relied on, but only those who had clearly walked to his side as they sorted out who was who at the top of the water-fall.

When it became clear that Onund, Murrough and Kaetilmund and the other survivors of the original eight he had taken were back at Orm's side, together with a good number of the old Red Brothers who considered the Oath binding, Crowbone felt the bitter gall of it in his mouth.

He had the Christmenn and some of those who still thought their prince was gods-blessed and would bring them to riches. Most of the Orkneymen, having gathered up the dead Od and Erling, let themselves be led by Ulfar the shipmaster, who gave no more than a grim nod to Orm, and filtered out, heading back to the coast and their ships.

'That may have been a mis-move,' Crowbone frowned to Orm, watching them leave. 'They may put a torch to our ships and try and strand us here.'

'Why would they?' Orm declared. 'They gave their word.'

Crowbone said nothing for a moment, though it was clear he thought Orm wrong-headed. Then he glanced at the sky, where a distant honking revealed the last skeins of geese, fleeing the land northmen knew as Cold Shores for the south.

'I have tripped every trap you put me at,' he said bitterly. 'Though there may be one or two ahead left for you. We had better hurry, all the same, for the winter is closing in and if we time this badly, we will be iced here for months.'

Orm nodded and forced a smile, trying to mend some bridges.

'I did not set you at traps,' he answered. 'I had work of my own and thought you would want this axe for your great-ness. I thought to bring you the key to the King's Key – the stick Martin wants in return for the Bloodaxe.'

'You do not want it, then?' Crowbone snapped back.

Orm did not answer, for the fact that the boy – he must stop thinking of him as the nine year old he had rescued from Klerkon's privy chains, he snarled to himself – had asked that at all was a crushing stone to all his hopes. In the end, all he could do was shake his head.

'I thought to make sure your sky did not fall,' he said, but the words felt as if he was dragging them from some endlessly-deep sea-chest. 'I handed you some good men and gave you to the care of Hoskuld. All you had to do was go with him to find out where the axe lay.'

'You knew Martin was at the bottom of it,' Crowbone countered sullenly. 'You knew he was pretending to be this Drostan, yet you did not tell me of that.'

'I was not sure,' Orm answered. 'This Drostan may have been a part of it, though Martin was the cunning in it. I am thinking Martin killed Drostan – it would not be beyond him. Once you got to Mann I thought matters would become clear to you.'

'Clear long before then,' Crowbone spat back. 'Hoskuld had carted Martin everywhere laying a trail of enemies to this prize. Hoskuld did not think fit to tell me of it – did he tell you?'

'No,' Orm admitted, 'though I was after thinking something of the same. You should have had patience, Olaf, for Hoskuld would have told you in the end. He did not trust you altogether. Thought you had much to learn.'

'I taught him a lesson or two,' Crowbone growled and Orm's sad eyes rested on him – worse, thought Crowbone, than if he had struck me.

'You hanged his crew, I hear,' he said and shook his head sorrowfully. 'They were good men; I knew them for a long time. What of Hoskuld?'

Crowbone pushed against the sudden shame he felt at the hangings and harshed out a grunt, waving one hand dismissively.

'Ask Gudrod. He lifted Hoskuld from Mann, but the trader was never heard from again.'

Orm sighed and scrubbed his beard. 'That was ill done.'

'It was all ill done,' Crowbone said, rasped with misery. 'You should not have used me like some thrall, to run ahead and take the blows.'

Orm's eyes narrowed and he straightened a little.

'I did not use you at all. I turned you loose and gave you what I could, so that you might make your own wyrd. I hoped you would stay true to the Oath you swore, hoped you were more of a man and less of a prince. I was wrong everywhere, it seems.'

Crowbone felt the spinning whirl of that, as if the earth had dropped away underneath him. There was a moment when he panicked from the fear of it, of being alone, like a boat cut away from the shore. Then it passed and the world settled.

'Here we are, then,' he said, staring Orm in the face. 'Do we go on together in this?'

The loss was sharp, as if someone had actually died. Orm met the odd-eyed, half defiant stare of him and nodded.

'Aye,' he declared, 'for you found Thorgunna for me, you tell me, and Odin's hand was in that, for sure. The least I can do now is hold up your sky, which I have done before. But quickly, as your birds in it tell us.'

He stopped and scrubbed his beard, thinking.

'Erling said Gunnhild and Gudrod had claimed the axe,' he mused and Finn growled at Crowbone.

'He might have said a little more on the subject,' he said, barbed as a hunting arrow, 'but finds it difficult to speak with an axe above his eyebrows.'

Crowbone admitted the fault with a brief flap of both hands, then squinted at the looming, smoking mountain.

'Well,' he growled, 'he may have gone off with it, or Erling might have thought so, or been told to say as much. We will only learn the truth by going to this mountain.'

He broke off as Bergliot came up, curious to see this legend that was Orm and trying to look at least a little alluring, while swaddled in as many clothes as she could put on.

'You Norse call this *Mörsugur*,' she said to Orm. 'I am told this means "the time that sucks the fat". It is a good name.'

Crowbone felt her hand on his arm and shook it off, irritated, feeling her stiffen.

'Together,' he agreed looking at Orm, though both of them knew that was only until matters declared themselves.

'I have lost interest in the working of birds,' he added. 'I do not fear the Mother of Kings as much as I did.'

'*Dimidium facti, qui coepit, habet*,' said Adalbert from nearby. Orm turned, saw the raw-boned priest, hands shoved

332

deep in his sleeves, cowl up and the beginnings of a good beard. Adalbert smiled.

'He has done . . .' he began.

'He has done half, who has begun,' Orm interrupted. 'I know that one, priest.

'You keep strange company these days,' he added softly to Crowbone, who frowned back at him, sullen as slush.

'Adalbert,' he declared. 'He came with me from Hy. To save my soul – "*probae etsi in segetem sunt deteriorem datae fruges, tamen ipsae suaptae eniten*". Was that not what you said, priest?'

'Very good, young prince,' Adalbert murmured. Orm grinned.

'At least you will learn the Latin,' he declared, then looked at Bergliot.

There was a pause, long and awkward.

'Bergliot,' she said stiffly, when it became apparent that Crowbone would not introduce her. 'I am from Wendland.'

'A thrall,' added Crowbone, then looked pointedly at her. 'To a princess.'

Orm did not say anything, though he was sure this Bergliot thought herself more than that and certainly much more than that to Crowbone. He merely nodded and turned away, his heart leaden; he was grown, was Crowbone, but still had much to learn, about love as much as friendships and the power of an oath.

They went on, shedding men like slug slime. The Oathsworn were fittest, almost untouched by the fighting – because, Crowbone thought bitterly, it has all been done for them.

Yet the cold and the bad food did for them all and men were staggering with the shite freezing down their legs, some falling down and begging to be carried even as others begged for death rather than be left to the Sami. Yet others simply vanished, dropped out unseen and unheard.

The ties that bound them all now were a snake-knot tangle

of oaths and fear and hope. It kept men from each other's throats, but did not dispel unease or mistrust – the snow-buried dead braided the tension on them and the last, panting climb to the smoking gash in the mountain twisted fear out of them like water from a tight rope.

It was grim and grey as a hag's head, with the almost sheer wall of a cliff where they wanted to go and a tumbled ruin of snow behind where rocks breached like the backs of whales, all the way to the faint line of dripping, mist-shrouded pines where the beast-men skulked. No birds sang here and only the dark gash with its pall of rotten-egg stink offered a way ahead. Finn alone took delight in it because it was warm.

'Warm enough to have vanished away all that fallen snow,' he pointed out, almost cheerfully, as if that was somehow a good matter. Everyone had noted the warmth that blew fetid from the mouth of the gash in the mountain; it did nothing to make them easier in their minds about entering the place, as Svenke Klak declared.

'I mean,' he argued, 'if the creature laired in it breathes warm enough to turn snow to water for yards, chances are it is not a hare hole we are looking at.'

'Melts my bowels to water, for sure,' growled Kaetilmund, then glared at Crowbone. 'Those oath-breakers without the protection of Odin should be trembling.'

Crowbone soured him with a withering stare. His shoulder throbbed and burned and his head felt light as a ball of air.

'I did not come here to tremble on the edge,' he growled. 'I will go – but if it will make folk easier, then I will go alone and take a first look ahead.'

He had courage, Orm saw – but he had always known that about the boy. It was the rest Orm did not like, all he had learned from Onund and Kaetilmund and the others. He had hoped Crowbone would understand about the Oath, keep to it, use the strength of it, but it was clear that he was too much of an Yngling prince for that. He was not Oathsworn, that was sure – but what he is becoming, Orm thought, is less clear.

'Best not, prince,' he advised. 'That dog can talk and we will need you here, I am thinking. Send someone else.'

The yellow hound was ruffed and stiffly pointing off into the snow haze; men shifted uneasily and started thinking about shields and weapons.

Crowbone moved to the entrance, where the walls rose up on either side and no more than three men could stand abreast – the yellow bitch whined and moaned as loudly as the wind, so that Bergliot reached down and patted her.

'By the Hammer,' Finn growled, looking round him at the smoking ground. 'I hope this is no goddess fud I have crawled into, though it reminds me of a woman I knew.'

'I was married to such a one once,' muttered Murrough, which brought crow-laughter from throats dry from fear and twisted with attempts to breathe. Even Bergliot managed a smile, bright-eyed with fear.

Crowbone turned his odd eyes on Klaenger, who groaned a little. Freyja's tits, he thought to himself, is mine the only face he sees? Yet he had seen the fight with Od and had more respect than ever for this young prince, was sure he was braided for greatness; it only remained to hope that his greatness was not threaded round Klaenger's doom. Then he put his head down, as if walking into a downpour and plunged into the reeking smoke ahead.

The tension seemed to hiss away then and the men left outside turned away from the cleft, putting backs to the shroud of white and the sick heat of dragon breath, to face the sort of enemy who was almost a comfort now – the dark little Sami with their reindeer skins and beast masks and the desperation of those who have already lost.

They all knew the men were coming now, for even the blind could have seen them flit between the misted trees lower down, had caught clear sight of knots of them skulking cautiously towards them over the open white slide of new snow, so that they did not need the yellow bitch's fresh warning growls.

There were not as many as before and a lot of them had no masks now, but they still had their little bows and vicious black-shafted, owl-feathered arrows.

'They will have to come at us here,' Orm shouted out to the backs of the men forming up, battered, scarred shields ready. 'Up Finn's woman's fud, which he has clearly not ploughed enough, for it is very narrow.'

They snarled out laughter and their backs straightened. The ones in front, The Lost, hunkered their ring-mailed bodies behind shields and the spearmen closed up a little to force their hedge of points through to the front.

Finn folded up the brim of his hat and clapped his helmet over it, then stuck his iron nail between his teeth. Folk chuckled at the sight and Murrough shook his head.

'I do not see why you bother with that hat, Finn Horsehead,' he declared, 'for it has never once nailed the weather the way we want it, so it has not.'

Finn frowned. The battered, rag-brimmed hat was spoil from the *rann-sack* of Ivar's steading, him who had been by-named Weatherhat, for his headgear was reputed to ease storms. It was this that Finn had taken and, in all the years he had worn it, he had never, as he confessed, mastered the way of working it. Yet he would not part with it and said so.

'You should at least tie that helmet under your chin,' Murrough noted, for Finn simply clapped the dented effort on his head.

Finn snorted. 'I have broken the neck of many a man using his own helmet,' he pointed out, 'and throttled a few more besides.'

Men tying their own helmet-thongs nearby looked stricken

336

and paused. Crowbone almost smiled, but could not bring himself over the edge of it, for he wished his own men were as snarling grim and sure of themselves, of each other, as the Oathsworn.

He looked at his men, cat-nervous and still strangers, yet he took comfort from the fact that they stood, looking to him, oathed to him. He swelled himself up a notch; he was Prince Olaf, son of Tryggve, an Yngling and a chooser of the slain.

'Do not listen to Finn,' he bellowed. 'To break a neck as Finn describes has to be done from behind and so it is rare, for all his boasts. Finn kills from the front and it is that iron nail you want to watch at work.'

Finn gave a huge burst of laughter and acknowledged Crowbone with a wave. Men yelled out and smacked weapons on their shields, taunting the creeping Sami. There was a shout from the front and men hunkered down, shields up, almost without thinking; the air flickered and arrows shunked into scarred wood, or skittered off the rocks. Knots of Sami ran to within range and hurled little throwing spears which clattered and bounced; folk jeered and yelled, while Crowbone pounced on the shafts and, one in either hand, hurled them both at once back over the heads of his men, shouting: 'Idu na vy!'

The Slavs knew that one – the great Prince Sviatoslav's war-yell to his enemies. I am coming against you. Orm raised his sword in salute hoping, even as the ranks roared at the expertise of the young Crowbone, that few remembered how Sviatoslav was now part of a Pecheneg war chief's drinking cup.

'That's a fine skill,' Svenke Klak said to Crowbone. 'Is it as hard to learn as that snatching in mid-air trick?'

Crowbone grinned and shook his head.

'You cannot learn it,' he announced loudly. 'It is a gift of the gods.'

Men who knew him, though, shook their heads, half-admiring, half-amazed at the truth of it. They had seen him practise such throwing daily, while his sea-rotten ringmail showed where he swam in it; they knew he had his face set on being a saga-hero.

Crowbone was about to tell Svenke more about how only some men had his hand luck, but the next flurry of missiles came, a mix of short spears and arrows, zipping and clattering dangerously. Svenke had half-turned to listen, his mouth open and a grin lopsided on it when the spear spanged off the black rock wall, splintered and broke, the point spinning harmless away and the broken shaft hitting him in the throat, just above the leather-thonged rim of his beloved ringmail, with the sound of a spade striking wet dung.

He staggered back, looked amazed at the lump of wood which had somehow just sprouted from him and turned his bewildered face to Crowbone, who half reached out as if to pluck the words Svenke's mouth worked to form – but all that came out was a gout of black-scarlet and he fell backwards with a clatter.

He was dead by the time Crowbone reached him, which was a mercy, for he could never have lived long with such a wound. Murrough cursed and saw Crowbone's face take on a pinched look – Halfdan moved steadily down the thick-ranked Oathsworn, telling those who craned to see who had been hit to watch their front and keep their shields up.

The stink of the place, the swirling misted smoke, the rattling rain of missiles and a thin, high shrieking wind ate at courage like worm on a keel, so that Finn and Orm had to move into the ranks, slapping shoulders and telling folk to stand, for they were starting to shuffle backwards. After a pause, Crowbone straightened from Svenke Klak's body and did the same. He shoved the man's death in the black sea-chest deep inside him and clashed the lid shut on it. Just another lost counter in the game of kings . . .

The actual charge came almost as a relief, but folk had been watching it curl on them like a falling wave and had braced for it. This time, Crowbone did not see any of the enemy, for the Oathsworn of Orm were the ones with numbers here and formed the front two ranks. He heard the furred Sami crash on the shields, saw wood splinter up, heard the Oathsworn howl like wolves and their enemy scream and die.

It was an eyeblink, no more, but enough for the Sami to leave a heap of reindeer-clad bodies almost three deep in front of the locked shields; spearmen killed the moaners close enough to reach and those who were too far away were left to groan and cry for help, for no-one wanted to leave the shieldwall to finish them until such cries started to itch their teeth.

The moments crawled away and the thin wind's shrieking bounced like thrown spears down the rocks of the cleft. Men passed leather water flasks back and forth; Svenke was carried off and other men bound up welts and scratches. Styr and Atli banged helmets together, panting and howling at each other – still here, they roared. Still here.

Then Klaenger appeared, panting slightly, face streaming and his eyes red from the acrid white smoke.

'You have to see this,' he said to Crowbone. 'Better to bring a few men, I am thinking. Bring Boomer and the priest, too, for we may need what lore they both know.'

The curiosity burned everyone when Crowbone called the pair of them over, ignoring Orm and Finn, who scowled and questioned Klaenger themselves.

'I found a way through the mountain.'

He paused, looked from Orm to Crowbone and back, licking dry lips.

'There is no snow beyond it. No snow at all.'

Orm took Finn and Murrough, left Kaetilmund in charge, with Halfdan to take over if he was killed. Crowbone, with a look at Orm's two grim warriors and his own men, the tremble-lipped skald, the determined priest and the grimly fearful Klaenger, slid across black stones, slush and puddles, into a wind that seemed to bounce and scream down the rocks, streaming all the stink and smoke round and behind them.

The cleft kinked to the right and Klaenger held up one hand, which froze them in mid-step – Crowbone realised the yellow bitch had come with him and crouched, trembling, by his side. He did not want to turn and see Bergliot, for he would have to order her back and knew she would defy him.

'This is where I saw the light,' Klaenger said. 'I thought it might be a way out.'

'Did you get to the part where such a thought found your feet?' Murrough demanded.

'*Cogitationis poenam nemo patitur*,' Adalbert declared, then looked at Crowbone.

'Not the time for lessons,' he snarled back and the bland face inclined itself in a gentle nod.

'Nobody should be punished for his thoughts,' Orm translated, then looked mildly at Crowbone, who was sure he was being mocked and whose glare said he did not like it.

'I say that for Finn,' Orm added blandly. 'He does not like not knowing what is being said.'

Finn, grinning, confirmed it with a nod.

'Well?' Crowbone demanded into the silence that followed. 'Do you all stay here, go back or go on with me?'

Klaenger, hackled up like an annoyed dog at Murrough's implication, growled, 'My feet found the thought you mentioned. Follow me.'

Then he paused and twisted a grin at the big Irisher.

'Do not believe what you hear or see.'

That curdled the flesh on all of them and Finn cursed his back for the mystery he was leaving, but he was already gone, threading into the skeined smoke, before anyone could get him to speak plain.

The wind moaned and screamed like gulls, it seemed to Crowbone, mournful shrieks, hot and fetid. Murrough gripped his axe more tightly and glanced sideways at Orm, who glared back at him, raising an eyebrow as if daring him to start in about the very breath of a sleeping dragon.

Then they stepped beyond the smoke, to where ranks of heads screamed on their poles, sightless eyes staring, snaggle-toothed mouths open, the last of their hair wisping round the ruin of their faces. The heads shrieked at them so that everyone froze and crouched – save for the yellow bitch, who bounded forward and growled and barked. Up ahead, Klaenger stood, unconcerned and enjoying a measure of revenge for what he had been asked to do. Then he laughed and smacked one of the heads, so that it spilled from its stake and rolled towards them. The dog chased it, barking.

'First time I saw them I shat myself,' he pointed out. 'But I threw a stone at one and nothing happened, so I had a closer look.'

He indicated that others should and Finn stirred the grinning horror with the point of his nail, so that the flesh still hanging like black strips waved in the wind. There were three holes punched in the back of the skull and Klaenger nodded when he saw folk understood.

'They are all like this,' he said and then laughed at the scowls.

'A rare joke,' Finn said bitterly to him. Three holes fluted the hot wind through each head, so that it appeared that they shrieked, as clever an idea as pretending to bark from secret like a guard dog and for the same reason.

'These are northmen,' Crowbone said, calling the yellow bitch by the name he had given it – Vigi. In the end, he had to catch it by the ruff and drag it away, for it was no good thing to maul the recently dead.

'The folk who know them will not share the joke in it,' he added.

'Well spoken,' said Orm and, for a moment, there was a warmth between them, an echo of what had once been. Finn and Murrough knelt and inspected the grisly skulls, as if examining lathe-made bowls. Bergliot moved up, one hand to her mouth and Finn glanced up at her.

'You should go home, woman,' he growled. 'This is no place for you.'

'The Norns wove her into this,' Crowbone answered harshly. 'Let them unpick her.'

'Move,' Orm told them, to bring them back to watchfulness. Cautious as sheep round wolf scent, they moved down past the shrieking skulls, through the last veils of smoke and steaming pools – then, like balm to the eyes, the shrouded white was swept away and, lolling beneath them like a naked blonde maiden with two bags of gold, was a little bowl-shaped scoop of valley, with grass cleared of snow and the huge mass of the mountain looming above and all around.

It was warm in that place, so that the grass of it, though winter sere, seemed like the rippling autumn pelt of a fox and the copses had bare trees that were tall, and those that were evergreen had branches that trembled like a rich man's belly in the ever-present swirl of warm wind.

Under one of them was a whipping vein of smoke; furred men stood up, spears ready and for a moment matters winked at the brim of blood. Then a woman's voice said something and the beast-men sank down like dogs.

Crowbone was hammered into the ground, as if a fist had struck him in the belly, driving air and sense out of him. Hate and fear welled in him and he almost went on one knee, then recovered himself, though he had to push to do it, lifting his head to see the puzzled worry in Orm's face.

'Gunnhild,' he said and Orm's eyes widened. He peered, then shook his head.

'Not Gunnhild, lad,' he declared. 'This is another witch.'

Unconvinced, Crowbone was barely aware that he moved at all; the last few steps towards her seemed like a walk through sucking bog wearing iron shoes.

FOURTEEN

Finnmark, the mountain of Surman Suuhun . . .

CROWBONE'S CREW

THÓRGERTH Hölgabrúth she said her name was and
Gjallandi went pale at the sound of it, for he knew that
name well. Orm only knew that the name somehow meant
a bride and had the taint of *seidr* on it – but Thor was in
it and that bluff, red-haired god was not noted for spawning
women of magic.

Crowbone did not care what her name was, for up close
she was not Gunnhild and that was all that mattered to him.
Oh, she had the cat's arse mouth and a skin soft as chewed
reindeer hide, but she was taller, thinner, both old and young
at the same time, with eyes that were curious, resting on his
own with the blue intensity of old ice.

'You have an axe in your care, mistress,' Crowbone managed
to growl, keeping polite in his voice for he was aware that
Klaenger had gone down on his knees, while Adalbert had
done the opposite and drawn himself up as tall as he could,
sticking his chin defiantly at her and making the sign of the
cross back and forth on his chest.

She ignored all of this, while her Sami guard dogs fanned out warily.

'I had,' she answered, her voice cracked as a bad pot, the Norse in it blurred with neglect. 'A wise woman came for it. Though I am not so sure she was all that wise, for she had fetched it once before and it had killed her man and all her other sons but one. Now she wants it for this last.'

'*Ave María, gratia plena,*' Adalbert intoned, his face raised and eyes closed. '*Dominus tecum, benedicta tu in muliéribus, et benedictus fructus ventris tui Iesus.*'

'So Erling had the truth of it,' Crowbone spat bitterly. 'Gunnhild and her son have the Bloodaxe.'

'Was there a Christ priest here?' Orm demanded. 'With a bad leg and looking like something freshly dug up?'

'There was – gently, gently,' she said, the last spoken to the Sami, grown restive with the priest's chanting, for they clearly thought he was casting some spell. She held her hands straight down by her sides, palms level with the earth and the furred warriors sank down on one knee, gathered protectively round her.

'That axe is mine,' Crowbone declared, his eyes narrowing. The woman nodded, as if she had known that.

'*Sancta Maria, Mater Dei, ora pro nobis peccatoribus, nunc et in hora mortis nostrae . . .*'

'In the name of Thor's hairy arse, priest, shut up,' Finn roared.

'*Amén,*' said Adalbert. Finn looked askance at the woman.

'I meant no disrespect to the Thunderer,' Finn added hastily and she smiled.

'It is cold,' the woman said. 'I am going to the fire. When you are ready to talk, come and join me.'

She turned and walked off, confident and sure-footed, trailing her hands through the pack of Sami, who rose up and trotted after her.

'You know this Thórgerth, Boomer,' Orm said and Gjallandi

jerked his eyes away from the woman's retreating back and nodded, licking his big, firm lips.

'She was the bride of King Helgi of Halagoland,' he said, then shook his head. 'That cannot be, for it was long ago, before the time of our grandfathers' grandfathers.'

'Perhaps she is that old,' Finn muttered and made a warding sign. 'She has the look, like the last leaf before winter.'

'More than likely there is a sisterhood,' Adalbert offered, 'of which she is the latest. They all call themselves the same name.'

'Like Christ nuns, you mean?'

Adalbert glared and denied it, but Crowbone shrugged.

'I have seen such nuns, in the Great City and elsewhere. A sisterhood, who all seem to be called Maria.'

'These heathens are not the same,' Adalbert insisted.

'A sisterhood? So you do not think anyone can be so old, Christ priest?' Orm asked. 'What of the one in your holy book – Methus . . . something?'

'Metushelach,' Adalbert answered levelly, 'son of Enoch, father of Lamech. He died old – but he was one of God's chosen.'

'Which this witch clearly is not,' interrupted a harsh voice and all heads turned to where Finn stood, glaring after the goddess of the Sami. He turned to Adalbert and astounded everyone.

'Nine hundred, sixty and nine years when he died,' he growled, then turned from astonished face to astonished face.

'What? You cannot spend time in the Great City and not pick up a few things,' he spat. 'I had the saga of that old Christmann from an Armenian whore. Which is not the point. The sharp end of this affair is what we do now – that little fuck Martin had a plan, but I cannot fathom it. Unless it was to mire us in this place, surrounded by Sami and with no way out, in which case it is a very good plan.'

'He laid a full-cunning plan,' Orm admitted, his face quern grim. 'I am thinking it was a Norn-weave of plot, but Martin does not have the skill of those blind sisters. I am thinking it unravelled a little in his hand.'

He stared, blindly thoughtful and spoke almost to himself.

'Gudrod was meant to be here, not away with the axe – Haakon's men were meant to secure that. All of us were meant to be killing each other and Martin, like a raven, would pick from the dead what he wants most in life. Not good enough, little priest – but many good northmen were wyrded to die in this affair and that must be answered.'

'Where is the axe?' demanded Crowbone and Orm blinked, then shrugged.

'Orkney, if it is anywhere. The priest, too.'

'Beyond us all if it is there,' Finn agreed. 'Even if we get out of this place.'

'Aye,' Orm agreed, which made men shift nervously and look about. The whole place, the situation, had them walking on dewclaws, looking to where the woman they had heard was a goddess sat beside the fire, to the Sami around her, to the woman again, who had stood up for some reason.

'Do you want this axe for yourself?' Crowbone demanded flatly and Orm fixed him with a silent, cold stare.

'That is the second time you have asked me that,' he answered coldly. 'Do not ask it again.'

'Will you help me against Gunnhild if I get us out of this place?'

Orm nodded with narrowed, questioning eyes and Finn snorted.

'I will help you against Loki himself if you get us out of this place,' he answered, with a lash in his voice that suggested it was beyond even Crowbone's strange *seidr*.

Crowbone looked along the line of men and grinned; they grinned back, wolf snarls with no laughing in it at all and that only increased Crowbone's delight, for he knew now how matters stood, knew it with the certainty of the next move in a game of kings, for he had seen the Sami goddess rise up from the fire and clap her hands, had seen what had delighted her.

He went to the fire and looked at the woman, who did not look much like a goddess now, with her mouth drooping a little and her eyes full of what she had seen.

'What can we trade to leave here with no fight from these hounds of yours?' he rasped, knowing the answer already and Thórgerth blinked her eyes up into his – then slid them back to Bergliot. Crowbone smiled, a long, slow triumphant smile and nodded.

For a moment, Bergliot stared at him bewildered, disbelieving, then her eyes widened, Finally, she screamed.

Sand Vik, Orkney, three weeks later . . .

THE KING PIECE

Gudrod sat at the far end of a long table, drinking from a green-glass cup. His gilded helmet was perched on the end, the nasal of it scoring a new mark in the scarred wood, the ringmail puddling round it. A board of nine squares sat in front of him, glowing soft as red-gold in the sconces, the pieces winking back fire.

In front of that, stretching the width of the table, lolling like the whore of fortune that she was, lay Odin's Daughter, the long handle of the Bloodaxe dark with age and sweat and old wickedness, the head gleaming, worked with the inlaid silver mystery of endless snake-knots and strange gripping beasts.

In front of the axe lay another long batten of wood, also dark with age, slightly swollen in the middle and with a nub-end of dark metal licking from the tapered wooden point. It had been taken, swaddled in cloth, from Orm's shoulder when their weapons had all been removed. It was an Old Roman spear, Crowbone knew, which the priest Martin coveted as a *seidr* of his own.

Crowbone had not known what to expect from this last

son of the Mother of Kings, but what he saw was a big man whose neck was thick and roped with great veins down either side, a fleshy face with a neat-trimmed beard more iron than black and eyes a little too bright with drink. Gudrod gestured, the cup in that meaty hand seeming as dainty as an eggshell.

'Olaf, son of Tryggve,' he said. Crowbone nodded curtly and walked forward a little, to where the swirling blue dim of the hall broke against the torchlight. Here he was, the killer of his father, the son of Gunnhild who had scattered the lives of him and his mother like chaff to the wind. And there, behind him . . .

She shifted from the dark like a detaching shadow and the light fell on the stiffened planes of her face, so that he caught his breath. Gunnhild, the hand who wielded the sword, the power which had conspired. He tried to see the eyes, but saw only the knobbed fingers of a hand. He tried to find the hate, but discovered that, strangely now that he was so close after the years running from her, he had no fear, only curiosity.

'Orm,' said Gudrod. 'Finn.'

Each name was a flat slap and, at each one, the owner stepped into the light. Out of the side of an eye, Crowbone saw the iron pillars which followed them, one for each, like watching hounds.

'Who was it who told you I play 'tafl?' Gudrod asked Crowbone suddenly.

'The abbot on Hy,' Crowbone replied. 'Or perhaps Erling, before I killed him. I forget which.'

'Just after he killed that strange lad,' Orm added. 'Od.'

The sibilant hiss came from the dark, a herald of the dust and rheum voice to follow.

'You have them in your power here,' she said warningly and Gudrod stiffened a little, then hunched his shoulders, as if against a chill breeze on his neck.

'You are resourceful,' he said, ignoring her. 'Survived the Sami and the cold, Erling and that boy. Especially that boy.

He was strange and gifted, that one. I respect that – admire it even – but I am not witless. Do you really think to beat me at the game of kings? And that I will hand over the axe if you do?'

That had been the plan when Orm and Finn, Crowbone and the others had reached the Finnmark shore, using axes to break up the forming ice and having to leave two ships behind because they did not have men enough to sail them. Even those who climbed on to their rimed sea-chest oar benches were burst-lipped growlers, trembling with cold.

Crowbone had stood with Orm and Finn on the snow-clotted shingle amid the frozen puddles of the beach arguing this plan; he knew they thought it madness, yet Orm went with it because he saw the hand of Odin in it and Finn went with it *because* it was mad and bold. Crowbone had known that, too, for they were all pieces in the game of kings.

Orm, watching the boy now, felt the grey slide into his heart, for he knew that whatever happened here, Crowbone was gone from him. He wondered what would become of the boy he had loosed from Klerkon's privy all those years ago.

Not yet into the full of his life, he had said for as long as he could recall, fooling himself with it. Crowbone was into the full of his life now and, just as Orm had predicted long since, was not a man you wanted to be around; the Wend woman had shown that, if nothing else. Orm hoped that Odin had not abandoned them completely – and that Crowbone could play 'tafl.

'I had heard you could play a bit,' Crowbone said to Gudrod, with an off-hand shrug, then nodded towards the black-handled axe. 'Now that you have that blade of victory, I thought to come and lay matters to rest between us. If I win, you and your mother stop working against me.'

Gunnhild's hiss was enough to bend Gudrod's backbone and he half turned as if irritated by something between his shoulderblades. Then he drank from the blue-glass cup and set it down gently.

'You seem to believe you can trade,' he said. 'You have nothing to trade. Two words from me and you are a corpse.'

Finn growled and Gudrod glanced up and twisted his fleshy face into a grimace of smiles.

'I hear you, Finn-who-fears-nothing,' he sneered. 'And I feel your stare, slayer of bears. You were foolish to entangle yourselves in this.'

Orm spread his hands and smiled, easy and loose.

'I am a trader, if you have heard anything of me at all,' he answered. 'I thought to help a prince I know. I thought I would be dealing with a Christ priest, mark you.'

'Ah,' Gudrod said knowingly and raised one hand above his head. There was a stirring in the shadows and then another iron pillar came forward, thrusting a figure by one shoulder. So, Crowbone thought, three guards . . .

'Martin,' said Orm and the figure raised its slumped head. He was blackened with ice rot and lurched, hip-shot to take the weight off his crippled foot. One hand was held awkwardly, the fingers of it clearly broken and sticking out at odd angles and his mouth was a fester of brown and black that showed when he breathed, for his nose was smashed and he sucked air in over raw gums.

Yet the eyes were a glittering grue at the sight of the Roman lance and he stretched out his good hand towards it.

'Mine,' he said and Gudrod backhanded him, so that the priest's head flew sideways. Finn and Orm both half started to their feet and Crowbone stared at them, astonished. Here was their arch-enemy – why did they care how badly he was handled?

Orm laid a hand on Finn's arm and they both sank back to their benches, so that the ring-mailed hounds behind them eased a little and let their swords slide back into sheaths.

'Mine,' Gudrod replied mockingly as Martin struggled to his feet.

'Tscha,' spat Gunnhild, forcing herself forward into the light. 'Kill them now and be done with this. It is bad enough you let Haakon's people go free and kept this festered monk . . .'

'Thank you,' Martin lisped, puffing blood on to the wild matting of his beard. 'That tooth pained me more than the others.'

Then he smiled, showing the bloody ruin of his swelling tongue and the blood in his mouth.

'I have had the winter eat my foot to endless pain,' he puffed at Gudrod. 'Brondolf Lambisson, whom you never knew and should thank God for it, broke my mouth long since. I have suffered the wrath of my God, little man, and there is no pain the equal of that. Think you are a king in making, a hard man from the *vik*? My first baby shite was harder than you can hit.'

Crowbone heard the delighted 'heya' from behind him. He turned to where Finn grinned, shaking his head with admiration.

'You have to say it,' he declared, beaming into Gudrod's thunder, 'our Martin speaks true enough. He is the hardest man I know, for sure.'

Our Martin. Crowbone could hardly believe he heard it – there was even affection there. Martin wobbled his head round and fixed it on them.

'Is that yourself, Finn? Ja, I think so. Orm also must be there. For certain you have sold yourselves to the Devil, to have come this far. You should both be dead.'

'I know you planned matters differently,' Orm answered coldly. 'Good men died for that and there is not much left of you. I have decided that this foolishness between us ends here.'

'You have decided?'

It was Gudrod's cracking bone of a voice and his eyes blazed behind it. 'You? In my own hall, you say this. To me?'

'Arnfinn's hall,' Finn answered with a scowl. 'You have no hall of your own.'

'Nor will have if you do not behave like a king . . .' Gunnhild interrupted, her voice cracking like the paint on her twisting face.

'Quiet!'

The thunder of it rang them all to silence and Gudrod stood, his face dark and his whole body heaving with the effort of controlling his anger. His eyes raged at them all and, momentarily, he put a hand to one temple, then let it drop.

'I should kill you now,' he declared and sat down, suddenly, like a dumped bag of winter oats.

'That you can is undeniable,' Crowbone answered. 'You will not, of course. Because your mother wishes it and you wish to defy her. Because you wonder if you have the beating of me in the game of kings.'

'Son, there is danger . . .' Gunnhild began and Gudrod rolled his head and shoulders and bellowed incoherently until she was quiet, glowering in the dark, seeing his blood-suffused cheeks and feeling the threads slipping away from her.

'After I beat you,' Gudrod said slowly to Crowbone, 'if you have played half well, I shall keep you for the amusement of it. The others I will kill.'

'When I win,' Crowbone countered, 'I may stay the winter with you, for the amusement of it. The others will go free, the priest with Orm and Finn.'

Gudrod paused for a moment, then shoved the board forward slightly, pushing the axe into the spear so that, for a moment, they nestled together.

'Choose,' he said.

Orm watched. He had played *hnefatafl*, as most northmen of worth did but he was middling fair at it and saw that Crowbone had opted to be the attacker. That gave him sixteen dark counters – *taeflor*, or table-men – surrounding Gudrod's eight white-bone pieces, plus the *hnefi*, the King piece.

The object was simple – surround the King and capture him before he was escorted to safety in any corner, using moves up and down, left and right only. The safety-corner was the Norwegian way of playing, for most folk settled for escape to the table-edge on small boards, allowing the more difficult corner escape for larger boards with more pieces.

At first sight, then, it seemed to onlookers that Crowbone had all the advantages – twice as many men and no easy escape for the *hnefi*. Yet that was the deception of the game of kings – the King's men need only arrange for their Lord to escape the board, so the King player must try to capture as many attackers as possible to clear an escape route, while not trying too hard to protect his own men since they, too, can block the King's escape. He was the chooser of the slain and it did not matter to him how many died, only that the King got away.

The attacker had not only to prevent the King's escape, but also capture him, which was not as simple as it seemed. The best way was actually to avoid taking any pieces early in the game, instead scattering the attackers so that they got in the way and also blocked possible escape routes.

They played in silence, until Gudrod, hovering over a piece, hesitated and smiled.

'You play well,' he said. 'I am pleased.'

'You should drink less,' hissed his mother from the dark, where she gnawed her knuckles and tried to make spells. Crowbone saw her and laughed aloud, making Gudrod turn, scowling.

'Enough of that, mother,' he said lightly. 'He is good and I shall keep him – but I am better and will win without your help.'

'She has no power over me,' Crowbone chuckled, hoping it was true. A move later, he stroked his thickening beard and smiled ruefully.

'Perhaps we should have played *brandubh* instead,' he said

354

and Gudrod laughed, hugely enjoying himself. *Brandubh* was the same game, but played by the Irish using dice; every norther knew that the true game of skill was played without those marked cubes.

Yet the next move, Crowbone announced, as the game bound him to do: 'Watch your King', meaning he had the capture of it in the very next move. Frowning, Gudrod managed to avoid the trap and Finn let out his breath and shifted in his seat.

They played in silence for the next few moves. Crowbone looked over to where Orm and Finn sat, tense as birds on a washing line. The plan had been spelled out beforehand, but it now seemed less obvious; he wriggled his toes in his boot, where the dagger nestled. He knew Finn's nail was down his and that the guards had missed it, too. Three guards only – and Crowbone knew that, no matter what shouts and noise happened here, no-one was coming to Gudrod's aid in this hall.

How quickly could he pull out the dagger? It did not seem to Crowbone that he would get it out of the boot before the guards saw him and even without them, Gudrod seemed a big, powerful man, which Crowbone had not expected. The idea of pulling a knife on a man that size seemed suddenly ludicrous and Crowbone's mouth went dry, while the sheath-straps burned round his ankle. Then he saw the shadowed planes of Gunnhild's cheekbones, the eyes fixed on him, feral as a mad cat and he was sure she was trying to read his thoughts.

'Passage,' Gudrod declared triumphantly. 'Doubled.'

Which meant he had two ways to freedom and Crowbone saw at once that he could block only one. Gudrod watched Crowbone's face, looking for the moment hope left it and was surprised to be denied that. To provoke it, he added: 'The King has escaped you.'

Crowbone slumped a little, as if dejected, his hands dropping beneath the table. Then he raised his head.

'There is more than one way to play the game of kings,' he said and the knife came out of his boot.

Too slow, too fumbled – and it was the saving of them all. If he had managed it properly and slashed the throat of Gudrod, the guards would have hacked them all to pieces – instead, Gudrod came roaring out of his seat and backhanded Crowbone off the bench to the floor, then pounced on him.

'You dare,' he bellowed. 'You dare this?'

Instead of hacking and slashing, his guards sprang forward to help him; one found himself shrieking and dying with a nail in his eye; half-turning, the other was confused, caught between leaping on Crowbone, or fighting Orm and Finn. He hesitated too long and was piled over by the pair of them.

The third guard sprang from behind Gudrod's chair to help wrestle the knife away from Crowbone – but a small, wizened figure leaped into his path, not even looking at him, one hand clawing for the table and the spear that lay on it. Cursing, the guard stumbled over him and the pair of them crashed to the ground, while Gunnhild shrieked for help in her cracked bell of a voice.

Gudrod held both Crowbone's wrists, knife hand and free hand, trying to lurch the weight of himself to pin the struggling youth down. Crowbone, for his part, snarled and writhed and kicked, so that Gudrod freed one hand to try and punch the youth senseless.

Instead, he found himself turned, felt a sharp blow in his cods and yelped as he lost control of Crowbone's knife hand. In desperation, he saw the blood staining the youth's shoulder, saw an old wound and an opportunity and smashed at it, making Crowbone howl and roll away, knife spilling free.

Blind and blurry, with fireflies dancing at the edge of his vision, Crowbone saw Gudrod snatch up the knife, just as the third guard tore himself free from the tangle that was Martin. Orm sprang forward and he and the guard clashed like rutting stags, straining and grunting, sliding and scrabbling for purchase on the floor and getting in Gudrod's way.

Finn rose up from where he had broken the neck of the second guard, into the mad shrieks and shrills of Gunnhild, screaming for help that never came; he gave a growl as he stepped for her. She waved her hands frantically at him, yelling: 'Blunt, blunt,' but Finn, lumbering and grinning like a bear woken too early, shook his head.

'That old spell worked on me once when I fought another witch like you,' he snarled. 'Now I do not bother with edged steel.'

His fist took her on the point of her jaw, breaking it, shattering the mask of her face to shards of powder and artifice, snapping her head back and cutting off her howls. Gudrod saw it as he weaved to his feet at last, panting, the knife in his hand and ready for Crowbone's throat. Instead, he saw his mother slumped, blood trickling from her nose and he howled like a trapped wolf and started toward Finn.

Crowbone leaped up, a salmon leap as good as any he had ever done before. He hit the table and scattered the board and the pieces into the shoulder and face of Gudrod, who reared back, his mouth opening with horror at what he saw.

The Bloodaxe, snatched up by Crowbone, coming down on him, all glitter and dark shaft, the edge growing bigger and bigger until it was the whole world crashing on Gudrod's forehead and splitting him to the chin.

Finn was leaping to the aid of Orm even before the black blood and gleet had washed down Gudrod's falling chest. Before he hit the floor, Finn had broken the neck of the last guard – and there was stillness, suddenly, where the rasp of their breathing was loud and ugly, the iron stink of blood cloying their throats. The King piece rolled backwards and forwards and finally toppled off the table, landing with a sticky little slap of sound in Gudrod's blood.

'Game to me,' Crowbone said and his own voice sounded like a stranger far off.

Finn got off his knees, canting his head sideways to where Crowbone still stood on the table, arms dropped to his side, staring at the body of Gudrod with the axe buried deep in what remained of his skull.

'You were ever handy with an axe and a skull,' Finn declared climbing wearily to his feet and wiping his hands down his breeks. 'I thank the gods for it now, of course.'

Crowbone barely heard it. The death of Gudrod, the axe that had done it, sent a thrill through him from soles to crown; the side of his head, where it had been smacked, seemed suddenly to have an ice spear thrust into it.

Here was a sign. The axe had betrayed Gudrod, who was clearly not worthy and the weapon had sprung almost unbidden into Crowbone's own hand to prove that he clearly was. And yet . . .

He blinked away from the corpse of Gudrod to the slumped figure on the High Seat.

Her. It was her. He peered across at her, no more than four steps away. Gunnhild, the Witch-Queen, who had ordered the death of his father – and, next to her, Gudrod, the son who had carried out the deed. Because of her, that bundle of rags there, everything that the Norns had woven for Crowbone's life had been unpicked then re-woven in suffering and the death of his mother; Crowbone could not move for breathing.

When he did, he slid from the table into the sticky mess of Gudrod's blood and plootered through it to the figure on the chair, her head lolling, the veil fluttering free to show her ancient, ravaged face and open, dead eyes. The gnarled fingers which had worked her last spell curled like a cold-killed spider.

She was dead, for sure, though Crowbone, feeling the fresh burn in his shoulder, had to reach out and touch the cheek, snake-scaled with age and marbling into cold death; when he brought his fingers back they were wet. A tear? Yet the thin lips were drawn slightly back, fretted all round with lines like a badly-fired clay pot and revealing teeth yellow as walrus tusks, a last snarl of defiance.

Here she was, then, the Mother of Kings, his enemy from the moment he drew his first breath – from before even that. Crowbone stood, feeling the insistent heartbeat agony of his shoulder, blinking with the pain and trying to feel as if something had ended, that his father was close by nodding approval, his mother's presence draping him with love and thanks.

But there was only an old dead woman, with a mouth dropped open to make her look foolish and eyes turning to dull ice.

A grunt and a whimper broke him from the moment and he turned, to where Martin levered himself upright to the table and reached out one clawed hand to grasp the spear. In one swift movement, Crowbone snatched it up, just as men spilled into the hall.

Orm and Finn were poised like dogs spotting wolves, but Crowbone merely glanced up at Arnfinn and his Orkneymen, smiling. He nodded towards Gudrod and Gunnhild.

'Done and done,' he declared and Arnfinn, after the briefest of glances, stared back at him.

'It were best if you were gone swiftly from here,' he said and Crowbone nodded. This, too, had been part of his plan, for Crowbone knew how to play the game of kings in life and he had surrounded the King piece before he had even sat down with Gudrod.

'Mine,' Martin managed out of the crazed ruin of his mouth and Crowbone looked at him, then at the spear in his hand.

'There was a dog,' Crowbone said and Martin scowled.

'No more tales,' he mushed. 'I have heard enough of your tales.'

For an eyeblink, Crowbone was back on the steppe, huddled with Orm round a mean fire, with Martin and the men he had persuaded to kidnap them. He had told a story then, though he could not remember it – but he remembered Martin's fury at it. Next day, in a raging blizzard the warrior women of the steppe had attacked and killed everyone save Orm, Martin and himself. That had been his last sight of Martin, Crowbone thought, scuttling into the snow like a wraith, clutching his holy stick and wearing only one shoe.

Crowbone glanced at Orm and saw that he, too, had remembered. Finn's grin was wolfen.

'The dog had stolen meat. "What a good time I shall have eating this meat when I get home," thought the dog as it started to cross a stream of water,' Crowbone went on. 'Then he looked down at his own shadow in the water and saw a dog with a large piece of meat in its jaws. "That dog has a larger piece of meat than mine," he thought. "I want it. I will have it!" He growled, but the dog in the water did not move, nor did he drop his piece of meat. He snapped at the dog in the water. The meat he carried slipped from his mouth and sank to the bottom of the stream – and the dog in the water lost his meat at the same time.'

'You have your axe,' Martin mumbled. 'Give me my spear.'

Crowbone looked at the axe, slanting blackly up from the body of Gudrod. He smiled.

'Odin's Daughter does not look so attractive in this light. I do not believe I wish to marry her this day, or the next – though I will in time. I have no need of this cursed axe to cut a path to the High Seat of Norway. It is only a *hunn* in the game of kings – besides, it may not be Christian enough if what Adalbert says holds true.'

A *hunn*, a 'lump', was the slang word for all other pieces on the board, easily sacrificed for the victory of the King. Orm and Finn looked at each other. Arnfinn tilted his head slightly and stared at the axe in Gudrod's head.

'Heya,' Finn sighed, 'I wish you had realised all this before we came to this hall. Before you set off on the entire Thing of it.'

'Just so,' Orm said, then shrugged. 'It seems wise to me, mark you. Perhaps you will be a great king after all.'

Martin shrieked then, a long howl of anguish and utter rage. He did it until he coughed and spat more blood up, then collapsed on the ground, panting. Orm stared at him, remembering the years – gods, the long years – since he had first set eyes on the priest, neatly tonsured, smoothly robed, with a smile that had white, even teeth in it and eyes that welcomed him and Einar to the warmth of Birka's borg.

Now the crippled mouth spewed curses, the eyes were wild little beasts leaping in the matted forest of his hair and beard. Martin sank to his knees, babbling curses and prayers to his god, beat the ground with his fists; even Finn, Orm saw, was beginning to feel some sorrow.

'The lance, the lance,' Martin babbled and Crowbone, halfway to the door of the long hall, turned and held the spear up. Martin's cries stopped at once, like a bairn handed honeycakes; he seemed to freeze on the spot, fixed on the sight like a hound on a spoor.

'This stick?' Crowbone said and raised it. He had never seen it closely before, now felt the heft of it, the fattened end, weighted to bring more power when the spear reached the falling point. The long iron end had gone, of course, but there was a nub of black metal left, a half-thumb of it in the tapered sleeve of the shaft.

A good spear in its day, Crowbone thought and I should know spears. He tested it; it was awkward, for the metal was missing, but he found the balance point, bounced it once or twice, then drew back and hurled it.

'Take it, then, since you want it so badly,' he said quietly. It slid through the air, revolving along its length, a perfect, curving throw and Martin rose to meet it, held out his hands as if to catch and cradle it, his face bright, his eyes exultant.

It went through his fingers and into his breastbone, which

it cracked like a pry-bar on a ship plank. There was so much force in it that it buried itself deep in him, the last nub end of black metal splitting his heart as if it were a skin bag, slicing through the entire of him and out the far side.

Martin was thrown back by it. The lance came out of his back, to the left of his spine and went into the beaten earth floor, softened to mud by Gudrod's blood, so that the priest hung on it, his hands grasping at the air, his face turned to the sky and his mouth working.

'*Iesu*,' Martin wheezed, his hands scrabbling bloodily on the shaft, his voice fading to dust and moth wings as he gasped.

'*Dimitte nobis debita nostra, libera nos ab igne inferni.*'

'What's he say?' demanded Finn hoarsely, staring fixedly at the choking, dying Martin. Arnfinn and his men had all taken a step or two back from the impaled monk and they made frantic cross-signs.

'A prayer to keep himself from Hel's hall,' Orm replied, then looked dully at Crowbone, stunned by the sudden death of the bane of his life.

He was gone. Sixteen years, Orm realised suddenly, since the Norns had woven Orm and Martin's threads into the weave of life and the rushing flood of images that broke on Orm's mind almost drowned him. Martin, lean and smooth and urbane in the polished hall of Birka; hanging upside down on the mast of *The Fjord Elk* while Einar's Truth Knife whicked his little finger off; burned by the Serkland sun; sitting beside the blood-eagled ruin that had been Starkad in an old church of the Constantinople Romans; hobbling off into the snows of the steppe; sly and black-toothed in the main square of Kiev.

Gone. All his plans and viciousness, gone like smoke. Orm shivered and shook himself back into the Now, stared astonished at the youth who had done it, easy as throwing.

362

Crowbone shrugged, then looked at the stunned Orm and Finn, took a breath and puffed out his cheeks.

'You should have done that years since,' he declared. 'If you ever planned to play the game of kings.'

EPILOGUE

Sand Vik, Orkney, the next day . . .

THE three of them stood on the sighing shingle watching their men load the ships. They had just been to see Martin kisted up in a stone-lined grave, the spear lying on his breast; only the three of them and Adalbert had witnessed it and, after mumbling what words were necessary, he had started asking Crowbone about the spear. Orm wondered how long the grave would lie undisturbed.

'What of the axe?' Finn asked and Crowbone grinned.

'It will end up with Haakon Jarl, of course,' he said and the other two looked at him quizzically. Crowbone ticked the matters off on his fingers.

'Already Arnfinn and his brothers are shouldering each other to have it, even before the blood of Gudrod's head is wiped clean,' he told them. 'When they have ruined each other for it, Haakon Jarl will move in and take it from them and Orkney, too, perhaps – much good may either do him.'

'Why do men want it so badly if all it brings is ruin?' Orm wondered aloud and Crowbone's smile was scornful.

'For one it will bring victory. The worthy one.'

They looked at him then and it was clear who he thought that Yngling hero was.

'I shall take it back from Haakon's hand, together with the throne of Norway,' Crowbone added blandly. 'He is not the one worthy to marry Odin's Daughter – but I will prove my worth by taking Haakon's High Seat with my own strength and fame. Then Odin's Daughter will be worthy of me, as well as me of her. Together we will make an empire in the north.'

Orm smiled back at him, a little sad twist of a smile.

'Make sure you get it before that axe goes all the way home to that goddess. I am thinking you may not survive another encounter with the Sami.'

'Especially their new goddess,' Finn growled and then stopped, shaking his head.

'That was a poor way to treat a Wend woman,' he added.

Crowbone's glance was cool.

'I am after thinking it was no good matter with her,' Finn persisted, squinting and rubbing his iron beard. 'It seems she had feelings for you and did not take kindly to becoming the next goddess of the mountain.'

'Fear and love are fox and dog,' Crowbone said and his voice was a chill down their necks. 'They do not walk well together and so it is best to choose one or the other. In balance, it is safer for princes and kings to be feared than loved.'

Then he sighed and shrugged.

'I am sorry for it, all the same,' he added, killing their sympathy in the next second. 'I could not persuade the yellow hound to leave her. I will miss that hound – but I hear there are good ones to be had raiding the Englisc these days.'

They watched him slosh, boot-careless through the half-frozen shallows, and be hauled up into the ship where his Stooping Hawk banner flew. Oars clattered and the *drakkar* sloughed away through the grue of ice, men yelling and setting a blood-red mourn of sail – in time, Crowbone had told them, he would paint the ship black too, and call it Shadow.

It was an echo of the Oathsworn and their *Fjord Elk*, but a distant one that left Orm more forlorn than comforted.

'May the gods save us when he becomes Norway's king,' Finn grunted, then scrubbed his beard.

'Ireland, is it?' he said and Orm smiled grimly. Ireland and Thorgunna.

'Digging an unwilling wife out of a Christ place in Ireland,' growled Finn, shaking his head and following him to their own ships.

'It might well be safer following bloody Crowbone.'

HISTORICAL NOTE

Eric Bloodaxe was the second king of Norway (930–934) and the eldest son of Harald Fairhair. One theory for the wonderful name is that he quarrelled with his other brothers and had four of them killed. My own is that the name (*Blotøks*) translated as 'blood axe' but is probably more accurately rendered as 'sacrifice axe' – the Old Norse equated sacrifice with blood – and I liked the idea of such a weapon, thought to be the treacherous gift of Odin.

Eric, of course, is a historical character, as is his wife, Gunnhild, the arch-nemesis of Crowbone since before he was born. Gunnhild's reputation for *seidr* magic was already legendary when she married Eric and included her living with two Sami wizards to learn all their magic – then she set Eric to kill them and married him.

There are also accounts of her helping in the killing of some of her husband's brothers and other enemies by poisoning or raising storms to drown their ships. She was reputed to go into prolonged trances – the essence of *seidr* – transform herself into a bird and in that guise cross great distances over land and sea, spy out the movements of hostile armies from the air, or listen to the conversations of unsuspecting enemies. She had Crowbone's father killed, but missed the wife, Astrid

– and the unborn son, young Olaf Tryggvasson, otherwise known as Crowbone.

Eric's youngest half-brother, Haakon, ousted Eric from Norway in 934 and, after unsuccessful attempts to get it back, Eric and Gunnhild and their sons moved to Orkney and then to the Viking Kingdom of Jorvik (York). His rule here was turbulent and he was ousted at least once, by the Viking king of Dyfflin, Olaf Cuarans, but regained the throne. He lost it, finally, when he was expelled by the populace and betrayed by Osulf, high-reeve of Bamburgh, and killed at Stainmore in 954.

The hunt for the axe takes Crowbone to a part of the world I had avoided with the first Oathsworn novels, simply because it was a route well travelled in other books – but the North Sea coast, from the Isle of Man to Orkney is an interesting place in the late tenth century. The Dyfflin Norse are humbled by the emergent Irish, first under the High King Mael Sechnaill at the Battle of Tara and then at Clontarf some thirty years later, under Brian Boru. At the same time, the Scots are slowly emerging as Alba while the last of the Picts cling to parts of the far north, a shadow of their former greatness; their fortress at Torridun (or Torfness) can still be seen today, as formidable earthworks at Burghead.

The Sami (Lapps) of the far north have already gained a place in Viking folklore as a strange, highly magical people and so were perfect for keepers of Eric's Bloodaxe.

Gunnhild, according to the Jomsviking Saga, returned to Denmark in 977 and was drowned in a bog on the order of King Harald – a suicidal visit and not, in my opinion, in keeping with the cunning old *spaekona*. I prefer the alternative version of her fate that has her imposing herself on Orkney and dying there circa 980. She had eight sons – including the most famous of them, Harald Fairhair – and a daughter and, as far as I can ascertain, Gudrod was the last of them.

This, however, is the story of the emergence of Crowbone,

Olaf Tryggvasson, already forging the reputation for hardness that will carry him all the way to the throne of Norway and, even as a stripling, determined to be first on his own boat rather than second on one belonging to the Oathsworn of Orm Bear-Slayer.

As ever, this is best told round a warming fire in the crouching dark; any errors or omissions I claim as my own – but do not let them spoil the tale.

ACKNOWLEDGEMENTS

The list of those without whom etc:

The Glasgow Vikings (www.glasgowvikings.co.uk) and the rest of the Vikings, national and international (www.vikingsonline. org.uk) who provide entertainment and education in several countries and have actually drunk Lindisfarne dry.

My agent at United Agents, Jim Gill, for being canny, steady and perceptive. Katie Espiner and Louisa Joyner at HarperCollins for having faith and Joy Chamberlain, one of the legion of unsung editors who do so much more than sort the apostrophes and split infinitives.

The Historical Writer's Association (www.thehwa.co.uk) whose members offer constructive criticism and are (usually) right.

The process of writing this has been encouraged by a firm band of fans, who have followed the Oathsworn and now want to carry on reading – more power to you all for your praise, criticism, comments and unfailing humour. I hope Crowbone carries on the Oathsworn saga in the direction you all want to travel.